28.95

In Good Company

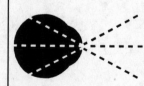 This Large Print Book carries the
Seal of Approval of N.A.V.H.

IN GOOD COMPANY

JEN TURANO

THORNDIKE PRESS
A part of Gale, Cengage Learning

GALE
CENGAGE Learning®

Farmington Hills, Mich • San Francisco • New York • Waterville, Maine
Meriden, Conn • Mason, Ohio • Chicago

GALE
CENGAGE Learning®

Thorndike Press® Large Print Christian Historical Fiction.
The text of this Large Print edition is unabridged.
Other aspects of the book may vary from the original edition.
Set in 16 pt. Plantin.

LIBRARY OF CONGRESS CATALOGING-IN-PUBLICATION DATA

Turano, Jen.
    In good company / Jen Turano. — Large print edition.
        pages cm. — (Thorndike Press large print Christian historical fiction)
    ISBN 978-1-4104-8153-5 (hardback) — ISBN 1-4104-8153-0 (hardcover)
    1. Large type books. I. Title.
PS3620.U745515 2015b
813'.6—dc23
                                                    2015024111

Published in 2015 by arrangement with Bethany House Publishers, a division of Baker Publishing Group

Printed in Mexico
1 2 3 4 5 6 7 19 18 17 16 15

For Jeb, Madison, and Morgan Turner
Love you!

Jennifer

1

Long Island, New York — July 1882

"Consider yourself dismissed. Effective . . . immediately."

Miss Millie Longfellow squinted against the bright light that suddenly filled the cluttered broom closet she was standing in, resisting a sigh when Mrs. Cutling loomed into view. Swallowing past the lump that had formed in her throat, she took a hesitant step forward. "Forgive me, ma'am, but did you just say *dismissed?*"

"Indeed."

"But . . . why?"

Planting a hand against a fashionably clad hip, Mrs. Cutling, Millie's employer for all of one week, narrowed her eyes. "I would think the reasoning behind your immediate dismissal is obvious."

"I'm afraid not."

Mrs. Cutling's eyes narrowed to mere slits. "Did I, or did I not, hire you to watch

7

after the children?"

"Yes, of course, but . . ."

"And you believe you're doing an adequate job of that watching as you lurk in the dark depths of this broom closet?"

"Oh, I wasn't lurking, Mrs. Cutling. I was simply biding some time in a location that was certain to keep the children out of view."

"Should that make me feel more disposed to keep you on?"

"I don't exactly understand what *disposed* means, ma'am, but since I was only keeping out of sight so that the children wouldn't think I was cheating as we go about playing a rousing game of hide-and-seek, then yes, I do think you should allow me to keep my position." Millie smiled. "While it might seem as if we're only playing, we're actually working on mathematical skills. You'll be pleased to learn that little James, being only five, was the one who suggested I, currently being the seeker, count all the way to one thousand before I start looking for him and Edith."

Mrs. Cutling's lips thinned. "I'm sure James has no concept of how long it would take for you to count to one thousand. Furthermore, you should have known it was hardly wise to leave the children to their own devices for that extended amount of time."

"They wanted to be sure I'd be out of the way long enough for them to find a proper hiding place."

"And find one they did." Mrs. Cutling moved closer to Millie and took a viselike grip on her arm.

Millie didn't so much as flinch. Through her many years of service she'd had cheeks slapped, hair pulled, and once, a warming pan tossed directly her way. She'd been lucky to dodge the hot coals on that particular occasion, but in all fairness, she hadn't truly blamed her employer for throwing the pan, since Millie had unintentionally set the lady's bed on fire with it.

What she had learned, though, through all the violence she'd suffered over the years, was that the slightest reaction seemed to bring some of the high-society ladies she worked for great satisfaction. That satisfaction was normally followed by more violence, which was why she was very careful to keep her emotions in check these days.

Fighting the urge to dig in her heels when Mrs. Cutling began tugging her away from the broom closet, Millie soon found herself hustled through a series of dark and narrow passageways. To her surprise, instead of escorting her through the kitchen — a place that was certain to bring Millie unwanted speculation from the cook and scullery maids — Mrs. Cutling pulled Millie down a bright hallway that had numerous crystal chandeliers hanging from the thirty-foot ceiling.

Before Millie had a chance to remark on the beautiful paintings lining the wall, she was marched through French doors that led to the back garden. Heat immediately began traveling up her neck when she stepped out onto the tiled courtyard and found herself pinned under the disapproving stares of at least ten society ladies. All of ladies were dressed in the first state of fashion, their day dresses cut to perfection, while stylish hats embellished with ornamental feathers and large brims lent delicate skin protection from the summer sun.

"As you can see," Mrs. Cutling began, "my friends have come to call."

"How lovely," was all Millie could think to respond.

"It *should* have been lovely," Mrs. Cutling countered. "However, I don't believe any of my friends expected to encounter such an execrable display when they accepted my invitation to lunch."

Biting her lip, Millie reached into her

10

apron pocket and pulled out the small, tattered dictionary she always kept handy. The sight of that dictionary evidently took Mrs. Cutling by such surprise that she actually took a step away from her.

"Is that a dictionary?"

Leafing through the E's, Millie nodded as she scanned the page.

"What are you doing with it?"

"Since I don't know what *execrable* means, I thought I should look it up so I'll be better equipped to deal with whatever I'm about to see." Ignoring the ladies' tittering, Millie continued perusing the pages until she found the word she was looking for. Lifting her head after she read the definition, she glanced around. "Begging your pardon, Mrs. Cutling, but I don't see anything out here of a wretched or" — she returned her attention to the dictionary — "abominable nature. Although" — she flipped the pages to the A's — "I don't know what that means either."

"That will be quite enough, Miss Longfellow. I'm not going to stand around twiddling my thumbs while you scour that dictionary." Mrs. Cutling crossed her arms over her chest. "Besides, girls of your station don't need a vast vocabulary at their disposal, since no employer wants to hire a

11

girl who puts on airs. If you ask me, your time would be better served learning how to be a proper nanny rather than wasting that time on such a trivial pursuit."

Millie lowered the dictionary. "Begging your pardon yet again, Mrs. Cutling, but the pursuit of knowledge can never be overrated. Why, Mrs. Charles Hart firmly believes that all ladies, whether they be society or working, should endeavor to improve themselves through knowledge on a daily basis."

Mrs. Cutling's nostrils flared. "I don't pay you, Miss Longfellow, to argue with me. But tell me — may I assume you used to be in service to Mrs. Hart?"

"I'm not certain that posing as a maid while at one of Mrs. Hart's balls can be considered being in her employ, but . . . getting back to the children . . . ?"

"Why in the world would you have been *posing* as a maid — a situation that almost suggests you were up to something . . . reprehensible?"

Millie lowered her hand. "I'm sure you'll be rather surprised to learn I know what *reprehensible* means, but there was nothing wicked whatsoever about me posing as a maid. Truth be told, Mrs. Hart has graciously offered me her hand in friendship, and with that friendship comes an inexhaustible amount of advice that Mrs. Hart enjoys imparting to me."

Mrs. Cutling nodded to her friends. "Did you hear that, ladies? This girl would like us to believe she's friends with none other than Abigail Hart, one of the city's most intimidating society matrons."

"It's a good thing you've decided to dismiss her," a lady wearing what appeared to be an entire bowl of fruit on her head proclaimed. "It's obvious that, besides being negligent in her duties, the girl's a liar. Such inclinations could have been detrimental to the children."

Millie itched to look up the meaning of *detrimental* but put aside that desire when she noticed Mrs. Cutling's friends were now advancing her way. Not caring to become the recipient of razor-sharp tongues belonging to bored society matrons, she caught Mrs. Cutling's eye. "Perhaps now would be a good time to show me what mischief the children have gotten into."

Mrs. Cutling blinked. "I almost forgot about the children." She turned her attention to the far side of the courtyard and nodded at an elaborate fountain.

With apprehension tickling her spine, Millie moved forward, her steps dragging

13

the closer she got to her destination. She came to a complete stop when she realized that the fountain, one that sported stone mermaids spouting water out of their mouths, seemed to have acquired additional statues. These statues, however, did not fit in with the mermaids but instead seemed to be mud-covered blobs with lily pads stuck all over them. When one of the blobs suddenly raised a hand and rubbed what surely had to be a nose, Millie moved forward again as amusement bubbled up inside her.

"How absolutely brilliant!" she exclaimed as she stopped right next to the fountain, earning a smile from little James, his teeth looking remarkably bright against the mud he'd used to cover his face.

The blob next to him, six-year-old Edith, rose to her feet and let out a dramatic sigh. "Mother ruined everything by pointing us out to you." She pulled a lily pad from her arm and dropped it into the shallow water pooling in the bottom of the fountain.

"It's a good thing she did point me in the right direction, or I could have been searching for the two of you for hours." Millie grinned. "I've played many a game of hide-and-seek, and yet I've never seen children use such inventive means to disguise themselves. It was completely *ingenious* —

which means *clever,* by the way — to choose the fountain to hide in."

"It was nothing of the sort," Mrs. Cutling argued, marching up to join them, apparently unimpressed with Millie's attempt at broadening the children's vocabulary. She leveled a stern look at her children before turning her disapproval on Millie. "I'm holding you responsible for their current condition."

"It wasn't Miss Longfellow's fault, Mother," James hurried to say. "It was my idea to hide here, so you shouldn't be cross with her."

"And it's been great fun," Edith added.

Mrs. Cutling drew herself up. "I see nothing fun about this, Edith. In fact, you and your brother have embarrassed me no small amount this afternoon. Because of that, the two of you will be spending the rest of your day in your rooms — after you bathe, of course — contemplating the ridiculousness of your actions." She pointed a finger to the dry courtyard. "Both of you . . . out . . . now."

Millie watched as the two children scrambled out of the fountain, lily pads and slime dripping off them, which earned them a thinning of the lips from their mother. They sent Millie pitiful looks that clearly begged for help, but then two sets of little shoulders sagged when it evidently became clear Millie had no help to offer them.

A maid appeared from behind Mrs. Cutling, and without speaking a word, she took hold of the children's filthy hands and led them away.

An ache formed in Millie's heart as the children were marched toward the back entrance, their small feet leaving muddy footprints against the tiles. When they disappeared from sight, she forced herself to face Mrs. Cutling. "Since I'm sure you don't want me to keep you from your friends any longer, I'll just be on my way."

"Not so fast, Miss Longfellow," Mrs. Cutling said, reaching out a hand to stop Millie from making a speedy escape. "Before you leave, I must insist you apologize — not only to me, but to my friends, whom you've distressed today."

A trace of stubbornness — something Millie had thought she'd put behind her long ago — took that moment to resurface. "I truly do not understand how seeing two sweet children being children could possibly distress anyone."

"They were filthy."

"Children can be expected to be filthy

upon occasion, especially when they're playing."

"My children are not permitted to be anything other than clean and tidy and, more importantly, free of slime."

"A little slime never hurt anyone."

A distinct touch of frost entered Mrs. Cutling's eyes. "My dear, your parents may have allowed you to participate in unacceptable childhood amusements that allowed you to get slimy on a regular basis. But, in my world, children are expected to behave properly at all times, no matter their tender ages."

"I grew up in an orphanage, Mrs. Cutling, and that experience led me to believe that all children deserve to enjoy a true childhood, one that occasionally comes with dirt, fun, and quite often, slime."

"Good heavens!" another one of the ladies exclaimed. "I don't believe I've ever met a nanny with such radical ideas." The lady sent a sniff Millie's way. "For your information, dear, Mrs. Cutling's father is a Patriarch. Because of the exclusiveness of that particular honor, Mrs. Cutling's children will always be held to a higher standard."

Mrs. Cutling rolled her eyes. "I hardly imagine Miss Longfellow knows what a

Patriarch is."

Not appreciating the whole rolling of the eyes business, Millie threw caution to the wind as she stuffed her dictionary back into her pocket, clasped her hands in front of her, and cleared her throat. "The term *Patriarch* was coined by Mr. Ward McAllister, *the* social arbiter of New York society. He, along with the assistance of Mrs. William Astor, in an obvious attempt at keeping the newly rich from entering their sacred inner social circles, devised a list that consisted of twenty-five names of gentlemen whom they considered . . . worthy. These twenty-five men were then each given the *daunting* task of choosing four of *their* worthy gentlemen friends, along with five appropriate ladies, all of whom were then included on Mrs. Astor's invitation list to her annual Patriarch Balls."

Millie wrinkled her nose. "Although, if you ask me, I don't really understand why everyone puts so much stock in what this Mr. McAllister thinks. It's clear he's a somewhat pompous and overly ambition sort who has entirely too much time on his hands, since he has nothing better to do than devise questionable lists."

Dead silence settled over the courtyard. All of the ladies were staring back at Millie with their mouths gaping open, although a few of them were beginning to turn a little pink, and Millie didn't think that was because of the sun.

"You've evidently misunderstood some of that information you claim Mrs. Hart has given you, Miss Longfellow," Mrs. Cutling finally said.

"Mrs. Hart didn't tell me about Patriarchs. Miss Harriet Peabody did. Though, in all fairness, she might have gotten her information from Mrs. Hart."

"Do not even tell me you're now going to try and convince me you're acquainted with Lady Harriet."

Forcing a smile, Millie began edging away from Mrs. Cutling. "Harriet and I have been friends for years, but . . . she doesn't really care to be addressed as Lady Harriet, just plain Harriet. Although . . . since she'll probably be married by the time she returns to the states, I suppose everyone will begin addressing her as Mrs. Oliver Addleshaw."

For a second, Mrs. Cutling appeared a little taken aback, but only for a second. "I highly doubt you share an intimate relationship with Lady Harriet, but enough about that nonsense. Since I have yet to hear a single word of apology come out of your mouth, do know that I will *not* be sending

19

you off with a reference letter. I will also not be giving you any of the wages I'm sure you feel you're due because I believe you put my children in grave danger. We're lucky they didn't drown in that fountain."

Looking down at the water, Millie frowned. "There's barely any water in there, Mrs. Cutling, and forgive me for saying so, but if you were truly concerned over your children drowning, one would think you would have seen them safely out of the fountain before running me down and spending precious time taking me to task."

That pronouncement earned Millie barely five minutes to pack up her belongings after Mrs. Cutling proclaimed her to be insubordinate. There were no fond farewells to give the children, no pristine letter stating how wonderful Millie was as a nanny, and not a single penny offered to see her back to New York City.

Before she knew it, she'd been deposited at the train station, where she purchased a ticket using funds she'd stashed away for emergencies. Unfortunately, the train was delayed due to a mechanical problem, and by the time Millie reached the wharf, the last ferry had departed from Long Island for the day. To her relief, a crusty yet completely delightful captain of a weathered fishing boat offered her a spot on his vessel, even going so far as to haul her heavy traveling bag up the plank himself when she accepted his offer.

The crossing proved to be memorable. Strong winds sprang up out of nowhere, and by the time they docked at the New York City harbor, she knew she was definitely looking the worse for wear. Her clothing was soaked, she was missing her cap, and she was absolutely sure that the neat and tidy bun she'd started the day out with was nowhere to be found, especially since a few strands of her brown, curly hair kept blowing around her face.

Besides looking less than her best, she was also fairly certain she smelled strongly of fish.

Giving the captain her warmest thanks once the vessel was securely docked, she dragged her heavy bag past numerous sailors, pretending to be hard of hearing when they sent whistles her way. By the time she put some space between herself and the sailors, her face was burning, but her embarrassment disappeared the moment she counted out the few coins she had left in her possession and found herself woefully short on funds. That meant even a trip on an omnibus was not in her future. Accepting a ride with a man delivering the very fish she'd escorted to the wharf, she consoled herself with the idea that although his wagon was less than comfortable, at least her unpleasant scent wasn't offending anyone.

When the delivery man dropped her off in front of the employment agency, nerves almost had her running after the delivery man and begging him to take her anywhere else. Mrs. Patterson, the woman who owned the agency, had warned Millie about losing another position, and Millie knew she was going to be in for a rough time of it once Mrs. Patterson learned she'd been dismissed yet again.

Reminding herself that she needed to secure new employment sooner rather than later, Millie squared her shoulders and headed for the steps. But before she had an opportunity to reach them, something hard and unyielding slammed into her. Dropping like a stone to the ground, Millie felt the oddest desire to simply stay there and let the world move on without her.

She was tired, smelly, discouraged, and didn't believe her life could get any worse than it was at that particular moment.

A second later, as she squinted up at what turned out to be a very large, very manly form, she realized she'd been wrong.

Her life could, indeed, become worse.

Peering down at her was none other than Mr. Everett Mulberry, a gentleman she knew through her acquaintance with Mr. Oliver Addleshaw. With his sculpted face, green eyes, and brown hair that was normally stylishly arranged — not that it was at that particular moment — he was an exceedingly handsome gentleman.

The first time she'd laid eyes on him, she'd actually become completely tongue-tied. Because Mr. Mulberry had recently inherited three young children to raise, Millie had found him slightly irresistible, until he'd had the audacity to immediately dismiss her offer of becoming a nanny to his slightly troublesome wards.

The moment he'd learned about her unfortunate propensity for getting let go from her positions, well . . . he turned adamant in his refusal to offer her employment.

The gentleman had not even given her a moment to properly explain all the past misunderstandings she'd suffered in those ill-fated employment situations, but had, instead, kept a careful distance between them whenever they happened to be in each other's immediate vicinity.

". . . and I cannot apologize enough for knocking you to the ground," Mr. Mulberry was saying, pulling Millie abruptly from her jaunt down memory lane. "Do know that my preoccupied state of mind is in no way an excuse for my less-than-careful regard for your person."

Pushing aside numerous curls that were obstructing her view, Millie was just about to take the hand Mr. Mulberry was offering her when his eyes suddenly widened and his offered hand was taken away.

"Miss Longfellow? What in the world are *you* doing here?"

Not appreciating the clear trace of horror in the gentleman's voice, Millie began struggling to her feet, reluctantly accepting the hand Mr. Mulberry finally thrust back at her. She soon found herself standing on her feet, even as she caught Mr. Mulberry's eye. "How *lovely* it is to see you, Mr. Mulberry. I do hope you and the children are well."

"You haven't been dismissed from another position, have you?" he asked, completely neglecting to exchange the expected pleasantries with her.

Millie lifted her chin. "I've been excellent of late — thank you for asking. And — to answer your oh-so-charming inquiry — why else would I be here instead of looking after

24

some little ones?"

"This is certain to complicate matters."

"How can my dismissal possibly complicate matters for you? Unless . . . Your wards haven't run off another nanny, have they?"

Mr. Mulberry frowned. "Mrs. Smithey preferred to be referred to as a nurse, but . . . yes, my wards somehow managed to run her off."

"And they did this . . . how?"

Raking a hand through his untidy hair, Mr. Mulberry shrugged. "From what I've been able to surmise, it all had to do with an unfortunate game of walking the plank, a plank that was, strangely enough, set over a fountain."

"Fountains do seem to be responsible for quite a bit of mischief today." She ignored his immediate look of confusion. "How is it possible — if I'm summarizing correctly — that three children were able to run off a woman by playing a simple game of walking the plank? Did this nurse not come with stellar references?"

"She came with the very best of references, but I don't believe she was expecting a frog to materialize on the scene — a creature, it unfortunately turns out, Mrs. Smithey is deathly afraid of."

25

"It's an unspoken requirement that women who choose to look after children for a living have a strong liking for all manner of creatures."

"I'm sure that's a valid point, Miss Longfellow. However, in Mrs. Smithey's defense, I don't believe she was expecting the little monster — and those are Mrs. Smithey's words about Thaddeus, not mine — to prod a frog in her direction as she was halfway across the plank. That nasty business resulted in the woman falling off the plank and into the fountain." Mr. Mulberry gave a sad shake of his head. "She was packed and out of the house before I could offer her a substantial raise to keep her in my employ."

"How much of a 'substantial raise'?"

Mr. Mulberry immediately began inching away from her. "I don't believe I care for that particular glint in your eyes, Miss Longfellow. Although, glinting eyes aside, I'm afraid I'm going to have to ask just the tiniest favor from you."

"You want me to look after your wards?"

"Ah, no. That's not what I want at all." He ignored her sputters even as he continued to inch backward. "What I need you to do is wait out here until I've secured a new nanny from the agency."

"Why would you want me to do that?"

"Because the last time I came here and managed to obtain the services of Mrs. Smithey, I was warned that there would be dire consequences if the children managed to drive that woman away. Since they *have* managed to do that — and somewhat quickly, I must add — I'm afraid the dire consequences I might face will involve you, once the agency learns you're out of work again."

He let out what sounded exactly like a sigh. "I wouldn't be surprised to hear Mrs. Patterson say something like we deserve each other, and I'd really like to avoid that, if it's all the same to you."

Millie summoned up what she hoped would be taken as a pleasant smile, nodded to Mr. Mulberry, and — right after he smiled back and began to look relieved — bolted for the agency door.

2

As a distinct whiff of ocean, mixed with a large dollop of fish, wafted back to him when Miss Longfellow rushed past, Everett took one step to go after her but then stopped and simply watched as she disappeared through the agency door.

In the past, he would have found her less-than-cooperative attitude rather confusing, given that she was a nanny and he was a well-regarded member of society. However, since he'd come into possession of his three wards — whom he occasionally thought of as *the brats,* and not always fondly — members of the working class were behaving, at least toward him, very oddly indeed. Governesses, nannies, maids, footmen, and even a few of his best drivers, had abandoned his household in droves, leaving his normally pleasant and structured life in a bit of an upheaval.

Taking a moment to consider his options,

Everett pulled a handkerchief from his pocket and began removing the dirt Miss Longfellow had deposited when she'd taken his hand.

It wasn't that he disliked Miss Longfellow — quite the contrary. With her decidedly quirky personality and habit of uttering words that didn't always suit what she wanted to say, Miss Longfellow was somewhat charming, if slightly deranged.

She seemed to possess an unusual exuberance for life, although at the moment, she also seemed to possess rather short brown curls — something he'd noticed as he'd been conversing with her.

He had a sneaking suspicion the reason behind the shortness was an unfortunate incident with a hot curling tong Miss Longfellow had experimented with a few weeks before. From what he'd heard, Miss Longfellow had perfected the art of *scorching* instead of *curling,* which had resulted with her being discouraged from trying out the tongs on the hair of Miss Harriet Peabody, a lady who was now engaged to one of Everett's best friends, Mr. Oliver Addleshaw.

Everett smiled as an image of Oliver, with Harriet by his side, immediately sprang to mind. They'd been standing on the deck of

Oliver's yacht, waving madly to everyone who'd turned out to see them off to England. That their love for each other had been unexpected, there could be no denying. Even though Everett had been a little hesitant at first to support the idea of Oliver actually marrying Harriet — a woman who'd been earning a living as a hat maker, of all things — he'd eventually come to realize that Harriet was exactly what Oliver needed.

Shoving the handkerchief back into his pocket, he glanced back toward the agency door and found his thoughts immediately returning to one Miss Millie Longfellow.

It truly was a shame he couldn't consider hiring her on, especially since she did seem to be a rather pleasant sort, even if she certainly didn't look like a typical nanny. Her form was waif-like, her features delicate, and she had somewhat intriguing lips — intriguing because they were slightly plumper than a person would expect to find on a face that was so . . .

Realizing that his thoughts were beginning to travel in a direction that they really didn't need to travel, Everett reminded himself exactly why he truly couldn't contemplate bringing Miss Longfellow on as a nanny to his wards — and it had absolutely nothing to do with her lips.

It all had to do with the lady's eyes.

That they were a perfectly ordinary shade of green was not in dispute. But that ordinary green, framed by dark lashes, always held a distinct trace of . . . mischief.

That mischief exactly explained why he wouldn't, or couldn't, consider hiring Miss Longfellow on to watch after his wards, because everyone knew that where there was mischief, trouble was certain to follow.

Ever since he'd become the unlikely guardian to three unruly children over five months before, Everett had witnessed more trouble than he'd ever thought possible. His life had been turned upside down — orderliness replaced with chaos, that chaos drawing censure from his friends and disappointment from his very own Miss Dixon.

Caroline Dixon was his perfect match in every way, her standing in society as lofty as his, and her desire to increase that standing rivaling his own. That she was not a girl fresh out of the schoolroom, being twenty-four years of age, was a definite mark in her favor. She didn't expect tender words whispered into her ears, and appreciated the fact that theirs was a relationship based on mutual advantages rather than any of the romantic fantasies so many younger ladies seemed to want to embrace these days.

Gentlemen of his social position had, for years, chosen their future wives exactly as Everett was choosing his now. If the thought occasionally struck him that it seemed somewhat cold selecting a wife in such a manner, he quickly pushed the thought aside, consoling himself with the notion that he and Caroline stood to gain much from their practical alliance.

He would secure a wife who was self-assured, competent at holding her own in a conversation, and perfectly capable of securing them the coveted invitations to all the proper dinners and balls.

Caroline would secure herself a husband possessed of an extensive fortune, one he didn't mind sharing with her in the least. She'd also obtain a husband who wouldn't hover around her, since he spent a great deal of time managing his many businesses. As an added benefit, when he wasn't consumed with business matters, having an entire brigade of associates in his employ who were perfectly capable of running his affairs, he enjoyed sailing his yacht on the high seas — something Caroline didn't particularly care to do all that often, which would allow her further time to spend pursuing her own interests.

All in all, they were a perfect match for each other, which was why he had no hesitation in humoring her, or rather, indulging her, when she turned a little . . . difficult — something she'd done just that afternoon.

When Mrs. Smithey had resigned, or rather, fled, from her position only a few hours before, Caroline had stated she'd had quite enough, and he couldn't actually blame her. Ever since he'd inherited the children, the life he and Caroline had grown accustomed to had disappeared. Plans, including those for their engagement, had been put on hold, and he couldn't count the number of times he'd been unable to escort her to a scheduled society event because of difficulties with the children.

Even though she'd been disappointed time and time again over the past five months, she'd handled herself with poise . . . until Mrs. Smithey had up and fled. That unfortunate business had resulted in Caroline losing her composure, apparently unable, or unwilling, to delay their trip to Newport since she'd delayed so many other events in her life because of his wards.

Tears had begun dribbling down Caroline's pale cheeks seconds after Mrs. Smithey flew out the door, and Everett had not been immune to the power of Caroline's tears. Not wishing to disappoint her yet again, he'd immediately headed out for the employment agency, praying a miracle could be found there.

That miracle, however, could not be found in the form of Miss Millie Longfellow. Bringing her, along with her mischievous nature, into his household was inviting further instances of disastrous situations. His wards needed a woman with a stern disposition and little tolerance for nonsense, and that woman certainly was not Miss Longfellow because . . .

The sound of the agency door opening pulled Everett from his thoughts, but he did not discover Miss Longfellow exiting the building, as he'd expected. Standing on the stoop was none other than Mrs. Smithey, the woman who'd just left his employ. She was sniffling into a large handkerchief as she moved down the steps, but she stumbled to a stop when she caught sight of him.

"I won't go back," she said in a voice that held a telling note of hysteria in it. "Not even if you offered me a thousand dollars."

"What if I offered you two thousand for simply watching the children for the rest of the summer?"

A lift of a chin, followed by a very loud

34

sniff, was Mrs. Smithey's only response before she turned on her sensible heel and marched off, leaving Everett staring after her.

"I would be more than happy to relieve you of two thousand dollars — especially if all that is required of me to earn that small fortune is to look after your little angels."

Turning back to the agency, he narrowed his eyes on Miss Longfellow, who was peering at him from the doorway.

"Has anyone ever told you that eavesdropping is unbecoming for a lady?"

She waved a slightly dirty hand in the air. "I've heard that numerous times, Mr. Mulberry — usually from disintegrated ex-employers."

"Disintegrated?"

Miss Longfellow bit her lip. "I knew I shouldn't have tried out a D word, especially since I haven't studied them for a few months now." She whipped out what appeared to be a dictionary from her pocket, riffled through it for a second and then looked up. "I might have meant *disenchanted,* although *disgruntled* would probably be a better description."

"Yes, well, *disintegrated, disenchanted,* and *disgruntled* aside, you still shouldn't have been eavesdropping on me."

"I wasn't eavesdropping. You practically shouted your offer at that unpleasant-looking woman, and it was hardly my fault she didn't shut the door firmly behind her after she spoke her mind to Mrs. Patterson." Miss Longfellow smiled. "You'll be pleased to learn I told Mrs. Patterson you're here, and . . . she's anxiously waiting to speak to you."

"Why did you tell her I was here?"

"To distract her from her annoyance with me, of course."

"Has anyone ever told you that you're incorrigible?"

"If that means *delightful,* then certainly." Miss Longfellow grinned, but her grin disappeared in a flash when Mrs. Patterson joined her in the doorway.

"Mr. Mulberry," Mrs. Patterson began as she sent him a look that seemed to suggest she found him rather distasteful. "I thought I was fairly clear the last time we saw each other — as in *yesterday* — that you were to strive diligently to get control of your wards so you wouldn't lose another employee."

"Was it only yesterday I was here?" he asked weakly.

"You know it was." Mrs. Patterson gestured to the door. "You might as well come in."

Knowing he had no other choice, he moved forward, although he did so rather slowly, stopping on the first step to nod at Miss Longfellow. "I suppose this is where we part ways, Miss Longfellow. Do know that I'm incredibly sorry I knocked you to the ground before."

"Miss Longfellow isn't leaving quite yet," Mrs. Patterson said. "She and I have yet to have a proper chat since up until a few minutes ago I was forced to deal with a distraught Mrs. Smithey." She wagged a finger in Everett's direction. "I hope you have a reasonable explanation as to why you allowed that poor woman to be set upon by a vicious pet."

Miss Longfellow's unladylike snort saved Everett from a response.

"From what Mr. Mulberry told me," Miss Longfellow began, "Thaddeus's pet is nothing more than a little frog, and what harm could one of those do to a person?" Miss Longfellow shook her head. "In my humble opinion, this Mrs. Smithey is obviously in the wrong profession. I do hope you'll refuse to place her with another family, Mrs. Patterson, especially since she seems to have a troubling tendency for dramatic displays."

Everett found himself shuddering ever so

slightly when Mrs. Patterson drew herself up.

"Mrs. Smithey has never been dismissed from a position due to unfortunate shenanigans, which certainly cannot be said about you, Miss Longfellow."

Mrs. Patterson lifted her chin. "Now then, before I decide to wash my hands of both of you, I suggest we set aside all attempts at nonsense and repair to my office." She turned and disappeared through the door.

"I do believe she's rather annoyed with us," Miss Longfellow said before she brightened. "But she didn't say she *was* washing her hands of us, so all hope hasn't been lost just yet." She caught his eye. "Would you be a dear and fetch my bag for me? The one I dropped when you knocked me over. It's lying there all forlorn on the sidewalk."

Unable to remember the last time someone had call him *a dear,* and asked him to *fetch* something, Everett's lips curled into a grin, and he ambled over to the bag and bent down to pick it up. Grabbing hold of the worn handle, he straightened . . . but wobbled when the weight of the bag took him by surprise. "What in the world do you have in here?"

"Essentials."

"What type of *essentials* could possibly weigh this much?"

"Well, if you must know, since I was intending on spending the next nine weeks employed by the Cutler family before I got unfairly dismissed, I had to pack enough reading material to see me through that extended period of time. In that bag rests a few of my favorite dictionaries, one thesaurus, my Bible, numerous works by Shakespeare, although I'm not exactly enjoying his writing, and two books by the incomparable Jane Austen." She smiled. "Those I enjoy tremendously, but besides my treasured books, I also have a few changes of clothing, an extra pair of shoes, and, well, I won't go into further details, since what's left to mention will most likely embarrass us both."

Hefting the bag up the steps, Everett followed Miss Longfellow through the door and dropped the bag, not surprised in the least when a loud thud sounded around them. "Are you telling me you fit everything you needed for two months into this one bag?"

"Well, not everything. I did want to include a lovely collection of poems by Lord Byron I found for a pittance at an outdoor market, along with my well-read copy of

39

Frankenstein, but there simply wasn't enough room to stuff them into my bag."

Everett frowned. "Miss Dixon sent her 'essentials' off to Newport two days ago, and it took three wagons to get her bags to the steamship."

"Miss Dixon, being of the society set, is expected to change clothing at least six times per day," Miss Longfellow countered. "She's also expected to not wear the same clothing too often, if at all, so I'm not surprised she had numerous trunks and bags. I, being a nanny, only have need of two sets of sensible clothing that I wear as I take care of the children, and two other outfits for when I'm at my leisure, which isn't often during the summer months."

"How many hours are you expected to work in a day during the summer, and . . . don't you get days off in every week?"

"I get a half day off every week, and the hours I work per day vary according to when the children go off to bed and if they stay in bed."

Disbelief held him silent for a moment, but only for a moment. "You might want to work on your negotiating skills, Miss Long-fellow. The women I've hired to look after my wards — and there have been many of them — have all received at least one full

40

day off per week, sometimes two depending on how desperate I am, and they only work, at the very most, ten hours per day."

"Miss Longfellow has a dismal employment record," Mrs. Patterson said, sticking her head out the office door. "Which means she has very little negotiating room, although that circumstance may soon change since I know perfectly well the extent of your desperation." She gestured him forward. "If you ask me, the only solution to both of your problems is for the two of you to join forces, especially since I'm rapidly coming to the belief that you might just deserve each other." With that, she vanished from sight again.

"I *told* you she was going to come to that conclusion," Everett said as he followed Miss Longfellow into Mrs. Patterson's office.

"I don't appreciate your attitude, Mr. Mulberry," Miss Longfellow said before she took a seat in an uncomfortable-looking chair. "Nor do I appreciate the idea that you think this situation we're currently in is my fault. If you would have simply considered hiring me when you first learned I was a nanny, you would not now be in a desperate frame of mind."

"Only because I probably wouldn't still

41

have the responsibility of my wards if I'd hired you. You might have lost them by now or —"

"It would not be in your best interest to finish that sentence, sir," Miss Longfellow interrupted. "I have never — and I repeat, never — caused any of the children in my care to come to any harm."

"What about that little Billy? I distinctly remember you telling me you almost drowned him."

"You're forgetting the story. It is true that I was a little misinformed about how children can learn to swim, but if you'll recall, after tossing little Billy into the water, I had second thoughts and jumped in after him. He proved that I wasn't completely off the mark, since he immediately paddled to shore — whereas I promptly sank."

"I'm certainly glad you cleared that up for me. I now feel so much more confident in your abilities."

"Honestly, the two of you are enough to set a person's head to pounding." Mrs. Patterson leaned forward across her desk, raising her voice because Miss Longfellow had begun to mumble under her breath. "Am I to understand, given the familiarity the two of you are currently showing each other, that you've been acquainted for quite some time?"

When Miss Longfellow stopped mumbling and pressed her lips together, Everett had no choice but to answer for both of them. "We are acquainted with each other, but I wouldn't go so far as to claim we're overly familiar with each other."

Mrs. Patterson settled back in the chair. "Why then, pray tell, haven't you simply hired Miss Longfellow to watch over your wards?"

"Do you really believe there needs to be another explanation other than the fact I'm slightly acquainted with her? Really, Mrs. Patterson, this is Miss Longfellow we're discussing."

"I *am* still in the room." Miss Longfellow crossed her arms over her chest. "And I'm beginning to take issue with the way this conversation is going."

Mrs. Patterson ignored her and kept her gaze on Everett. "You, my dear man, are not in a position to be overly selective at the moment. As I seem to recall, you told me you're behind schedule traveling to Newport — a situation that has your Miss Dixon decidedly put out. Her attitude will certainly not change if she's forced to miss more of Newport's summer festivities because you're unable to find anyone willing to take on the children. Since I have no one available at the moment to travel with you to Newport, other than Miss Longfellow, you're going to have to put aside whatever qualms you have in regard to her abilities and offer her employment."

Mrs. Patterson had the nerve to smile. "She's really not that bad, and to her credit, children do seem to adore her."

"Forgive me, Mrs. Patterson, but I find I'm not quite desperate enough to hire Miss Longfellow. I have been given the responsibility of three children. With that responsibility comes the expectation that I will keep them alive until they reach adulthood. Putting Miss Longfellow in charge of them is truly not the best way for me to achieve the whole keeping-them-alive part of my plan."

"I never realized you were possessed of such a melodramatic nature, Mr. Mulberry," Mrs. Patterson began. "But while I sympathize slightly with your plight, knowing you never expected to have three children dropped off on your doorstep, I'm afraid you've run out of options. Your wards' reputations precede them, and no one wants to work for you, with the exception of Miss Longfellow."

Miss Longfellow suddenly rose to her feet

and lifted her chin. "I find I no longer have any desire to work for Mr. Mulberry."

Mrs. Patterson waved Miss Longfellow's protest aside. "Of course you do, dear. Why, he pays top dollar, and you'll get to spend your summer in Newport. It's *the* place to summer these days, and I've heard Mr. Mulberry has one of the most impressive cottages there." She smiled. "It faces the ocean."

"Which is exactly why I won't be taking Miss Longfellow with me to Newport," Everett argued. "She'll either drown the children by tossing them into the waves to assess their swimming abilities, or drown herself in the process, leaving me short a nanny once ag—"

"I wouldn't work for you even if you offered me two thousand dollars, begged me on bended knee, and brought me flowers." Miss Longfellow turned her attention to Mrs. Patterson. "If you come across a family other than Mr. Mulberry's who could use my services, I may be reached at Mrs. Hart's residence in Washington Square."

With that, Miss Longfellow spared him not a single glance before she spun on her heel and stalked out of the office, leaving a distinct smell of ocean in the room.

One hour later, Everett walked into his Fifth Avenue mansion, unable to fully appreciate the spectacular detail the architect, Mr. Richard Morris Hunt, had accomplished in the entranceway. His gaze didn't settle as it normally did on the high ceiling with the painted fresco gleaming down at him or on the treasured furnishings that had been found throughout Europe to bring attention to the mahogany woodwork. Due to his dismal frame of mind, he barely remembered to nod at his butler, Mr. Macon, who'd been holding the door open for him since before Everett had even reached the steps. He paused mid-nod, though, when he finally noticed that Mr. Macon was looking a little . . . distracted — something that was completely out of character for the gentleman.

"Is something wrong, Mr. Macon?" he forced himself to ask.

Mr. Macon shut the door. "Wrong? Why would you assume something is wrong?"

Everett cocked a brow. "Since something is always amiss these days, I don't believe my assumption is farfetched, and . . . the house seems unusually quiet."

"As you very well know, sir, most of the staff departed for Newport a few weeks ago to ready the cottage."

"And as *you* well know, Mr. Macon, the staff hasn't been responsible for the overabundance of noise of late."

"True, this is true. But speaking of the staff, I'm certain they've gotten Seaview Cottage sufficiently ready by now. They're probably at loose ends, since they were expecting you in Newport last week."

"I'm sure the staff will miss their boredom once I show up with the children in tow." Everett shook his head. "I certainly wasn't planning on delaying my trip this long, but due to the antics of my wards, well . . . need I say more?"

"If I may be so bold, sir, those antics might lessen if you were to take a moment to reassure the children that you have no intention of sending them off to a faraway boarding school in the immediate future."

"They know about the boarding school idea?"

"They're very good at lurking, sir, especially outside doors where important conversations are taking place."

"They lurk outside doors?"

"Indeed, and can usually be found doing that lurking whenever Miss Dixon comes to visit. And speaking of Miss Dixon, she's waiting for you in the library."

"Caroline's still here?"

"Surely you didn't think she'd go home before learning the outcome of your quest, did you?"

"I'm afraid she's doomed for disappointment, because I was less than successful. But . . . I would have to imagine, given the lateness of the hour, that her companion is none too pleased about Caroline waiting for me."

"She sent Miss Nora Niesen home an hour ago, sir. From what I understand, Caroline wanted to spend some time alone with the children."

"While I should find that encouraging, hearing that Caroline wanted to spend time with the children, it was hardly proper of her to send Miss Niesen away."

"Forgive me, sir, but because Miss Niesen is more of a friend to Miss Dixon, especially since she doesn't get paid, it's not quite the thing to expect the woman to stay up late because of your situation with your wards."

"Perhaps I should encourage Caroline to hire on a real companion."

"Or perhaps you should simply hire on a nanny capable of doing her job. I find it difficult to believe that there isn't at least one woman out there who's up for the task of bringing your wards in hand."

"An excellent point, Mr. Macon, but . . . speaking of my wards, I should probably see how Caroline is faring with them."

Sending Mr. Macon a nod, Everett turned on his heel and strode down the hallway. Passing the curved staircase that was the centerpiece of the house, he was almost to the library when he noticed something that slowed his pace to a mere crawl. A priceless painting of a young lady — painted by none other than Bouguereau — seemed to have acquired a mustache placed inexpertly above the young lady's lip.

Leaning closer to the painting, he released a sigh when it quickly became evident that someone had, indeed, added his or her own touch to the masterpiece. Deciding that now was not the moment to spend dwelling on this particular situation, he tore his gaze from what was now a less-than-priceless painting and headed into the library. What met his gaze there took him completely by surprise.

Instead of the chaos and disaster he'd expected, he found Miss Caroline Dixon, looking lovely with her brown hair pulled attractively away from her face and wearing a beautiful gown of striped blue, sitting in a

49

delicate chair upholstered in forest green, sipping a cup of tea. Sitting opposite her, in a matching chair of green and reading out loud, was Elizabeth, the oldest of his wards at eight. The twins, five-year-old Thaddeus and Rosetta, were sitting stiff as pokers on a settee, both of them wearing identical, poorly sewn frocks, not that Thaddeus wearing a frock was an odd sight to see these days.

Everett accepted full responsibility for the little boy's refusal to wear anything but dresses. In all fairness, though, there was no possible way he could have known that when Elizabeth had sewn a frock for her little brother, she'd only done so because she didn't know how to sew pants. When Everett had made the unfortunate error of pointing out that little boys didn't wear frocks, Thaddeus had turned stubborn. In an obvious attempt to stick up for his sister, he now balked at wearing anything other than the frocks Elizabeth stitched up for him.

Even though Everett found the situation somewhat amusing, and was impressed with how long Thaddeus had been able to stick to his principles, he knew seeing Thaddeus dressed as a girl day after day was beginning to embarrass Caroline to no small end.

That meant he was going to have to figure out a way of getting Thaddeus back into pants one way or another before Caroline took matters into her own hands, a situation that would hardly encourage harmony in his household.

"What a charming picture all of you make," he said, stepping farther into the room as Caroline set aside her cup of tea and smiled at him.

"Everett, I was hoping you'd return soon." Caroline craned her neck right before her smile slid off her face. "But . . . where's the new nanny?"

"I'm afraid I wasn't successful with that tonight, dear, but don't fret. I'll go back to the employment agency in the morning." He smiled at Elizabeth who was peering at him over the top of her book. "What's that you're reading, Elizabeth?"

Elizabeth Burkhart scrunched up her nose, and for a moment, he didn't think she was going to respond, but then she held up the book. *Little Women.*

"That's a bit of a depressing tale, because if I'm not much mistaken, one of the sisters dies, doesn't she?"

Elizabeth snapped the book shut. "I guess there's no need for me to finish reading it now."

Everett winced. "Ah, yes, quite right — sorry about that." He looked back to Caroline. "Everything go well while I was away?"

"Everything's been fine," Caroline said as she nodded to the twins. "We've come to an understanding."

Alarm coursed through him. "What kind of an understanding?"

Caroline waved a hand in the air. "I just went over a few of my expectations for them. Once I explained some of the punishments they might face if they continue on with the mayhem — such as no meals, no frogs, and no fun — well . . . they understand my position. I don't believe we'll be seeing any more trouble. Will we, children?" Caroline arched a dainty brow at the twins.

"No," Thaddeus and Rosetta said together.

"No . . . what?" Caroline asked pleasantly.

For a second, pure mutiny flashed from both the twins' eyes, but then Rosetta smiled. "No more trouble, Miss Dixon."

"Exactly right." Caroline looked back to Everett. "Now then, returning to the nanny situation. What happened?"

"Mrs. Patterson doesn't have anyone available at the moment. Well, not anyone suitable for our needs."

"So there *was* at least someone?"

"Not really."

Caroline picked up her tea and took a sip. "I will be beyond disappointed if we have to delay our trip to Newport again, Everett, especially since I've already missed numerous social events. I, along with Miss Niesen, have plans to play tennis at the Casino two days from now with our friends. I will be sorely put out if I have to give up my match because you can't find help to watch over the children."

Rubbing a hand over his face, Everett took a step closer to her. "You and Miss Niesen should go to Newport without me, which is what I suggested to you two weeks ago, when nanny number twelve left my employ. You do have your own cottage after all, given to you by your very indulgent grandmother, and it seems a shame that said cottage is still standing vacant at the moment, except for your staff, of course."

Caroline let out a sniff. "Society would not look kindly on me if I were to abandon you in your time of need." She lifted her chin. "But, I'm going to admit here and now that I'm beginning to get extremely annoyed with you. If there is a woman out there available to work, whether she's suitable for the position or not, I'm going to have to insist you offer her a position — tonight."

Everett opened his mouth to argue, but before he could utter a single word, Caroline set aside her cup and began rising from her chair, stopping suddenly as she sucked in a sharp breath of air. A mere second later, Everett discovered what was behind her peculiar behavior.

The chair was now firmly attached to Caroline's behind, sticking out at a very awkward angle. One glance to the twins — both of whom were looking far too innocent — proved who was responsible for the latest disaster.

A second later, there was an ominous ripping sound, and to his relief, Caroline was no longer attached to the chair, but when she turned around, he discovered that she was also no longer attached to the back of her skirt. As her shrieks of outrage began bouncing around the room, Everett realized what he was going to have to do.

He was, much against his better judgment, going to have to seek out Miss Longfellow and beg her — on bended knee and with flowers, no doubt — to come work for him.

3

With bubbles tickling her nose, Millie leaned her head back against the rim of the clawfoot tub, appreciating the luxury of taking an honest-to-goodness bubble bath. Before Abigail Hart had come barreling into Millie's life almost two months before, along with the lives of her friends, Miss Harriet Peabody and Miss Lucetta Plum, she'd never had the opportunity to slide into a tub filled with bubbles. There could be no denying that there were many luxuries available to her now that she'd accepted Abigail's offer of a permanent place to live when she wasn't working, but Millie certainly didn't take any of them for granted.

The reasoning behind Abigail welcoming her into her home was still a bit of a mystery. Abigail claimed she'd done so because she owed Reverend Thomas Gilmore a favor, but Millie didn't think that was the only reason behind the woman's extreme generosity. Abigail, from what little Millie had learned about the lady, seemed to have numerous regrets from her past. Those regrets, more than any favors owed, were most likely what had prompted Abigail to take three young ladies out of the tenement slums and see them settled in Washington Square.

While Millie was incredibly grateful for the generosity offered her, she couldn't help feeling just a smidgen of wariness about her current situation, especially because Abigail seemed to have a distinct propensity for . . . plotting. Abigail's last plot had revolved around getting Miss Harriet Peabody and Mr. Oliver Addleshaw well settled. Since Abigail had met with great success in that endeavor, Millie was quickly coming to the conclusion that the dear woman was now in search of fresh prey. Which meant —

"Ah, wonderful, I was hoping to find you in the tub," Abigail said, strolling right into the very midst of the bathing chamber. Moving over to a dainty chair gilded in gold, she took her seat, glancing around the room. "Do you like the improvements I had done while you were off with that horrible Cutling woman?"

Sinking ever so slowly down into the bubbles, Millie managed to summon up a smile. "Everything is delightful. Although I'm not really sure why you had so many chairs brought in here."

"I needed to make certain I'd have a place to sit."

Millie's smile disappeared in a flash. "I know I still have much to learn about etiquette and the peculiar ways of people with wealth, Abigail, but I don't recall working for a society family who liked to congregate for conversation in the bathing chamber."

"We in society share the bathing chamber quite often, my dear. Why, most society ladies your age have their own personal maids, and those maids are responsible for helping their young ladies bathe, as well as helping them into their clothing numerous times per day."

"Well, yes, I did know that, but I don't believe those maids pull up a chair and settle in for a long duration during bath time."

"Which is a most excellent point, but I'll have you know that when my daughter was growing up, she and I shared the most interesting conversations when she was in her bath."

"Because she wasn't able to escape while she was bathing?"

"Exactly." Abigail settled back in the chair. "Now then, tell me, are you quite certain you don't want me to have a little chat with Mrs. Cutling?"

"While I appreciate the offer, Abigail, I don't think that's necessary. I really just want to put that unfortunate incident behind me and move on with my life."

"How lovely, and do know that I'm more than happy to assist you with that moving on with your life business. In fact, I insist on lending you my invaluable advice."

Not caring at all for the distinct note of glee in Abigail's voice, Millie dunked under the bubbles, hoping that if she stayed there long enough, Abigail just might forget the direction the conversation seemed to be heading. When she started getting a little dizzy from lack of air, she resurfaced and discovered that while she'd been depriving herself of oxygen, another person had entered the room — that person being none other than her very good friend Miss Lucetta Plum.

"Lucetta, what a wonderful surprise."

Miss Lucetta Plum, acclaimed actress and beauty of the New York theater scene, grinned. "I don't know why you'd be surprised to see me since I do live here. However, seeing you is certainly a surprise.

What happened?"

"Do you really need to ask?"

"Oh . . . dear, you were let go again, weren't you. But . . . honestly, Millie, being employed for only a week has to be a new record for you."

"It's not," Millie admitted. "If you'll recall, due to that unpleasant situation with the goats, I only lasted a day when I went to work for Mrs. Wilson a few years back." She shuddered, stirring the bubbles. "How could I have possibly known those particular goats had a fondness for violets? I certainly wouldn't have dabbed violet water on my wrists that morning if I'd known it was going to send the goats into a frenzy. But, goat incidents aside, yes, I did get dismissed once again today, and no, I don't feel like talking about it. Let's talk about you and how rehearsals are going for your latest play."

Turning on a lovely high-heeled shoe, Lucetta moved to sit in a chair right beside Abigail, gesturing around the room with a wave of a gloved hand. "This is nice and cozy, Abigail. What an interesting idea to add furniture in the bathing chamber."

"She's only done so because she wants to be able to hold us captive as we bathe," Millie pointed out.

Lucetta stopped gesturing. "I should tell

you that I prefer to bathe with no one in the room, Abigail — not even a maid. That means *I* certainly won't need furniture in the bathing room you're redecorating for me."

"That's too bad, since I've already ordered some." Abigail folded her hands in her lap. "But new furniture aside, why are you home early tonight?"

Lucetta pushed a strand of golden hair out of her face. "The new electric lights the owner of the theater had installed began to smoke. I decided it wouldn't be in my best interest to linger, so . . . I returned here to enjoy the rest of my evening with you."

Abigail gave a sad shake of her head. "Life in the theater does seem to be filled with unexpected hazards, dear. Which is why you really should, as I've suggested a time or two, reconsider your chosen profession."

"I adore being an actress."

"Hmm . . . I'm not certain I completely believe that, dear, but . . . you do have a steady income at the moment, whereas Millie does not . . ."

Abigail settled her attention squarely on Millie again. "Because you've been very vocal regarding your desire to work, and I don't know of any families who need a nanny at this particular time, I think the

60

only option available to us is to introduce you to my grandson. He's a bit of a recluse, but I'm sure he can be convinced to take you on."

"Take me on?" Millie repeated slowly.

"Indeed, but I'm not certain in what capacity we should ask him to do that taking on just yet."

"He doesn't have children?" Millie pressed.

"Not a one, but I have to imagine, with a little persuasion on my part, he'd be downright delighted to offer you some type of position. . . . Perhaps as a social secretary or keeper of his extensive library."

"Don't you think his wife might have a slight problem with her husband hiring on a young lady with no social secretary skills or any ability to keep a library?"

"He's not married, dear."

Millie's mouth dropped open. "Really, Abigail, one would think you'd be a little more subtle, but if I must remind you, I'm not in the market for a husband."

"Every unattached lady, whether they admit it or not, is in the market for a husband, my dear. However . . ." Abigail turned to Lucetta. "I actually believe you'd be a more appropriate match for my grandson, who goes by the very charming name of . . . Bram."

Lucetta's mouth gaped open, much like Millie's had done only seconds before. "I am definitely not in the market for a husband, especially a recluse. Why, that particular word immediately brings to mind an image of a curmudgeon, one sporting some type of horrible disfigurement, that disfigurement the reasoning behind the whole reclusive business."

"Bram isn't disfigured," Abigail argued. "In fact, he's quite a dish, from what young ladies have told me."

Lucetta lifted her chin. "Dish or not, you will leave me out of your matchmaking plans."

"And I second what Lucetta just said, although I'm curious now as to what *curmudgeon* means. Because I'm in my bath, though — something both of you seem to have forgotten — I don't have a dictionary handy."

"*Curmudgeon* means grouchy, but you're exactly right, Millie." Lucetta rose to her feet. "We've been very rude, keeping you from enjoying your bath, so Abigail and I will repair to the library and leave you in peace."

"But we haven't yet settled on a plan as to what to do with Millie." Abigail rose from her chair, although she looked extremely disappointed to do so.

"I've already spoken with Mrs. Patterson," Millie began. "And, while she voiced doubts about finding another family willing to take me on, I'm sure she'll be successful in the end, especially if I continue to show up at the agency every other day, begging for a position."

Abigail, to Millie's concern, plopped back down on the chair. "I do hope Mrs. Patterson wasn't too unpleasant with you, dear. She should know by now that you can't actually help the mischief you and your charges always seem to find yourselves in."

"Mrs. Patterson wasn't the reason behind the unpleasantness I experienced tonight. Mr. Everett Mulberry was."

Lucetta abruptly retook her seat as well. "You never mentioned a single thing about running into Everett."

"Because you just got home, and again, I'm trying to take a bath, and just so everyone knows, the water is turning a little chilly." She sent what she hoped was a pointed look toward the door, but her message was ignored.

"Chilly water is incredibly beneficial for a lady's skin, but back to Everett." Lucetta scooted her chair forward. "Did his wards run off another nanny, and did he ask you to accept a position with him, and . . . did you feel compelled to turn down his offer because of that pesky attraction you feel for the man?"

"I'm not attracted to Mr. Mulberry," was the only protest she could think to respond.

"How could you not be attracted to the gentleman?" Abigail countered. "A person would have to be blind not to notice that he's incredibly handsome. Add in the fact he's now responsible for three children, and well that must make him downright scrumptious to a lady who has a soft spot for little ones."

"I do not find Mr. Mulberry scrumptious," Millie argued, wincing when Abigail sent her an incredulous look. "Oh, very well, I might have, when I first laid eyes on the man, thought he was a little handsome — although *not* scrumptious, mind you. But after he refused to consider me as a nanny for his wards, his handsomeness faded in a flash. Furthermore —"

A knock on the door interrupted her speech.

"Mrs. Hart? Are you in there?" Mr. Kenton, Abigail's butler, called through the door.

Abigail rose to her feet and moved across the room. "I am, Mr. Kenton, but Miss Longfellow is in the middle of her bath, so in order to preserve her modesty, I suggest you don't open this door."

"Very good, ma'am, but I'm here to tell you that Miss Longfellow has a visitor. He gave his name as Mr. Everett Mulberry. May I tell him Miss Longfellow is receiving this evening?"

"Of course she's receiving, Mr. Kenton. Tell Mr. Mulberry she'll be down directly."

"Tell him I'm not available," Millie called.

"Do no such thing, Mr. Kenton," Abigail countered. "Millie is certainly available, and she'll receive Mr. Mulberry in the drawing room in five minutes, ten at the most."

"Very good, ma'am."

Listening to Mr. Kenton's departing footsteps, Millie frowned at Abigail, who'd turned away from the door and was beaming back at her. "I have no desire to see Mr. Mulberry, and since I *am* in the middle of my bath, which does, indeed, make me unavailable, you'll need to go and make my excuses to the man."

"You've been complaining that your water is getting cold. That means you'll have to get out of the tub soon to avoid freezing to death, making you available to speak with

Mr. Mulberry."

"Perhaps I've decided to heed Lucetta's advice and enjoy the benefits cold water is supposed to deliver to my skin."

Abigail shook a finger in Millie's direction. "I'll give you ten minutes to make yourself presentable, and do make certain to choose a suitable frock to wear." With that, and before Millie could voice another protest, Abigail opened the door and slipped into the hallway, closing the door firmly shut behind her.

"Your unexpected return has certainly put a lovely bounce in Abigail's step." Lucetta said as she rubbed her gloved hands together. "Why, she's fairly bursting with schemes, and I, for one, could not be more delighted, especially since she's definitely fixed her scheming ways on you."

Lucetta glided over to the door. "I'll just go keep that *scrumptious* Everett company while you make yourself presentable." Lucetta drifted out of the bathing chamber, the distinct sound of laughter following her.

Seeing no point in remaining in a tub of cold water with bubbles that were rapidly disappearing, Millie climbed out, wrapped herself in a soft bundle of fine linen, and moved to her adjoining room. To her surprise, Miss Bertha Miller, an older woman

Abigail had recently hired on as a maid, was already waiting for her, a situation that sent apprehension racing down Millie's spine.

Bertha made no secret of the fact she absolutely adored Abigail, that adoration cemented forever when Abigail had hired the woman on the spot after she'd learned Bertha had been unable to secure employment due to being almost sixty years old. That kindness meant Bertha was incredibly loyal to Abigail, and that loyalty, mixed with the pesky little fact Bertha seemed to be holding a lot of blue silk in her arms, had Millie's apprehension turning to downright alarm.

"I was just about to come and prod you out of the tub, but you've saved me that bother," Bertha said as she marched determinedly Millie's way. "Mrs. Hart is of the belief you might be a little confused about her request to dress in something suitable, so she sent me to assist you with . . . this." Bertha shook out the silk and smiled. "Isn't it lovely?"

"Without question it is, but I think a dinner dress might be a little too much for wearing about the house, particularly since I'm not exactly planning on going out to dine this evening."

"Mrs. Hart went to the extreme bother of

taking your measurements to Arnold Constable & Company to get you this perfect gown, which she has requested you wear tonight. Because of that, I'm sure you won't want to repay that bother by refusing to wear her gift, or any of the other garments she purchased for you."

Millie's brow scrunched together. "Other garments?"

"She ordered you a new wardrobe."

"Why would she have done that?"

"To help you on your way toward getting settled, of course. Something I and the rest of the staff are in full agreement with." She held up the blue silk and gave it another shake.

"Why does everyone I encounter seem to have some type of mad plotting on their minds these days?"

"You're a lovely young lady with no prospects, Miss Longfellow. Plotting is definitely required by everyone who knows you to better your situation in life."

"I don't believe Mr. Mulberry is here in order to become a future *prospect* for me. If I were to hazard a guess, he's here to swallow that annoying pride of his in an attempt to secure my services as a nanny, which is far removed from a prospective anything."

"While that might be the case, it won't hurt to have you looking your best." And before Millie could voice another protest, blue silk was thrust her way as Bertha bustled into motion.

Fifteen minutes later, not ten, Millie made her way down the stairs, feeling like a complete idiot. Not only had Bertha stuffed her into the dinner dress, she'd also tied a bow into Millie's short curls, pinched Millie's cheeks to give her added color, and had even suggested Millie might want to add a little . . . stuffing to the bodice area to really attract Mr. Mulberry's notice. Pretending she hadn't heard that less-than-helpful suggestion and knowing her cheeks were flaming, which had made the whole pinching thing unnecessary, Millie had fled from her room before Bertha could think up any other wonderful ideas.

Reaching the bottom of the stairs, she forced feet that didn't seem to want to move into motion and headed for the drawing room. Hovering in the doorway, she tried to steady nerves that had taken to jingling, surveying the scene in front of her as she did so.

Mr. Everett Mulberry was standing in the middle of the room, holding a large bundle of flowers wrapped in what seemed to be newsprint. Lucetta was standing right in front of him, chatting about what sounded like the weather, but it was immediately clear Everett wasn't exactly listening to her. His eyes were a little glazed and he seemed somewhat dazed. Millie couldn't really blame him for the whole dazed situation, since Lucetta *was* known as one of the most beautiful ladies in all of New York.

A trace of wistfulness took Millie by surprise, brought on by the disturbing notion that there was a part of her, albeit a small part, that wished a gentleman like Everett would look at her with . . .

A loud sneeze interrupted her thoughts, and then Everett sneezed again, right as his eyes began watering.

"Forgive me, Miss Plum, but I haven't been able to concentrate on a word you've said," he began as he held out the bouquet of flowers. "Would it be too much of a bother to have you hold these for me until Miss Longfellow appears? I'm afraid I'm somewhat sensitive when it comes to flowers, and I'm beginning to lose the ability to breathe."

Lucetta, strangely enough, sent Everett an approving sort of look before she nodded in Millie's direction. "Millie's just arrived, so you can hand those to her."

Spinning around, Everett narrowed still-watering eyes on her, took a second to look her up and down, which had her feeling a little flustered, and then strode right up next to her. Without saying a single word, he thrust the flowers at her and then practically raced to the other side of the room. Whipping out a handkerchief, he wiped his eyes before he frowned.

"Good heavens, Miss Longfellow, I must beg your pardon. By your appearance, it's clear you're readying yourself to go out this evening. Would it be more convenient for me to call upon you tomorrow, say . . . midmorning?"

Millie forced a smile. "There's no need for you to return tomorrow morning, Mr. Mulberry, since I'm, ah, not planning on going anywhere this evening."

"Why are you wearing a dinner dress, then?" he asked before he dissolved into a bout of sneezing, giving Millie much-needed time to consider a suitable response.

"I, um, enjoy dressing in dinner gowns when I'm at my leisure?" was all she managed to come up with since she certainly wasn't going to tell him Abigail had been behind her unusual clothing choice.

Everett lifted his head from his

handkerchief. "That seems like a rather odd thing to do."

"Perhaps, but . . . since you obviously have a reason for being here, do you truly believe it's in your best interest to argue with me or . . . insult me by insinuating I'm odd?"

Another sneeze was Everett's first response, before he blew his nose, then smiled somewhat weakly in Millie's direction. "Excellent point, Miss Longfellow, and to correct that, may I say that although I find your choice of dress somewhat peculiar, you do look remarkably charming at the moment, quite different from how you normally look."

For a second, her knees felt all wobbly, but only until she actually considered what he'd just said. "I'm not sure that was much of an improvement, but tell me, Mr. Mulberry, are you, by chance, hoping that your attempt at complimenting me will have me feeling more disposed toward whatever business you're evidently here to propose?"

"What a wonderful use of the word *disposed*," Lucetta said before Everett had a chance to reply.

Millie turned to Lucetta. "I learned it just today — from Mrs. Cutling, of all people — as well as the word *execrable*, but I haven't yet been able to fit that appropriately into any of my conversations so far."

"Your interest in words is truly inspiring, Miss Longfellow," Everett said, speaking up, apparently not quite done with the whole complimenting business. "And it's also inspiring how much you seem to enjoy children, which is why I just *happened* to bring my wards with me this evening." He turned and nodded toward a fainting couch placed in front of the fireplace.

Millie didn't know whether to laugh or shake her head when she finally took note of the three adorable children smiling brightly her way. All of them had strawberry-blond hair, hair that undoubtedly hadn't seen a good brushing in a while, and all three of them were wearing very unusual frocks, ones that certainly hadn't been professionally sewn.

Glancing back to Everett, Millie arched a brow. "I would have never taken you for a coward, Mr. Mulberry, but honestly, do you really believe carting out your wards is going to convince me to agree to whatever madness has you seeking me out so late at night?"

Everett smiled almost as brightly as the children. "Now, now, Miss Longfellow, there's no cause to call me a coward. Smart like a fox, perhaps, but —"

"You shouldn't antagonize her, Everett," Lucetta suddenly said, interrupting Everett's speech before she turned to Millie. "And *you* shouldn't be surprised he brought the children with him, considering everyone knows you have a distinct weakness for the wee ones. However, before the conversation moves forward, I really am going to have to insist that the two of you drop all of this Miss and Mister nonsense. We have a common friend in Oliver Addleshaw. Which means, like it or not, we're now friends of a sort. And because of that, there's really no reason for such formality."

"There is if he's here to ask me to work for him."

"Of course he's here to ask you to work for him," Lucetta said. "But that has absolutely nothing to do with calling him by his given name."

Millie opened her mouth, but before she could respond, something that looked remarkably like mud began seeping through the paper wrapped around the flowers she was holding. Moving to the closest table, she unwrapped the paper before setting her sights on Everett again. "Did you pull these flowers right out of the ground, Mr. Mulberry?"

Everett smiled. "Please, call me Everett

since Lucetta was kind enough to point out we're friends, and of course I didn't pull those right out of the ground."

Millie held up the flowers, exposing the roots still clinging to dirt. "You would have me believe you purchased these from a flower shop?"

"It's after ten. There are no flower shops open, but if you must know, I had Rosetta pluck those out of the ground for you."

A little girl of about five raised an incredibly dirty hand and waved at her right as Everett cleared his throat, drawing Millie's attention.

"I think you should view it as a mark in my favor that I remembered the flowers, especially since, again, I'm a little sensitive to them, but . . . you were quite vocal about what it would take to get you to work for me." He sent her a far-too-charming smile.

Ignoring the charm, Millie lifted her chin. "You might as well tell me what disaster struck your household now."

Everett shot a glance to the children and seemed to shudder. "Why would you assume something disastrous happened?"

Setting the flowers, roots and all, aside, Millie crossed her arms over her chest. "Don't insult my intelligence, Everett. You wouldn't be bringing me flowers or children if something of a disastrous nature hadn't occurred."

"The children *are* adorable, aren't they?"

"Of course they're adorable, dear, which I'm sure you were hoping to use to your advantage," Abigail said as she arrived in the drawing room, pushing a cart that seemed to be heavy with treats. She brought the cart to a stop. "Mr. Kenton is currently making us some tea, since both the housekeeper and chef have retired for the night." She smiled at the children. "I didn't want your hot chocolate to get cold, though, and I thought all of you might like a few cookies."

The three children were on their feet in less than a second, but before they reached the cart, Millie stepped in front of them. "You'll need to wash up first — especially you, Rosetta."

Three pairs of eyes narrowed on Millie, but when she didn't budge, the oldest girl took her two siblings by the hands and met Millie's gaze. "I don't know where the washroom is located."

"I'll show you," Abigail offered, and a moment later, with the children by her side, she disappeared through the door.

Millie watched them leave before looking at Everett. "What happened?"

For a second, she didn't think he was going to answer, but then his shoulders sagged. "They glued Miss Dixon to a chair and ruined one of her new dresses in the process."

Lucetta smothered what sounded exactly like a laugh behind her hand before she made a mad dash for the door, vanishing from sight a second later.

"It wasn't funny," Everett said shortly.

Millie pressed her lips firmly together and watched as Everett began pacing around the room, bracing herself when he suddenly stopped and sent a scowl her way.

"Miss Dixon is demanding I hire on a nanny immediately, and since you're the only nanny who seems to be available . . . you're going to have to do."

Millie blinked. "Do you honestly believe that little speech will have me accepting your offer?"

Before Millie had an opportunity to so much as blink again, Everett was right beside her, dropping down on one knee even as he pulled her hand into his. "*Please*. I'm begging you. Come to Newport with me."

Looking down into eyes that truly did seem to be desperate, Millie considered him for a long moment. "No."

Her hand was dropped in a split second as Everett rose to his feet. "Why not?"

"Because I'm a very good nanny, and I don't like hearing you say differently."

"I brought you flowers and begged you on bended knee."

"That was just for show and you know it."

"I'll pay you that two thousand dollars I offered Mrs. Smithey."

"How incredibly generous of you, Everett," Abigail said, walking back into the room with the children trailing after her.

"It's not generous at all," Millie argued. "He offered that same amount to a woman who had a very sour disposition and was probably a horrible nanny."

"I seem to have forgotten napkins," Abigail said before she headed for the door again, bustling through it rather rapidly.

Glancing to the cart, Millie noticed a stack of folded napkins and felt her lips curl. Shaking her head at the antics of Abigail, yet having no idea if the older woman was up to something at the moment or had simply not wanted to witness an argument, Millie began placing cookies on the small plates that were also on the cart. She turned and found the oldest child standing right next to her.

"You must be Elizabeth," she said, earn-

78

ing only a nod in return as Elizabeth took the plate Millie offered and handed it to the younger girl hovering behind her. "And you, of course, are Rosetta, and you . . ." She looked at little boy. "Well, you must be Thaddeus, twin brother to Rosetta."

Thaddeus took the plate she offered. "How do you know I'm a boy?"

"I'd be a very sorry nanny indeed if I couldn't tell the boys from the girls, wouldn't I?"

"I'm wearing a dress."

"And I'm sure there's a perfectly good reason for that, but we'll discuss it at another time . . . if I decide to take up Everett's offer of employment."

"They're really very good children, when they put their minds to it," Everett said as the children got resettled on the fainting couch with their treats. "They're also very sorry about what they did to Miss Dixon and have promised not to glue anyone else to any chairs."

By the mutinous expressions on all three little faces, Millie was fairly sure they weren't sorry at all, but she saw absolutely no benefit in pointing that out.

"And they've agreed," Everett continued as he looked directly at the children, "to be on their very best behavior if you'll agree to become their nanny."

The mutinous expressions disappeared to be replaced with three angelic smiles.

Realizing that Everett had evidently resorted to bribery to get the children's co-operation, Millie swallowed a laugh as she nodded toward the door. "Before I give you my answer, Everett, I'm going to need a minute alone with the children."

Everett's eyes went wide. "I'm not sure that's exactly wise."

"Wise or not, I'm afraid I'm really going to have to insist on this."

With a look of skepticism on his face, Everett quit the room, closing the door ever so slowly behind him.

Placing her hands on her hips, Millie regarded the children, who were now sending her looks of deepest dislike. Arching a brow, she decided her best option was to let them start the conversation.

It didn't take long for them, or at least Elizabeth, to speak up.

"We don't want a nanny, and we only said we did because each of us will get a dollar if we're friendly." Elizabeth lifted her chin and glared at Millie.

The defiance spoke volumes.

"I must admit I, too, would have been hard-pressed to refuse such a generous offer, but . . . tell me . . . what is it that you really want, since it's clear you don't want anyone looking after you?" Millie said softly.

For a second, Elizabeth's lip trembled, but only for a second. "We just want things to go back to the way they were — before . . . well . . . before."

Right there and then, Millie knew she had no choice but to accept Everett's offer. It didn't matter that he'd injured her pride, or that he really was far too attractive for his own good. All that mattered was sitting right in front of her, trying not to cry, and looking more pathetic than Millie had seen a child look in a very long time.

"Fair enough," she said before she made for the door, pulling it open only to discover Everett standing remarkably close to it, as if he'd been doing his very best to eavesdrop.

"So?" he asked.

"I'll do it, but it's going to cost you twenty-five hundred dollars."

"That's flat-out robbery."

"True, but you were the one who mentioned not that long ago that I needed to work on my negotiating skills, and . . . since you're obviously desperate, I do believe this is the perfect time for me to try my hand at negotiating."

Everett narrowed his eyes. "And if I agree

to your outlandish demand?"

"I'll come to Newport with you."

His eyes narrowed another fraction. "Fine, it's a deal, but tell me, are you doing this strictly for the money?"

Millie narrowed her eyes right back at him. "It's never about the money, Everett. It's only about the children. Maybe with time, you'll understand that."

4

The next day, Everett urged Titan, one of his favorite horses, down the cobblestone path that led to the back of his Fifth Avenue mansion. He pulled the horse to a stop directly in front of a groom already waiting for him. Climbing from the saddle, he handed the reins to the groom, gave Titan a pat, and headed for the house. Pulling out a pocket watch, he stopped dead in his tracks when he took note of the time.

"It cannot be only a little after noon." He peered closer at the watch, disgruntlement settling over him when he realized that it was, indeed, just past twelve.

After all the events he'd squeezed in since he'd stumbled out of bed that morning, it seemed to him as if entire days had passed, not simply hours.

When he'd returned home the night before, after securing Millie's agreement to work for him, he hadn't been surprised to find Caroline still firmly ensconced in his library. She'd immediately demanded to learn the outcome of his quest, and when he informed her he'd found them a nanny, if a slightly questionable one, a genuine smile had spread over her face, the first he'd seen from her in days.

His delight over seeing that smile didn't last long. Once he got Caroline into a carriage to escort her home, she'd taken to turning a little bossy.

She'd told him, in no uncertain terms, that she wanted to be on her way to Newport early the next morning. The only problem with that, though, was she did *not* want to travel in the company of the children, proclaiming that the children's recent fascination with the whole walking the plank business gave her heart palpitations. Since the best way to get to Newport was over a vast amount of water, and Everett was fairly certain the children hadn't exactly put aside their mischievous ways just yet, he actually thought her concerns held some merit. Because of that, he'd decided the only way to placate her was to offer her the use of his private yacht the next morning, complete with a full staff to wait on her every need, while offering to bring the children to Newport on a different day.

Caroline had quickly accepted his offer, but then she'd continued to voice additional demands — demands that went from seeing her to the docks the next morning, to promising to be in Newport a day after that in order to watch her play tennis. She'd even gone so far as to suggest he leave the children behind in New York with their new nanny, proclaiming that leaving them behind would be beneficial to all involved.

Caroline had not been pleased when he'd immediately rejected that particular suggestion, but she'd rallied quickly. Evidently realizing she'd annoyed him with her less than compassionate attitude toward his wards, she'd batted her lashes in a very attractive manner, and told him that she'd only suggested such a thing because she missed the comradery they'd shared before the children had come into their lives. He'd felt slightly mollified by that, until Caroline mentioned the bothersome little fact that she'd left a long list of what she believed were appropriate boarding schools on his desk. By the time they'd arrived at Caroline's residence on Park Avenue, he'd been rather relieved to bid her a quick farewell.

His sense of relief, however, had been short-lived, because when he got back to his house, he discovered the children had not cooperated with Mr. Macon and gone to bed but were waiting for him to see them settled.

Getting three children into bed had turned out to be a very difficult task indeed. Glasses of water were requested — and not at the same time — and then Elizabeth had decided to launch into a very long speech about why she and her siblings didn't need a nanny. That had gone far in explaining why they'd waited up for him in the first place.

By the time he'd finally gotten them settled, without the nanny issue resolved to anyone's satisfaction, it had been after midnight. Stumbling into his bed, he'd immediately fallen asleep but had been rudely woken up at the unheard of hour of six by the children. They'd claimed they were ravenous and needed him to find them some breakfast. Why they hadn't simply sought out the cook on their own was still beyond his comprehension.

To his relief, Millie had shown up at exactly seven o'clock, lugging her one traveling bag into his house, far too chipper than a person had a right to be at such an early hour.

When she learned they would not be traveling to Newport that morning, she'd not batted an eye and proclaimed the delay would give her much-needed time to become better acquainted with the children. He hadn't missed the sneaky glances his wards shared after that pronouncement. But since he'd needed to get ready to escort Caroline to the dock, he'd warned the children to behave, warned Millie to try her best not to drown anyone, and left the house a short time later, leaving muttering children and an annoyed nanny behind.

Now, five hours after giving those warnings, he was finally returning home. Repocketing the watch, he trudged around the front of the house and then up the steps, finding himself staring at a door that, peculiarly enough, remained closed against him.

A sense of alarm was immediate.

Moving forward, he pushed the door open, stepped inside, and found dread mixing with the alarm when Mr. Macon, who was truly the most competent butler Everett had ever met, didn't immediately come into view.

Striding down the hallway, he cocked an ear, but when only silence met that ear, his heart began beating a rapid tattoo. The rapid thumping came to an abrupt end when Millie suddenly glided out of the library. Unlike the night before, she was not dressed in a fancy gown but was wearing a sensible dark skirt paired with a white blouse that was covered with a practical apron. Her hair was tucked beneath a cap that for some reason bothered him, and when she took another step forward, he noticed her shoes didn't sport much of a heel. Her nose was firmly stuck between the pages of a book, and she didn't appear to be in any way distressed, but . . . she also didn't appear to be in possession of any of the children.

"What are you doing?" he finally asked when she remained oblivious to him.

The book dropped from Millie's face as she raised a hand to her chest. "My goodness, Everett, you scared me half to death." She smiled, the action causing a dimple he'd never noticed before to pop out on her cheek. "I do hope you don't mind, but I simply couldn't resist taking a peek around your library. I'm thrilled to report you have a Jane Austen novel I haven't read in ages." She held the book up and beamed at him. "Would it be permissible for me to take this book with us when we leave for Newport tomorrow?"

"You may take whatever books you desire from my library, even though there is a library at my cottage in Newport."

Her eyes widened. "How in the world do you manage to get any work done when you're surrounded by so many books?"

"I rarely have time to read these days."

She sent him a sympathetic smile. "That's truly unfortunate, but I do understand. There've been many times when I've been gainfully employed when I can only squeeze reading in late at night. Sometimes I end up regretting that decision in the morning, but I don't think reading is a pleasure I'll ever be able to abandon."

Her earnestness had him smiling, until he remembered the silence of the house. "I must admit that learning you're a voracious reader does take me by surprise, but books aside, do you happen to know where Mr. Macon is?"

Millie ignored his question. "Why does my reading take you by surprise?"

From the manner in which her eyes had begun to spark, Everett realized he just might have made a bit of a blunder. "Ah, well . . . I've never known a person in service who enjoys reading."

"Have you ever taken the time to get to know any people in service?"

His collar began to feel rather tight. "Well . . . ah . . ."

"Of course you haven't," Millie finished for him as she tucked a strand of hair that had escaped the cap back into place and sent him a somewhat irritated look. "But getting back to your question regarding your butler, Mr. Macon very kindly offered to go to Abigail's house and pack up some toys Abigail has in her attic so that the children will have something new to play with once we arrive in Newport." She crossed her arms over her chest. "I've been informed by Elizabeth that most of their toys are still back in their old home, which is slightly puzzling to me since you've had responsibility for them for . . . how long?"

His collar turned a touch tighter. "A little over five months, but . . . I wasn't aware the children were missing most of their toys."

"I see."

Those two words, spoken in a voice that had turned rather knowing, set Everett's teeth on edge. Deciding to turn the conversation away from his apparent failure as a guardian, Everett took a step closer to her. "Speaking of the children, aren't you supposed to be watching them at the moment?"

"Of course."

He glanced around the hallway. "Where are they?"

"They're perfectly fine." She dropped her voice to the merest whisper. "I've tied them up in the nursery."

For a moment, he thought he'd misheard her. "Forgive me, but you didn't just say you've tied up the children, did you?"

"Indeed I did."

"It's little wonder you get dismissed so often if you make a habit of tying up your charges while you wander through libraries perusing romance novels."

"Oh, I've never tied children up before today. . . . Well, except for some children in my youth, but that hardly counts, since I was a child myself." She held up a hand. "Before you dismiss me — something your expression clearly states you long to do — the whole tying-up business was the children's idea."

"You would have me believe they *wanted* you to tie them up?"

The dimple on Millie's cheek popped out again as she grinned. "Don't be silly. If you must know, they insisted on tying me up first, but obviously, since I'm standing in front of you, I was able to free myself." Her grin widened. "In the spirit of fair play, I convinced them it was their turn to be held captive, although I don't think the children thought their little game was going to have this particular outcome."

Everett headed for the stairs. "I'm going to go release them."

"You'll put a damper on our fun if you do."

Not bothering to address that ridiculous statement, he took the stairs two at a time, breathing somewhat heavily by the time he reached the third floor. Wiping a hand across his perspiring brow, he headed for the nursery, coming to an abrupt halt after he stepped across the threshold.

Elizabeth, Rosetta, and Thaddeus were firmly tied to three straight-back chairs, looking completely forlorn, and for some reason, they seemed to be rather wet. Spinning on his heel, he narrowed his eyes at Millie, who'd followed him into the nursery, and annoyingly enough, she wasn't perspiring in the least from her climb up three steep flights of stairs.

"Why are they wet?"

Millie gave an airy wave of her hand. "Oh, that was from before, when we were playing an exhilarating game of walking the plank, and *exhilarating* means *invigorating* if you didn't know."

"I distinctly remember cautioning you against trying to drown the children before I left this morning."

"What an interesting imagination you have, Everett, especially since the game of walking the plank was yet another one of the children's ideas," Millie returned. "Since I agreed to go first, if there were any thoughts of drowning a person, I do believe those thoughts originated with the three little angels currently glaring at me. Why, it's truly only because I'm fleet of foot that I was able to make it across the plank without falling in, especially when obstacles were thrown my way, such as sticks, mud, and I do believe, a shoe."

She shook out the folds of her dry skirt. "As you can see, I was able to cross successfully. I then encouraged the children to follow me, which they did, but . . . alas, they were not as successful as I was at navigating across the plank."

"She threatened us with a really big snake when we were in the very middle of the fountain," Elizabeth said, speaking up in a voice that shook with indignation. "We could have died a horrible death if the poisonous thing had bitten us."

Millie smiled. "What a wonderful imagination you have, dear, quite as good as the one Everett possesses, and a flair for the theatrical, I must add. Why, I thought since the three of you seem to have a liking for slimy creatures, and you also seem to like sharing those slimy creatures with others, such as Mrs. Smithey, you'd want to add the snake I found to the rest of your collection of peculiar pets. How could I have possibly known all three of you are frightened of snakes?" She nodded at Elizabeth, just once, although to Everett it almost seemed as if something unspoken swirled between Millie and the young girl.

Before he could dwell on that idea, though, Millie turned back to him. "Since you look as if you're contemplating bodily harm, that being my body in question, I must tell you that it was just a little garden snake. And it's not as if I tossed it at the children — I simply held it up as I got back on the plank to join them." Her lips began twitching. "I don't think I've ever seen anyone jump off a plank so quickly, and then, well, watching the children try to run through water to get away from me and my tiny little snake was absolutely . . . amusing."

"She's a lunatic, Mr. Mulberry," Elizabeth declared, "and I want you to get rid of her right this second."

Before Everett could think of a single reply to that, especially since he wasn't certain Elizabeth was exactly wrong with the whole lunatic theory, Millie stepped forward, all signs of amusement gone from her face. "Did you just call Everett . . . Mr. Mulberry?"

"That is his name," Elizabeth said.

Suddenly finding himself pinned beneath Millie's glare, Everett forced a smile. "May I presume you have a problem with the children calling me Mr. Mulberry?"

"I do." Millie swung her attention back to Elizabeth. "From this point forward, all three of you shall address Mr. Mulberry as . . . Uncle Everett."

Elizabeth immediately turned hostile. "We don't want to call him Uncle Everett," she said as the twins nodded in obvious agreement.

"It's not up for debate," Millie countered.

"Is it up for debate that he calls us *the brats*?" Elizabeth shot back.

Millie squared her shoulders, shot him another glare, and returned her attention to the children. "He will no longer be using that particular endearment, but now, if you three will excuse us, I feel a distinct need to go over a few things with your Uncle Everett in private." She stepped closer to him, took a firm hold of his arm, and immediately began prodding him toward the door.

"You're just going to leave us tied up like

this?" Elizabeth called after them.

Stopping in her tracks, Millie looked over her shoulder. "Did you, or did you not, tie me up and not offer me even a smidgen of help getting untied?"

For a moment, Elizabeth looked a little uncomfortable, but only for a moment. "It took you less than a minute to get undone."

"True," Millie replied with a nod. "And since that is a skill that has come in handy for me over the years, I'm going to allow you the supreme treat of being able to practice your untying skills for just a bit longer." Ignoring the sputters that were coming from the children, Millie practically pushed him out of the nursery, pulling the door firmly closed behind them.

"I'm not comfortable leaving them tied up."

"I'm sure you're not, but if you go back and untie them, you'll ruin any chance I might have of bringing the children in line."

For a second, he resisted her words, but then, something about the intensity of her gaze had him releasing a sigh. "I'll give you five minutes to explain what you're up to, but after that, I will see the children released."

Without giving him a response, Millie began striding down the hallway, and then down the steps, leaving him with no choice but to follow her. She reached the first floor and headed into the library, where she immediately took a seat on a settee done up in ivory that was situated between two dainty tables he'd had imported from Europe. "You may sit beside me." She patted the spot right next to her.

After taking a seat beside her, while feeling a little off-balance over the idea Millie didn't seem to have any qualms about ordering him around, he looked up and found her watching him closely. "Was there something specific you wished to discuss with me?" he asked.

Millie lifted her chin. "Contrary to popular belief, I'm a very good nanny. A misunderstood nanny, but a very good one nevertheless."

"You believe tying up helpless children is being a good nanny?"

"I'm teaching them an important lesson. They need to understand the consequences of their actions." She shook her head. "I'm sure your wards were not always so ill-behaved but are simply acting out due to the death of their parents. But even though the children have suffered a tremendous loss, they cannot continue behaving in such an . . . execrable manner." She grinned. "I knew I'd find a use for that word."

"And you put it to good use indeed, but getting back to what you're trying to teach the children?"

The grin disappeared. "They need a few lessons tossed their way, and the tossing of those lessons is probably not going to be very pleasant. That means I need you to put your indigestion aside, and allow me to do what needs to be done, unpleasant or not."

"While I readily admit that trying to follow your rather odd logic is enough to give me a whopping case of indigestion, I think the word you might have meant to say was *indignation.*"

Millie blinked. "I knew I shouldn't have gotten a little arrogant with the whole *execrable* business, but you're right — *indignation* is probably exactly what I meant to say. Still, pesky words aside, in order for me to be successful with the children, you're going to have to trust that I know what I'm doing."

"I'm having a difficult time with that, considering my wards are currently tied up in the nursery — and there is that troubling past of yours to contend with. You do seem to have a most unfortunate propensity for getting dismissed from positions on an alarmingly frequent basis."

"I will agree that my past employment disasters are a mark against me, but my many dismissals have never been caused by me not performing my job to the best of my abilities, and those abilities are quite impressive, if I do say so myself."

Everett quirked a brow her way.

Millie began fiddling with the folds of her apron. "I'm not explaining very well, am I?"

"I don't believe we can consider anything you've said thus far as an actual explanation."

"I should just start at the very beginning, from clear back in the day when I first went out into service."

"Clear back in the day?"

"Well, yes, because I went out into service when I was twelve, and since I'm twenty-four now, that was certainly clear back in the day."

His stomach immediately turned a little queasy. Millie was the same age as Caroline, but whereas Caroline had been enjoying school, social events, and traveling, Millie had been put out to work when she'd been little more than a child.

". . . and then, when I got fired as a lowly kitchen maid, all because I wasn't the best potato peeler in the world, I thought I was going to be out on the streets since I didn't have a penny to call my own."

"You were a kitchen maid?"

Millie frowned. "Have you not been listening to a word I've said? Yes, I was a kitchen maid, an upstairs maid, and I even worked in the stables once. I had to disguise myself as a boy for that position, which, surprisingly enough, wasn't much fun. It even turned a little scary when the head groom discovered my little bit of subterfuge, which means *deception,* by the way, and threw me out of the stable."

It took a great deal of effort on Everett's part not to laugh, but there was something vastly amusing about Millie's habit of spewing out words and definitions. He'd never known anyone who was so fascinated with the dictionary, but he forced all lingering amusement aside when he noticed she'd taken to scowling at him. "Sorry," he managed to say. "Continue, if you please."

"As I was saying, I'd been turned out without a reference and didn't know how I was going to obtain another position. But then I met Reverend Thomas Gilmore." Millie smiled. "I believe you've made the acquaintance of that delightful gentleman as well."

Everett returned the smile. "I have indeed, and from what little I know about the man, he seems to be a kind and sensible soul."

"That's exactly right." Millie settled back against the settee. "He makes a habit of looking out for the underprivileged, and I was certainly that on the day I met him. He took me under his wing, found me a place to live, introduced me to Lucetta, and later, Harriet, and began to help me develop a plan for my life."

Millie bit her lip, a surprisingly endearing action. "I thought for certain Reverend Gilmore wouldn't be of much help in that regard. But it soon became clear that he has a distinct talent for planning people's lives. After questioning me for hours about my life, especially the time I spent in the orphanage, he concluded that my calling was not in cleaning but in looking after children."

"You grew up in an orphanage?"

"Why else did you think I was sent out to work at twelve?"

"I thought perhaps your parents needed help with expenses."

"My parents died when I was an infant."

Everett simply stared at her for a long moment as a clear sense of horror spread through him. He'd never been without the support of his parents, and as he considered that Millie had never even known hers, well —

A pat on his knee had him blinking back to the conversation at hand.

"There's no need for you to feel distressed about my upbringing, Everett. Children lose parents all the time, and it could have been much worse for me. I could have landed in an orphanage that sends children out to work in one of those dismal factories instead of placing me as a domestic." Her gaze suddenly sharpened on his face. "You don't own any of those factories, do you?"

"I invest mostly in land, not factories."

If anything, the sharpness of her gaze increased. "Is any of that invested land in the Five Points area?"

"Ah . . ."

"Because I've been told," she continued before he could fully respond, "my parents lived in a tenement slum in Five Points. Due to the dismal conditions the slumlords allowed there, an influenza epidemic spread from one building to the next — an epidemic that I've been told killed my parents." Her eyes narrowed. "You *don't* own any of the land the slumlords operate on, do you?"

Raising his gaze to peruse a bookcase lined with leather-bound books he couldn't remember having read in the recent past, if ever, he took a moment to consider his response. There was no denying that the properties he owned were extensive, and some of that property was located in the Five Points area. Nevertheless, in his opinion, there was a vast difference between a slumlord and himself. Slumlords might erect shoddy buildings on land that Everett owned, but the slumlord, and the slumlord alone, was the one responsible for stuffing as many people as possible into those buildings. All Everett did was collect a monthly fee for the use of the land he and his family had owned for generations. But, he didn't think it would benefit him to admit that to the woman sitting next to him, a woman he desperately needed to keep in his employ.

He pulled his attention away from the books and settled it on Millie again. "My family has a diversified list of properties that was acquired over many years — starting with my great-great-grandfather after he got out of the fur business. Because of that, I can't say with complete certainty, without digging into my ledgers, exactly what land I might own in Five Points."

Millie's brows drew together. "You would have me believe that you don't know what specific parcels of land you own, and that you had a great-great-grandfather?"

"Everyone had great-great-grandfathers, Millie, including you."

"Well, yes, of course, but I don't even know what my mother's maiden name was, and only think my father's surname was Longfellow." She waved a hand at him when he drew in a breath. "Again, there's no need for you to feel bad about my lack of a family . . . so getting back to yours — how did your great-great-grandfather go about the difficult business of setting himself up in fur trading?"

Relieved that the conversation seemed to be safely traveling away from the whole Five Points subject, Everett settled more comfortably on the settee. "Family legend has it that my great-great-grandfather was a very determined young man, traveling here from England all by himself when he was in his early teens. He then somehow managed to align himself with different tribes of Indians, and his business grew from there. After he became successful trading his furs, he must have decided it was time to take his newfound wealth and invest elsewhere, and that's when he began acquiring land."

"And that's what you do to this day — acquire land?"

"Though I have started businesses here

and there, I mostly manage the collection of rent from the land we already own."

Millie began to slowly inch away from him. "Then you *are* somewhat like a slumlord."

Everett opened his mouth to deny the statement, but then swallowed his denial as the thought struck him that Millie's accusation might just have a tiny bit of truth to it. While he wasn't responsible for the shoddy housing slumlords rented out to the poor, his bank accounts were filled with money that had come out of the meager pockets of the poor, which —

"Maybe you should reconsider how you earn money," Millie said quietly.

Shaking out of thoughts that were most likely ridiculous, because he wasn't *truly* a slumlord, Everett forced a smile. "My investments are completely legitimate, Millie, but enough about them and enough about me and my family. I still find myself curious about how Reverend Gilmore came to the conclusion you were well-suited for working with children."

For a second, he thought she wasn't going to answer him, but then she shrugged. "He's a man of the cloth, Everett. He turned to God and eventually came to the conclusion that God had selected me to work with children because of my experiences in the orphanage." She smiled. "I thought he was a bit out of his mind because I wasn't exactly a supporter of God at that particular time. In my mind, God had taken away my parents, so I really had no reason to put any trust in Him."

"But you changed your opinion about that?"

"It took a while, but Reverend Gilmore kept at me, encouraging me to attend church, and grow my faith. I still struggle at times, when I try to reason out why my parents died, but —"

"How splendid to see the two of you getting along so well, although . . . I must say it's not exactly wise for either of you to sit quite so closely together without some manner of chaperone present."

Everett shifted his attention from Millie and discovered Abigail strolling into the room, holding a stuffed bear in her arms. She immediately picked up her pace, arrived directly in front of him a second later, and without a by-your-leave, thrust the bear into his arms before she plopped down between him and Millie on the settee.

"This is cozy, but would have been completely unnecessary if only the two of you had kept the children around to keep an eye on the situation." Abigail caught Everett's eye. "And speaking of the children, I have an entire carriage filled with toys your Mr. Macon helped me pack up, but I think the children will want to help us unload everything. May I assume they've simply gone off to the kitchen for a treat and will be returning to the library promptly?"

"Millie's tied them up in the nursery."

Abigail's eyes widened. "How . . . delightful. Although that seems like a rather unusual method of keeping track of children."

"Millie's apparently teaching them some type of lesson, something she was also evidently doing when she bested them in a game of walking the plank. Quite honestly, I'm hoping the children aren't scarred for life from that troubling experience."

Abigail beamed his way as a touch of relief filled her eyes. "Well, of course she's teaching them something of worth, Everett, and I have to admit that I'm now somewhat disappointed I clearly missed so much fun this morning. I'll just have to console myself with the idea that I won't miss additional fun and games in the future, since I've decided to join you in Newport."

"What?" Everett and Millie asked at the same time.

Abigail glanced at him and then at Millie. "I'm going to take the expressions residing on both of your faces as unmitigated joy over my decision to travel to Newport."

"I have no idea what *unmitigated* means, but I do know that there's no need for you to travel to Newport," Millie said. "I'll be watching the children the entire time, and you'll have absolutely nothing to do."

"Oh, I think I'll be able to find *something* of worth to occupy my days." Abigail folded her hands in her lap. "Besides, there's every need for me to travel with you, because you really do need a chaperone."

"I've never brought a chaperone with me before when I've taken on a nanny position."

"And look where that landed you — dismissed every time." Abigail nodded to Everett. "You understand, don't you, the need for me to travel with Millie as her chaperone, especially since Millie's a lovely young lady and you're an eligible gentleman bachelor?"

"None of the nannies I've employed over the last few months have come with their own chaperones" was the only thing he could think to reply.

Abigail's brow disappeared beneath the

brim of her fashionable hat. "Millie's different."

Everett couldn't help himself — he laughed. "Oh, I don't think there's any disputing that, but she'll be surrounded by the rest of my staff once we reach Newport, so she truly has no need of your chaperoning services."

"Are you uninviting me?" Abigail demanded.

"I didn't realize I'd extended you an invitation in the first place."

"This is going to be much more difficult than I anticipated," Abigail mumbled. And right there and then, he finally understood exactly what the lady was up to.

Heat traveled up his neck and settled on his face. "I realize you must be feeling rather smug, given the outcome of the whole Oliver and Harriet business, Abigail. But you're completely off the mark if you're turning your matchmaking skills my way because —"

"You're committed to Miss Dixon," Millie finished for him, leaning forward to catch his eye, her leaning allowing him to see that her face had turned rather heated as well. "You'll have to forgive Abigail, Everett, because she doesn't seem capable of resisting the allure of matchmaking. Do know, though, that I'm fully aware of the fact that a nanny is never considered an appropriate option for a matchmaking scheme with someone of your social status."

"I can't tell you how relieved I am to hear you say that," he said, immediately regretting the words when Millie's eyes narrowed and temper flashed through them. "I mean . . ." He stopped speaking when she raised a hand, cutting him off.

"There's no need to say anything else, Mr. Mulberry, because, believe me, I understood exactly what you meant." Millie rose to her feet. "And you should be further relieved to learn that I do not care to discuss this particular subject ever again." She sent him a nod. "I'm, again, only a nanny, you'll only ever be my employer, and . . ." She directed a nod Abigail's way. "You're destined to remain disappointed, at least in regard to your matchmaking plans for me. Now, if everyone will excuse me, I'm off to resume my duties as *only* the nanny, which entails . . . untying the children."

With that, and with her head held high, Millie marched out of the room, leaving him all alone with an obviously disappointed and very disgruntled Abigail Hart.

5

Keeping a firm grip on Thaddeus with one hand, while pushing strands of hair soaked with sea mist away from her face with the other, Millie couldn't help but wish she'd brought a spare cap with her. The one and only cap she'd thought would be sufficient for her trip to Newport had been whipped straight off her head minutes after she'd stepped foot on Everett's yacht. That sad state of affairs was responsible for her being forced to drag unruly curls out of her eyes every other second, which was making it somewhat difficult to keep the children in constant view. Even though all of them were wearing oversized coats made out of cork, she certainly wasn't going to relax her guard, especially since there'd been so much talk of late of her allowing children to drown.

It truly was unfortunate that Everett had abandoned the deck almost as soon as they'd pulled away from shore. From what she'd been able to tell, he was in possession of a very fine set of what she'd been told were "sea legs," those legs being something that would have come in remarkably handy at the moment, given the slightly turbulent nature of the sea. But since Everett had been doing his utmost best to keep his distance from her, and keep a safe distance from Abigail as well, it was now left to Millie to keep the children firmly out of the sea. That was why she currently had a death grip on Thaddeus, who was turning out to be quite the typical little boy — even while wearing a frock of brightest purple — and a little boy who certainly didn't enjoy the notion of doing anything as dull as actually standing still.

"Look starboard, children. It's a whale," Abigail called out.

Having no idea what direction starboard was, Millie glanced to where Abigail was now pointing, smiling at the sight of the older woman holding Rosetta's hand and laughing at something the little girl was saying. Abigail's cheeks were red from the breeze, and her eyes were sparkling, and for once, not sparkling with speculation.

Although Abigail had mortified Millie to the very tips of her toes the day before with her less-than-subtle matchmaking attempt, Millie really didn't have the heart to stay annoyed with the woman for any great length of time. And even though the whole matchmaking debacle had been exactly that — a debacle — it had at least given Millie an honest glimpse into Everett's true character.

By being so quick to agree with her assessment concerning their different stations in life, he had allowed her to understand that even though he was certainly handsome and debonair, and charming upon occasion, he was at heart . . . a snob.

Generations of Mulberrys increasing the family coffers at every turn had obviously been responsible for giving Everett his not uncommon sense of entitlement. And even though she'd witnessed snobbery from almost all of the society families she'd worked for, she'd found herself surprisingly disappointed with Everett for being exactly what society expected him to be, a man with —

"Look, there's another whale," Thaddeus yelled as he tugged his arm out of her grip right as the yacht caught a swell, rose into the air, and then dropped.

Millie lost her balance and plummeted toward the deck even as she tried to keep a grip on Thaddeus's cork jacket. The sea mist had made it slippery, and she felt her fingers clutching nothing but air right as she hit the hard surface. The yacht rose again, and Thaddeus began sliding straight for the railing, but then Elizabeth was right next to him, pulling him to safety.

Lurching to her feet, Millie stumbled as quickly as she could to Elizabeth's side. "Forgive me, Elizabeth. I fear my wobbly legs got the best of me, but thank goodness you were able to react so swiftly."

"I would have watched over Thaddeus from the very beginning if you'd told me you weren't steady on your feet."

"If I'd known you were so comfortable on a boat, I probably would have asked you to do just that."

Elizabeth's lips thinned before she marched Thaddeus over to where Abigail and Rosetta were now sitting on some chairs and made sure her brother was safely situated next to Abigail before she marched back to Millie. "My father owned a yacht, and since he and my mother enjoyed traveling, I spent a lot of time on it, and that's . . ." Elizabeth stopped speaking, as if she'd just realized she'd broached a subject she didn't care to talk about.

Resisting the urge to scoop Elizabeth into

a hug, Millie forced a smile instead. "I think after we get settled in Newport, we should have your Uncle Everett send for your father's yacht. That way, you and your siblings can enjoy the use of it over the summer."

"My father's yacht is gone."

"What do you mean . . . gone?"

"It disappeared."

"I'm not sure I understand how an entire yacht can disappear," Millie said slowly.

Elizabeth shrugged. "I don't understand either, but it wasn't where it was supposed to be after the . . . funeral." One lone tear began trailing down Elizabeth's cheek, a tear she quickly dashed away. "I went all the way down to the docks just to look at it because . . ." She stopped talking again, drew in a ragged breath, and squared her small shoulders. "It wasn't anchored in its usual place, so I checked every dock, but it wasn't anchored at any of them either. I think Mr. Mulberry might have sold it."

Millie narrowed her eyes. "I highly doubt Everett would have sold your father's yacht, especially during that particular time, but . . . let us move on to a more disturbing matter. What do you mean, you went down to the docks, and with whom did you go down there?"

"I don't think my pony can be considered a *whom,* Miss Longfellow."

Millie stiffened. "Are you telling me that you, a girl of eight, rode your pony all by yourself down to the New York City docks so that you could look for your father's yacht?"

"Of course not. I went to the Boston docks, since that's where we lived before Mr. Mulberry made us move to New York."

A million questions flooded Millie's mind. "Where was your *Uncle Everett* or your nanny when you made this little jaunt to the docks?"

"*Mr. Mulberry* was off trying to track down Daddy's attorney, and my nanny, Miss Oglestein, was packing her bags to go off with another family who'd swooped in right before the funeral and stole her away from us." Another tear dribbled down Elizabeth's cheek, but this one she ignored. "Miss Oglestein didn't want to leave Boston, and she didn't even *care* that we were going to be all on our own, with a new house and no one to love us."

The sight of Elizabeth's lip, now trembling ever so slightly, had Millie longing to reassure the child that *she'd* never abandon them, but she knew Elizabeth would hardly be receptive to that promise at the moment.

"It was not acceptable in the least for this Miss Oglestein to abandon you and your siblings, Elizabeth. Although that certainly explains why you're so opposed to nannies."

"Does that mean you're going to go away now?"

"Well, no. But getting back to Everett — why was he out searching for your father's attorney?"

Elizabeth shrugged. "All I know is that Mr. Victor, my father's attorney, was not in Boston at the time of my parents' accident. I think Mr. Mulberry was trying to find out where Mr. Victor had gone so that he could see if it was possible to get someone else to take over our care."

"I'm sure that's not true, but is that one of the reasons you don't want to call Everett 'Uncle'?"

"Maybe."

Millie blew out a breath as she came to the immediate, and rather troubling, conclusion that there were many different problems swirling around this family, all at the same time. "I don't claim to know much about attorneys, Elizabeth, but I'm going to hazard a guess and say Everett was trying to locate this Mr. Victor because he needed assistance sorting out your father's affairs, unless your father had an estate manager to look after those affairs."

"I don't know what an estate manager is, but Mr. Victor was Daddy's good friend and business partner, that's why he always looked after everything — even the investments I heard Daddy talk about all the time."

"Your father had a lot of stocks and bonds?"

"Daddy invested in inventors and was always being sent new inventions to look at. We even had a large barn that was set clear back from our house that was filled with all kinds of interesting gadgets." Elizabeth smiled a genuine smile. "My mother was forever getting annoyed about all the things exploding out there, but if Daddy found an invention he believed in, he'd give the inventor money." Her lip began trembling again. "He shouldn't have given the inventor of a peculiar-looking buggy any money, though, since the wheels weren't stable on that invention, and that's what . . ."

As Elizabeth's lips pressed firmly together, Millie didn't need her to finish what she'd been about to say. Fred Burkhart, along with his wife, had seemingly been killed while trying out some new invention, but before she could question Elizabeth further, Rosetta appeared by Millie's side and gave her skirt a sharp tug.

"Miss Abigail told me she's not going to be staying with us now."

"Should I assume you think that's my fault?" Millie asked.

Rosetta nodded. "She's probably scared you'll tie her up like you did to us."

"Abigail knows I would never tie her up. And even if I did, I'm sure you and your siblings would use those new untying skills you acquired just yesterday to set her free."

Rosetta crossed her arms over her little chest, looking just a bit smug. "You sure did seem surprised to find us untied when you walked into the nursery."

"I certainly was surprised, and curious beyond belief to learn how you were able to manage such a great feat. You should know that I'm still waiting with bated breath to learn how you got untied, and also know that I was very impressed by your perseverance to get yourselves untied, and *perseverance* means *determination,* by the way."

Rosetta wrinkled her nose, leaving Millie with the distinct impression the little girl was not exactly in the right frame of mind for a vocabulary lesson. Fighting back a smile, Millie leaned closer to the child. "I'm sorry you're disappointed about Miss Abigail no longer staying at Seaview Cottage with us, but I'm sure we'll see her often."

"Why did she change her mind?" Rosetta pressed.

Not wanting to tell the little girl that she thought Abigail was repairing to her own cottage so that she'd have peace and quiet in order to formulate a new plotting strategy, Millie settled for a shrug and a smile. "Sometimes, when a person reaches a rather advanced age, they prefer a calm atmosphere, something Abigail probably realized she wouldn't find at Seaview."

"I do believe you just called me old," Abigail said as she joined them, holding firmly onto Thaddeus's hand. "But since Mr. Andrews, our charming steward, is standing right behind you, we'll put the discussion of my ancient age aside for now."

Turning, Millie caught sight of the steward in question, a very nice gentleman who was dressed in a smart suit of navy, and a gentleman who seemed to be smiling very brightly her way. Glancing out of the corner of her eye, Millie couldn't help notice the fact that Abigail was suddenly looking far too interested in Mr. Andrews.

"I've come to tell you, Miss Longfellow, that the chef is almost finished preparing a most delicious lunch for you, Mrs. Hart, and the children." Mr. Andrews extended his arm. "It would be my honor to escort you to the dining room."

Before Millie could do more than blink in Mr. Andrews's direction, Thaddeus, to her relief, drew everyone's attention.

"I don't want lunch," he said. "I might miss seeing more whales."

Stepping around Mr. Andrews, Millie moved right up to Thaddeus and knelt beside him. "While I agree that watching whales is great fun, you must know that you can't stay on deck by yourself. Since I'm not exactly steady on my feet, someone will need to stay out here with us, and I'm afraid that someone will have to be Elizabeth since she's very good at keeping you safe." Millie lowered her voice. "She won't tell you this because she's a wonderful big sister, and as such, doesn't like to disappoint you, but I think she might be hungry."

Thaddeus looked at Elizabeth, who for once wasn't saying anything, then back to Millie as his forehead creased. "Do you think there'll be cake?"

"Chef made a chocolate cake," Mr. Andrews answered before Millie could. "And he also made ice cream to go with that cake."

Giving the ocean one last longing look, Thaddeus let out a pathetic sigh before he walked over to Mr. Andrews, obviously taking the man by surprise when he grabbed hold of the arm that had only recently been offered to Millie. Then, with Rosetta and Elizabeth joining him, he proceeded to tug the steward across the deck before vanishing through the doorway.

"That Mr. Andrews is just a lovely gentleman, and he seems to have a great liking for children," Abigail said, her tone practically oozing with satisfaction.

"He seems very pleasant, but I'm no more in the market for a steward than I am for an annoying society gentleman."

"Have I mentioned to you how remarkably pleased I am with the progress you're making with the children?"

Millie blinked. "That's a fairly rapid change of topics, even for you, but since it's apparent we're now on the subject of the children, you must know that they're in the midst of planning some type of mutiny."

Abigail reached out and took hold of Millie's arm. "Oh, undoubtedly, but you just got Thaddeus to agree to what you wanted him to do. That's progress." She smiled. "And speaking of annoying society gentlemen, you are going to ask Everett to join us for lunch, aren't you?"

Millie blinked again. "I don't believe we

were speaking of annoying society gentle-men, and no, I don't think it's my place to ask Everett to join us for lunch. If you've forgotten, although *he* certainly hasn't, I'm just the nanny."

"And as such, it's your duty to let him know when he's being negligent in regard to his responsibilities. It has not escaped my notice that he spends relatively little time with the children. Those children need a guiding influence in their little lives, and since Everett has been given the privilege of raising them, that guiding influence needs to come from him."

"He won't appreciate me lecturing him, Abigail."

"Perhaps not, but as you've stated before, working with children is a calling for you. Because of that, I would imagine God expects you to intervene with Everett and convince him to change his neglectful ways."

"Everett probably doesn't have the least idea he's being negligent. Why, having worked in society all these years, I've yet to find society parents who spend much time with their children, because distance is all the rage and has been for years."

Abigail lifted her chin. "Distance is a mistake I made with my daughter, and I will not watch Everett make that same mistake.

But, since he's evidently still a bit put out with me over what I now believe was an ill-timed matchmaking attempt, you're going to have to act in my stead."

"Maybe you should just tell Everett you've learned your lesson regarding the whole matchmaking business, which will allow you to get back in his good graces."

"Thaddeus," Abigail continued, completely ignoring Millie's suggestion, "is in desperate need of male companionship. He would enjoy having Everett sit down to lunch with him. That would allow Everett the opportunity of getting to know the boy better, as well as the girls, which just might put an end to Miss Dixon's ridiculous idea of sending the children off to boarding school."

"How did you know about the boarding school plan since I have yet to mention it to you, having only heard about it yesterday?"

"Elizabeth told me. She's very upset with the idea, and who can blame her?"

Millie blew out a breath. "Fine, I'll go see about getting Everett to join us for lunch, but I'm not promising I'll be successful."

"You won't know until you try, dear." Abigail reached up and smoothed a hand over Millie's hair. "You might want to consider fixing this mess on top of your head before you do anything though. It's looking a tad frightening at the moment." With a last pat to Millie's cheek, Abigail smiled and hurried away.

Left alone on the deck, Millie allowed herself the luxury of taking a moment to gather her thoughts. Lifting her face to the sky, she sent up a small prayer asking for guidance as well as a good dose of patience since she was about to go off and deal with Everett. She then straightened her spine and headed into the yacht. Walking down the narrow passageway, she peered into one room after the next, impressed in spite of herself by how well turned out the yacht was. It was equipped with everything one would find in an actual house, complete with walls painted in a soft shade of cream paired with matching furniture — although that furniture had been bolted to the floor. Poking her head through yet another doorway, she stilled when she caught sight of Everett. He was sitting behind a desk, reading what appeared to be a . . . novel.

Irritation was immediate. Taking a step into the room, she stopped, crossed her arms over her chest, and waited for him to notice her.

Unfortunately, the wait turned into a rather long one.

"You'll be pleased to learn that these fancy cork jackets really do a remarkable job of keeping a person afloat," she heard spill out of her mouth after a full minute had passed.

Everett, annoyingly enough, kept reading, but then his head snapped up and he narrowed his eyes on her. "I do beg your pardon, Millie, I was completely engrossed in my book, but . . . what did you just say? Something about keeping a person afloat?"

"I said these jackets are remarkably effective." She twirled around to show off the jacket she was wearing.

Everett shot out of the chair before she could finish her twirling. "Where are the children?" he demanded as he rushed for the door, scowling down at her when she, seemingly unable to help herself, moved to block his way.

"They're languishing, which means *lingering,* in the ocean, having a most marvelous time of it, I might add."

Everett actually picked her up and set her aside right before he froze. "Elizabeth was right, Miss Longfellow. You really are a lunatic."

"And you, *Mr. Mulberry,* are rapidly turning out to be a rather unlikeable sort," Millie shot back. "Do you honestly believe if the children had gone overboard that I'd

126

waste time seeking out your assistance instead of jumping into the ocean after them?"

"You don't know how to swim."

"Which is why I'm wearing this jacket, and which is also why, because you know I can't swim, you should have stayed topside with the children instead of burying yourself in here with what appears to be some type of novel." She peered over at the desk, but couldn't make out what he was reading. "Did you forget the children's fascination with walking the plank?"

"They were considering walking a plank?"

"Don't be silly," Millie said with a sniff. "After what happened the last time they tried that game, I do think their interest in that has dimmed simultaneously."

Everett's brows drew together. *"Simultaneously?"*

Fumbling with the cork jacket, Millie stuck her hand in a pocket and retrieved her dictionary. Flipping through the pages, she glanced over different words. "Ah, here we go. I think *significantly* might have been what I meant to say." She lifted her head and refused to sigh when she realized Everett was now scowling her way.

"Why would you bring up the whole plank business when you knew the children had abandoned their interest in it?" he asked.

"You annoyed me."

"The amount of money I'm currently paying you to nanny the children should hold any and all annoyance you may think you feel for me at bay."

"Even if you paid me twice what you are, I'd still get annoyed with you on a frequent basis."

"I'm *not* paying you additional funds to keep your annoyance in check."

"I don't remember *asking* you to," Millie said as Everett stalked back to his desk and then pointed to a chair that was bolted to the floor opposite him.

"Mr. Mulberry, you don't believe that's an acceptable way of asking me to take a seat, do you?"

A stabbing of a finger to the chair once more was his only reply.

Taking a second to fasten herself back into the cork jacket, even as an odd and somewhat inappropriate sense of amusement settled over her, Millie walked over to the indicated chair and took a seat. Placing her hands demurely in her lap, she watched as Everett lowered into his own chair.

Thrusting a hand through hair that was distinctly untidy, he caught her eye. "Was there a reason behind your interrupting my reading?"

"I'm sure there was, but that reason escapes me at the moment." She sat forward. "What are you reading?"

Everett's face turned a little red as he snatched the book off the desk and stuffed it into a drawer.

Millie leaned back in the chair. "Very well, since you don't seem to want to exchange the expected pleasantries, let us move on to what I've suddenly recalled I wanted to speak with you about. We need to discuss the children and the part you need to play in their lives, as well as discuss how you're going to go about telling Miss Dixon it would be a horrible idea for you to send the children away to a boarding school."

Opening the drawer, Everett yanked out the book he'd just stashed away, and pushed it Millie's way. "I think I'd rather discuss this."

Picking up the book, she looked at the title. "You're reading *Pride and Prejudice?*"

"I am, but don't tell anyone. It could ruin my reputation as a manly gentleman."

The amusement that was still bubbling through her increased. "I doubt that, but tell me, what do you think about the story so far?"

"I think it's unfortunate that Lizzy is not

better connected, because she would be perfect for Mr. Darcy if she came from money."

Millie shoved the book back at him as every ounce of amusement disappeared in a flash. "You don't believe that Mr. Darcy might be just a tad too prideful since he believes he's superior to Lizzy?"

"He's one of the richest men in England," Everett said, returning the book to the drawer and giving it a somewhat longing look before he caught Millie's eye. "Of course he's superior to Lizzy."

Fighting the impulse to tell him he was a bit of an idiot, because that was a guaranteed way of getting dismissed, Millie forced a smile. "Perhaps it would be best to continue this discussion *after* you finish the book. But, tell me, why in the world are you reading a romance novel?"

"I needed something to keep me occupied while evading Abigail and her meddling ways, and since you spoke so highly of Jane Austen, I thought I'd give her a try."

"You're reading it because I enjoy Jane Austen?"

"Well, yes. You also mentioned you enjoy *Frankenstein,* but I couldn't find a copy of that in my library, so I decided I'd read a book of Jane's instead."

Pleasure shot through her, until she remembered that she really didn't like Everett at the moment, especially considering his completely mistaken opinion about *Pride and Prejudice.*

"And speaking of Abigail, where is your chaperone?" Everett asked.

"Did I neglect to tell you that she's changed her mind about that?"

"She's come to her senses, has she?"

"I don't know if I'd go that far, but she has decided to stay at her own cottage in Newport, and . . . I'm hopeful she'll abandon all attempts at matchmaking in regard to the two of us, especially since we were so vocal with our opposition to the idea."

A discreet knock on the doorframe interrupted whatever Everett had been about to say. Turning her head, Millie found Mr. Andrews, the steward, pushing a cart covered with silver domes into the room. He stopped the cart directly beside a small table, and after nodding at Everett, he turned his attention to Millie and sent her a charming smile.

"Mrs. Hart was concerned your meal would get cold, Miss Longfellow, which is why she suggested I deliver it to you, along with a meal for Mr. Mulberry." He whipped

131

off silver lids, placed china plates on the table, added glasses of lemonade, and then pulled out a chair and resumed smiling at Millie.

"I thought I told Abigail I was going to join her and the children directly," Millie said as she rose to her feet and moved a step Mr. Andrews' way.

If anything, Mr. Andrews' smile widened. "The children turned out to be ravenous, Miss Longfellow, which is why Mrs. Hart allowed them to begin eating without you. Since they seem quite capable of demolishing a meal at a very rapid rate of speed, she told me to tell you that the children will probably be finished with their meal before you'll be able to join them. She also wanted me to mention that there's no reason for you to hurry with your own lunch, since she's planning on teaching the children a new card game." His smile dimmed just a touch. "And begging your pardon for this — although it comes directly from Mrs. Hart, not me — she believes that the children will not appreciate your company as they're playing cards."

"They're probably afraid Millie will decide to do something dastardly to them, such as bilk them out of their allowances, or . . ."

"Honestly, how you do go on, especially

since I don't gamble," Millie interrupted before she returned her attention to Mr. Andrews, who was still holding out the chair for her. Before she had an opportunity to take even a single step forward, Everett was right by her side, taking her by the arm. As he prodded her toward the table, he arched a brow at Mr. Andrews, who immediately stepped aside.

"That'll be all, Mr. Andrews," Everett said as he helped Millie take her seat.

Mr. Andrews considered Everett for the briefest of seconds before he nodded. "Very good, sir." He sent Millie a last smile, took hold of the cart, pushed it across the room and straight out the door, leaving that door open in the process.

"I'm surprised Mr. Andrews didn't stay and offer us his chaperoning services, and . . . surprised Abigail seems to have changed tactics, sending in a gentleman who is obviously smitten with you," Everett said as he took his seat.

Millie snapped her napkin open and placed it on her lap. "Mr. Andrews, while being a very nice man, is hardly smitten with me. Not that it would be any of your business if he was. And, as for Abigail . . . Well, I have nothing to say about that, other than to remind you I am in no way romantically inclined toward any gentleman at the moment, whether he be a steward or . . . you."

Picking up her fork, Millie stabbed a potato, placed it in her mouth, and ignored the fact Everett had taken to watching her with a grumpy expression as she went about the daunting business of trying to enjoy her lunch.

"Why did you really seek me out?" Everett finally asked after Millie had made it through the potatoes and had moved on to the peas.

Abandoning the peas, Millie lifted her head. "I was going to ask you to join everyone for lunch, although, just so we're clear, the invitation was Abigail's idea, not mine, so don't get any notions about me trying out my feminine wiles on you."

Everett choked on the sip of lemonade he'd been taking. Setting down his glass, he coughed a few more times, then turned now watering eyes on Millie. "It never entered my head that you would take to turning your, er, *feminine wiles* on me."

"Wonderful, and since we've gotten that out of the way, let us return to the subject of the children. You need to spend more time with them."

"If you haven't noticed, the children don't

care for me. I highly doubt they want to spend additional time in my company."

"That's because they don't know you, and Thaddeus would especially benefit from spending time in your company, even with all your character flaws."

Everett's lips actually began to curl at the corners. "While I do believe you just extended me a rather odd compliment, I fear I'm destined to disappoint you, because I won't have much time this summer to give Thaddeus, or the girls, for that matter." Everett rose to his feet, walked to his desk, picked up a sheaf of papers, then moved back to the table and retook his seat. He handed the papers over to her. "That's the summer schedule Caroline's made for me."

Glancing down the first page, Millie lifted her head. "Are you aware that you're supposed to be at some place called the Newport Casino today at two?"

Everett nodded. "For Caroline's tennis match." He pulled out a pocket watch. "I'll be cutting it close, but I'm sure I'll still be able to make it."

"You're just going to dump the children off at your cottage and go watch a tennis match?"

"I won't have time to travel with all of you to the cottage, so it's more a case of abandoning them after I have the hansom cab we'll hire drop me off at the Casino." He held up a hand when she opened her mouth. "And no, I'm not changing my plans, because I promised Caroline I'd try my very best to be at her match, and a gentleman always honors his promises."

"You promised to take responsibility for the children, yet I'm not sure you're exactly honoring that promise."

"I hired *you*," Everett said. "That was me, being responsible."

"Not that it's going to benefit me in the least to bring this up, but you only hired me because you were desperate. If you were truly responsible, you wouldn't have hired a nanny you believe is capable of drowning your wards."

"I think I might have changed my mind about your capabilities."

"You *think*?"

"We still have the rest of the summer to get through, Millie."

Millie's lips twitched, but since she didn't want to give him the impression she found him amusing, she bent her head and began reading the schedule he'd given her again. "Did you know you're hosting a ball toward the end of the summer?"

"Caroline thought that would be a lovely

way for me to show off my cottage."

"Have you ever planned a ball before?"

"My mother normally hosts any balls my family holds, but since she and my father are currently sailing around the world — Father deciding it was time for him to completely step back from the family business — Caroline's seeing to everything. She's hired on a woman to organize the event, which means all I have to do is pay an exorbitant amount of money to ensure everyone has a lovely time. Not that I begrudge that expense," he hastened to add. "I'm afraid I've disappointed Caroline quite often of late, which means holding the ball she hopes will be the highlight of the Newport season is the least I can do to make up for all of that disappointment."

"Is that why you're also being so obliging with all the activities she's planned out for you?"

"I must admit that it is. I normally don't spend my entire summer away from New York, but ever since I inherited the children, Caroline has not received the attention she deserves."

"While I will admit, reluctantly, of course, that your consideration for Miss Dixon is very well done, you will *try* to spend some time with the children, won't you?"

"I'll try, but I can't make you any promises, nor can I promise to reject out of hand Caroline's desire to send the children off to boarding school, something I do believe you mentioned when you first burst into this room."

"That's a subject you and I will certainly discuss further, but for now, will you at least promise to speak with Elizabeth regarding her father's yacht?"

Everett frowned. "What about Fred's yacht?"

"Elizabeth believes it's missing, and she thinks you stole it, or perhaps she said 'sold it.' "

"I certainly did no such thing, and quite honestly, I completely forgot all about Fred owning a yacht until you just mentioned it."

"Well, he apparently did own a yacht, and it might benefit your relationship with Elizabeth if you were to tell her you didn't sell it."

"I'll tell her straightaway, although I have to wonder what really did happen to the yacht. It's not like it's a usual occurrence for one of those to go missing, and . . . how does she even know it's missing?"

"She went down to the docks — on her own, no less — and couldn't find it. As for wondering what happened to it, I'm sure all you need to do is pen a letter to the attorney, a Mr. Victor, from what Elizabeth said, and ask him where it is."

Everett suddenly sat forward. "Did you just say that Elizabeth traveled to the docks on her own?"

"I did."

Running a hand through his hair, Everett blew out a breath. "I swear she's going to be the death of me, and . . . who knew eight-year-old girls could be so headstrong? But getting back to Mr. Victor, I'd love to ask the man about the yacht, but I have yet to even speak with the gentleman."

Millie frowned. "That seems rather odd, since Elizabeth mentioned Mr. Victor was also her father's business partner as well as his attorney. Shall I assume you've located a man of affairs or a secretary Mr. Burkhart used?"

"There is no man of affairs or a secretary — at least none who've come forward as of yet." Everett set aside his napkin. "That's why Fred's estate is still unsettled. From what I've been told, Mr. Victor has apparently gone off on holiday and has yet to return. I'm not even sure he's aware Fred and his wife died."

Millie tilted her head. "If Fred's attorney is off on holiday — what would appear to be a very extended holiday, at that — how did you come to find out you'd inherited the children?"

"Fred sought out the services of another attorney in Boston, a Mr. Colfax, just a month or so before he died, and had that man draw up a new will. Unfortunately, that's all Fred had that particular attorney do for him, apparently leaving all of his other business matters in the hands of Mr. Victor."

"Why would Fred leave the matter of his children with one attorney, while leaving matters of his estate and business ventures with another?"

"I have no idea, but I will admit that I was taken completely by surprise when I was contacted by Mr. Colfax and learned that Fred left me the care of his children. Granted, I am a godparent to them, but I didn't know I was signing up for taking over their care when Fred and his wife, Violet, asked me to take on the godparent role. I thought a godparent was just responsible for giving nice gifts at Christmas."

"While your idea about what a godparent is responsible for is incredibly disturbing, I find I'm more disturbed by something else." She leaned forward. "Don't you think it strange that Fred and his wife died in a buggy accident shortly after hiring a new attorney to draw up a new will? And," she continued before he could answer, "isn't it odd that Fred's attorney, a man Elizabeth said was very good friends with her father, would be gone on holiday when Fred and his wife died, *and* that he hasn't contacted you yet . . . *and* Fred's yacht is missing as well?" She crossed her arms over her chest. "If you ask me, something troubling is afoot."

For a second, Everett simply looked at her, but then, to her extreme annoyance, he had the audacity to laugh. "What an interesting imagination you have, Millie." He let out an honest-to-goodness snort. "Next thing you know, you'll be trying to convince me something more troubling than a missing yacht is afoot — something like . . . murder."

Placing her napkin on the table, Millie rose to her feet. "You may laugh all you want, but I'm telling you now, something is gravely amiss. I, with or without your assistance, intend to get to the bottom of it." Turning on her heel, she headed for the door, ignoring Everett's chuckles as she did so.

6

As Millie questioned Abigail about the effectiveness of private investigators, in a lowered and somewhat mysterious voice, Everett fought the urge to grin. Looking out the window of the hansom cab he'd hired, he found Newport spread out before him in all her charming summer glory, reminding him that he was, indeed, on holiday. That meant he needed to go about the task of enjoying himself — even if he knew Millie was going to do her very best to plague him about the *Boston Affair* as she'd begun to call what she now believed was some type of dastardly conspiracy.

Feeling the cab begin to slow, all thoughts of enjoyment faded in a flash as he braced himself for certain battle when Millie sat forward and peered out the window.

"This does not look like your cottage," she said, swiveling her head to pin him with eyes that had begun to spark. "Why aren't we at your cottage?"

"I told you that I have a commitment today, which is why I'm being let off at the Newport Casino." He gestured out the window, pretending he hadn't noticed that Millie seemed to be swelling on the spot. "Did you know that the Newport Casino, which is a social club by the way, not a gambling resort, only came into being last year because Mr. James Gordon Bennett got into a disagreement with the powers that be at the Reading Room?"

"I really don't . . . Did you say there's a reading room here in Newport?" Millie asked.

His lips curled at the sight of her now smiling his way, until he realized why she was smiling. Refusing to sigh, he leaned forward. "There is an establishment *called* the Reading Room, but I'm afraid I must tell you that it's not exactly what you'd assume it would be. It's a gentlemen's club, there's never any reading done, and . . . ladies aren't allowed entrance."

Millie wrinkled her nose. "Why would anyone name a club the Reading Room if there's no reading to be had?"

"It's just one of those oddities of life, I suppose."

"It's a disappointing oddity," she

mumbled before she crossed her arms over her chest, looking, to his surprise, rather adorable at the moment.

Shaking away the whole adorable idea, because that certainly wasn't an appropriate thing to think about one's nanny, Everett reached for the door, got out of the cab, and looked back at Millie, who was craning her neck, trying to see past him. Without taking time to consider his actions, Everett held out his hand to her.

"Would you feel better if you could get an unobstructed view of the Newport Casino?" he asked.

His hand was immediately taken, and he found himself feeling a little peculiar when Millie grinned at him as he helped her from the cab. Not particularly caring for the peculiar feeling, he released his hold on her, turning to help the children out of the cab next. When he held out his hand to Abigail, though, she shook her head in a rather sad sort of way and sent him a pitying look.

"Getting them out of the carriage was probably not the brightest thing you've done today, dear," she said.

Turning, he discovered that Millie was no longer standing by the hansom cab, but was already halfway across the lawn, heading directly for the Casino, with the children scurrying right beside her.

"I'll be right back," he told Abigail.

"I doubt that, but you can always hope," Abigail called after him as he bolted away.

Catching up to Millie a moment later, he took her arm, hoping to slow the rather rapid pace she'd been setting. "I wasn't really intending on giving you a tour when I got you out of the cab."

"Then why did you have us get out?" she asked before she abruptly began steering him to the right. "Children, come see. I think it's a croquet court."

With squeals of delight, the three children flew past him before he had the presence of mind to call them back. By the time he made his way over to the croquet area, while still holding tightly to Millie's arm since he was unwilling to lose track of her, Elizabeth had a mallet in her hand, and Thaddeus and Rosetta were going about the tricky business of picking out balls.

"I think black would be the perfect color for your mallet, Mr. . . . er . . . Uncle Everett," Elizabeth said, sending Millie a small smile before she picked up the black mallet and held it out to him.

"While I would love to challenge you in a game of croquet, Elizabeth, I can't do so today, since Miss Dixon's expecting me to watch her play tennis, and I'm running late for her game as it is."

"Everett really shouldn't break a promise," Millie said when Elizabeth started scowling his way. "But I'm more than happy to play with you."

Thaddeus began scowling as well, but at Millie, not Everett. "How do we know you won't try to do something sneaky to us while we play?"

"How do I know you won't try to do something sneaky to me?" Millie countered.

All three children immediately began to voice their opinions about that, but before Everett could intervene, a booming voice rang out behind him, calling his name.

"Everett, there you are, my friend. Caroline was beginning to worry."

Turning, Everett discovered Mr. Dudley Codman striding his way. The gentleman's face was ruddy, probably from too much time in the sun, and the large paunch the man hadn't had the last time Everett had seen him was straining the buttons of his jacket.

Letting go of Millie's arm because Dudley's gaze was locked on that arm, his expression a little confused, Everett stepped forward and held out his hand.

"Dudley, it's good to see you. I think it's

146

been, what, a year since we last spoke?"

Dudley shook Everett's hand and smiled. "I believe it has been about a year. I've been off to England on business for quite a few months, so . . . we haven't seen one another since last summer." He nodded to Millie. "I don't believe I've been introduced to this lovely lady."

Since Everett had never introduced a nanny to any of his friends, he wasn't exactly sure what the proper protocol was, but Millie, being Millie, simply took matters into her own hands. She stepped forward and dipped into a curtsy.

"I'm Miss Longfellow, nanny to Mr. Mulberry's wards."

Dudley blinked. "You must be a brave one, Miss Longfellow, to take on that particular job, especially after the stories I've recently heard from Miss Dixon."

Not caring at all for the rather disturbing glint residing in Millie's eye, Everett stepped between Millie and Dudley. "Miss Longfellow, allow me to introduce my very good and always charming friend, Mr. Dudley Codman."

Everett was less than reassured when the glint in Millie's eyes intensified.

"I find the whole charming statement to be rather confusing, *Mr. Mulberry,* especially since he just insulted the children. You —"

"And these lovely children," Everett said, raising his voice to be heard over Millie's complaints as he gestured the children forward, "are Miss Elizabeth Burkhart, Miss Rosetta Burkhart, and Master Thaddeus Burkhart."

"May I hope that you were robbed on the crossing and that's why the children are dressed in such an . . . interesting manner?" Dudley asked as he looked the children up and down, taking in every detail of their poorly sewn frocks.

Finding a slight bit of solace in the notion that Dudley probably didn't realize the material that made up the children's frocks had come from curtains, Everett forced a smile, but just as he was considering the idea of agreeing with Dudley's assessment regarding them being robbed, Millie stepped around him.

"Of course we weren't robbed, Mr. Codman, and shame on you for suggesting such a thing in front of the children. You have now succeeded in making them uncomfortable."

Dudley took a step backward, clearly uncertain how he should proceed since it certainly wasn't every day a nanny took a society member to task. "Er. . . ." he began.

Knowing there was nothing to do but step in to a situation that was certain to get worse if he didn't, Everett cleared his throat but was spared any type of response when they were suddenly joined by an entire group of ladies and gentlemen, all of whom were dressed in fashionable outfits suitable for summering in Newport. Leading that group was none other than a smiling Caroline, but her smile lost almost all of its warmth when she shifted her gaze away from him and settled it on the children.

"Goodness, Everett, this is a lovely surprise, seeing the children with you here at the Newport Casino," she finally said as her face began to take on a telling tinge of pink.

"I was just about to see them back to the cab," Everett said as he stepped up to Caroline, took her hand, and brought her gloved fingers to his lips. Before he could explain further, though, Millie was edging around him.

"Miss Dixon," Millie exclaimed as she smiled brightly Caroline's way. "I don't know if you remember me, but we were both in attendance at Mrs. Hart's ball a month back, although I was there in the capacity of a maid, while you were, of course, a cherished guest." The brightness of Millie's smile edged up another notch, showing a great deal of teeth. "I'm Miss Millie Longfellow, Miss Harriet Peabody's friend."

Caroline sucked in a sharp breath before she snatched her hand away from him. "You hired *Miss Longfellow*?"

Everett frowned. "I know I must have mentioned that to you."

"No, you didn't." Caroline stepped closer to him, and lowered her voice. "What could you have been thinking? All of our friends have heard of Miss Longfellow and her radical behavior around children. Hiring her on is certain to bring us additional censure from our peers."

A trace of temper sliced through him. "If memory serves me correctly, I did tell you that the only option available was not exactly suitable, but you insisted I go out and hire that option."

"I wouldn't have done so if I'd known we were speaking about Miss Longfellow," Caroline hissed back at him.

"I am still standing right here, listening to the two of you disparage my character, and that means *belittle* if either of you didn't know," Millie said.

Caroline drew herself up and seemed just about ready to explode, until she glanced around at the crowd watching her. She smiled at their friends and then returned her attention to Millie. "May I hope you're enjoying the privilege of being here at the Newport Casino?"

"It's lovely, though Mr. Mulberry has yet to finish telling me the history of the place."

"There's not much of a history since the Casino has only been around for a year," a voice said from the crowd.

Everett refused to groan when a lady by the name of Miss Gertrude Rathbone, one of Caroline's dearest friends, stepped forward and began strolling in their direction. She came to a stop directly in front of Millie. "I don't believe we've ever been introduced."

"She's just the nanny, Gertrude," Caroline snapped, right as Millie dipped into another curtsy, although if Everett wasn't much mistaken, she'd added a bit of attitude to the whole curtsying business.

"I'm Miss Millie Longfellow," Millie said in a remarkably loud voice, which had the crowd now gathered around them falling silent.

"Wonderful," another lady said as she hurried forward, edging Gertrude out of the way so she could stand in front of Millie. "I'm Miss Nora Niesen, and I've heard the most delightful stories about you, Miss Longfellow. I'm Miss Dixon's companion, by the way, although I'm not a true companion, since I don't get paid. I'm more like a last resort Caroline had to make do with when her last companion left. However, that has nothing to do with you, and since I'm dying to ask you some questions, since I know rumors can be a little unreliable, tell me . . . did you really get set upon by Mrs. Wilson's goats?"

Millie grinned, and before Everett knew it, the two women began chatting about everything under the sun, acting as if they'd been the best of friends for years.

"This is an interesting turn of events," Gertrude purred as she linked her arm with Caroline's and sent Everett an arch of a brow. "Interesting employees you're taking on these days."

"Good help is difficult to find," Caroline said. "And if I'd have known exactly who Everett was —"

"Aren't you and Gertrude, along with Nora, supposed to play tennis soon?" Everett interrupted, not particularly caring to listen to Caroline disparage, as Millie would have said, Millie's character.

Caroline's toe started tapping against the well-manicured lawn. "We can't play. Birdie

Taylor broke her leg two days ago, and because of that, she's refusing to participate."

Everett's lips began to curl. Before he could point out that he highly doubted Birdie had broken her leg on purpose, or that she'd be much use on the court with a leg in a cast, Dudley, who'd not spoken a word since Caroline had shown up on the scene, cleared his throat. "I'm sure you're very disappointed over the inability to play tennis today, Caroline, but perhaps Everett can suggest something we can do instead to ease that disappointment." He arched a brow Everett's way.

"Well, as to that, I'm sure I can come up with something," Everett said slowly, a little confused as to why Dudley was stepping in. "But, before I address that, I really do need to get the children on their way to Seaview."

"Not until you tell me the history of this Newport Casino," Millie said, speaking up before she, oddly enough, began inching away from Nora. She stopped inching a moment later and jerked her head ever so slightly to the right.

Directing his attention that way, he spotted Elizabeth, Rosetta, and Thaddeus, all lined up in a row, and all of them standing in front of balls that seemed to be aimed

153

directly at Caroline. Giving them a small shake of his head, he couldn't claim to be exactly surprised when the children pretended they didn't see him.

"Of course, I did promise you a history lesson, didn't I, and ah, well, that Mr. Bennett I mentioned before was, ah . . ." He started moving as casually as he could to stand beside Millie, hoping that presenting the children with his back wasn't another bad choice he was making today. "He was the respected owner of the *New York Herald,* and he had this friend by the name of . . ." The sound of what clearly had to be a mallet swinging behind him distracted Everett for a second, but luckily, the someone swinging that mallet seemingly missed the ball.

"Captain Candy," Nora finished for him even as she craned her neck and tried to see around him.

Everett shifted a little to the left. "That's right, and Mr. Bennett invited this Captain Candy to join him at the Reading Room, where he then encouraged the captain to ride his horse up the steps and right into the building as a bit of a lark."

"You know, maybe this really isn't the best story to tell right now, especially with these particular children standing behind us,"

Millie mumbled. "It might just give them ideas."

Glancing back to the children, Everett noticed that all three of them seemed to be tilting their little ears his way. "Clearly it was a mistake, but they might find the ending of the story interesting."

"Does Captain Candy fall off his horse and suffer a horrible injury?" Elizabeth asked.

Everett frowned. "No, he simply got himself banned from the Reading Room, and that annoyed Mr. Bennett, which had him building the Newport Casino." He nodded. "That is why one should not ride a horse into a club, house, or anywhere else a horse doesn't belong."

"But since riding a horse got this new club built, it doesn't seem like such a bad idea," Elizabeth said before she squinted her eyes and then moved the croquet ball a few inches to the right, once again putting it directly in a path with . . . Caroline.

"Elizabeth . . . you don't want to do that," he said quietly.

"She doesn't want to do what?" Nora asked, appearing right beside him, where she promptly glanced to Elizabeth, then to Rosetta and Thaddeus who were now positioning their balls just so. Spinning around, Nora spread her arms out wide as if that could possibly add more protection.

"I've just had the most marvelous idea," Nora chirped. "Since we were so looking forward to playing tennis, but Birdie let us down by breaking her leg . . ." She nodded at Millie. "Do you happen to play, Miss Longfellow?"

"Ah, well . . ." Millie began.

"Don't be ridiculous, Nora," Caroline interrupted. "Of course Miss Longfellow doesn't play tennis, and it's not well done of you to embarrass the poor dear in front of all these people."

From the second Millie lifted her nose into the air, to the moment she opened her mouth, Everett knew disaster was about to strike Newport.

"I've played tennis before, Miss Dixon. A previous employer of mine had two sons who loved the game and always needed someone to practice with." She shook her head. "I certainly couldn't keep up with them, but they did teach me the basics. So, if you still want to play a match, I'd be willing to fill in for that Birdie lady."

"Her name is Miss Taylor, but . . ." Caroline stopped talking, looked around at the crowd, who all seemed to be highly amused, and then looked back to Millie before she . . . smiled. It was not a pleasant smile, not one filled with amusement, and it did not bode well for Millie. "If you're certain you want to play, who am I to deny you the treat of playing tennis at the Casino?" She shifted her attention to Nora. "Since this was your idea, Miss Longfellow can be on your team."

As Everett opened his mouth to voice his opposition to what was clearly a very bad idea, Nora linked her arm though Millie's and began strolling away. Caroline and Gertrude fell into step behind them, and before Everett realized it, he'd lost the opportunity to protest.

"We're just off to get our racquets," Caroline tossed over her shoulder. "We'll be on the court in less than five minutes if any of you care to watch the match."

Determined to stop the madness, or at least stop the crowd that had begun moving toward the tennis courts, Everett started forward. But he came to an immediate stop when a croquet ball went whizzing past him, missing him by no more than an inch. Turning, he leveled a glare on Elizabeth, who leveled a glare right back at him.

"Why did you and Miss Longfellow have to go and stand in front of us?" she demanded.

"Because it's never acceptable to try to hit someone with a croquet ball, or any type of ball, for that matter, as you very well know." Everett moved closer to her. "And furthermore, your poor judgment, and the fact you talked your little brother and sister into joining you, has just earned you a bit of punishment, such as an afternoon spent in your room at Seaview."

"That's hardly fair," Elizabeth said.

"And this is hardly the moment for additional dramatics, although it's encouraging to see you take a firmer line with them, dear," Abigail said, bustling up to Everett, her face pink and her expression troubled. She immediately took hold of his arm. "Thank goodness I was getting overly warm in the hansom cab and got out to cool off, or else I wouldn't have heard about the disaster that's about to occur."

"It's only tennis," he said as Abigail began prodding him forward.

"It's not, and you should realize that," she countered. "I do wish we hadn't sent that wagon on ahead with all of our trunks, though. I packed the most adorable white lawn gown in one of those trunks for Millie, and it would have been perfect for this occasion."

"I've never gotten the impression Millie's

exactly keen about fashion."

"Oh, she's not keen about fashion at all, which is why I've had to step in, but . . . no need to delve further into that. She has enough on her mind at the moment, poor dear, without wondering exactly how I've stepped in, and she'll see for herself once . . . Well, again, this is hardly the time to talk nonsense. It is a shame she has to play in that hideous skirt and blouse, though, with an apron on no less. I'm afraid people might laugh at her."

"I think that man was laughing at my dress, and I didn't like that at all," Thaddeus said, coming up beside Everett with Elizabeth and Rosetta right behind him. He pointed a little finger at Dudley's retreating back. "He's not a very nice man." With that, Thaddeus slipped his hand into Everett's and tilted his head back, catching Everett's eye. "Are you mad at us for trying to conk Miss Dixon in the head with a croquet ball?"

"A bit, but we'll discuss that at a later time. I'd much rather talk about your refusal to wear pants, and . . . when you think you might get over that refusal, which would probably lead to people not laughing at your choice of clothing in the future — not that Mr. Codman was in any way justified in doing that."

Thaddeus began swinging Everett's hand back and forth. "I can't change back to wearing pants because I don't have any pants anymore." He looked a little smug. "I buried them back on Fifth Avenue."

Everett slowed to a stop. "Why would you do that?"

"That's what you do when you don't want someone to find your things."

Unable to keep from smiling over that odd bit of logic, Everett squeezed Thaddeus's hand. "I suppose you do have a point, but . . . if you want to wear pants again, you should know that there are stores here in Newport that sell clothing for little boys. I'd be more than happy to purchase you whatever you want."

When Thaddeus didn't immediately agree to that idea, Everett didn't bother to pursue it, knowing now was hardly the time to get into a debate with a five-year-old. Steering everyone around the Casino and over to the wooden stands that had been erected for the convenience of the guests, trepidation began to steal through him as those stands quickly began filling with what seemed to be every guest enjoying the Casino that day.

Numerous members of the staff rushed around setting up additional chairs to accommodate the overflow, and then servers appeared, handing out glasses of lemonade. After getting lemonade for the children and Abigail, Everett took a seat on the wooden bench and turned his attention to the lawn tennis court.

The crowd suddenly grew quiet when Millie, with Nora by her side, appeared on that court, swinging a racquet and looking downright cheerful, even if she did look completely out of place in her dark skirt, although she had taken off her apron. She'd also done something to shorten her hem, showing ankles clad in dark stockings, the sight of those ankles having his pulse, strangely enough, speed up. What made that circumstance seem even stranger still was that when Caroline walked onto the court, wearing the latest in fashionable tennis attire, she was also showing a bit of ankle, but the sight of her ankles didn't seem to . . .

"This is going to be a nightmare," Abigail said as she took a sip of her lemonade and shook her head rather sadly as she looked around.

Shoving all thoughts of ankles aside, Everett summoned up a smile. "Millie will be fine. She seems very adaptable, and she also seems to be a good sport."

"I'm not actually that worried about

Millie at the moment."

Before he had a chance to process that statement, the ladies took their places, Caroline either not seeing his wave or deliberately ignoring it. Millie, on the other hand, was waving enthusiastically to the children, all of whom, surprisingly enough, were cheering for her — something that was no doubt irritating Caroline no small amount.

"I'll serve first, shall I?" Caroline called across the net as she plucked a ball out of her pocket, stepped up to the line, and tossed it into the air, leaving Millie, who was supposed to be the recipient of the serve, barely any time to get ready.

All the breath seemed to leave him as the ball traveled rather slowly over the net. But then Millie drew back her racquet and . . . slammed the ball back Caroline's way, the force of her swing completely unexpected given her small size. Before Caroline even moved, the ball shot past her.

"Was that out?" Caroline demanded, swinging around.

"It was in," called a lady from the stands.

Caroline spun to face Millie as Nora flashed a cheeky grin.

"Love-fifteen," Nora called.

"I know how to keep score," Caroline snapped back.

Unfortunately, the game did not get better for Caroline after that.

Millie had obviously not been exaggerating when she'd claimed she'd played tennis before, but it was clear that she hadn't been playing with *young* boys. She was all over the court, hitting anything Caroline or Gertrude managed to get over the net, while Nora simply strolled back and forth, swinging her racquet, and at one point, whistling a jaunty tune.

When it was Millie's turn to serve, matters turned downright concerning. Gertrude was the first to try and return Millie's serve, but when the ball came rushing at her, she screamed, dropped her racquet, and ran the other way, earning a screech from Caroline until she seemed to recall that her turn was next.

"Give her a fast one, Miss Longfellow," Thaddeus called.

Millie lowered her racquet to send Thaddeus another wave.

"Miss Longfellow, we are in the middle of a match here," Caroline yelled across the net.

"Forgive me, Miss Dixon. You're quite right."

As if the world had suddenly slowed down, Everett watched as Millie threw the ball up, and then the racquet connected squarely with it, the thud of the connection reaching his ears. It began to move, and then the world sped up as the ball hurled at Caroline, and . . . smacked her right in the middle of the forehead, the impact knocking Caroline off her feet. Her skirt fluttered up, showing a bit of leg.

Millie immediately began running across the court. Darting around the net, she raced to Caroline's side, and yanked Caroline's skirt back over her legs.

Before Everett had a chance to see what Millie would do next, Abigail was tugging on his arm, and he realized he needed to act . . . the sooner the better.

By the time he got to Caroline, made certain she wasn't seriously hurt, and on her feet, he knew he had to get Millie as far away as possible from her. Caroline was shaking with rage and muttering threats under her breath. Telling Caroline he'd be right back, he nodded to Millie, who was still trying to apologize to Caroline, even though Caroline was not acknowledging the apologies and was resolutely looking the opposite way from Millie.

"I really am so very, very sorry," Millie said one last time before Abigail suddenly appeared right by her side and the crowd that had gathered around them fell silent.

"Good heavens, Millie, it's not as if you hit Miss Dixon on purpose — something Caroline knows all too well." Abigail leveled a cool look on Caroline. "Why, your forehead is just a little pink. Granted the pink is perfectly circular, but . . . I'm sure it'll fade soon, so no harm done."

Abigail stepped closer to Millie and took hold of her arm before she nodded to the crowd. "If everyone will excuse us, Millie and I need to get the children settled." She glanced Everett's way. "I'm sure you'll want to escort Caroline straight to her cottage, dear."

As Abigail pulled Millie away, the crowd began whispering again, but Caroline wasn't paying the slightest attention to the whispers. Her attention was centered squarely on Abigail's retreating back. "What's Mrs. Hart doing in Newport?"

Everett swallowed a sigh. "She's here because of Millie, er, I mean . . . Miss Longfellow."

Caroline's eyes narrowed to mere slits before her voice turned dangerous, even though she was barely whispering. "Is she now? Well, I won't stand for it, I tell you." She stepped closer to Everett. "Miss Longfellow needs to go, as well as Mrs. Hart *and* her meddling ways. Which means I expect you to dismiss the nanny — immediately."

"I've obviously lost my mind," Millie said as the hansom cab trundled down the road. "What was I thinking, playing to win?"

Abigail immediately began clucking. "From what I've come to know about you, my dear, you're a lady who embraces every venture with enthusiasm. I would have been very disappointed if you'd gone out on that court and not played the way you're apparently capable of playing."

"I smashed a ball directly into Miss Dixon's face."

"You didn't do it intentionally. How could you have possibly known Caroline would just stand there like a deer caught in the lantern light?"

Elizabeth sat forward and grinned. "Did you see how the ball bounced right off her head? That was great, and one of the best things I've . . ."

"It was *not* great that I bounced a ball off

of Miss Dixon's head," Millie interrupted, her words causing the grin to slide right off Elizabeth's face.

"Sure it was," Elizabeth countered. "She deserved it because she only wanted to play tennis with you in order to embarrass you, but . . . that didn't turn out how she wanted, did it?"

"I don't know about that. I was pretty embarrassed when all those people started wagging their fingers at me, and especially when Gertrude began yelling at me that I was unnatural and shouldn't be allowed in public." Millie shuddered. "But my embarrassment aside, you, Elizabeth, have some explaining to do regarding that nasty business with the croquet ball. You could have seriously injured Miss Dixon."

Elizabeth looked less than contrite. "I was hoping if I conked her in the head, she'd lose her memory and forget all about the boarding school plan." She suddenly looked a little hopeful. "Do you think *your* conking her on the head might have rattled her memory a little?"

"Miss Dixon seemed perfectly coherent, and that means *logical,* when she took to screaming at me, so no, I think her memory is still intact. I believe it might be easier all around though, if you'd just talk to Uncle

Everett about your feelings regarding boarding school instead of thinking up dangerous plots that will certainly see you sent off to one."

"If he really was my uncle, I would talk to him about it. But he's just my guardian along with being my godparent. He's a horrible guardian because he hasn't even *tried* to guard me from the dreadful Miss Dixon, and as for being a godparent . . ." Elizabeth stopped talking as her eyes turned suspiciously bright. "I asked him after Mommy and Daddy died why God had taken them and left me, Rose, and Thaddeus all alone, but . . . he didn't have any answers to give me."

"In Everett's defense, that's a really tough question to answer."

"He didn't even try."

"I can try now if you'd like, because I lost both of my parents when I was just a baby," Millie said softly, right as the hansom cab pulled off the road and began traveling over a surface that crunched beneath the wheels.

Elizabeth turned her head to the window. "I didn't ask you to explain anything to me, and I don't want to talk about God, because He doesn't listen to me. He completely ignored all of my prayers begging Him to send my parents back."

169

Swallowing past the lump that formed in her throat, Millie leaned forward. Unfortunately, the cab took that particular moment to pull to a stop. Elizabeth didn't bother to wait for the driver to get the door but wrenched it open and jumped out, Rosetta and Thaddeus scrambling after her a second later. A hand on her arm had Millie pausing in the act of following the children.

"She won't listen to anything you say right now," Abigail said. "But leave the God business to me. Given the delicacy of the topic, I think our best option is to bring in an expert. Since Reverend Gilmore is always willing to lend his advice, I'll pen him a letter as soon as I get back to my cottage and ask if he has any suggestions."

Millie blew out the breath she hadn't even realized she'd been holding. "I think that's a wonderful idea, Abigail. Quite honestly, I don't really know how to explain the situation properly, especially since I've never truly understood why my parents were taken from me."

Abigail patted Millie's hand. "I've always believed God has a certain purpose for all of us, and once we fulfill that purpose, He calls us home." She smiled. "Perhaps your parents' purpose was to bring you into the world."

"I would have preferred they'd been granted time to raise me."

"And that is exactly why we need Reverend Gilmore here." Abigail moved to the door, accepting the hand the driver offered her.

Millie followed a moment later and after thanking the driver for his assistance found herself incapable of speech when she got her first good look at Seaview Cottage.

Three stories of white stone rose up before her, the many-paned windows gleaming in the sunlight. Chairs piled high with comfy-looking cushions were set charmingly about, beckoning a person to enjoy the shade granted from the green-and-white-striped awnings covering the entire length of what appeared to be some type of veranda.

A stone fountain gurgled from the very center of a well-manicured lawn, while birds that Millie thought might just be peacocks strutted in and out of shrubs that had been carefully pruned. A glance to the right allowed her a glimpse of the ocean, and when a breeze began to stir, she smelled the distinct scent of the sea.

"This can't be anyone's idea of a cottage, can it?" she asked, catching the driver's eye.

"You did bring us to the right place, didn't you?"

"Mr. Mulberry instructed me to deliver you to Seaview Cottage off of Bellevue Avenue," the driver said. He gestured to the house. "This is definitely Seaview, and that" — he turned and pointed to the road — "is definitely Bellevue Avenue."

"But that," Millie argued with a wave of her hand toward the house, "is not a cottage. Cottages are supposed to be small and quaint, not . . . intimidating."

Abigail smiled. "My dear, surely you must realize that members of society only call their summer residences by such a ridiculous name to ascertain their superiority over the common folk, don't you?"

"Haven't I heard *you* refer to your summer home as a cottage?"

"My summer home is a true cottage, purchased years and years ago before society began deciding ostentatious was the new fashion. That ostentation, I'm afraid, is something we're going to see much more of in the future, what with fortunes being made at a drop of the hat these days. Why, since Mrs. Astor recently acquired Beechwood Cottage here in Newport, I'm sure we'll soon be inundated with even larger cottages, everyone trying to outdo one another to prove their worth."

Millie eyed Seaview Cottage again. "There can be no denying that it's overly . . . impressive, but . . . the sheer size of the cottage does explain a few questions I had about the ball Everett's hosting here this summer."

"Everett's hosting a ball?" Abigail eyes began sparkling. "I love organizing balls, and I do hope he'll seek out my advice as he goes about planning it."

"From what I understand, Miss Dixon is organizing the event. And, I don't know if you noticed this or not, but she was not regarding you in a very friendly manner after the whole ball bouncing off her head incident."

"Hmm . . . you might have a point, but I have to tell you, there aren't many young society ladies who have the nerve to refuse me." Abigail smiled before she turned to the driver. "I'm just going to make certain Miss Longfellow gets introduced to the staff, and then I'll need you to drive me over to my cottage. It's not far from here."

"Very good, ma'am," the driver said, tipping his hat to Abigail.

Taking Millie's arm, Abigail began strolling toward the children, who'd stopped by the fountain and were dipping their hands

into it. "This really is very lovely, but . . .
I'm not sure those peacocks are a good
idea." Abigail nodded to the birds in question. "From what little I know of them,
they're not supposed to be pleasant
creatures."

Elizabeth withdrew her hand from the
fountain, and to Millie's relief, she was actually smiling a little now. "The peacocks were
a present from Miss Dixon for Uncle
Everett's birthday a few months back."

"Everett wanted peacocks for his
birthday?" Millie asked slowly.

Elizabeth shook her head. "He wanted a
dog, but Miss Dixon decided dogs were out
of fashion. She got him peacocks instead
because she believes they're soon going to
be all the rage." She grinned. "Uncle Everett
was a little upset about the birds, especially
when it turned out they like to shriek every
morning really early. Since their shrieking
sounds like someone's being murdered, the
police kept showing up on our doorstep.
That's why he sent the birds here, that and
the fact his neighbors on Fifth Avenue were
beginning to leave him nasty notes."

"I wonder if he realized the peacocks
would soon begin multiplying, because if
I'm not much mistaken, I see a few babies
poking their heads out of the shrubbery,"

Abigail said.

"Baby peacocks?" Rosetta took off toward the shrubbery before anyone could stop her. A shrill screech split the air right as an entire flock of peacocks came charging out of the shrubbery and directly toward Rosetta. Dropping Abigail's arm, Millie broke into a run, dodging peacock after peacock as she tried to get to the child. By the time she finally reached her, Millie had been pecked numerous times. Scooping Rosetta up into her arms, she hugged the little girl tightly to herself before she looked over the child's curls, discovering, much to her dismay, that they were now completely surrounded by the birds.

"Shoo," she shouted, but all that managed to do was set off additional screeching. A small hand on her cheek had her looking down. Rosetta, much to Millie's surprise, wasn't looking frightened in the least. In fact, she was smiling.

"Aren't they beautiful?" Rosetta asked before she tucked her small head into the crook of Millie's neck. She then let out the smallest of sighs as her other hand reached up and closed around the fabric of Millie's blouse.

Right there and then, Millie lost her heart. Leaning closer to the little girl nestled against her, she breathed in the sweet scent of Rosetta's hair, but then remembered she was right in the midst of a flock of mad peacocks. Lifting her head, she eyed the birds that were closing in on her.

"They're not going to hurt you," Elizabeth called over the screeching. "Animals adore Rose. You'll be fine walking through them."

Millie's first thought, since the numerous pecks the peacocks had given her were beginning to sting, was that Elizabeth was up to no good, but then she remembered she was carrying Rosetta. It had been clear from the start that Elizabeth took her role as older sibling very seriously. Taking a steadying breath, Millie tightened her hold on Rosetta and began moving ever so slowly forward. To her relief, the peacocks stopped screeching and then filed, one after another, into a straight line behind her. Hoping she was not setting herself up for an attack, Millie headed for the house, wanting to put a solid wall between her and the birds.

"I can take my sister," Elizabeth said, hurrying over to join them.

Rosetta snuggled closer to Millie and tucked her head back into the crook of Millie's neck. "I don't want you to carry me, Elizabeth."

"Rosetta probably just thinks she's too heavy for you," Millie said softly when Elizabeth stopped in her tracks and looked as if someone had smacked her.

Not bothering to respond, Elizabeth sent Millie a glare before she marched over to her brother, who was trailing beside the peacocks, eyeing them in a rather strange sort of way. Grabbing hold of Thaddeus's hand, she began tugging him toward the house.

Thaddeus immediately dug in his heels. "Stop pulling me, Elizabeth. I want to pet the peacocks, or . . . try riding them."

"You can't ride the peacocks, Thaddeus," Millie said. "They're really not friendly in the least, and if you need proof of that, just look at all the pecks on my arm." She shifted Rosetta and held out an arm for Thaddeus to inspect, although he seemed less than impressed with the abuse she'd suffered. Fighting a smile, she tried again. "And although Miss Dixon is hoping peacocks become all the rage, after seeing the birds in action, I have numerous doubts that will ever happen."

"If I rode one of them into that reading place, I bet everyone would start wanting them as pets," Thaddeus argued.

"And that right there is exactly why I'll be

speaking with Everett when he returns to Seaview about what he can and can't talk about when the three of you are within listening distance," Millie said as she began walking again, Elizabeth and Thaddeus falling into step beside her. When they reached the veranda, the door burst open and what seemed like the entire staff streamed out. Surprisingly enough, every member of that staff was beaming back at her as if they were truly delighted to see her.

It was not a sight she was accustomed to seeing.

"You must be Miss Longfellow," a heavy-set woman wearing an apron said as she hurried down the steps. "I'm Mrs. O'Conner, the housekeeper at Seaview. May I just say all of us are thrilled beyond belief you've agreed to look after the children."

"I wouldn't count on her being here long," Elizabeth said before she nodded to her sister. "Come on, Rose, we should go see what our rooms look like."

Rose lifted her head from the crook of Millie's neck and let out a sigh. "You can put me down, Miss Longfellow."

As she set the little girl on her feet, Millie leaned over and brushed a strand of hair away from Rosetta's face. "I've noticed that your sister calls you Rose. Do you prefer that over Rosetta?"

Rosetta nodded.

Straightening, Millie caught Elizabeth's eye. "Why doesn't everyone call her Rose if it's what she likes to be called?"

"No one ever asked."

A touch of temper shot through Millie at that telling remark. "I'm asking now. May I assume you prefer a different name as well, such as Lizzie or Beth?"

"Do I *look* like a Lizzie or a Beth?"

Millie fought a smile before she nodded to Thaddeus. "What about you, Thaddeus? Do you prefer to be called Thad?"

Thaddeus scratched his nose. "I think Thaddeus is a nice name, but . . . Chip . . . That's a great name."

Millie grinned right as Elizabeth let out a huff.

"We're not calling you Chip," Elizabeth said. "Mother named you after our late grandfather, so Thaddeus you're going to stay."

Thaddeus's jaw turned stubborn. "Why are you always so bossy?"

For a second, Elizabeth simply stood there, but then she rounded on Millie. "This is your fault." With that, she pushed her way through everyone gathered on the veranda and disappeared from sight.

"Oh . . . dear," Abigail said, moving up to join Millie. "And here I'd been thinking we were beginning to make some progress."

"She wasn't always so . . . mean," Rose whispered as Thaddeus nodded in agreement.

Millie forced a smile. "I think the events of the day have simply caught up with Elizabeth. I'm sure she'll feel better after everyone gets settled."

Thaddeus shook his head. "I bet she won't, since she's really mad about Uncle Everett telling her she has to spend the afternoon in her room because of trying to do Miss Dixon in with a croquet ball." His little shoulders slumped. "We'd better go after her, Rose."

"I'll come with you as well," Millie said, right as a young woman stepped out of the crowd and moved to stand in front of Millie.

"You need to meet the staff, Miss Longfellow, so I'll take Thaddeus and Rose up to speak with their sister." She smiled. "I'm Miss Ann Quigley, one of the upstairs maids here at Seaview, and an upstairs maid back in Mr. Mulberry's residence on Fifth Avenue. I've been given the pleasure of watching the children over the past few months, when we've been short a nanny or two."

"While that's a generous offer, Miss Quigley, and one I truly appreciate," Millie began, "I fear Elizabeth might be a little tricky at the moment. Since I am paid to look after her, I wouldn't be comfortable accepting your offer."

"Elizabeth likes Miss Ann," Rose said as she actually took hold of Ann's hand and smiled. "Me and Thaddeus like her too."

Glancing to Thaddeus, who sent her a nod, Millie smiled and looked back at Ann. "If you're sure, it would be nice to meet the staff, and I promise I won't be long."

With a returning smile, Ann took hold of Thaddeus's hand, and with the children chatting about everything under the sun, she led them into the house.

"What a lovely young woman," Abigail said. "And since it does seem as if you're going to be well taken care of here, I'll be on my way." She nodded to Mrs. O'Connor. "I'm Mrs. Hart, by the way, and do know, if anything of a troubling nature occurs, my cottage is just down the road."

Mrs. O'Connor dipped a curtsy Abigail's way. "It's a pleasure to meet you, Mrs. Hart. Since Mr. Mulberry gave instructions for us to send your trunks on ahead, I have your address and will certainly send for you if something of a troubling nature happens."

Mrs. O'Connor turned to Millie. "And speaking of trunks, your trunks, along with a black bag, have been delivered to the room you'll be using on the second floor."

"I only brought the black bag," Millie said slowly.

Mrs. O'Connor's brow furrowed. "Then why were there four trunks with your name stamped on them?"

An image of a dinner dress suddenly sprang to mind, along with Miss Bertha Miller's remark about Abigail ordering an entirely new wardrobe for Millie. Shaking her head, Millie turned to tell Abigail exactly what she thought about the older woman's latest shenanigans but found that Abigail was already halfway across the lawn, moving at a remarkably fast clip for a woman of her age. "Should I ask what's in the trunks, Abigail?" she called.

"You'll see," Abigail tossed over her shoulder as she reached the hansom cab. A moment later, with a cheery wave sent out the window, Abigail got on her way.

Watching until the hansom cab disappeared down the road, Millie turned to the staff still waiting to meet her. "I don't care to be an alarmist, but I get the distinct impression we're going to be experiencing a very disturbing summer."

She was not reassured in the least when not a single one of them bothered to dispute her statement.

Less than ten minutes later, Millie came to the conclusion she'd been exactly right about the disturbing summer business.

After being introduced to the entire staff, she'd followed Mrs. O'Connor through the well-appointed cottage, up a curving staircase lined with red carpeting, then down a long hallway that had gilded papered walls, and into the nanny's room. She'd been taken aback by the drabness of the room, especially considering how nice the rest of the cottage had been decorated. However, once she spotted the incredibly large trunks that did, indeed, have her name stamped on them, all thoughts of decorations had immediately evaporated from her mind.

Mrs. O'Connor, obviously being a very astute woman, had beaten a remarkably hasty retreat, leaving Millie all alone to consider the trunks in front of her. Deciding after a few minutes that she wasn't brave enough to delve into the deep depths of the trunks quite yet, Millie walked over to the black bag she'd personally packed and picked it up, plopping it right back down on the small bed the room afforded.

Flipping open the clasp, she smiled when her books came immediately into view. Pulling out her Bible, two Jane Austen books, a dictionary, several works by Shakespeare, and last, but not least, her thesaurus, her relief turned to annoyance when she realized all of the clothing she'd packed seemed to be missing. Sticking her hand back in the bag, she felt nothing but empty space. Gone were the skirts, blouses, sensible undergarments, stockings, and even her aprons, along with her spare pair of comfortable shoes.

Withdrawing her hand, she stalked over to the trunks, disbelief flowing through her when she opened the first one and discovered day dresses that would be perfect if she happened to be invited to a fancy tea.

The next trunk held hats and shoes, the third, beautiful dinner dresses, and the fourth . . . Millie actually shuddered when she'd pulled out a wispy piece of silk that was nothing less than a ball gown.

"Honestly, this time she's gone too far," Millie muttered, tossing the ball gown over a straight-back chair. "When I get my hands on her I'll —"

"Forgive me for interrupting, Miss Longfellow, but I do feel I should point out that issuing threats against the person responsible for those trunks, a person I'm assuming might be Mrs. Hart, could possibly see you dismissed from your position. Believe me when I say none of us here at Seaview want to see that happen."

Looking up, Millie found Ann standing in the doorway. "Believe *me* when I say the last thing Mrs. Hart would let happen would be my dismissal from this position, given her liking for plots. But . . . never mind about that." She tilted her head. "May I hope you're here to tell me you've met with some success in regard to Elizabeth and her bad temper?"

"She won't let us in her room," Thaddeus said, darting around Ann with Rose by his side. "She sent us to find you because she says she won't come out until you go and talk to her."

Rose's little lip started trembling. "I think she's . . . crying."

Those words had Millie heading out of the room and striding down the hallway. She came to a stop in front of the door Mrs. O'Connor had told her led to Elizabeth's room. To her relief, she heard not a single sound of crying coming from Elizabeth's room. Moving a step closer, she noticed that the door had been left open a few inches, and found herself wondering if Elizabeth had done that on purpose so that Millie would know she'd be welcome. Deciding the only way she'd discover exactly what Elizabeth was thinking was to actually go speak with the girl, Millie took a step forward and pushed open the door, regretting the decision almost immediately when water suddenly poured over her.

Tilting her chin, she immediately regretted that as well when a wash basin, obviously the one that had recently held all the water, dropped on her head, the weight and surprise of it sending her crashing to the ground.

"You killed the nanny, Elizabeth," Thaddeus wailed. "We're going to be in terrible trouble now."

Millie heard the sound of little feet pounding away and realized the children were fleeing, no doubt because they *were* only children and probably did think she was truly dead. Trying to summon up her voice to tell them she was very much alive, she found herself incapable of speech so simply stayed on the floor, counting the stars that were still swirling beneath her eyelids.

"Good heavens, Miss Longfellow, are you all right?" Ann asked as she knelt down beside Millie. "I cannot believe Elizabeth resorted to such a prank. Why, she really could have killed you."

"On my word, what happened?"

Forcing her eyes open, Millie discovered Mr. Macon, Everett's butler, peering down at her.

"I'm fine, or at least not dead," she managed to say.

Mr. Macon smiled. "Of course you're not dead, and thank goodness for that, Miss Longfellow. You must realize that everyone on staff is in full agreement that you, my dear, are our last hope." He knelt down beside her, opposite Ann. "Do you think you can sit up?"

"Give me another minute."

"I'll go track down the children," Mrs. O'Connor said, peering down over Mr. Macon's shoulder to catch Millie's eye. "They need to take responsibility for this."

"Thaddeus and Rose have done nothing wrong, Mrs. O'Connor. They just panicked, and if I were to hazard a guess, Elizabeth probably didn't realize what the consequences would be from her little bout of mischief."

"Surely you're not going to let her get away with what she did without some type of punishment, are you?" Mrs. O'Connor asked slowly.

Rubbing her head, Millie nodded to Mr. Macon, who helped her into a sitting position. "I'm not a big believer in the usual methods of punishment, such as spanking or withholding food, Mrs. O'Connor. Although, given what just happened, it's clear I have to come up with something spectacular to teach Elizabeth, along with Thaddeus and Rose since they have caused quite a bit of mayhem the last few months, a lesson they'll not soon forget." She rubbed her head again before she smiled. "If anyone is willing to help me — and I do believe I'm going to need quite a few people to help me set up what I have in mind — I'd greatly appreciate the assistance. And I need a place where no one will mind if it gets a little . . . messy."

Stepping off a ladder twenty minutes later, Millie looked up and surveyed her handiwork, pleased with how her plan was taking shape. She nodded to Mr. Macon and Mrs. O'Connor, who nodded back before they exited what they'd called the mud room by walking out a door that led to the backyard.

This particular spot was absolutely perfect for what Millie had in mind. The floor was made of stone, there was relatively little furniture in the room, save a couple of chairs, and there were numerous sinks that were certainly going to come in handy, especially since there was little question that a huge mess was about to happen. Smiling her thanks to a footman who was carting the ladder out of the room, Millie took a seat on a chair that was placed exactly right. Plopping an ice pack on the lump on her head, she watched the door as she waited for the children to arrive.

It turned into an extremely long wait.

Shifting in the chair, she was just about to get up and see if anyone had located the children, when she heard Mrs. O'Connor speaking in a very loud voice as she marched what were surely three reluctant children down the hallway.

"And you didn't kill Miss Longfellow, Elizabeth, but it was a near miss, so the very least you owe her is a heartfelt apology."

"I didn't know that basin would fall on her head," Elizabeth said with a distinct quiver in her voice.

"Buckets placed over doors do tend to fall when the doors open, Elizabeth," Mrs. O'Connor returned. "Which is why I expect you to tell Miss Longfellow how sorry you are, and assure her you'll never, as in ever, play that particular trick on anyone again."

Anticipation had Millie's nerves jangling as the children and Mrs. O'Connor drew closer.

"I'm going to allow the three of you to speak with Miss Longfellow alone. Come and stand together, and . . . in you go."

The doorknob turned, the door began to open, and if Millie wasn't much mistaken, Mrs. O'Connor pushed the children forward in an obvious attempt at making certain Millie's idea would go off as planned. Giving a nod to two footmen by the names of Will Davis and Henry Johnson, she watched as they yanked on the ropes they'd been instructed to hold, ropes that were attached to large buckets used to water the horses, but buckets that were now hanging from the ceiling.

Shrieks were immediate as cold water thoroughly soaked the children, but then the shrieks were cut off as flour, placed in sheets clear up by the ceiling and controlled by another piece of handy rope, dumped over their soaking wet bodies. It covered them from head to toe and rapidly began turning to . . . paste.

Dropping her ice pack, Millie rose to feet, unable to help but laugh when three pairs of outraged eyes blinked her way. She swallowed another laugh, but suddenly found herself devoid of all amusement when a lady dressed from head to toe in the latest fashions breezed into the room. That lady was immediately followed by a gentleman who looked remarkably similar to Everett, although older.

"Mr. and Mrs. Mulberry," Mrs. O'Connor said in a horrified voice as she trailed after the newcomers. "What in the world are you doing here?"

Mrs. Mulberry didn't bother to answer. Instead, she looked the children up and down, looked around the room, which was rapidly becoming coated with flour, then turned green eyes that were blazing with heat on Millie.

"Who are you?" Mrs. Mulberry demanded.

"I'm, ah, well . . . the nanny."

Mrs. Mulberry lifted her chin. "That, my dear, is no longer the case, since you may now consider yourself dismissed. Effective . . . immediately."

8

"I cannot believe you refused Caroline's request of dismissing the nanny."

Pulling his attention away from the many buggies that were slowly traveling down Bellevue Avenue, filled with *the* fashionable set of Newport out and about on their daily afternoon jaunt, Everett settled it on Dudley. That gentleman was sitting on the carriage seat opposite him, having offered Everett a ride home after Caroline had refused to allow him to set so much as a single toe in her carriage after *he'd* refused to let Millie go.

"I don't believe Caroline presented me with a request. It was a demand, and one I wasn't comfortable granting," Everett finally said.

"Your nanny succeeded in embarrassing Caroline in front of everyone at the Casino. That in and of itself should have had you agreeing to Miss Longfellow's termination."

"If Caroline suffered undue embarrassment, she has no one to blame but herself. She *is* the one who badgered Millie into playing tennis against her."

One of Dudley's brows shot up. "It's hardly appropriate for you to call your nanny by her given name, no matter that I've heard rumors she's friends with Miss Harriet Peabody. Miss Peabody might now be engaged to Oliver Addleshaw, and you might be very good friends with Oliver, but that does not make it acceptable for you to address your nanny so familiarly. It does a disservice to your position within society."

Something unpleasant unfurled in Everett's stomach. It had not escaped his notice that all of his friends, with the exception of Nora Niesen, had been a little too anxious in their desire to watch Millie take the court. Everett knew full well that anxiousness had stemmed from everyone wanting to see Millie fail. But when she hadn't failed, had actually risen to the occasion magnificently, the anxiousness his friends had been displaying turned to antagonism, and an undeserved antagonism at that.

His friends had been cruel in their pursuit of amusement and that —

"While I normally don't enjoy pointing

out the faults of my friends," Dudley was saying, pulling Everett abruptly out of his thoughts, "you're behaving like a complete idiot."

"And your reasoning behind that would be . . . ?"

Dudley raked a hand through thinning brown hair. "You have been fortunate enough to obtain the affections of the most desirable lady in society, yet you hardly treat Caroline in the manner she deserves."

"Quite frankly, I'm not exactly certain I've obtained her affections, especially since she's been less than pleasant to me of late."

"She's been less than pleasant to you because you haven't been showing her the proper amount of attention."

"I find it somewhat interesting that you feel qualified to give me advice since you have yet to settle your affections on a particular lady."

Dudley shoved his hand through his hair again, leaned forward, and pinned Everett under a rather intense gaze. "I was never going to mention this to you, believing there was no point in allowing you access to this somewhat delicate information, but . . . you stole away the only lady I ever *wanted* to settle my affections on."

Time ceased to move as Everett simply

sat there, his thoughts becoming more muddled the longer he considered Dudley's words. "I never had the faintest inkling you held Caroline in high esteem," was all he seemed capable of mustering up in response.

"I mentioned my *very* great esteem for the lady at one of the Patriarch Balls well over two years ago."

"I thought you were only telling me about Caroline because you thought I'd get along well with her, and that you felt she was an appropriate lady for *me* to set my sights on."

"That was not why I pointed her out to you."

"Oh . . . I see." Everett's collar suddenly felt incredibly tight. "Forgive me, Dudley, because, besides being rather devoid of appropriate words at the moment, I also have no idea what you expect from me now. I hope you realize I certainly wouldn't have formed an attachment with Caroline if I'd known you'd set your sights on her. But . . . tell me . . . Why *are* you speaking up about this now?"

"I might not have won Caroline's affections, but she does consider me to be a most loyal friend. As that friend, it's my duty to look after her best interests, which is why I'm telling you that you need to treat her with greater care."

Having absolutely no idea how to proceed with what was quickly becoming a most uncomfortable, and unfortunate, state of affairs, Everett felt a small sense of relief when the carriage took that moment to turn off Bellevue Avenue and began rolling up the drive that led to his cottage. As they slowed to a stop, he caught Dudley's eye. "I am truly sorry for the misunderstanding you and I apparently suffered. Do know that I appreciate your words, and that I'll take them to heart and try harder with Caroline."

"See that you do."

Sending Dudley one last nod, even though he felt that action was less than sufficient considering what his friend had just disclosed, Everett waited for the driver to open the door, then climbed out of the carriage. A moment later, the carriage trundled down the drive again, leaving Everett staring after it as his thoughts whirled with everything Dudley had said, but more importantly, what Dudley *hadn't* said.

That the man was still enamored with Caroline, there could be no doubt, but . . . what had been the *real* purpose behind Dudley revealing such sensitive information?

Had he hoped that Everett would reconsider his association with Caroline, and then, after reconsidering it, step aside to allow Dudley the opportunity of finally pursuing the woman of his dreams?

Oddly enough, after Caroline's behavior of late, that idea held a certain appeal, but . . .

Shoving that completely ridiculous idea aside, Everett forced his thoughts in a different direction, summoning up all of Caroline's positive attributes instead of her deficiencies. When he began struggling to summon up those positive attributes after less than a minute, he decided he simply wasn't in the right frame of mind to tax his brain at the moment.

Turning toward his cottage, he drew in a deep breath and forced all unpleasantness aside as he took a moment to simply appreciate the beauty of Seaview, a building he hadn't set eyes on for almost an entire year.

The businessman in him eyed the fine lines of the roof and the high-quality of the stone, while also appreciating the fact that he'd been able to negotiate a more than fair deal on the cottage since the original owner had wanted to complete the sale quickly and with as little fuss as possible.

Mr. Barclay and his wife had made the mistake many nouveau rich made in regard to Newport, or more specifically, Newport high society. They'd assumed that since they possessed a rather fine fortune made in the iron industry, they'd be welcomed with open arms.

When that hadn't happened, and when not a single soul had shown up for the lavish ball Mrs. Barclay had thrown, they had not wanted to linger with their embarrassment. Because of that, Everett had been given the wonderful opportunity of acquiring a summer cottage for a more than reasonable price, and a summer cottage that was certain to increase in value — especially since Mrs. William Astor had decided that Newport was now *the* place to summer. That meant that the majority of high society in New York would soon be scrambling for their own cottages in Newport, if they hadn't purchased one already, and that meant that Everett had made a very sound investment indeed.

With his mood steadily improving because nothing improved his mood more than proof he'd invested wisely, Everett headed up the steps of Seaview but then found himself staring at a door that remained stubbornly shut against him. Hoping there was not another disaster waiting for him on the other side of the door, he slowly let himself into Seaview, pausing on the threshold to get a sense of the atmosphere. Unfortunately, the only sense he came away with was that something was probably amiss since not a single person was in sight.

The faintest sound of people talking drew him down the long hallway, moving all the way to the very back of the cottage before he finally spotted what seemed to be his entire staff blocking his path. All of them were standing on tiptoes and craning their necks, and not a single person took note of him until he coughed rather loudly, drawing the attention of a maid. She nudged the maid standing in front of her, who turned and blinked before she nudged the person in front of her, and on it went until the staff suddenly parted straight down the middle and Mr. Macon began walking his way.

"Ah, lovely, another unexpected Mulberry," his butler said as he stopped right next to Everett.

"What do you mean, *another* unexpected Mulberry, and it certainly shouldn't be odd to see me here, since this is my residence, and . . . what is that sprinkled in your hair?"

"It's flour, of course, and I'm perfectly aware of the fact you own Seaview, sir.

However, since you were supposed to be escorting Miss Dixon home from some disastrous tennis debacle, I wasn't expecting you for hours. As for why I said *another Mulberry,* your parents are here."

"I thought they were in Paris."

"They've apparently cut their trip around the world short." Mr. Macon shook his head. "Unfortunately, they chose an inopportune time to descend on us."

"Perhaps you should try explaining that a little more sufficiently."

"I think it might be best if I simply showed you, sir. It's a bit of a tricky situation to explain."

Feeling less than reassured, Everett trudged after Mr. Macon, passing through the staff, all of whom were looking somewhat guilty. Before he could question the reason behind the looks though, Mr. Macon gestured some footmen out of the way, leaving Everett a clear path to the mud room. Waving Everett forward, Mr. Macon stepped aside. "After you."

Knowing full well he'd come across as a complete coward if he refused to move another inch, Everett took a deep breath and stepped forward, coming to an abrupt halt when he found himself in a room completely covered in white. Glancing to the right, he found his mother and father standing close together, both of them gawking at something on the other side of the room.

Sending them a nod of acknowledgement, one they missed since they obviously hadn't become aware of his presence yet, he switched his gaze to where his parents were gawking and found himself completely devoid of speech at the sight that met his eyes.

Elizabeth, Rosetta, and Thaddeus were standing still as statues, completely covered in a white, pasty substance, while Millie stood a few feet away from them, looking slightly water-logged, but with only a light dusting of flour spotting her clothing.

"What happened?" he managed to ask.

"Oh, Everett, thank goodness you're here." His mother, Dorothy Mulberry, hurried to his side and hugged him, something that was completely at odds with how she normally greeted him, which was giving him her hand to kiss. She stepped back. "You look a little peaked, dear. Have you not been sleeping well of late?"

"I'm fine, Mother, although sleep can be a little difficult to be had when one is chasing after three children. But my sleep-deprived life aside, what are you doing here?

I thought you were intending to travel to India after you finished holidaying in Paris."

His father, Fletcher Mulberry, joined them, shaking Everett's hand and looking rather somber. "Your mother's been having bad dreams about you, son. So many of them of late that we felt it might be for the best to abandon our travels and come home to make certain you're well."

"You crossed an entire ocean because Mother's having . . . dreams?" Everett asked slowly.

"And it's a good thing we did," Dorothy said before Fletcher could speak. "Why, it's clear you're in trouble, son, but no need to fear. I'm here now, and I've already taken care of one order of business for you." She turned her head and narrowed her eyes on Millie. "I've dismissed that horrible nanny, and I shall take it upon myself to find you someone more . . . suitable."

"You've dismissed Millie?" he asked, glancing to Millie, who was nodding her head and looking rather resigned. Although . . .

His gaze sharpened on her. "Good heavens, Millie, is that a *lump* on your head?"

Not allowing Millie an opportunity to reply, his mother stepped directly in front of him, blocking Millie from sight.

"Why do you keep calling the nanny by her given name? It's hardly in keeping with the expected code of conduct for someone of your social status."

Everett frowned. "Interestingly enough, you're not the first person to voice that very same thought to me today. I must admit to you here and now, though, that I'm finding the unmitigated snobbery I've encountered so much of late to be completely unacceptable."

"Forgive me, dear, but it almost sounds as if you're accusing me of being a snob." Dorothy craned her neck and then, for some peculiar reason, nodded toward Mr. Macon. "In my opinion, I'm no more of a snob than your butler."

"Pardon me, Mrs. Mulberry," Mr. Macon began, "but I may not be the best example to point out in this particular instance, considering I freely admit I'm a huge snob."

"You're not exactly helping the situation, Mr. Macon," Everett said before he looked back at his mother. "But, snobbery aside, to answer your question of why I call Millie by her given name, do you not recall the letter I sent you regarding Oliver and Miss Peabody?"

"Of course I recall it, and while we're on

the subject of dear Oliver, I hope you remembered to pass on my best wishes to him."

"I actually thought you might not have paid close attention to the circumstances I laid out in that letter, and because of that, I have yet to pass on your best wishes."

Dorothy's brow creased. "What circumstances?"

"That Harriet worked in a hat shop when Oliver first met her, and that she lived in a tenement slum with a nanny, Miss Longfellow, and an actress, Miss Plum."

"I fully remember that from your letter, Everett, but you also wrote that Miss Peabody turned out to be far more than a hat girl, which is why I was completely delighted to learn of the upcoming union."

"Would you not have been delighted if Harriet hadn't discovered she was more than a hat girl?"

"Are you going to accuse me of unmitigated snobbery again if I admit to that?"

Everett smiled. "Probably, but to get back to the point I was going to make, the *Miss Longfellow* I was speaking about is none other than Millie, and . . . not only is she good friends with Miss Peabody, she's also wonderful friends with Mrs. Charles Hart, a lady who, as luck would have it, has also come to Newport for the summer festivities, and . . ."

"I know who Abigail Hart is," Dorothy interrupted. "But . . . didn't you also write that Abigail had a hand in getting Oliver and Harriet betrothed?"

Everett refused to wince. "I might have written something like that."

Turning on her heel, Dorothy marched over to join Everett's father, who'd retreated a safe distance from most of the flour. "We've arrived just in the nick of time, my dear. It's clear Abigail Hart is up to something, which means I'll be having a little talk with her soon. But for now" — she sent a single nod to Millie — "you need to go and fetch your belongings. I won't suffer you under my son's roof another second, not when it's just been made clear you have nefarious ideas on your mind."

Millie stuck her hand in her pocket, pulled out a dictionary that seemed rather soggy, and began flipping through the pages, the wetness of the paper giving her a great deal of difficulty. She finally stopped flipping and ran her finger down a page. "Nefarious, nefarious, ah . . . here it is." She lifted her head. "Honestly, that's a bit harsh, Mrs. Mulberry, because I can assure you that I have absolutely nothing of a wicked or evil nature on my mind."

Everett wasn't certain but he thought his father let out a snort of laughter, until his mother elbowed the poor man in the ribs, which had him then letting out a grunt.

"Really, Fletcher, this is hardly the time for amusement," Dorothy said before she nodded at Millie again. "There's no need for you to linger. As I said before, your services are no longer wanted here."

Millie stuck the dictionary back in her pocket. "Since I don't make it a habit to linger where I'm not wanted, I'll just be off to fetch my bag. Although arrangements will need to be made to deliver those trunks Abigail —"

"Miss Longfellow shouldn't be dismissed from her position because nothing about today was her fault. It was mine."

Everett found himself completely taken aback when none other than Elizabeth stepped forward, her stepping hampered by the fact her shoes were covered in paste and kept sticking to the floor. She finally made it across the room and came to a stop in front of him.

"You can't dismiss Miss Longfellow, Uncle Everett. It was my doing, all of this." She waved a hand at the mess, her siblings, and then to Millie, the waving sending a glob of paste up to attach itself to the ceiling.

Pulling his attention away from the glob that was certainly going to drop soon, Everett caught Elizabeth's eye. "I'm not exactly certain how this could possibly be your fault, when you're looking far worse than Millie is."

Elizabeth drew in a breath before she straightened her spine. "Miss Longfellow annoyed me because . . . well, it doesn't really matter. But because of that, I decided I was going to make her leave once and for all. I filled up a wash basin with water and set it on top of a door I left cracked open just the slightest bit. I knew Miss Longfellow would eventually come in my room to check on me, especially since I made sure Rose heard me crying, or what she thought was crying."

She frowned, or at least Everett thought that was what she was doing. It was a little difficult to tell considering the paste on her face had begun to dry, limiting her movements. "I didn't think about the basin falling off the door, which was a very silly thing for me not to think about because it smashed down on Miss Longfellow's head, and . . . I thought I'd killed her."

"Rose and I got scared when we thought Miss Longfellow was dead, and that's why we ran away," Thaddeus added, sending Everett one of the most pathetic looks he'd ever seen, the look accentuated when a glob of paste dripped from his chin. "That was very bad of us."

"And I didn't want Miss Longfellow to be dead," Rosetta chimed in. "She tried to save me from the peacocks."

"You ran into trouble with the peacocks?" Everett asked.

"No, but Miss Longfellow didn't know that, and she came running to get me . . . and she got a lot of pecks from the peacocks. But you can't let her go, you just can't, because she calls me . . . Rose."

Everett leaned over and caught Rosetta's eye. "You like Rose over Rosetta?"

"I do, but Thaddeus doesn't like being called Thad, only Thaddeus, even though it's a huge mouthful to say all the time. He'd like to be called Chip, but don't start calling him that, because Elizabeth will just get mad again."

Amusement immediately shot through Everett, until it was quickly replaced with guilt when the reality of what Rose had admitted sunk in. He'd been responsible for the children for months now, but not once had he even thought about asking them what names they preferred to be called. Millie had discovered that important information in the span of a few days, which . . .

"So you really can't dismiss her, Uncle Everett," Elizabeth said, interrupting his thoughts. "If anyone needs to be punished, it should be me, and *only* me."

Millie was suddenly in motion, and she didn't stop until she reached Elizabeth's side. "While I find it rather dear that you'd want to take the blame, Elizabeth, I want it known here and now that none of this is anyone's fault but mine."

"I started it," Elizabeth argued.

"Of course you did, darling, but you see, I threw down the gauntlet by winning the game of walking the plank, and then winning the delightful business of tying all of you up. I knew full well that you weren't done trying to get rid of me, and I should have known you'd do the old bucket of water over a door sometime soon." She smiled and rubbed her head. "If I'd been more diligent in my duties as a nanny, I'd have shown you the proper way to go about this particular prank — speaking of which, if you'll look at that door, you'll see a wonderful example of how it's supposed to be done. A short length of rope, a nail and a hook in the ceiling, and there you have it, a marvelous way of making sure this prank goes off effortlessly while not leaving the victim senseless."

She let out a sigh. "In hindsight, though, I might have overdone it by adding that flour, which means before I depart for Abigail's cottage I need to tidy up this room."

"If you're moving out, I'm moving with you," Thaddeus said, slipping up beside Millie and taking hold of her hand.

Elizabeth was the next to move. She reached out and put her arm around Millie's middle, leaning in to rest her head against Millie's side. "I'm coming too," she said as she snuggled closer right as Millie smiled and placed a quick kiss on top of Elizabeth's paste-covered head.

Everett's heart immediately took to the unusual act of lurching, no doubt due to the sight of Millie's understated affection. Ladies of society always made a big production out of kissing their children when company was present, but Millie . . . Her kiss had been the real thing, a show of regard for a child who'd caused her no small amount of trouble.

Expecting Rose to throw her support in next and proclaim she was moving out as well if Millie got dismissed, Everett looked around the room and finally spotting her moving up to the glass door, staring at peacocks that were bobbing this way and that, as if they were trying to figure out how to get into the room.

"Rose, no," he called when he saw her reach for the doorknob, but it was too late.

Complete and utter mayhem took over as the birds flocked inside, scattering and stirring up all the flour that had settled to the floor. His staff soon flooded into the room, their presence adding another layer of chaos to the situation as they tried to corral the peacocks. Rose was shrieking at the top of her lungs as the peacocks ran around her, but then Millie scooped the little girl up and bolted out the door that led outside. To Everett's horror, all the peacocks bolted right after her.

Rushing through that same door only a few seconds later, he stumbled to a stop when a small hand grabbed onto his and gave it a tug. Turning, he looked down and found Elizabeth standing next to him, the same Elizabeth who had never once in the time he'd taken responsibility for her and her siblings, touched him.

"Just wait" was all she said before she smiled.

Forcing his attention away from Elizabeth, even though he found the sight of her smiling completely endearing, he looked to where Millie had come to a stop, his breath hitching in his throat when the peacocks began surrounding her.

"Trust me," Elizabeth said.

Not taking his eyes off Millie, who was still holding Rose, he itched to move forward, especially when Millie whispered something in Rose's ear and then, to his complete dismay, lowered the little girl to the ground.

"Is she mad?" he asked.

"She dumped water, along with flour, over the heads of three innocent children, Uncle Everett," Elizabeth said with a snort. "Of course she's mad, but . . . she's somewhat brilliant as well because nobody else was able to best us at our own games."

"And she's very nice, Uncle Everett," Thaddeus added as he joined them. "Even if she told me I couldn't try riding a peacock."

"Peacocks aren't exactly pets, Thaddeus."

"Tell that to the peacocks," Elizabeth said with a grin when a peacock moved right up to Rose and nuzzled her with its beak.

Everett returned the grin, but then felt his grin fade when Thaddeus moved closer to him and blinked big eyes his way.

"Since Rose has some pets now, do you think I might be able to get just one . . . like a dog?"

"You want a dog?" Everett repeated.

Nodding, Thaddeus began scratching at the paste that covered his arm. "It wouldn't cause you any trouble, Uncle Everett. I would take care of it, but . . . I would want it to be a boy dog." He started scratching his other arm. "I'm always around girls these days."

It was telling, that statement, and Everett realized in that moment, as the sun beat on his head and the sound of peacocks cooing instead of screeching filled the air, that he'd been horribly negligent when it came to Thaddeus, as well as Elizabeth and Rose. "I wouldn't be opposed to the idea of getting a dog," he said before he could stop himself.

Thaddeus's eyes began to sparkle. "We could name him Chip, because that's what I was going to name the dog my daddy said he was going to get for me someday." The sparkle immediately faded from the little boy's eyes. "Someday never came because Daddy went away."

Not allowing himself a moment to consider his actions, Everett leaned over and scooped Thaddeus into his arms, ignoring

213

that the little boy stiffened the second Everett touched him. To Everett's relief, the stiffening disappeared a second later, right before Thaddeus snaked an arm around Everett's neck and leaned his little body into Everett's.

"Does this mean you're getting me a dog?" Thaddeus whispered.

"I do believe it might mean exactly that, but . . . before we speak about it further, I think it might be a good idea if we set about the business of getting you and your sisters cleaned up. You're only going to get itchier as that flour dries."

"So I have to take a . . . bath?" Thaddeus asked rather glumly.

"I think there might be another option, one you might find a little more amusing."

Everett turned and nodded to Elizabeth. "I'll race you over to the fountain." Giving her a head start, he finally took off after her, jostling Thaddeus around in his arms, which succeeded in having a loud burst of giggling erupt from the little boy every other second. Running behind Elizabeth, while being careful to never pass her, Everett heard her giggling as well. The sound warmed his heart.

Before he knew it, he'd reached his destination, and without bothering to kick off his shoes, he jumped into the large stone fountain that was situated halfway between the house and the cliffs that led to the sea. Splashing his way through the water, he reached the waterfall that had been built in the very middle of the fountain and stuck Thaddeus right into it.

Shrieking with clear delight, Thaddeus began to wiggle, the paste that still covered him making him remarkably slippery. Afraid of dropping him, Everett set him down and then straightened, discovering that while he'd been busy with Thaddeus, Elizabeth had joined them in the fountain.

Without so much as a by-your-leave, she sent water flying his way. And when Rose suddenly appeared in the fountain as well, he found himself splashed from all sides as the children went about the business of being children. Stumbling his way to the side of the fountain, he was just about to announce his surrender when a wave of water smacked him in the face, leaving him sputtering. When he finally caught his breath and pushed his hair out of his eyes, he found Millie grinning back at him, even as she scooped more water up into a bucket she'd somehow managed to procure.

War was immediate, and one he knew he couldn't win. The children continued splashing him as Millie threw bucketful after bucketful of water his way. When Millie slipped and fell, he saw an opportunity he couldn't resist. Grabbing the bucket, which was floating beside her, he scooped up water and aimed it at Thaddeus, who'd abandoned his purple frock and was splashing around in nothing but his drawers. Drawing the bucket back, he let the water fly, but Thaddeus ducked out of the way — which had the water winging out of the fountain to land directly on . . . his mother.

Even the peacocks that had been screeching just as loudly as the children had been shrieking seemed to realize the gravity of the situation. They stopped screeching, the children stopped shrieking, but Millie pushed soggy curls out of her eyes and simply smiled at his mother.

"You're more than welcome to join us, Mrs. Mulberry, now that you're all wet."

For the briefest of seconds, Everett thought he caught a glimpse of longing in his mother's eyes, but then she lifted her chin. "It would hardly be proper for me to frolic in a fountain, Miss Longfellow, nor is it proper for you to be in there, either." She lifted her chin another notch as she glanced his way. "You've ruined my hat as well as soaked me to the skin."

With amusement tickling his throat, he looked his mother up and down. "I'll buy you a new hat, Mother, but all I can suggest about you being soaked to the skin is to perhaps recommend you either search out a towel or, as Millie suggested, join us. It's rather fun to frolic about in a fountain, even if society wouldn't approve."

Dorothy cast another glance at the fountain, this one more longingly than the previous one, before she began wringing water out of her skirt. "Your father and I recently had the privilege of viewing pools over in England that were built specifically for the purpose of swimming." She looked up from her skirt. "Since the children seem to be so fond of the water, but society does look askance at the idea of splashing around in something so common as a fountain, perhaps you should look into the feasibility of having your very own pool built here." Everett could do nothing but stand in wide-eyed surprise as she said, "I would imagine if you were one of the first to build a personal pool, why, society would soon find them all the fashion."

"That would probably be a more realistic goal than trying to convince society peacocks are soon to be all the rage," he heard Millie mumble.

Pretending he hadn't heard her because he really wasn't up to explaining the reasoning behind the peacocks to his mother at that particular moment, Everett smiled at Dorothy. "While the idea of a personal pool is incredibly enticing, it might be easier all around if I were to just take the children swimming in the ocean, especially since there are many beaches to choose from here in Newport."

"I suppose you make a most excellent point, although you will need to hire someone who knows how to swim to join you when you take the children into the ocean, unless . . ." She glanced at Millie. "Can you swim?"

"I'm afraid not, Mrs. Mulberry, but since you've dismissed me, I don't believe it really matters at this point whether or not I know how to swim."

"I've decided that I might have been a little hasty in that regard, especially since I've been reminded by my husband that nannies are always in short supply during this time of year." She narrowed her eyes at Millie. "Having said that, do know that, if I witness any further shenanigans on your part, I *will* see you dismissed."

"I don't purposefully become involved with shenanigans, Mrs. Mulberry, but you should know that sometimes they just seem to happen to me."

Dorothy's eyes narrowed a bit more. "Don't make me regret giving you another chance."

"Of course, and I do thank you, but again, it's not as . . ."

"You should stop while you're ahead," Dorothy interrupted before she turned to Everett. "I'm going to go dry off, but I expect to see you in the not-too-distant future in the library, where you and I, along with your father, are going to discuss a few things."

"What kind of things?" Everett asked.

"Your progress with the children, or lack thereof from what I've seen thus far."

Elizabeth sloshed her way through the water to join him, surprising him once again when she took hold of his hand. "Uncle Everett has been doing much better of late, taking care of us and all. Just today he told me that I'm going to face punishment for aiming a croquet ball directly at Miss Dixon's head, and if you ask me, that's progress, even if I don't particularly care to spend the rest of the afternoon in my room."

Dorothy blinked. "Why in the world would you have aimed a croquet ball at Caroline's head? She's a completely lovely soul."

"She wants to send me and my brother and sister off to boarding school so that she won't have to fuss with us anymore."

Dorothy blinked again right before she arched a brow at Everett. "Is that true — does Caroline want to see them sent off to boarding school?"

"I don't think now is the best time to discuss this, Mother."

Dorothy glanced to the children before she nodded. "Very well, but do know that we *will* discuss it."

She turned and smiled at Elizabeth. "You, dear girl, were always getting into mischief, even when you were little. However, you're quickly turning into a lovely young lady, which means that it's time for you to manage that mischief. That means no future instances of aiming croquet balls at anyone."

"How do you know I've always been prone to mischief?" Elizabeth asked.

"Mr. Mulberry and I, along with Everett, used to spend part of our summers holidaying in Saratoga Springs," Dorothy said. "We specifically went there in order to visit with your parents, since your father, Fred, was a frequent and much loved guest in our house while he was growing up." Dorothy smiled.

"He, you'll be pleased to learn, was quite the mischief-maker in his youth, so I was thrilled to find out that you possessed that very same trait. Why, one only had to look at the impish grin on your face to know you'd get your way in the end, even if it entailed staying in the mineral springs for hours at a time."

Everett's breath caught in his throat as pain took him by surprise and left him reeling. He'd been so agitated since he'd been given the children that he'd not allowed himself to revisit the fond memories he had of Fred, or of the many times they'd vacationed together even after Fred and Violet had their children.

He'd also never taken more than a brief moment to mourn, something that sent shame mixing in with the pain.

"You used to go on holiday with my family?" Elizabeth demanded, her hand no longer in his.

Everett summoned up a smile, one he hoped would mask the turmoil that was spinning through him. "Your father and I did grow up together, Elizabeth, and we went on holiday together every year throughout our youth, and even after we went off to college. Then, he met your mother and they got married, but I still met up with him often, traveling to Saratoga Springs, or visiting all of you at your home in Boston."

He shook his head. "When you were about four, and the twins were just babies, your parents started taking you sailing all over the world, and that's when our annual holidays stopped, although I'd always hoped that after life settled down a bit for me and for your father, we'd once again have time to spend with each other."

Elizabeth considered him for a long moment. "When you were in Saratoga Springs with us, did you throw me up high while we were in the water and then laugh when Daddy claimed you were giving him heart palpitations?"

"I must admit that I did."

A little ghost of a smile played around the corners of her lips. "I remember that."

Dorothy stepped closer to the fountain and cleared her throat. "I remember that you always enjoyed a good game of splashing, dear." She dashed a hand over her eyes, cleared her throat again, and then smiled at Elizabeth. "It was not well done of Everett to douse me with that bucket of water, so . . . do promise to put your heart into soundly drenching him."

With that, Dorothy sent Everett a nod,

smiled at the children, looked Millie over as if she still didn't know what to make of her, and then turned and strolled away without speaking another word.

"I like her," Elizabeth proclaimed when Dorothy was almost to the cottage. "She changed her mind about dismissing Miss Millie, and that shows she's a smart lady."

Glancing to Millie, Everett found *her* dashing a hand across her eyes, much like his mother had recently done. Not understanding in the least what had caused her to break into tears, he opened his mouth but was interrupted by Elizabeth.

"You don't mind if I call you Miss Millie, do you?"

The reasoning behind the tears was immediate, and Everett couldn't help feeling incredibly proud of Millie once again. She was already helping the children return to the adorable imps he'd once known, even if he'd forgotten how adorable they'd —

"Of course you may call me Miss Millie, Elizabeth," Millie said. "But, before we forget the request Mrs. Mulberry left you, I say . . . get the bucket, and get it now."

Before he could voice a single protest, Millie and Elizabeth jumped his way, and with renewed shouts of laughter, water began splashing once again, even as a sense that the world as he knew it had changed forever took root inside him.

9

Enjoying a rare moment of peace and quiet, Millie settled into the chair on the back terrace of Seaview, appreciating the serene beauty that surrounded her. To her right, the ocean sparkled in the bright morning light, and to her left, a peacock strutted before her, fanning out his tail feathers even though Millie didn't see any peahens around to appreciate his efforts. Picking up the cup of coffee Mrs. O'Connor had very kindly made her, she took a sip and allowed her thoughts to wander.

She was rapidly coming to the conclusion that her world was turning rather topsy-turvy.

The children, bless their little hearts, were no longer trying to do her in.

Everett was spending time with those children while being far too charming to her in the process, and Mrs. Mulberry had taken to watching her . . . at every turn.

To say it was all very confusing was an understatement.

"Ah, Miss Longfellow, I've been looking for you," Dorothy exclaimed as she stepped through the French doors and immediately headed Millie's way. "I went up to your room to check on you, but . . . good heavens, it's no wonder I didn't find you in there, what with the horrendous décor and all."

She pulled out a chair beside Millie and sat down. "I do hope you won't mind, but I took the liberty of instructing Mr. Macon to have those drab drapes taken away from your room. What Everett's decorator was thinking using all that brown, well, I really couldn't hazard a guess, but . . . would it offend you if I took to calling you Mille instead of Miss Longfellow?"

Barely blinking an eye over that rapid change of topics, probably because she'd been around Abigail so often of late, Millie set aside her coffee. "Forgive me, but . . . why would you want to do that? If you've forgotten, I'm the . . . nanny."

"Well, of course you're the nanny, dear. That certainly isn't in dispute. As for the other matter, well, I think it would be beneficial to the children if we provided them with a more relaxed atmosphere. That means you'll need to call me Dorothy."

Dorothy leaned forward, poured herself a cup of coffee from the silver pot Mrs. O'Connor had left on the table, took a sip, and then turned her gaze to the vast expanse of green lawn. "May I assume Everett and Fletcher are still off searching for bugs with the children?"

"They are, which is why I decided to take my coffee in this particular spot, in case they find themselves in need of some professional assistance. But returning to me calling you by —"

"Very wise of you, my dear, to make yourself available to Everett and Fletcher," Dorothy interrupted before Millie could finish her point. "I have to tell you, I've been watching you with the children for the past day and a half, as well as watching you interact with my son, and . . . I have to admit I'm finding myself, surprisingly enough, very impressed with you." She beamed Millie's way right as her eyes began to sparkle almost exactly like Abigail's did when she was . . . scheming.

Stuffing a large portion of a scone in her mouth in order to give her some much needed time to think, Millie proceeded to chew that scone for a rather long stretch of time. Finally, having no choice but to swallow it, she summoned up a smile. "I thought you weren't really impressed with my skills as a nanny."

Dorothy gave an airy wave of her hand. "That's all water under the bridge, my dear, and you can't actually blame me for my first misimpression, given the condition I found the children in. But, again, I've changed my mind about you, and not just about your abilities as a nanny." Dorothy beamed another bright smile Millie's way.

Pushing aside the thought that Dorothy was scheming, especially since Millie knew perfectly well that society mothers never schemed with regard to the staff, Millie wiped her lips with a napkin, having no idea what to say next. Luckily, Dorothy didn't seem to be experiencing that particular problem.

"I found the dinner we shared last night to be simply delightful," Dorothy continued. "I especially enjoyed the discussion you and Everett shared regarding books. Why, I had no idea Everett doesn't particularly care for Shakespeare's writing, but I was tickled to death to learn that you were a big supporter of the Bard's work."

"I don't know if I'd go so far as to claim I'm a big supporter," Millie corrected. "If you'll recall, I did mention that I'm not always certain what Shakespeare is actually saying."

"You might not understand all of his work, dear, but it's still impressive that you're giving Shakespeare a go in the first place." Dorothy took a sip of coffee. "It was unfortunate that Caroline made the decision not to join us last night, especially after Everett sent her a note, telling her Fletcher and I had come to Newport."

"Ah . . . well . . . I'm sure she probably had a prior engagement she couldn't neglect."

Dorothy lifted her chin. "Perhaps, but . . . one would think she'd . . ." Dorothy stopped speaking midsentence and sent another smile Millie's way. "I shouldn't be burdening you with such talk, so . . . tell me more about how Abigail's been doing of late. I thought for certain *she* would come to dinner last night."

Millie shifted in her chair. "I fear I was probably the reason for her claiming to be indisposed, Mrs. Mulberry."

Dorothy nodded. "Ah, you sent her a note telling her I was originally put out with what I thought were unacceptable shenanigans on her part, didn't you."

Millie frowned. "No, although now that you mention that, I probably *should* have sent her a note of warning, since she is my friend. However, I think she made herself scarce last night because I was a little put out with her over my unexpected acquiring of an entirely new wardrobe, while experiencing an unexpected loss of my normal clothes."

"But you look completely charming this morning, as you did last night, so there's really no need for you to be annoyed with Abigail."

The pesky notion of scheming ladies flickered once again through Millie's thoughts, a notion she quickly shoved aside. "I know Abigail means well, but I can't properly run after three children in garments that are better suited to being at my leisure than doing anything of a strenuous nature."

"Since you're currently at your leisure, you're dressed exactly as you should be dressed."

"But because your son is paying me to look after the children, I'm sure you'll understand why I'm going to change back into the only skirt and blouse I have left just as soon as they come back from being laundered."

"If you'll excuse me, I need to see about having another pot of coffee brewed." With that, Dorothy rose from her chair and practically bolted for the house.

Having no idea what to make of that, and knowing she wouldn't be able to figure it out anyway, Millie picked up the copy of *Emma* she'd brought outside with her and flipped to the page she'd marked.

She read all of three pages before the squeak of the French doors drew her attention, and she found none other than Caroline Dixon walking her way.

"I was hoping to find you gone," Caroline said as she came to a stop in front of the table.

Setting aside the book, Millie rose to her feet, wincing when she noticed a bruise on Caroline's head, one that just happened to be formed in a perfect circle, quite like a circle a tennis ball would make. "It certainly is nice to see you today, Miss Dixon, especially since I've wanted to apologize again for . . ." She waved to Caroline's head, earning a sniff in response.

"Apology not accepted, Miss Longfellow, but . . ." Caroline's eyes narrowed as she looked Millie up and down. "What in the world are you wearing, and why are you out here on the terrace, sipping coffee and reading . . . Is that a Jane Austen book?"

"It is. *Emma,* in fact. One of my favorites,

231

if you —"

"Where are your nanny clothes?" Caroline interrupted.

"If you can believe this, most of them have mysteriously disappeared."

Caroline's face began to darken. "Did Abigail Hart have something to do with the mysterious disappearance of your clothing?"

"As to that, ah . . ."

Drawing herself up, Caroline's nostrils flared. "I told Everett yesterday I won't stand for this nonsense. If you think, for one minute, that I'm simply going to stand by and watch as Mrs. Hart tries her hand once again at inappropriate matchmaking, well, you're sadly mistaken. I am Miss Caroline Dixon, and as such . . ."

"Caroline, what a pleasant surprise," Dorothy said, strolling back out on the terrace and smiling brightly, although her smile didn't seem to reach her eyes. "I thought you and Millie had already been introduced."

"We have been introduced."

"Then why were you telling Millie your name?"

Caroline shot Millie a glare before she turned back to Dorothy. "It's such a marvelous treat to find you and Mr. Mulberry here in Newport, especially since I'm quite certain Everett told me you'd be traveling to India after your stay in Paris."

"Our original plans did have us traveling to India, but . . . before I speak further, we should get comfortable." Dorothy gestured Millie back into her chair, before gesturing to another chair and nodding at Caroline. "Have a seat, dear."

Looking as if she wanted to do anything but take a seat, Caroline finally slid into the chair, where she promptly set about the task of ignoring Millie.

Dorothy poured a cup of coffee for Caroline, and then retook her seat as well. "Isn't this just lovely? I do so enjoy a bit of feminine conversation over coffee."

"I don't normally enjoy conversation with members of the staff," Caroline said as she took a sip of her coffee, her little finger raised exactly so. "But returning to why you cut your trip short?"

Dorothy's lips pursed just a touch. "I kept having this unnerving feeling that Everett was in some type of horrible trouble. That feeling left me out of sorts, which is why Fletcher finally insisted we needed to return to the States, if only to allow me to ascertain that Everett was fine."

Caroline leaned forward. "You really could have simply sent Everett a telegram, Mrs.

Mulberry. Especially since his troubles, all three of them — or four, if you count Miss Longfellow — will disappear as soon as he chooses a proper boarding school to send the children off to."

"Boarding school?" Dorothy let out an honest-to-goodness snort. "Goodness, and here I thought that was just a rumor, spoken out loud because the children don't seem to care for you. But . . . hear me well, my dear — that idea is completely ridiculous. Those precious children will not be sent off to any boarding school. The mere idea is preposterous."

She took a sip of coffee, regarding Caroline over the rim of the cup. "Their father, Fred, was like a son to me, and it's rapidly becoming clear I've been dreadfully negligent with this situation. Those children need a stable environment, stable adults in their little lives, and they need to know they have people surrounding them who truly want only what's in their best interests."

Caroline drew herself up. "Forgive me for pointing this out, Mrs. Mulberry, but you've been gone for months. You were here for the funeral, but then you left, leaving me and Everett to deal with the horrid little beasts. You seem to be under the mis-impression that Fred's children are little angels, but I'm telling you now, they're nothing of the sort. If you truly want to help your son escape his troubles, you'll back me in the decision of sending them off to boarding school — a place, if you'll recall, you sent Everett off to."

Dorothy drew herself up, much like Caroline had just done. "I've recently come to the conclusion I was wrong to send Everett away to be raised by other people in a boarding school. I'm not excusing my actions, but it was simply what parents did in my social circle. Since then I've come to the uncomfortable realization that bending to society's ways prevented me from building a close relationship with my only child, so I am now completely against the idea of boarding schools. Why, I'll take the children in before I'd see them sent off to one."

Instead of looking chagrined, Caroline looked happier than Millie had ever seen her before. "That's a wonderful idea, Mrs. Mulberry, and will solve everyone's problems, especially if you agree to take on Miss Longfellow since Everett seems reluctant to dismiss her."

For a second, Dorothy simply stared at Caroline, as if she'd never seen the lady before in her life. Luckily for Caroline, the sound of giggling distracted Dorothy, who turned her attention to where Elizabeth and Rose were stepping from the cliff walk and onto the lawn. Elizabeth immediately took hold of Rose's hand, and together the two girls began skipping toward Seaview.

Dorothy rose to her feet, shading her eyes with her hand. "It looks like the girls have beaten Everett, Fletcher, and Thaddeus home from their explore."

Caroline suddenly leaned across the table, her eyes narrowing on Millie. "Why in the world are Mr. Mulberry and Everett minding the children while you're sitting here enjoying your coffee?"

"The gentlemen wanted to spend time with the children on their own, and . . . nannies certainly are entitled to having a morning off now and again," Dorothy said before Millie could respond. She waved to Elizabeth and Rose. "Girls, we're over here."

Elizabeth and Rose stopped skipping, seemed to look in their direction, and then, instead of moving their way, charged off in the opposite direction and were quickly out of sight.

"Do you think they didn't hear me?" Dorothy asked as she retook her seat.

"Oh, they heard you all right," Caroline said. "Their blatant rudeness should give you a better idea as to what I've been made to suffer ever since those children stormed into my life."

Dorothy frowned. "They didn't storm into *your* life, Caroline, they stormed into Everett's. Quite honestly, I'm beginning to get the distinct impression *they're* not the reason I still continue to feel Everett's in trouble."

"He's not in any trouble," Caroline argued.

"That remains to be seen." Dorothy looked back over the lawn and smiled. "Ah, there're the gentlemen now. Oh look, Thaddeus is getting a ride on Everett's shoulders."

"I see the boy hasn't abandoned his ridiculous frocks," Caroline said as the gentlemen drew closer.

"The boy's name is Thaddeus, dear," Dorothy corrected.

"Well, I hope someone will get dear *Thaddeus* out of those dresses soon." Caroline nodded to Millie. "Since you're the nanny — and one no one seems capable of dismissing — I think that daunting task is going to fall on you. Don't take him shopping with you though. I was embarrassed quite enough yesterday, thank you very much, when all of my friends got to witness the oddness of that boy wearing a purple frock as he

237

cheered you on from the stands. The mere idea that he wasn't cheering for me, a lady he's known for far longer than you, completely proves my point about the rudeness these children seem to embrace."

"Thaddeus isn't odd," Millie said. "He's just a little boy, and little boys rarely do what adults expect of them, such as cheering for a particular person involved in a tennis match."

Caroline's face began to darken, but then she was smiling — the reason behind that smiling becoming apparent a moment later when Everett strode into view, without Thaddeus or his father in tow.

"Thaddeus spotted a rabbit," Everett said, which explained much as he moved to his mother's side, kissed her cheek, and then kissed the hand Caroline promptly held his way. "I wasn't expecting to see you this morning."

Caroline withdrew her hand. "I can't help but wonder why I went to the bother of writing out that schedule for you since it's becoming clear you rarely refer to it. To refresh your memory, we're supposed to go to the Ocean House today to enjoy music on the veranda."

"I assumed my schedule of events had been put on hold since I was under the impression you were put out with me."

"I am put out with you, but that's no reason to miss the summer festivities."

Everett raked a hand through his hair and glanced around. "Where's Nora?"

Caroline shrugged. "I've sent her on."

"You sent her to Ocean House by herself?"

"Of course not. And just so you know, we're not going to Ocean House now, but I'll get back to that in a moment. I sent Nora over to Birdie's cottage because I thought it would do Nora good to have some time away from me so that she can contemplate her responsibilities to me, her employer."

Everett crossed his arms over his chest. "Nora doesn't actually take any money from you, Caroline, so she's not actually in your employ — more like she's simply doing you a favor. And surely you didn't send her on, as you so quaintly put it, because of the tennis match, did you?"

"She was directly responsible for this," Caroline said, pointing to her head. "So yes, that is why I sent her on. I found her lack of loyalty appalling, as did the rest of my friends, all of whom were only too anxious to discuss the tennis debacle with me last night."

"But who will step in as your companion

now, Caroline?" Dorothy asked. "Your parents haven't cut their trip around the world short, have they?"

"My mother has yet to finish selecting her wardrobe for the fall season, and since the House of Worth has been booked solid with appointments, she'll be there another month, at the very least, waiting for her designs to be finished. As for the companion business, there's no need for anyone to fret. Mr. Dudley Codman has kindly provided me with a chaperone — that being his elderly aunt, who just happens to be moving into my cottage as we speak."

Everett pulled out a chair and lowered himself down beside Caroline. "How was it that Dudley came to be the one to provide you with a chaperone?"

Caroline shrugged. "He escorted me last night to the Belmonts' ball held at their cottage, By-The-Sea. The ball was a delightful affair, and allowed me to further my acquaintance with Mrs. August Belmont, a truly gracious lady if there ever was one. But, getting back to Dudley — when he realized I'd been placed in the unenviable position of not having a proper chaperone at the ready, he made arrangements for his elderly aunt, who has been staying at his cottage, to take up the position."

"*Dudley* escorted you to the ball last night?" Everett asked.

"I certainly wasn't going to miss it just because you and I quarreled."

Feeling increasingly uncomfortable and out of place, Millie plucked up her book and buried her nose behind it, pretending to read as the argument raged on.

"Do you honestly believe that was appropriate — having another gentleman escort you to a ball of all things," Everett demanded, "and without a proper chaperone, from the sounds of it?"

"Do you honestly believe it was appropriate for you to side with your nanny instead of doing what I'd asked, which, if you've forgotten, was to dismiss her?" Caroline countered.

"And do either of you believe this is an appropriate conversation to have at this particular moment?" Dorothy asked.

Millie peeked over the book, finding Everett now looking uncomfortable — probably because of his mother's reprimand. Caroline, however, looked livid . . . until she drew in a deep breath and nodded Dorothy's way. "Forgive me, Mrs. Mulberry. I certainly didn't mean to offend you."

Caroline looked back to Everett. "If you're

still willing to continue on with our plans for today, I must tell you that those plans have, indeed, changed, and we will not be going to the Ocean House, because" — her eyes began to sparkle — "we've been granted the supreme honor of being invited to one of Mr. Ward McAllister's picnics at his farm. I was given the privilege of speaking with him at length last night at the ball, and he very kindly told me he'd enjoy having my company, as well as yours, today."

Everett considered Caroline for a long moment before he finally nodded. "I would be delighted to escort you to Mr. McAllister's farm, my dear. Although I do hope we can put aside our differences so that we may actually enjoy the day."

Smiling somewhat sweetly, Caroline reached out and patted Everett's arm. "That sounds lovely, Everett. And, before I forget, when guests inquired last night about where you were, I told them you were indisposed, so do try to think up a good reason to explain that indisposed condition so you won't be taken aback if anyone happens to mention it."

Before Everett could respond to that, Caroline turned Millie's way. "Now then, since Mr. McAllister is in Newport, and he's a stickler for the proprieties, you really are going to have to find a way to get Thaddeus out of those frocks once and for all. Mr. McAllister will not see such attire as amusing, and I will not damage the bond I formed with *the* social arbiter of New York last night because no one can take the boy in hand."

"I'll do my best," Millie said.

"See that you do." Caroline nodded to Dorothy and then turned her attention back to Everett. "Shall we go? We certainly don't want to be late. Mr. McAllister does not abide lateness at all. My buggy is out front, so there's no need to call for yours."

Rising to his feet, Everett gave Dorothy a kiss on the cheek, sent Millie a nod, and with Caroline attached to his arm, walked off the terrace and soon disappeared from sight.

Dorothy picked up her coffee cup again. "Do you think he knows what a mess he's gotten himself into?"

"A . . . mess?" Millie asked as she lowered her book.

"He's tied himself to a shrew, my dear. Why, it's little wonder I've been having such dreams. God apparently realized I was not aware of the disturbing nature of Everett's relationship with Caroline, so He sent me a very clear message as I slumbered."

"You think God sent you messages through your dreams?"

"I do believe that's exactly what He was doing, but . . . what to do about it now . . ." She tilted her head and considered Millie once again in a very concerning fashion.

"Mrs. Mulberry . . ." Millie began.

"Dorothy, dear."

"Yes, well, I'd like to keep things formal at the moment since I need to be firm and tell you, exactly as I told Abigail, that I will not be a part of . . ." Millie's voice trailed off when Mrs. O'Connor stepped out onto the terrace and began marching her way, holding what appeared to be a bunch of rags in her arms.

Stopping directly in front of Millie, Mrs. O'Connor heaved a very dramatic sigh as she dumped the rags on the table. "I have no idea how this happened, but your shirt and skirt somehow got stuck in the wringer, and . . . the wringer ripped them to shreds."

Millie's mouth dropped open before she set her sights on Dorothy. "Did you even request another pot of coffee, or did you simply draw poor Mrs. O'Connor into some type of dastardly plan that I'm sure no one, not even you, can truly explain."

Dorothy fluttered innocent lashes her way before she looked over Millie's shoulder and smiled. "Would you look at that — impeccable timing, if I do say so myself."

Turning her head, Millie discovered the children and Fletcher walking across the terrace.

"I just bid Everett and Caroline a fond farewell for the day," Fletcher said as he came to a stop in front of Dorothy. He looked down and smiled at Thaddeus, who was holding his hand and looking rather grumpy. "Caroline, I hate to admit, annoyed Thaddeus no small amount by telling him —"

"That I have to get out of my frocks," Thaddeus interrupted as he let go of Fletcher's hand and stomped his way over to Millie. "She said you were going to make me do that, even if I don't want to."

"I'm not going to *make* you do anything, darling," Millie said. "If you want to continue wearing those frocks your sister made for you, so be it."

"Elizabeth tried really hard to make me pants," Thaddeus said. "But when she couldn't figure out how to sew them up properly, she made me dresses, and I don't want to hurt her feelings by not wearing them."

"Perfectly understandable," Millie said.

"May I offer the perfect solution to the

pants-versus-frocks dilemma?"

Turning, Millie discovered Mr. Macon standing on the terrace, his arms filled with quite a bit of brown material.

"I'm sure you'll be pleased to learn, Miss Longfellow, that I've replaced these lovely drapes that were hanging in your room with some cheery yellow ones. And, since I now have in my hands yards and yards of material, and we certainly don't want it to go to waste, may I suggest that someone — as in you, Miss Longfellow — teach Miss Elizabeth how to make . . . pants?"

Eyeing the material in Mr. Macon's hands, Millie grinned. "I think that's a wonderful idea, Mr. Macon, and it will be the perfect solution to not only the children's dilemma regarding clothing, but mine as well."

10

As Mr. Ward McAllister droned on and on about the many different ways one could fold a linen napkin, Everett stretched his legs out on the checkered blanket Caroline had brought for them to eat their picnic lunch on. Try as he might to focus, he found his thoughts drifting away from the project at hand.

Regrettably, the main thought his mind wanted to dwell on was that something was dreadfully wrong with him.

He normally enjoyed spending the summer in the company of his good friends, but this year, something was different. Something had changed.

Friends he'd known for years were no longer very entertaining, and Caroline . . . Well, she was becoming more difficult by the day.

That she'd told everyone he'd been indisposed the night before annoyed him no small amount. He'd spent half his time at the picnic fending off questions regarding his indisposed condition, even though he was fairly certain everyone knew he hadn't attended the ball the night before because he and Caroline had not been in accord. His friends, people he'd always believed were the very best company, had now taken to badgering him endlessly about the matter.

Quite frankly, even though he was less than interested in learning how to fold a proper napkin, he'd been relieved when Ward had gathered everyone together for this particular lesson.

"And, if everyone will now pick up the napkins that are square, not rectangular, we'll move on to a delightful knot I learned about just last week," Ward said.

Caroline thrust a square piece of linen into his hand, leaving Everett with no choice but to accept it. Trying his best to follow Ward's instructions, he looked around and discovered that the rest of Ward's guests seemed to be having a marvelous time of it. They were laughing and chatting away as they tried to fold their napkins, a task that Everett, unfortunately, was finding very dull indeed.

If he were honest with himself, the most

fun he'd had in a very long time had been when he'd recently spent time with the children and . . . with Millie.

It wasn't as if they'd done anything extraordinary, although the fountain incident had certainly been one of the most unusual and amusing ways he'd ever spent an afternoon. What he'd enjoyed most of all, though, had been getting to know the children once again, which was why he kept considering the unusual idea that it had actually been a fortunate day when he'd run into, or rather run over, Miss Millie Longfellow.

She had, in a remarkably short period of time, gotten the children in hand, begun to help him form a relationship with those children, and had somehow been able to win his mother over in the span of less than —

"You're not knotting your napkin."

Pushing all thoughts of Millie straight out of his mind, especially since he had the sneaking suspicion she really shouldn't be there in the first place, Everett found Caroline frowning back at him. Handing her his square of linen, he smiled.

"I'm afraid I just don't have a talent for matters of a domestic nature, my dear." He nodded to her napkin. "But since you apparently do, we should consider ourselves fortunate that we'll never have our guests sit down to a table with improperly folded napkins on it."

Looking somewhat appeased, Caroline began folding the napkin he'd given her. "Speaking of guests, I was recently given the name of a wonderful social secretary here in Newport whom I've already taken the liberty of contacting. That woman sent me a note just this morning telling me that she can fit creating and addressing our invitations into her schedule. And because I promised to pay her extra, she'll be done with them by tomorrow morning — which means we can have them hand delivered to all of the people on our guest list by tomorrow afternoon."

"Forgive me, Caroline, but I'm afraid you have me at a disadvantage. I thought we'd agreed to host our ball toward the end of August, which would mean we certainly shouldn't need to get our invitations out so soon."

"I knew you weren't listening when we were gathered on Dudley's blanket and I was talking about the wonderful news Mr. McAllister had imparted to me."

"I wasn't with you on Dudley's blanket."

Caroline blinked. "Oh, well, then I

apologize for snapping at you, but do try to do something about that frown on your face. I think Mr. McAllister is done with his lesson, so . . . I'll let him tell you the good news." She held out her hand, and after Everett helped her to her feet, he immediately found himself being steered around other picnic guests as Caroline marched them toward Mr. McAllister, who was now leaning against a tree.

As they approached Ward, Caroline began smiling a very lovely smile, even as Everett found it somewhat difficult to suppress a laugh when he realized Ward had taken to posing. One of the gentleman's hands was placed just so in the pocket of his waistcoat, while the other was positioned on his hip, and there was a small trace of a smile on the older man's face, a smile that held more than a hint of superiority.

"That was an interesting lesson on napkin folding, Ward," Everett said, earning a regal nodding of the head from Ward in return. "Where do you learn these things?"

Ward pushed away from the tree. "Books are obviously a wonderful source, but, to be perfectly honest, I spend a great deal of time stalking servants at different houses. They're founts of information — although . . . not everyone has the stomach to converse with domestics."

A twinge of irritation snuck under Everett's skin, but before he could respond, Caroline let out a small laugh.

"I know I certainly don't have the stomach you obviously do, Mr. McAllister. But . . ." She sent another lovely smile Ward's way. "I have yet to tell Everett the good news and thought that, just perhaps, you'd enjoy telling him."

Ward released a chuckle and sent Everett an approving sort of nod. "You've done well for yourself there, dear boy, earning Miss Dixon's great esteem. But . . . as for what she's referring to, well, I'm sure you'll be delighted to learn that there's an opening in the social schedule just two weeks from now."

"Mr. and Mrs. Kane had to cancel their ball due to a death in the family," Caroline added in a rather breathy sort of voice, one that suggested she was having a difficult time containing her excitement. "And because of that, society will be looking for a replacement event, and that means they will not even expect the customary three-week notice."

"That's unfortunate about the Kane family suffering a death," was the first thing Everett could think of to say.

Caroline wrinkled her nose. "Well . . . yes, I suppose that was unfortunate for the Kane family, but it's *fortunate* for us, since Mr. McAllister, who created the guest list for the Kane ball, has now given that special list to . . . me."

She turned back to Mr. McAllister. "I simply cannot thank you enough for parting with that list, Mr. McAllister. I'm convinced the ball Everett and I intend to hold will be considered one of the smashing successes of the summer season by all two hundred of the people we're now going to invite."

"Do you think two hundred people will fit in the ballroom at Seaview, Caroline?" Everett asked.

"Everyone knows that in order for a ball to be considered successful, it needs to be a true crush, so two hundred guests will be absolutely perfect. We might need to squeeze in the orchestra a bit, but I'm sure those musicians are used to working in crowded conditions."

Ward smiled in Caroline's direction. "Indeed they are, but speaking of the hired help, do be certain to send a note off immediately to the French chef I recommended, Monsieur Roquet. You'll need to let him know that you're a friend of mine, but if he is less than cooperative, you send *me* a note straightaway. These French people can be a bit . . . difficult, but they normally cooperate when faced with my displeasure." He chuckled. "There are advantages, my dear Miss Dixon, to counting Ward McAllister as one of your friends."

Caroline smiled a very satisfied smile. "I'll pen him a letter as soon as I return home, as well as send for Miss Pickenpaugh so she can get Seaview ready with all the decorations and so forth." She inclined her head at Mr. McAllister. "We'll leave you to speak with your other guests, since I know you don't want to neglect them." She sent Everett an expectant look.

Clearly his throat, Everett thanked Ward as profusely as he was able, even though the man's interference was going to cause Everett no small amount of trouble, as well as money, in the end. After speaking all the words of thanks he could possibly muster up, he took hold of Caroline's arm and led her away, steering her over to a tree that was quite a distance away from their fellow guests, a tree that would afford the two of them a bit of privacy.

"This has just been the most delightful of afternoons," Caroline said before he could get so much as a single word out of his mouth. "Why, our ball really *will* be considered the ball of the summer season, especially since I hinted to Mr. McAllister that it'll end with a very *special . . .* event."

A surge of panic hit from out of nowhere, stealing the breath straight from him.

Caroline's idea of a special event could only mean she expected him to propose to her at the end of the ball. While it *was* true that they'd always planned to become engaged at some point . . . he hadn't been planning on doing that proposing in the next two weeks.

"Do be sure to mention the change of date to your mother," Caroline continued, apparently unaware of the fact he was in the midst of an anxiety spell. "I wouldn't want her to be taken by surprise when Miss Pickenpaugh shows up at your house and begins rearranging the furnishings."

Bending over, Everett forced himself to take a deep breath, and when he decided he was not going to embarrass himself by fainting dead away, he straightened. "You do realize that my mother will expect to help with the planning of this ball, don't you?"

"Miss Pickenpaugh does not appreciate help, which is why she's in such high demand. We pay her money, she arranges everything, and that's how it's done." Caroline wagged a finger practically under his nose. "You'll need to explain that to your mother and make sure she understands that she's not to interfere. The last thing we want to do is have Miss Pickenpaugh take offense at something because she'll never agree to organize a ball for us again."

"I'll try my best," Everett finally said.

"Wonderful." Caroline patted his arm, but her patting stopped when she looked past him and frowned. "It seems to me that Dudley is trying to get our attention . . . but . . . I wonder why all Mr. McAllister's guests are currently smiling our way?"

Thirty minutes later, after learning why everyone had been smiling their way, Everett shifted on the buggy seat, the heat of the day unrelenting since the buggy's top had been pushed down. Taking a handkerchief from his pocket, he dabbed at his face. He couldn't help wonder for what felt like the hundredth time how it had happened that Dudley, along with every other guest who'd been in attendance at the picnic, had come to be invited back to Seaview, and were even now stuffed into buggies and following Caroline's buggy down the road.

From what little he'd been able to gather, Dudley had taken it upon himself to speak in glowing terms about . . . the peacocks.

That bit of glowing nonsense had apparently been what had prompted the idea, much to Caroline's delight, of everyone traveling to Seaview to see the peacocks.

The only problem with the plan was that no one except Everett seemed to be grasping the notion that this particular outing could go horribly, horribly wrong.

"Isn't this just so exciting, acting so impulsively and inviting all of our friends to Seaview to meet our delightful peacocks?"

Everett shot a look to Dudley, who was looking rather smug, as if he and he alone was finally going to make Caroline's dream of owning the most fashionable of pets come true. Returning his attention to Caroline, Everett tilted his head. "I have to admit that I'm finding this more nerve-wracking than exciting. I've yet to be convinced the peacocks are all that delightful."

Caroline waved that comment aside as she looked at Gertrude, who was sitting right next to Dudley on the opposite side of the buggy. "Did I tell you that I saw one of the peacocks peeking out at me from the bushes as I sat on the terrace at Seaview this morning, and . . . well, it was just too adorable for words. It was so beautiful that I immediately came to the conclusion I'd been right to purchase Everett an entire flock for his birthday." She nodded in clear satisfaction. "You mark my words, after today, everyone will be running out to buy themselves a flock of peacocks because they truly are going to be *the* fashionable pets of the season."

"I'm afraid you might be a little mistaken regarding your assessment of the peacocks' character," Everett said quietly, his words stealing the smile from Caroline's face.

"Must you argue with everything I say these days?" Caroline asked as her cheeks turned a vivid shade of pink even though her delicate skin was protected by her parasol. "You're putting a huge damper on the fun we're trying to have this fine afternoon, as well as embarrassing our two very good friends who made the unfortunate choice of getting into this buggy with us, and . . ." Caroline waved a hand at him as if she couldn't think of any other words to say as Gertrude and Dudley began taking a pointed interest in the passing scenery.

Opening his mouth to argue that point, Everett immediately snapped it shut again when he glimpsed the unmistakable sheen of tears in Caroline's eyes and the slight trembling of her lips.

An exceedingly unpleasant notion walloped him squarely over the head.

Caroline was right. He did argue with her frequently these days, even over something as ridiculous as what type of character the peacocks possessed.

It didn't matter if he agreed with her. Caroline obviously thought it was of grave importance to impress their friends with the birds, and because of that, she deserved better from him.

Taking a second to collect his thoughts, he studied Caroline, who was not looking his way but directing her attention to Dudley, who was now sending her looks of deepest sympathy. Knowing how Dudley felt about Caroline, the sympathetic looks were a tad annoying — but not completely unwarranted.

Caroline was, and had always been, a lady who demanded attention. She was spoiled, self-centered, and rather bossy, when it all came down to it, but she was what every gentleman within society aspired to marry. She was beautiful, accepted in all the right circles, charming when she put her mind to it, and . . . she'd decided that he, out of all the other eligible gentlemen in society, was worthy of her affections.

He reached for her hand. "You're absolutely right, Caroline. I've been arguing with you quite often of late, which has not been well done of me at all. I must beg your pardon here and now, and I hope you'll somehow be able to forgive me for my boorish behavior."

"You *have* been a complete boor, Everett. Quite dreadful, in fact."

The buggy took that moment to turn off of Bellevue Avenue and began moving up his drive, but he didn't take his gaze from Caroline's face. "You'll forgive me?" he asked quietly.

"I suppose I'll have to since you must know that everyone has . . . expectations regarding us at this point."

Leaning closer to her, he lowered his voice. "Caroline, if you're having second . . ."

"Good heavens," Gertrude yelled, sitting forward on the seat as she interrupted Everett and pointed at something in the distance. "Are those peacocks trying to run that boy down?"

Swinging his attention to where Gertrude was pointing, Everett felt his mouth drop open at the sight that met his eyes. Peacocks were streaming over the lawn, the largest ones in the front, followed by what appeared to be babies, and . . . they were chasing after a small boy — who had to be Thaddeus, but . . . he was wearing pants — and . . .

from all appearances, he seemed to be running for his very life.

"Driver, follow those peacocks," he shouted.

The buggy thrust forward, throwing Everett back against the seat. A glance to the right had his mouth dropping open again. Two members of his staff were chasing after the peacocks, although why the men were carrying a ladder between them as they ran was more than Everett could comprehend.

The second the buggy began to slow, he jumped over the side and immediately headed for the peacocks, which had stopped moving right underneath a large tree, but were now screeching so loudly it actually hurt his ears.

"Uncle Everett," Elizabeth shouted, waving him forward. "I sure am happy to see you."

Since he'd been expecting words laced with panic, but had gotten a somewhat pleasant greeting instead, Everett slowed his pace. "It's good to see you as well, Elizabeth," he called over the screeching as he made his way to Elizabeth's side. "What's wrong with them?" he asked, nodding to two peacocks that were screeching louder than ever.

"They're probably looking for Rose," yelled a voice from above. "But . . . not to worry, I think I see her now."

Glancing up into the tree, Everett spotted some feet, but then the peacocks abruptly went silent as Rose ran up to everyone, water slopping out of the glass she was clutching and soaking the front of her. She spared Everett not a single glance but sent a glare to Thaddeus, who was stepping out from behind one of the footmen.

Thaddeus *was* wearing short pants, as were Rose and Elizabeth, now that Everett took a closer look at them, and all the pants were made out of the same brown material — material that looked slightly familiar. Before he could determine where he'd seen the material before though, Rose stalked closer to her brother, looking very grumpy indeed.

"Why did you leave without me?"

Thaddeus scrunched up his nose. "Because we're in the middle of an emergency, and . . . Did you stop in the house to get a glass of water when we ran in there to call for help?"

Rose lifted the glass, gulped down half the contents, wiped a hand over her mouth, and nodded. "I was thirsty."

"You don't stop to get water when there's

an emergency going on, and your peacocks were really upset when they couldn't find you."

Thaddeus looked up at Everett. "Girls don't know anything about emergencies."

"I do too know about emergencies," Rose argued. "They make a person thirsty, and I bet Miss Millie will like having a nice drink of water once we get her out of that tree." She held up the glass. "I saved her some of my water."

Everett felt the corners of his mouth begin to twitch. "Millie's gotten herself stuck up in this tree?"

"I'm not stuck," Millie's voice called down. "I'm simply taking a small break up here to, er, appreciate the lovely scenery."

Swallowing a laugh, he looked at Elizabeth, who was grinning back at him. "What happened?"

"The string on Thaddeus's kite broke, and it landed in the tree."

"Did no one think about simply buying him another kite?"

"He was crying," Millie called down to him. "Tell me if you'd been here and seen Thaddeus crying that you wouldn't have hightailed it up this tree."

"I would have, but I'm not afraid of heights, something I get the distinct feeling you suffer from," Everett called back before he looked back to Elizabeth. "Why didn't anyone think to send my father up the tree? I know he's not afraid of heights."

"He and your mother went off to fetch Mrs. Hart," Elizabeth said. "But they've been gone for over an hour, which has been making Miss Millie awfully nervous."

"Why would that make her nervous?"

Elizabeth's brow wrinkled. "I'm not sure, but Miss Millie keeps mumbling something about plotting, and that everyone seems to have lost their minds."

"Who lost their mind, dear?"

Elizabeth jumped when Caroline suddenly appeared under the tree, but then the young girl began backing up ever so slowly when Caroline drew in a sharp breath and pointed a finger Elizabeth's way.

"What are you wearing?"

"They're wearing pants," Millie called down to them. "Per your request."

"I only requested that Thaddeus start wearing pants, not the girls, as I'm sure you very well know, Miss Longfellow. And . . . I recall ordering some drapes to be put up in the nanny's room only a month or so ago that were made up in material remarkably similar to what Elizabeth's wearing," Caroline called up to her.

"I thought that material looked familiar," Everett said to no one in particular. "And it's not as if we should really be surprised the children are wearing clothing made out of drapes, since they've been doing just that for months now."

Caroline drew herself up. "This is not amusing, Everett. I hate to even consider what all of our guests will think about us if they see the girls wearing pants, but if anyone realizes the children are actually wearing former drapes . . ."

"No one but you and I have even been in the nanny's room, Caroline, and as for the girls wearing pants, well, they're just children, and I'm sure many of our guests have faced similar situations with their own girls."

Caroline turned and directed her attention to where the buggies that had followed them to Seaview had now come to a stop. The occupants of those buggies were slowly climbing out of them, and to Everett's disappointment, everyone seemed to be whispering rather furiously behind their hands.

Caroline immediately rounded on him. "Do they look like people who have seen situations like this before?"

"Well, no, and since we hardly want to

distress our cherished guests, I'm going to suggest you take everyone to the back terrace and have Mrs. O'Connor serve some of that delicious lemonade she makes. I'll join you just as soon as I get Millie out of the tree."

"I don't need you to get me out of the tree." Millie said.

"Is someone stuck in that tree?" Dudley called.

"It's just the nanny," Caroline said before she started walking Dudley's way. "But there's no need for us to linger here. It'll hardly be amusing to watch her get rescued, so I need everyone to follow me. We're going to adjoin to the terrace, where there's a lovely view of the ocean, and Everett's housekeeper will serve all of us her special lemonade."

Waiting until the last of the guests disappeared around the corner of Seaview, Everett moved to the ladder his footmen had set up, shaking off his jacket as he did so. Handing it to Thaddeus, who'd immediately scampered over to his side, he eyed the tree.

"If you're scared, Uncle Everett, I could go save her," Thaddeus said solemnly. "It's my fault since she only climbed up there because of my kite." He hung his head. "I wasn't watching out for the trees, and it got stuck when a big gust of wind caught it."

"Thank you, Thaddeus, but I'm not afraid to climb the tree."

"I'm not afraid either," Millie yelled.

Completely ignoring that statement since he knew it was less than true, Everett glanced to the two footmen, Davis and Johnson, who were standing on either side of the ladder. "You'll hold the ladder steady for me?"

Davis, a young man who always had a ready smile and a very pleasant personality, nodded. "We will indeed, sir, but I'd be happy to fetch Miss Millie." He looked up the tree then back at Everett. "She's a nice lady, she is, a real friendly sort, and it would be a true honor for me to go and save her."

A stab of something unpleasant settled in Everett's stomach as he immediately came to the conclusion that he'd been wrong about Davis, and that the man didn't possess a pleasant personality at all, but was a pushy and far-too-handsome sort. Reaching out, Everett took hold of the ladder and raised a foot to the first rung. "While I certainly appreciate your offer, Davis, Miss Longfellow is my responsibility, and as such, *I'll* save her." Not allowing Davis an opportunity to argue, he began climbing, pausing when he reached the very last rung of the ladder and realized Millie was still sitting quite a ways away from him.

He couldn't see much of her, given the foliage that surrounded them, but she was perched on a limb that seemed rather thin. She was also holding perfectly still, that stillness causing him no small amount of concern.

Millie was never still, and the very idea she wasn't so much as moving a muscle proved she was in a very precarious state.

Pulling himself up and off the ladder, he climbed closer to her, stopping when the branch he was standing on began to bend. "I'm afraid I'm not going to be able to climb all the way up to you, Millie, so you're going to have to scoot down here and meet me."

"Not likely."

"You really don't have another option."

"I told you, I'm going to sit here for a spell, rediscover my nerve, and then I'll climb down on my own."

"What if your nerve doesn't want to be rediscovered?"

A snort was her only response.

He tried again. "There's no need to be scared. I assure you I won't let you fall. I was considered a very good tree climber in my youth, so you're in good hands with me."

"When was the last time you climbed a tree?"

"I will admit it's been some time, but it's liking riding one of those bicycles everyone seems so keen about these days. They say once you learn to ride, you never forget — and the same goes with climbing trees. If you've neglected to notice, I made it all the way up here to you without a single mishap."

"You used a ladder for most of your climb. That's cheating."

"While I would love to delve into the reasons behind your difficult attitude at the moment, in case you're confused about what I'm doing up here, I'm trying to help you."

"Fine, help me then. Go find Caroline and help her entertain all of those people, and when I'm sure no one is lingering around . . . watching me . . . I'll come down."

"No one is watching you. They've all retreated to the back terrace."

"I bet some of them are peeking around the corner of the house, just hoping I'll . . ." Millie suddenly stopped speaking when the branch she was sitting on gave an ominous creak.

"Stop moving," he said as calmly as he

could, even though his heart had begun beating furiously.

"I wasn't moving," she whispered.

Shifting a little on his branch, he looked down and discovered Davis standing on the top rung of the ladder, looking up at him.

"I thought you might need some help, sir," Davis said before he craned his neck and shifted to the right. "How are you doing up there, Miss Millie?"

"She's fine, but I might have a bit of a difficult time getting her down if you're using the ladder," Everett pointed out.

"Right you are, sir," Davis said. "I'll just wait for you on the ground."

"He's a very nice man," Millie said after Davis disappeared, her words having the strange effect of causing Everett's teeth to clink together.

"Yes, yes, he's delightful, and certainly seems . . . Well, no need to get into that right now. We need to get you out of the tree. Can you move to another branch? The one right beneath you looks a little sturdier."

Leaves rustled as she shifted around, but then she stilled again. "I can't do it."

"Of course you can. You're the lady who got Thaddeus out of frocks and into pants with remarkable ease. You can do anything."

Unfortunately, Millie didn't seem to want

to discuss what she could or couldn't do at the moment. The branch gave another creak, she let out what almost sounded like a whimper, and then, to his surprise, she completely changed the subject. "Do you know that Davis is an extremely competent tailor? He helped sew all the garments the children and I are currently wearing."

The unpleasant something or other once again unfurled in Everett's stomach. "He helped sew the children's outfits?"

"He did, along with quite a few other members of your staff, as well as your mother. That's how we were able to finish so quickly. Just so you know, I told Davis I'd introduce him to Harriet once she gets back from England. She could use such a talented man when she gets around to opening her dress shop, so I might have lost you a good footman."

Everett didn't know if he should laugh or pull all of his hair out in frustration. Here they were, high up in a tree, and Millie had apparently decided to act as if they were sitting down to tea, discussing matters of a rather mundane nature.

"Fascinating as it is to learn Davis likes to sew," he settled on saying, "we really do need to get you down from there, so . . . I'm going to try and get closer to you."

Everett stepped on a branch to the right that, thankfully, held his weight, swung around the trunk, and found another branch that brought him right up next to Millie. When he got a good look at her, though, he found himself in the unusual position of having completely lost the ability to speak.

Millie's curly hair was tied back with a ribbon, making her appear remarkably young, while also lending her a rather flirty attitude. His gaze traveled from her hair to her face, and he felt his breath catch in his throat when he took note of the paleness of her skin, the panic in her eyes, and the slight trembling of her lips. A scratch marred her cheek, and as his gaze drifted down her person to make certain she wasn't injured anywhere else, he blinked and blinked again.

"Are you wearing . . . pants?"

"Well, yes," she said, right before she sent him the smallest of grins.

The grin hit him like a fist to the stomach, and right there and then, in the midst of the tree, he finally realized what it was about his life that had changed.

He, Everett Mulberry, one of society's highest members, was attracted to Miss Millie Longfellow, the . . . nanny.

It was completely unacceptable, ridiculous even, and almost seemed like a story Jane

Austen would have penned. In fact . . . him being attracted to Millie was remarkably similar to the *Pride and Prejudice* story he hadn't picked up for a day or two. And he realized now that he certainly wasn't going to finish because . . . if Mr. Darcy did indeed end up with Miss Elizabeth, well, it was a silly fairy tale, plain and simple.

He didn't believe in fairy tales, even if Oliver seemed to have experienced one, but . . . no — he would not allow himself to think in that direction. The question that remained now, though, was how was he going to overcome this attraction — if that's what he was actually feeling — for Millie?

She was unlike any lady he'd ever known — caring, funny, and more intelligent than she gave herself credit for — but . . . she was not his equal in any way, shape, or form. He had to remember that, had to remember that he had a standing within society he'd carefully cultivated over the years. He also had a certain standing within the business community, a community that would not look kindly on him if he allowed himself to pursue this attraction he held for Millie. Besides all that . . . there was Caroline to consider.

Resignation settled deep within him as he realized exactly what he needed to do. He was going to have to distance himself from this woman he found far too enticing, spend even more time with Caroline, since she was the woman he'd committed himself to, and . . . he'd have to find a new nanny sometime in the foreseeable future.

"What is the matter with you?" Millie demanded, pulling him back to the situation at hand.

"I'm thinking about how to get you out of here" was the only response Everett was comfortable giving. Reaching out, he took hold of her arm. "Are you ready?"

"Do I have another choice?"

He refused to grin, reminding himself that he needed to maintain a careful distance with her from this point forward. "I'm afraid not."

"Oh, very well, but I'm going to need a moment." With that, Millie closed her eyes, kept them closed for a good long moment, whispered an "Amen," then opened her eyes.

"Were you just . . . praying?" Everett asked.

"I always pray before I proceed with life-threatening situations."

"Does it help?"

"I'm still alive, aren't I?"

Resisting the impulse to grin yet again,

Everett settled for a nod.

"You'll catch me if I start to fall?" she asked.

After reassuring her that he would, indeed, catch her, they finally began to make their way incredibly slowly down the tree. By the time they reached the ground, Millie was shaking like mad, but instead of pulling her close and offering her comfort, Everett allowed the children to do that, unable to help but smile just a little when they couldn't seem to hug Millie hard enough. Lifting her head, she caught his eye. "Thank you," she whispered.

"You *should* be thanking him, Miss Long-fellow," Caroline said as she marched back to join them, having obviously abandoned their guests on the back terrace. "I have no idea what you were thinking, climbing up a tree, for goodness' sake, but . . . Are you wearing pants?"

Before Millie could respond, Rose stepped forward. "Miss Millie thought if all of us wore pants, Thaddeus would feel better about wearing them again, so you shouldn't scold her."

Caroline's face darkened even as she shook a finger in Rose's direction. "Pants are never acceptable for ladies or young girls to wear, Rosetta, and I must tell you that you and your sister have succeeded in embarrassing me quite dreadfully since you allowed our guests to see you in such a disgraceful state." She shook her finger again. "Why, your lack of proper attire is *the* topic of conversation right now on the back terrace."

Rose's little lips began to quiver, her eyes filled with tears, and then she began to cry in earnest, but before anyone could offer her a smidgen of comfort, the air split with a hair-raising shriek.

To Everett's very great concern, the peacocks that had been gathered off to the side of the tree turned their heads in unison and set their beady eyes on Caroline. As if choreographed, they spread their tail feathers right before they charged — directly in Caroline's direction.

11

A week and a half after the disastrous peacock debacle, Millie sat in the shade of a large tree, but not the one she'd been unfortunate enough to get stuck in. Peering closely at the rather worn copy of *Romeo and Juliet* she was attempting to read, she reached for her dictionary when she ran into yet another word she'd never seen before. As she switched one book for the other, she caught a glimpse of someone walking toward her across the back lawn of Seaview.

"Millie. There you are."

Abandoning her books, Millie scrambled to her feet and dashed forward, stopping right in front of none other than Lucetta.

"What a marvelous surprise, Lucetta, but . . . what are you doing here? I thought your new play opened this week."

Pulling Millie into an enthusiastic hug, Lucetta gave her a good squeeze before she stepped back. "The play *did* open this week.

However, because of a pesky little problem with the new electric lights that were installed to replace the old, smoking electric lights, there's been a slight setback."

"What happened?"

Lucetta shook her head rather sadly. "It turns out the new and improved lights weren't exactly improved, since they burst into flames. The theater caught on fire during our first performance."

"The theater burned down?"

"Well, no, but there was enough damage to require extensive repairs, so the theater will be closed for a good month, perhaps two, leaving me free to travel to Newport."

"But . . . what will you do for funds?"

Lucetta gave Millie's arm a pat. "No need to worry about that. I have funds set aside for emergencies, along with a bit of money I make through invest . . . Well, no need to get into that boring business. But my savings aside, I'm pleased to report that since management wanted to ascertain I wouldn't move on to another theater, they're paying me my full wage until the repairs have been completed."

"That's generous of them."

"I'm not sure it *was* exactly generosity that had them offering to continue paying me. From the whispers I've overheard, Mr.

Grimstone, the author who penned the play, would only allow his masterpiece to be produced if *I* was given the lead role. That means management can't afford to lose me."

"Who exactly is this Mr. Grimstone?" Millie asked.

"No one seems to know. He's very reclusive, which has rumors swirling around the country. He writes brilliantly, in a dark and brooding style, but with just enough witty dialogue to capture and hold everyone's attention. This is actually his first play, but his books sell out almost as soon as they hit the shops." She smiled. "Management is convinced we have *the* hit of the theater season this year."

Millie smiled. "Well, I am sorry your theater caught fire, but not sorry that you and I are now going to be able to see each other often this summer."

Lucetta took hold of Millie's arm and strolled over to where Millie had set up her reading spot under the tree. "We will see each other often, but enough about me. What has been going on with you, and . . . where are the children?"

Striving for an air of nonchalance, Millie shrugged. "They'll be back soon. They're off exploring along the cliff walk with Everett — something they've taken to doing every day now for the past week and a half."

"Why aren't you with them?"

"Oh, ah, Everett believes I need some time to myself."

"That's very . . . considerate of him."

Millie's shoulders drooped, and to her absolute horror, she felt tears sting her eyes. Blinking rapidly, she tried to hold them at bay but realized she'd failed miserably when tears started dripping down her cheeks.

"Good heavens — what's wrong?" Lucetta demanded.

Dashing the tears away with her hand, Millie blew out a shaky breath. "That's just it. I have no idea."

Lucetta practically shoved Millie down on the blanket before she took up a spot right beside her. "Tell me exactly what Everett's done."

Drawing in a shaky breath as she gathered her thoughts, Millie smoothed down the fabric of the pretty peach day dress Abigail had provided her. "He hasn't really *done* anything, except maintain a careful distance from me over the past week and a half. He excludes me from the morning explorations he takes with the children, and he leaves Seaview immediately after returning the children back to me. He spends hours and hours away from the cottage in the company of his society friends, and . . . he's taken to calling me Miss Longfellow again."

"Why in the world would he do that?"

"I don't know, but it all started right after he rescued me from being stuck in a tree, and right after the peacocks went on a rampage."

"I think you need to start at the beginning."

Fifteen minutes later, Millie finished with, "So Caroline and Everett took refuge from the peacocks in the icehouse, which turned out to be a bit of a mistake. The peacocks, you see, took up positions directly in front of the door and wouldn't budge, not even when the footmen and I tried to shoo them away. Elizabeth finally had the ingenious idea of having Rose step in — since she does seem to have an unusual relationship with the birds — but . . . before Rose had the opportunity to lead the birds away, Caroline did the unthinkable."

"She yelled at Rose again?"

"Not exactly, but what she did do was almost worse." Millie felt her lips begin to curl. "She stuck her head out of the icehouse, and when she spotted her friends — all of them having abandoned their lemonade for the drama that was unfolding with the peacocks — she yelled to them that she'd made a small miscalculation regarding the birds. Caroline then proceeded to state that peacocks were not meant to be pets but were meant to be served as a tasty dish for dinner with a lovely cream sauce on the side."

"Oh . . . my."

"Indeed. That nasty business had Rose turning stubborn, and she flatly refused to lure the peacocks away. The minutes ticked by until, finally, Everett stuck *his* head out the door. He yelled to Rose — through teeth that were chattering from the cold, mind you — that Caroline had come to her senses and decided that peacocks wouldn't be tasty after all, and that they were never going to show up on the menu."

"And that had Rose cooperating?"

"It did, although I'm not exactly certain she believes Caroline won't someday try and cook the birds in a cream sauce. But after the peacocks were out of sight, Everett and Caroline emerged from the icehouse and Caroline promptly demanded to be taken home. She's now refusing to step so much as a toe in Seaview again until the peacocks are permanently removed."

Millie shook her head. "It's a bit of a problem for Everett, I think — especially since he doesn't seem to be immune to the tears Rose summons whenever her precious peacocks come up in conversation. Those tears are why Everett is having Davis, a charming man if there ever was one, build a peacock enclosure on the other side of the stables."

"Who is the world is this Davis gentleman?"

"He's a footman, but he's so much more than that. Why, I think his skill with a needle and thread rivals Harriet's skill, and he's been using those skills to whip up short pants for Thaddeus, now that our favorite little boy has finally agreed to abandon his frocks. However, poor Davis has not had a lot of time to do much sewing lately, since this peacock enclosure is turning out to be rather tricky, given that the peacocks keep finding ways to escape."

Lucetta's eyes began to gleam. "Do you spend much time with Davis?"

"A fair amount, but he's very busy, especially since Everett keeps giving him new projects to complete every day, even though the peacock enclosure is far from being finished."

The gleam was replaced with calculation. "Are these projects Everett gives Davis completely necessary?"

"Well . . . I suppose they must be or else

why would Everett assign them?"

Lucetta ignored the question. "And you said that Everett *had* been behaving downright charming to you, but then . . . completely out of the blue, he began acting somewhat surly?"

"I think *distant* rather than *surly* might be a better way to describe him at the moment."

"Interesting" was all Lucetta said as she turned her head and looked out toward the ocean.

"What's interesting?"

Lucetta considered the ocean a moment longer before she finally looked back to Millie. "I might be completely off the mark, but have you ever considered the idea that Everett might be slightly . . . intrigued by you? And because you seem to get along so well with Davis, Everett's been behaving distantly toward you because he's . . . jealous?"

Amusement was immediate. "You're delusional, especially since Everett is a gentleman who embraces his role within society. Because of that, he'd never look at a member of his staff as anything other than an employee, and he certainly would never allow himself to become *intrigued* by anyone on his staff."

Lucetta crossed her arms over her chest. "Why else would he be maintaining a careful distance from you? He certainly can't blame you for the whole peacock fiasco or for getting stuck up in that tree. Besides, gentlemen enjoy rescuing damsels in distress. It makes them feel manly."

"I hate to come across as argumentative, Lucetta — especially since you went to the great trouble of coming to Newport to visit me — but I don't think Everett enjoyed rescuing me at all. In fact, I've actually been considering the idea that his being forced to fetch me out of that tree is exactly why he's gone all peculiar of late. He obviously was completely disgusted by my lack of bravery and has now lost all respect for me."

"And you have the nerve to call *me* delusional," Lucetta said with a roll of her eyes. "I can assure you that Everett did not lose respect for you because you got stuck up in a tree."

"When I lived in the orphanage, the children I grew up with never had any respect for the poor souls who showed any sign of fear."

"That was a completely different situation, Millie. Adults don't view life as children do."

"I work with children all the time. They

think remarkably like us, and besides, you didn't see Everett when he finally reached me up in that tree. He certainly didn't look like the hero coming to rescue the damsel in distress. Instead, he just stared at me with this look on his face — the one people get when they're feeling a little queasy."

"Perhaps he's scared of heights as well and just didn't want to admit it."

"No, I think he was just really annoyed that he had to spend time rescuing me when he could have been spending that time socializing with his friends."

"I think he's attracted to you."

Millie wrinkled her nose. "You're apparently not listening to a word I'm saying, but allow me to be crystal clear. Everett, I'm very certain, is not attracted to me — nor, I'm going to add, am I attracted to him."

Lucetta arched a brow.

Millie arched a brow right back at her. "I'm not, not really, although I freely admit he's a very handsome gentleman, and it's been quite sweet to see him with the children." She blinked and pretended not to see the smug expression on Lucetta's face. "I'm truly only upset because I thought we were becoming friends, but now . . . he wants nothing to do with me."

Lucetta pushed herself up from the

blanket and held out her hand to Millie. "I've just decided that I'd adore nothing more than taking a walk."

"Now?" Millie asked, taking the hand Lucetta was still holding out to her and allowing her friend to pull her to her feet.

"It's a glorious day," Lucetta continued. "And as such, I'd like to mosey on down to the ocean and dip my toes into the water."

"Or mosey on down to the ocean to see if Everett's perhaps moseying around down there as well?" Millie countered.

Lucetta smiled. "Has anyone ever told you that you have a somewhat suspicious nature?"

"I have every reason to be suspicious right now. You're up to something."

Linking her arm with Millie's, Lucetta's only response was to change the subject as they began meandering across the lawn. "Did I mention that Reverend Gilmore traveled to Newport with me?"

Millie opened her mouth, intending on sticking with the conversation about Lucetta's behavior, but then tilted her head. "Reverend Gilmore's here?"

"He is indeed, his presence in Newport a direct result of his receiving a letter from Abigail a week or so ago, asking for some assistance with the children. He'd already made arrangements for another minister to take over his sermons, so when he discovered I was traveling to Newport on the first steamship out this morning, he decided to join me."

They reached the beginning of the cliff walk, and Millie let go of Lucetta's arm. "I'll go first, shall I?"

With Lucetta close on her heels, Millie made the descent, slipping every so often on the loose stones scattered about the well-worn path. With a sigh of relief, she reached the sandy beach, turning to check on Lucetta's progress.

Lucetta, however, was no longer right behind Millie. She had stopped a few yards up the path, her hand shielding her eyes from the sun. "There's Everett, right over there on the beach, but he's not moseying, as you suggested, Millie. He's just sitting there, holding Rose from what I can make out from this distance."

Directing her attention back to the beach, Millie immediately caught sight of Everett, who really was sitting on the beach with Rose in his lap. When Rose lifted her head and caught sight of Millie, Millie knew she had no choice *but* to travel Everett's way. The irritation she felt over that disappeared in an instant, though, when Rose started running toward her. As Rose drew closer, Millie noted the telltale signs of tears on the little girl's face.

Bending down, Millie held open her arms, which Rose immediately jumped into.

Straightening, Millie snuggled Rose close to her. "What happened?"

"She got pinched by a crab," Thaddeus said, appearing out of nowhere and looking rather guilty.

Hugging Rose tightly to her for another second, Millie set Rose on her feet, and then knelt in front of the little girl, taking the hand Rose immediately held up. A fine linen handkerchief was wrapped around Rose's index finger — one that obviously had come directly out of Everett's pocket, since it held the faintest scent of sandalwood. "May I take a look at your finger?"

"It's not bleeding," Thaddeus said quickly, earning a glare from his sister.

"It wouldn't even be hurting if you hadn't handed that crab to me," Rose returned.

Fighting a smile, Millie unwrapped the handkerchief. To her relief, Rose's finger was not bleeding, although it sported two red marks where the crab had apparently grabbed hold of it.

"Do you think it's broken?"

Looking up, Millie found Everett standing

beside her, his face rather pale and his eyes filled with worry. Returning her attention to the finger, she moved it gently up and down before shaking her head. "No, it's not broken."

Everett blew out a breath. "Thank goodness. I didn't know what to do, and she was screaming something awful, and the crab wouldn't let go, and then Thaddeus started crying because he'd been the one to give Rose the crab, and . . . I think I've just aged ten years."

"Where's Elizabeth?" Millie asked. "She would have known what to do."

"She's farther down the beach with my mother."

Millie smiled. "It's lovely to see your mother and Elizabeth getting along so well. I think they really enjoy each other's company." Her smile widened. "Dorothy's turned out to be rather nice, even though I thought she was a complete nightmare that first day I met her."

"Since she tried to dismiss you, I'm not exactly surprised by your admission."

Millie's smile turned into a grin. "I do think that's the one and only time that someone's threatened me with dismissal and yet here I am . . . still employed."

When Everett grinned back at her, Millie's

breath got stuck in her throat, but then, after only a few seconds had passed, his grin faded and he began taking a pointed interest in sky.

Her breath returned in a flash, and with annoyance now humming through her veins, Millie brought Rose's finger up to her lips, placing a kiss on the marks the crab had left behind. "Better?" she asked as she wiped the lingering tears on Rose's cheeks with the sleeve of her dress.

Rose's little lips curved into a smile. "Kisses always make everything all better. That's what my momma used to do when I got hurt."

Leaning forward, even as her heart took to aching, Millie kissed Rose's forehead, but Rose wasn't content to stand still long. Twisting away from Millie, she pointed down the beach. "There's Elizabeth and Mrs. Mulberry. Can I go show them my finger?"

"You may."

Turning to Thaddeus, Rose glared at her brother for a second before she let out a little huff. "You can come, but only if you promise not to be mean."

"I didn't do it on purpose," Thaddeus said before he took hold of his sister's hand, and together, they hurried off over the sand.

"Is it my imagination, or are those two squabbling a lot more lately?" Everett asked as he stopped perusing the sky.

Relieved that she didn't lose her breath again when Everett looked her way, Millie shrugged. "They're acting exactly how five-year-olds are supposed to act. So, yes, they are squabbling more, but it's a good sign. It means they're beginning to feel secure again."

"And it also means that our wonderful Millie is having a great impact on the children, even though she hasn't had responsibility for them for an entire month yet," Lucetta said as she strolled into view, making her way over to Everett before she held out her hand.

Everett didn't hesitate to bring Lucetta's fingers to his lips, but unlike most gentlemen, he didn't linger, earning a nod of approval from Lucetta. "This is a pleasant surprise, Lucetta, finding you in Newport."

"Thank you, Everett, and I'm sure you'll be absolutely delighted to learn I'll be skulking around Seaview for the next few weeks — although you needn't look so worried. I won't be staying under your roof, but at Abigail's. I thought I'd help Millie out with the children a bit, at no cost to you, of course, but . . . speaking of Millie — have you been given the pleasure of kissing her hand yet today?"

For just a second, something interesting flashed through Everett's eyes, but it was gone in the next, replaced with something . . . cold. "I don't normally make a habit of kissing the nanny's hand, Lucetta."

"And I don't normally make a habit of telling people they're complete idiots, but . . . there you have it . . . you're an idiot, Everett," Lucetta said as calm as you please, not even batting an eye as she delivered her insult.

A vein began throbbing on Everett's forehead, but instead of responding to Lucetta, he turned on his heel, stalked over to Millie, and grabbed hold of her hand. Bringing it to his lips, he pressed a kiss on it that lasted barely a second, before he dropped her hand as if it had burned him and turned back to Lucetta again. "Does that make you feel better?"

"Hardly, since no woman likes to be kissed by a man who scowls at them, but . . . it's a start." Lucetta smiled sweetly at Everett, the sweetness of the smile having Millie suppressing the urge to cringe. "I hear you and Caroline suffered quite the adventure with a flock of peacocks the other week."

"I don't know if I'd call what Caroline and I experienced with the peacocks an adventure, but it did succeed in embarrassing Caroline in front of none other than Mr. Ward McAllister, something she's having a difficult time putting behind her."

Lucetta's smile slid right off her face. "I will never understand why everyone puts so much stock in what Mr. McAllister thinks. If you ask me, he's a bit nauseating, what with his constant fawning over Caroline Astor and his habit of calling her his Mystic Rose. People who work in theater absolutely loathe when he and the whole Astor crowd descend on a performance. They always arrive smack in the middle of the second act, and then they proceed to chat on and off throughout the rest of the play. That makes it very difficult to understand why they bother going to the theater in the first place. And from what I've been told, their behavior is even worse at the opera, where they don't bother to pay attention to the performance at all."

Everett brushed some sand from his sleeve. "You must know that they only go to the theater and opera to be seen."

"They can be seen without speaking. I don't believe it's too much to ask of society to show some common courtesy, especially since they're the ones who are always going on and on about proprieties." She pursed her lips. "Why, Mr. McAllister is one of the worst offenders when it comes to rudeness, and yet he has the audacity to speak about actresses as if all of us are . . . women of questionable repute."

"While you have a very valid point, Lucetta, and one I haven't actually considered before, Mr. McAllister *is* a gentleman of a certain age, and as such you should expect such behavior."

"Mr. McAllister is a snob, Everett, and I do believe he's suffered from that condition since birth, as do most of the society people I meet."

Everett stopped brushing at the sand. "I'm not a snob."

"Who else would say — in a snotty tone of voice, no less — that they don't normally kiss the nanny?" Lucetta shot back.

"I have to believe a lot of gentlemen don't spend their time kissing the nanny since their wives probably wouldn't appreciate that."

"You're completely missing the point, and . . ." Lucetta stopped talking when Dorothy snuck into their midst.

"I do hope I'm interrupting some type of riveting discussion," she said before she nodded to Lucetta. "Were you just arguing with my son?"

Lucetta was smiling again, far too sweetly, but before she could answer Dorothy, Everett stepped forward.

"I don't believe you've met Miss Plum before, Mother."

After Everett took a moment to perform proper introductions, Dorothy beamed a smile Lucetta's way. "I must say, Miss Plum, that even though you and I have never met, since I've seen almost all of your plays, I feel as if you and I are already friends. But, tell me, dear, what in the world are you doing in Newport? I thought I read in the paper that you were performing in a new play, written by that oh-so-mysterious Mr. Grimstone."

Lucetta nodded and then launched into the sad tale regarding the electric lights, chatting back and forth with Dorothy as if they really had been great friends forever.

". . . so, since the electric lights were responsible for causing quite a bit of damage, the theater had to close, which is why I'm here."

"If I ever become an actress," Elizabeth said as she skipped right into their midst and sent a smile to Lucetta. "I'm never going to perform in a theater that has electric lights."

Lucetta returned the smile. "While I do believe your Uncle Everett might have something to say about your even contemplating becoming an actress, dear, why don't you like electric lights? They're being proclaimed as the great invention for the future these days."

Elizabeth shook her head. "People might be keen on them right now, Miss Plum, but my daddy had tons and tons of electric lights in his barn back in Boston, all by different inventors, and none of them ever worked like the inventors said they were going to work."

"One light inventor even caught the barn on fire with his invention," Thaddeus said as he pulled Rose along beside him to join everyone. "Daddy was really mad because that man's light exploded and flames started shooting out everywhere. He and that inventor had some words after the fire got put out, and then the inventor stormed out of the barn and raced away on his horse."

The hair on the back of Millie's neck stood to attention, as she suddenly remembered — what with all the peacocks rampaging and tennis matches that had gone amok — that she'd not spent any time at all thinking about the mystery surrounding what had actually happened back in Boston with Fred and Violet Burkhart.

"When did that take place — the argument your father had with the inventor?" Millie finally asked.

Elizabeth's forehead creased. "It was a while ago, but Daddy was always having words with inventors. They didn't like when he wouldn't give them money, but he only gave money if inventions worked."

Millie caught Everett's eye. "You don't suppose . . . ?" she began, but stopped midword when she realized all three children were watching her closely. Summoning up a smile, she found herself voicing the first thing that popped to mind. "Who wants to go back with me to the cottage and collect our kites? It's a lovely day to fly kites, and if we're lucky, Miss Pickenpaugh will be having her late-morning tea right about now, so we should be able to avoid running into her."

"Who is Miss Pickenpaugh?" Lucetta asked.

"She's the lady Caroline hired to prepare the house for the ball we're hosting in a few days," Everett said before he actually winced. "She's a bit of a nightmare, which is why all of us try our very best to avoid her."

"If you'd simply allowed me to help with the organization of this ball, Everett," Dorothy said as she stepped closer to Everett. "You wouldn't currently have Miss Pickenpaugh wreaking havoc at Seaview, and you'd be saving quite a bit of money as well."

"Caroline brought in Miss Pickenpaugh because she wants to make certain this ball is particularly special."

The air crackled with tension as Dorothy stepped closer to Everett and began to whisper furiously in his ear. Millie didn't need to hear the words to know what Dorothy was upset about.

Everett and Caroline were apparently making plans to move forward in their relationship, and that meant . . . they'd be planning a wedding before too long.

Millie's stomach immediately began to churn even though she'd been trying to convince herself that, what with Everett's peculiar behavior toward her of late, she didn't care for him. She'd been having difficulty with that convincing, though, especially since she kept catching Everett watching her, something tha—

"If Caroline is refusing to visit Seaview, how in the world is she going to attend your ball?" Lucetta asked, breaking through Millie's disturbing thoughts.

"I'm hoping we'll have the peacock situation well in hand by that time," Everett said.

"And if you don't?"

"I'd rather not think about that."

"That would be one way to settle the whole special-ball moment once and for all," Dorothy said as she ignored Everett's immediate argument and turned to Millie. "But I find I'm growing weary of this particular subject. Didn't you mention something about kites?"

"Good heavens, I almost forgot," Lucetta exclaimed before Millie could respond. "We can't go fetch any kites, because Abigail wants me to invite everyone over to her cottage for a special treat."

"Is the special treat a dog?" Thaddeus asked, looking hopefully up at Lucetta.

"No, I'm sorry, it's not. Although, speaking of dogs . . . No, never mind about that right now." Lucetta squatted down next to Thaddeus, who was looking a bit glum. "The special treat is actually an odd contraption Abigail pulled out of her carriage house called a bathing machine. She's already had it taken down to her private beach, and we're going to try it out today."

"We're going to use it to bathe in the

300

ocean?" Thaddeus asked slowly.

"Or something like that," Lucetta said. "I have yet to see this bathing machine, so I'm not really sure what it does. But in order to find out the answer to that, we need to go gather up appropriate bathing gear."

"Bathing machines were all the rage when I was a young girl, but I haven't seen one in years," Dorothy said before she nodded. "I'd love to come, although Fletcher isn't at home today. He's gone off to the Reading Room." She quirked a brow at Everett. "You could join us though."

"I'm afraid I can't, Mother. I promised Caroline I'd take her to Bailey's Beach."

Dorothy wrinkled her nose. "Bailey's Beach is a horrid spot to swim. There's seaweed everywhere."

"It's secluded," Everett said. "And it even has private bathing huts a person can use to change out of wet attire after their day in the sun is done."

"What do you think a bathing machine's for? And again, even though Bailey's Beach seems to be the beach of choice these days for society members, it's not the best beach around to enjoy the water." She smiled. "I imagine there's more fun to be found at Abigail's private beach, especially since the children, Millie, Lucetta, Abigail, and, of

301

course, I will be there." Her smile widened. "I must admit that I'm looking forward to spending the afternoon with Abigail. She's far more pleasant than I remembered and has been an absolute joy to have at all those society luncheons I keep feeling compelled to attend."

Lucetta cleared her throat. "Forgive me, but did you just say that Abigail's taken to mingling with Newport society?"

"Since Millie's been occupied with the children so much, you really shouldn't find that to be a surprise, Miss Plum. Or is it acceptable for me to call you Lucetta?" Dorothy asked.

"You may certainly call me by my given name, but . . . *why* is Abigail mingling with society?" Lucetta pressed.

Dorothy looked a little shifty, and when she hesitated with a response, Lucetta sent a glare Everett's way. "This is *your* fault, and if I suddenly find myself inundated with gentlemen callers, it's not going to be pleasant for you." She sent him a sniff, grabbed hold of Elizabeth's hand, and nodded to Thaddeus and Rose. "Children, come with me."

Without bothering to say anything else, Lucetta marched away with her head held high, although the sounds of additional sniffs followed her all the way back to the cliff walk.

"All of this would be much easier if everyone weren't so stubborn and would take advice from ladies who only have their best interest at heart," Dorothy mumbled before she hurried after Lucetta.

Everett turned his attention to Millie. "What do you think *that* was all about?"

"If I were to hazard a guess, I'd say Lucetta's blaming you for not complying with Abigail's schemes. Because of that noncompliance, Lucetta now feels Abigail is turning her plotting ways in Lucetta's direction, with your mother's assistance, of course."

Everett frowned. "Abigail wasn't really serious about the two of us forming some type of alliance, was she? Matches between a nanny and a society gentleman might happen on the pages of a romance novel, but in real life, they simply never occur."

Temper came from out of nowhere, and not all of it directed at him.

She'd been a complete ninny — she was absolutely certain about that now.

Even though she'd claimed over and over again that she wasn't attracted to the gentleman standing before her, she . . . was. But it was ridiculous, that attraction.

He was, and would always be, a member

of the social set, even if he had made himself agreeable to her by drawing closer to the children and picking up one of her favorite novels to read.

It was almost as if she'd subconsciously convinced herself that by his reading *Pride and Prejudice,* he'd suddenly turn into Mr. Darcy, proclaim his very great affection for her, and . . . whisk her off to his estate in England, or the mansion on Fifth Avenue — given that that was where he lived — and . . . they'd live happily ever after.

Her temper burned hotter.

How could she have been so foolish? She wasn't a foolish sort of lady, even with the mischief she got into now and again, but there was just something about Mr. Everett Mulberry that had obviously made her a little . . . insane.

"Did you ever finish *Pride and Prejudice*?"

Everett blinked. "I beg your pardon?"

"*Pride and Prejudice* — did you ever finish reading it?"

"Well, ah . . . it wasn't really to my taste."

"Of course it wasn't." Ignoring the arm she'd just noticed he was holding out to her, she began stomping her way through the sand.

"Millie . . . wait."

For a second, she continued stomping,

but then, hearing him running after her, she stopped and turned around. "Shall I assume we're both back to addressing each other informally now, or do you still expect me to call you Mr. Mulberry?"

He regarded her for a long moment, the intensity of his gaze leaving her a little flustered. "I've hurt your feelings, haven't I."

Squaring her shoulders, she took a step back from him. "If you need reminding, Mr. Mulberry, I'm just the nanny. That means a gentleman in your lofty position doesn't need to be concerned about my feelings, especially since you're paying me so handsomely. I'll thank you to remember that."

Sending Everett the smallest curtsy she could manage, Millie marched her way to the cliff path, determined to put any lingering feelings she might have for the gentleman firmly aside.

12

Resting his hands on his knees, Everett watched Caroline, along with Gertrude and Nora — who'd moved back into Caroline's cottage but was staunchly refusing to ever be Caroline's companion again, paid or not — frolic in the sudsy foam of the ocean. They were laughing and splashing each other, all three ladies garbed in the latest sea attire, which consisted of a black smock that reached past the knees, pants that went all the way to the ankle, and black stockings that covered every single toe. On their heads were black hats with large brims, covered in bows and netting, and Everett couldn't help wonder why ladies would even want to go to the beach, given that they had to feel a little . . . stifled.

"Care to join me in the water?" Dudley asked, pushing up from the blanket next to the one Everett was lounging on.

"I think I'll just sit here."

"Suit yourself," Dudley said, looking completely delighted by Everett's refusal to join him as he set off over the sand, his steps downright jaunty.

Feeling a small stab of annoyance when his friend immediately gravitated to Caroline, Everett pushed the annoyance away when the thought struck him that at least someone was making certain Caroline enjoyed the day. He was obviously not up for that particular task, especially since he was in a foul frame of mind.

Flopping back on the blanket, Everett threw an arm over his eyes as his thoughts began to wander and then turned rather disturbing.

For weeks he'd been *thinking* something was wrong, but now there was no sense denying it any longer — he *knew* something was dreadfully amiss.

Unfortunately, what was amiss had nothing to do with Caroline, their friends, the children, or even Millie. No, what was wrong had everything to do with him, but it was extremely uncomfortable coming to that troubling conclusion.

He was not, as he'd always convinced himself he was, a charming, debonair, and likeable sort. Instead, because he'd purposely distanced himself from Millie and hadn't even bothered to offer her so much as an explanation as to why, he couldn't claim to be charming in the least. He'd also taken to blaming Caroline and their friends for his ill-temper, which meant he certainly wasn't debonair. And quite honestly, *likeable* wasn't a word that described him either.

Better descriptions might be inconsiderate, boorish, and . . . selfish.

Coming to that conclusion was disconcerting, but there was no avoiding the hard truth any longer.

His certain belief in his superiority over everyone except those in his social set had finally succeeded in turning him into a gentleman he was not proud of in the least. He'd somehow been holding Millie responsible for his attraction to her, which was ludicrous. It wasn't as if Millie had been practicing her feminine wiles on him, especially since he was fairly sure she didn't even realize her appeal.

She was sweet, innocent, and had a most charming way about her. She'd been given little to no advantages in life, but instead of turning her bitter, that lack of advantages had given her a strength he envied.

He'd had every advantage in life — had gone to the best schools, visited foreign countries, could purchase anything he wanted on a whim — and yet, he'd taken to brooding quite often of late, unhappy with his lot in life, yet blaming everyone but himself for that unhappiness.

It was unacceptable, the brooding, and he realized he needed to change before he became one of those nasty old men who spent their time grumbling about everything and everyone, and one whom no one wanted to grow old with.

"Everett, be a dear and fetch me my parasol," Caroline called.

Opening his eyes, Everett sat up, reached for Caroline's parasol, and rose to his feet. Making his way across sand that had gotten remarkably hot, he waded into the surf and reached Caroline's side a moment later, earning a frown from Dudley in the process. Handing Caroline the parasol, he smiled when she whipped it over the large hat that was already covering her head and smiled back at him.

"You should stay in the water with us," she said as Gertrude and Nora, who were standing right beside her, nodded in agreement. "You're looking somewhat flushed, and you really shouldn't allow yourself to get too warm."

"That's a wonderful idea," he said before

he drew in a breath and decided there was no time like the present to start making amends. "You look very lovely today, Caroline."

Caroline blinked somewhat owlishly back at him. "That's a charming thing for you to say, Everett. Thank you."

"You're welcome, and . . . may I also say that I've come to the realization that I've been less than pleasant of late, even though I promised you I'd stop being so boorish, so I must now beg your forgiveness once again. I've had a lot on my mind, but that isn't an acceptable reason for not paying you the proper amount of attention."

Caroline blinked again, right as Gertrude, Nora, and Dudley exchanged significant looks before they turned and splashed away from them.

"Are the thoughts that have plagued your mind lately of any great importance?" Caroline asked as she began twirling her parasol around.

"They're a touch troubling, but nothing for you to worry about."

Instead of looking reassured, Caroline's eyes widened before she sloshed closer to him and lowered her voice. "You haven't had a change of heart about the ball, have you?"

"Since Miss Pickenpaugh would have my head if I did, no, of course not."

"I meant about what's to happen at the ball."

Taking a moment to collect his scattered thoughts, Everett considered Caroline, taking in the trace of panic now resting in her eyes, and the heightened color on her cheeks that he knew wasn't from the sun. He'd been with her every afternoon and evening since the peacock disaster, but they hadn't talked about anything of importance. They certainly hadn't talked about what exactly she was expecting of him at the ball. Instead, Caroline had taken to clinging to him quite often when they were with their friends, laughing at almost every little thing he said, even though he now knew he'd been less than amusing of late.

Now that he actually thought about it, her behavior made him realize that he'd been unfair to Caroline. He'd apparently caused her to become insecure in their relationship, but . . . he wasn't exactly sure why she was so determined to continue on with him since he obviously hadn't been treating her very well.

Releasing a breath, he lifted her hand and placed a kiss on her salty fingers. "I think it's past time you and I go somewhere private so that we may speak frankly with each other."

Caroline's eyes widened to the size of small saucers. "About what?"

"About us, the ball, what you expect, and . . . just everything."

"I don't think there's any reason for that, Everett," Caroline said quickly. "You have to know what I expect, what our friends expect, and what society expects at this point. You've made me promises, and I'm going to hold you to those promises."

Everett frowned. "But . . . why do you want to hold me to those promises? Forgive me, but there are times I get the distinct feeling you don't particularly care for me, let alone love me."

"Of course I don't love you, Everett," Caroline whispered furiously. "Love is for those feeble-minded common people — not people like us. But I respect you, respect your position within society, and you and I both know we'll be a force to be reckoned with once we're married."

Everett blinked, not certain how to proceed. "While I truly used to believe that would be enough for us to build a marriage on, I've recently changed my mind," he said slowly. "Marriage is for life, Caroline, and I do think a bit of affection, and even . . .

love, should play a part in the equation."

Caroline snatched back her hand. "You don't love me any more than I love you, but . . ." Her eyes narrowed. "This reluctance on your part doesn't have something to do with that dreadful Miss Longfellow, does it? Because honestly . . . if it does . . . Well, need I remind you . . . she's the nanny?"

"I'm well aware of Millie's status, Caroline, and —"

"You're back to calling her Millie again?" Caroline drew herself up. "It's unacceptable, Everett, this fascination you seem to hold for that woman. Don't think I didn't notice how you stepped in to rescue her when she got stuck in that tree, even though you should have let one of the footmen do it." She shook a finger at him. "I'm a reasonable woman, Everett, and know full well you'll have your little amusements after we're married. I'm perfectly willing to overlook your indiscretions, but I will not tolerate you flaunting them under my nose."

"You'll overlook my indiscretions?"

"Of course, it's what we ladies do, just as I'm sure you'll overlook mine."

His blood began rushing through his veins. "You intend to have indiscretions?"

"Not until after our children are born, of

course, but . . . it's only fair. And I do think, in order for us to have a successful marriage, we should at the very least be honest with each other."

As he stood there, with the surf gently lapping over his feet, Everett had no idea whether he should laugh at the absurdity of the conversation or flee from the woman who was calmly speaking about completely unacceptable ideas — as if those ideas shouldn't surprise Everett in the least.

"What about the vows we're going to take — especially the one regarding being faithful to each other?"

Caroline waved the question away. "No one I know takes their vows seriously, and it's not as if either one of us is overly religious."

Something unpleasant settled on his tongue, something that tasted remarkably like regret. While it was true that he and Caroline had never spoken much about God — even though they did attend church every week when they were in the city — Everett had never realized Caroline held such a jaded view. Even though he was not, as Caroline had put it, overly religious, he was of the firm belief that vows spoken in front of God should be honored at all costs. In fact, ever since he'd become acquainted with Millie, he'd been somewhat fascinated by how easily she prayed, spoke of God, and —

"Both of you need to laugh right now as if I've just told you the most amusing joke," Nora said as she splashed her way up to them. She let out a very credible laugh before she leaned closer and began whispering very rapidly. "If you've neglected to notice, everyone — and I mean everyone — has started edging your way, and . . . they're looking a little rabid."

Looking to the right, and then to the left, Everett discovered that Nora was speaking nothing less than the truth. Everyone at Bailey's Beach seemed to be moving his way — people who'd been bobbing in deeper depths were bobbing closer, people who'd been milling in the shallow surf were now milling in his direction, and people who'd been sunning themselves on the sand had apparently decided to take this particular moment to cool off. Turning back to Caroline, he offered her his arm, which she completely ignored. She gave him a cool smile, right before she turned her back on him.

"Dudley, be a dear and see me home, will you? I find I'm suddenly not feeling very well," she called before she started wading

Dudley's way. She apparently had no qualms about taking the arm Dudley offered her and then flounced out of the water without a single glance his way.

"That wasn't exactly what I had in mind when I interrupted your argument," Nora muttered. "And it certainly didn't put a stop to all the speculation spreading over Bailey's Beach."

Taking Nora's arm, Everett helped her out of the water, but as soon as they reached the beach, he realized that Caroline and Dudley were gone.

"Will you go after her?" Nora asked quietly.

"Do you think I should?"

Nora considered him for a long moment. "No, but I do think you should take some time to really think matters over before you make the biggest mistake of your life." With that, Nora sent him a rather sad smile before she headed back into the water, leaving him with only confusing thoughts for company, and everyone still sending speculative glances his way.

13

Millie was quickly coming to the conclusion that being tethered to a rope while trying to dodge waves that seemed intent on drowning her was probably not the best way to go about the tricky business of learning how to swim.

Pushing sopping strands of hair out of her eyes, she watched as Lucetta swam gracefully toward her, her body rising fluidly over a swell, before she dove under the water, surfacing a second later right in front of Millie.

"You just have to keep your feet kicking at all times, and then move your arms in a clockwise motion, turning your head every now and again to get a breath of air," Lucetta said.

"Every time I turn my head to breathe, I get a mouthful of salty water. Honestly, the last time I tried the whole breathing thing, I swear a small fish darted into my mouth."

"You love fish."

"Well, yes, when it's grilled, baked, or fried, but not when it's still swimming."

"I don't think you're kicking your feet enough," Elizabeth said as she waded away from the bathing machine, a *machine* that had turned out to be little more than a shack on wheels, and a very weathered, gray-looking shack at that.

"And you're not moving your arms right," Thaddeus called from his perch on the steps of the bathing machine, Rose nodding in agreement from right beside him. He held out an apple that already had bite marks in it. "Want a piece of apple? I bet it tastes better than that fish you just swallowed."

"I didn't swallow the fish," Millie said before she grinned and shook her head. "And I didn't know the two of you snuck food into the bathing machine."

"It's not much of a machine, Miss Millie. It's just a big box on wheels and doesn't even have a motor, which was a little disappointing to find out," Rose said. "I was hoping we could drive the machine around the beach, like a boat, but . . . the peacocks sure do seem to find it a good place to roost."

Millie grabbed hold of the rope that kept her attached to the bathing machine and pulled herself right up next to it. Getting a grip on the wooden railing she'd been told was to help timid bathers lower themselves into the water, she heaved herself up and then moved through the narrow doorway. Her gaze swept over three peacocks that were sitting calmly on the benches that lined the little room, one of them actually sleeping. Turning, she arched a brow at Rose. "How in the world did you get those in here without me seeing you do it?"

"They've been here the whole time, but were hiding, er, I mean resting, underneath our towels." Rose blinked far-too-adorable eyes Millie's way. "And I only brought three of them, just the ones that seemed the saddest about leaving Uncle Everett's house."

"The peacocks staying at Abigail's is only temporary," Millie reminded her. "Just until after the ball."

Rose shook her head. "I don't think Miss Dixon's going to let them come back, not when she finds out Miss Abigail agreed to take them in."

"Abigail only agreed to take them for a few days, mostly because poor Miss Pickenpaugh was having a nervous episode when she heard the peacocks screeching. In Miss Pickenpaugh's opinion, that screeching was certain to ruin the ball, and quite honestly, she might have had a very valid point."

"That poor woman needs to search out a different profession, or else she's going to find herself committed to an asylum," Lucetta said, tripping over the numerous lengths of rope lying about, one of which was still wrapped around Millie's middle. Giving the ropes a glare, she lifted her head and sent Rose a smile. "It was very brave of you, though, darling, to agree to allow the peacocks to stay at Abigail's."

"I think her bravery might have had something to do with the promise of a puppy, or . . . three," Millie added.

"Did someone just mention something about puppies?"

Pushing curls yet again out of her eyes, Millie looked to the doorway and found Everett peering in, the striped bathing shirt he was wearing plastered to his chest, the sight of that chest causing her mouth to go just a little dry. "What are you doing here?" was the first thing she could think of to say, although what she really wanted to tell him was to swim right back to shore and leave her alone.

Everett hefted himself out of the water and sat down on the step beside Thaddeus and Rose, squishing the two children together in the process. "I'd had enough of Bailey's Beach for the day, so thought I'd stop by and see how this bathing machine experiment was working out for everyone."

"You and Caroline had a fight, didn't you," Lucetta said.

Everett frowned. "Why would you assume that?"

Shrugging, Lucetta grabbed a towel off a bench and wiped her face. "I'm intuitive. And I'm going to hazard a guess and say the reason the two of you got into an argument was because you were foolish enough to tell her that I've come to Newport for the rest of the summer."

"Your name didn't come up at all today."

For some odd reason, Lucetta laughed. "How delightful. Although . . . well, now I'm a tad stymied — which means *bewildered*, Millie, if you didn't know — about why you and Caroline argued." She set aside the towel, lifted a bare foot up on the bench, and began wringing water out of a pant leg.

"Did my footman, Davis, make those pants for you?" Everett asked slowly.

Lucetta continued wringing out her pants. "Of course, and he made the pants Millie's wearing as well."

Millie suddenly found herself the recipient of Everett's attention, attention that seemed to be lingering on her . . . limbs. To her relief, Lucetta regained his notice when she began speaking again.

"I just have to add that Davis is one of the most charming footmen I've ever had the pleasure of meeting. Do you know that, even though he admitted he can't swim a lick, he's sitting out on the beach, keeping an eye on us?" She dropped her foot and smiled. "Bless his heart, I don't know how much help he'd be if one of us did start to drown, but it's very considerate of him to want to try."

"Yes, bless Davis's all-too-charming heart," Everett mumbled. "But . . . what happened to Abigail and my mother?"

"They're taking a stroll with Reverend Gilmore," Elizabeth said as she climbed over Thaddeus and crawled her way into the bathing machine. "Grandmother Dorothy got a little emotional right after I called her *Grandmother* for the first time, so Miss Abigail thought it would be a good idea for them to go on a walk with Reverend Gilmore in order to allow Grandmother Dorothy time to collect herself."

"You're calling my mother Grandmother Dorothy now?"

Looking up from the rope she'd been trying to get untied from her waist, Elizabeth smiled. "It seemed a little silly to keep calling her Mrs. Mulberry."

"That was very thoughtful of you, Elizabeth."

"Thank you, Uncle Everett, and I hope you'll remember how thoughtful I can be when you hear about the . . . puppies."

Everett immediately arched a brow Millie's way, but before she could summon up a suitable explanation, Thaddeus stood up on the step he'd been sitting on and turned eyes that were rather wide and filled with hope on Everett.

"Miss Lucetta brought three puppies with her all the way from New York, but they're up in Miss Abigail's cottage sleeping right now because they were exhausted from the boat ride." He gulped in a big breath of air. "She said two of them are girls, and one's a boy, and . . . we can keep them if you're still keen to get a dog."

"I'm pretty sure I mentioned one dog, Thaddeus, not three."

"But the two sister puppies will be awful sad if we take their brother away." Thaddeus's lower lip began to tremble.

Reaching out, Everett ruffled Thaddeus's hair, right before he turned accusing eyes on Lucetta. "You just *happened* to bring three puppies with you to Newport?"

Lucetta wagged a finger Everett's way.

"Now, now, there's no need to sound so suspicious, Everett. If you must know, I only acquired the puppies yesterday, and couldn't very well leave them behind."

"They're Buford's," Millie added.

Everett blinked. "Oliver's dog?"

Millie nodded. "Buford apparently took up with a lady friend, and that lady friend's owners weren't exactly happy about it."

"How do they know for sure Buford was responsible, for . . . well . . . you know?" Everett asked.

"When you see the puppies, you'll have no doubts," Lucetta said. "Their paws are like dinner plates, and they're only a few months old. Plus, they're a little . . . motley looking."

"But how did you end up with them?"

"Oliver's butler, Mr. Blodgett, brought them around to me." Lucetta pushed a strand of hair out of her eyes. "He was getting ready to go on holiday, and since Oliver hasn't returned from England yet, he knew the pups might come to a bad end if he didn't take them. But, again, he was going out of the city, so he moseyed on over to Abigail's and left them with me, since he remembered how well Buford took to me."

"I really think we should take all three of them, Uncle Everett," Thaddeus said earnestly. "Even though we'll be outnumbered again since two of them are girls."

"I suppose we really can't separate them if they're siblings, now, can we," Everett said slowly before he gave a rather resigned shake of his head. "Puppies can be a lot of work though."

A chorus of how happy they'd be to work hard with the puppies immediately commenced, and before Millie could step in and save Everett from certain mayhem, he was nodding his head and smiling.

"Very well, we can take them, but . . . this is it now. I don't want to see any other creatures being brought home."

Squeals of delight sounded around the bathing machine, and then Everett eased off the steps and back into the ocean. "Anyone want to go for a swim with me?"

"Can I swim without this rope?" Elizabeth asked.

"Certainly, but let me help you, since it seems to be knotted well."

Millie watched as Everett got Elizabeth untied and then held out his arms, which Elizabeth immediately jumped into. The young girl's laughter rang out again and again as she and Everett dove through the waves, going deeper into the ocean than

Millie would have dared.

"I know you're incredibly annoyed with the gentleman, Millie," Lucetta said quietly. "But I can't help but like him."

"He's still a snob."

"He's changing, and I think he just hasn't discovered exactly who he is yet. You can't really blame him for that though, given the lifestyle he leads and the people he surrounds himself with."

"He'll always be surrounded by those people, especially since it seems he and Caroline are planning on making a special announcement at the ball, which is only three days from now."

"There's still plenty of time for him to come to his senses about that."

Sending Lucetta what she hoped was a look of disbelief, Millie turned her attention back to Elizabeth, watching the young girl enjoy time with Everett. When Elizabeth apparently got tired, she and Everett swam for shore, Everett slowing his strokes toward the end so that Elizabeth made it to shore first.

"I beat you!" Elizabeth shouted.

Shading her eyes with her hand against the glare of the sun, Millie saw Abigail, Reverend Gilmore, and Dorothy hurrying over to meet Elizabeth, Dorothy draping a towel around Elizabeth's shoulders.

"He let her win," Lucetta whispered in Millie's ear. "Very considerate of him, don't you think?"

Pretending she hadn't heard Lucetta, Millie sat down beside a peacock, keeping an eye on Thaddeus and Rose, who both seemed content to sit on the steps of the bathing machine for the moment. Drawing in a deep breath, she tried to find a sense of peace, but all hope of finding that disappeared when Everett swam back up to them.

"Who wants to go out with me next?"

With Millie's help, Thaddeus was out of his rope and into Everett's arms in no time at all. With a shout of laughter, Everett carried him away, dipping Thaddeus into the waves and then sweeping him up into the air as Thaddeus shrieked in clear delight.

Turning away from Everett because the mere sight of him kept making her forget she'd vowed to loathe the man forever, Millie smiled at Rose. "Should we get you out of your rope so you can swim after your brother's done?"

Rose yawned. "I'm really sleepy, Miss Millie. Could I go back to shore?"

"I'll take her," Lucetta offered, helping Rose out of her tether and then wading back to shore with the little girl securely held in her arms a moment later.

Having nothing else to do, Millie sat down on the steps of the bathing machine, her attention, to her dismay, returning again and again to Everett. Pretending an interest in a bird that was flying overhead when Everett finally carried Thaddeus back her way, she found herself hoping he'd think the color she knew was now staining her cheeks was a direct result of being out in the sun.

"Where'd Rose go?" he asked. "I thought I'd take her out next."

"She got tired."

Everett tilted his head. "I never thought I'd see that day come, but . . . I guess it's your turn then. I'll be right back after I get Thaddeus to shore."

Without bothering to see if she was in agreement with what could only be considered a deranged idea, Everett headed for shore. She stared after him for a good, long moment, before she realized he would be coming back. Grabbing hold of the rope that was still firmly tied around her middle, she tried to get undone, but her fingers suddenly seemed to turn into all thumbs. Before she could get the knot untied, Everett was standing right in front of her.

"Don't tell me the master of knot tying

and untying is having difficulties," he said with a grin.

She didn't like it when he grinned. Not one . . . little . . . bit. He was far too handsome, his eyes took to twinkling in a very intriguing way, and . . .

"I'm not having difficulties," she finally said. "I just didn't realize the water would make this so tricky."

"Allow me to help you with that."

The second Everett took hold of the rope that was wrapped around her middle and pulled her closer to him, all thoughts of loathing the man disappeared, immediately replaced with a shock of something that Millie could only liken to what the theater's faulty electric lights must have felt like right before they exploded. Given that Everett snatched his hand back only a second later, she got the distinct impression he might have felt exactly the same shock.

"Maybe you should do it," he said before he took a step away from her.

"You don't have to stay here with me." Her hands fumbled against the knot, until finally, with a breath of relief, she got herself free.

"I'm going to teach you how to swim."

Whatever she'd been expecting him to say, that had not been it.

"Lucetta did a fair job of that, so there's really no need."

"You couldn't have learned very well while tethered to a rope."

With shoulders drooping just a bit, Millie met Everett's gaze. "Why is it so important to you that you teach me how to swim? I am, as you've pointed out numerous times, only the nanny. Are you afraid that I really will end up letting one of the children drown?"

For a second, she didn't think he was going to answer her, but then he reached out and took her hand in his. Even though another disturbing bolt of something shot up her arm, she didn't seem to have the will to pull her hand from his.

"You would never put the children in harm's way, and no, that's not why I want to teach you to swim."

"Then I must admit I'm a little confused. You've been avoiding me like the plague this past week or so, but now . . . you want to spend your precious time teaching me how to swim? Don't you have some tea or croquet game on that schedule Caroline made for you that demands your attention?"

Everett blew out a breath. "Keeping to my schedule is not really that important to me at the moment, but what is important is setting matters right with you. I cannot apologize enough over how I've treated you this past week. My actions have been reprehensible, and you must know that nothing you did brought about my surly attitude."

"I thought perhaps you'd gotten disgusted with me because I got stuck up in that tree."

"What?"

"I wasn't very brave."

Everett considered her for a long moment. "You're not serious, are you?"

"I'm also scared to go out into the ocean without the rope around me."

"Why didn't you tell me that before you took it off?"

"I didn't want you to lose what little respect you might have left for me."

He moved closer to her, so close she could feel the heat from his body. "Honestly, Millie, you're being completely ridiculous at the moment. Why you would feel I've lost respect for you is beyond confusing, especially since I believe you're one of the most accomplished women I've ever met."

"I'm hardly accomplished, since I've had little to no formal education."

"I would have to disagree with that," Everett said softly. "You've managed to survive a childhood set in the meanest of

331

slums when the odds were certainly never in your favor. Then, you carved out a living by embracing your love of children. I have to imagine many of those children benefited tremendously from having you in their little lives, even if you didn't always remain employed in their households for long." He smiled. "Truth be told, I find you to be quite extraordinary."

With knees that had turned distinctly wobbly, Millie found she could only stand there, in the cramped confines of the bathing machine, with her heart beating so hard it felt as if it was going to pound right out of her chest.

"What's wrong with you?" she finally whispered.

"I have no idea, but before you truly begin to question my sanity, and before I do something I know I really shouldn't, let me teach you how to swim. It's the least I can do to make up for my churlish behavior of late, and I believe you'll enjoy not being afraid of the water."

"What's the something you know you really shouldn't do?" She couldn't resist asking even as Everett tugged her through the door and then lifted her up and . . . dropped her right into the water.

Sputtering as water shot up her nose, she

found her feet but didn't have a second to question him further because he hauled her close to him, smiled, and . . . flipped her on her stomach, the surprise of that sending more water up her nose.

"I thought you were supposed to be trying to teach me how to *keep* from drowning," she finally rasped when she caught her breath.

"The first thing I'd like you to do is show me how good you are at floating."

"I can't very well float when I've sucked down so much of the sea."

She felt Everett's hands underneath her stomach as he held her up, and not particularly caring for the sensations that was causing, she set about the daunting business of learning to float properly.

Five minutes later, after much prodding and insults from Everett, she was floating on her own. Five minutes after that she was managing a clumsy stroke and was completely delighted about it.

"I did it," she said, paddling her way over to Everett, who was beaming back at her.

"You're doing a great job, Miss Millie."

She wasn't certain, but she thought Everett let out a grunt right as Davis, her favorite footman, waded up to join them. She smiled at the man, until an incredibly disturbing thought hit her. "Good heavens, Davis, what in the world are you doing out here? You can't swim."

"It's not too deep quite yet, Miss Millie, but the tide is coming in and Mrs. Hart sent me out here since she didn't think you'd noticed. Johnson is bringing the horse around, and we're going to tow the bathing machine back to shore."

Millie turned back to Everett. "Since you were kind enough to teach me how to swim, I'm now going to swim to shore."

"And since I do believe you're doing remarkably well with that swimming, I'm going to let you swim back to shore on your own, but . . . only because it's shallow and you can touch."

"You're not coming with me?"

"I'm going to send Davis back with you, since he can't swim and the tide is coming in." Everett nodded to his footman. "I'll help Johnson get the bathing machine hitched up, but . . . I do think it might be a good idea, going forward, for everyone on staff who doesn't know how to swim to learn. I'll look into hiring an instructor after the ball."

Millie found herself smiling at Everett, seemingly unable to help herself. "You're acting rather oddly today. You do realize that, don't you?"

Everett's response to that was a grin, before he waved her away, waved Davis away as well, and then began wading toward the bathing machine.

Swimming somewhat clumsily to shore, she finally reached the spot where small waves were breaking, and accepted the hand Davis held out to her. Before she could take so much as a single step onto the beach though, she looked up and found Elizabeth running across the sand, and then the young girl threw herself into the ocean.

"Daddy!" Elizabeth screamed as she began swimming right out to sea.

Millie caught a glimpse of a yacht sailing past before she saw Everett take off after Elizabeth, his strong arms cleaving through the water so fast they were a blur. He caught up to Elizabeth in no time, but then, once he grabbed hold of her, she began fighting him, kicking and screaming as she tried to get away, even as he hauled her back to shore.

"Let me go, let me go. Daddy's come back for us."

Not relinquishing his hold, even though Elizabeth had taken to sinking her teeth into his bare arm, Everett finally reached Millie and sent her a look that had despair written all over it. Stumbling out of the surf with Millie keeping pace right beside him, Everett moved up on the beach, then sank down on it, still holding Elizabeth, who was now sobbing in his arms.

"You have to . . . let me go. You have to. It's my daddy," Elizabeth got out between sobbing breaths. "I've been good. I've been so good lately . . . not getting into any trouble, and being friendly and all. I've been . . . praying . . . all the time . . . and I know God finally heard me. He saw I was being good. And because of that . . . God's sending Daddy and Mommy . . . back to us."

"Shh, darling, *shh,"* Everett whispered as he began rocking Elizabeth back and forth. "It's not your daddy, honey. It's not."

"It's his boat. He . . . always flew that bright . . . pink flag. Mommy made it for him, and it has my handprints on it — Thaddeus's and Rose's too. It's really big, so we'd always be able to tell which boat Daddy's was." Elizabeth lifted her head and struggled to get an arm out from underneath Everett's. "Look, you can still see it. You have to let me go. I have to get to my daddy."

Millie heard Abigail let out what sounded like a sob, and when she looked that way, she found Abigail standing beside Lucetta, who was holding a crying Thaddeus in her arms, while Dorothy was standing on the other side of Lucetta, cradling a crying Rose. Turning back to Everett with tears now falling freely down her cheeks, Millie swallowed past the large lump in her throat and moved forward.

"You can give her to me, Everett," she said softly, but Everett didn't move. Instead he kept rocking Elizabeth, whispering something in her ear, something Elizabeth obviously didn't want to hear.

"They're not gone. I told you. I promised God I'd be good, and I have been good, so He's sent them back to me, I know He has. That's my daddy's boat."

Everett lifted his head. "It might be your daddy's boat, darling, but your daddy isn't on board. He's not coming back, sweetheart, even though you and I really wish he could."

Elizabeth tipped back her head and stared at Everett for what seemed like an eternity before she began to sob, harder than before, and buried her head against Everett's shoulder. No one spoke as the child sobbed as if her heart were breaking in two, but then, after quite a few minutes had passed, Reverend Gilmore stepped forward.

"Give the child to me, Everett."

Everett looked up, the despair on his face evident, and shook his head. "She needs me now."

"She needs you always, but I think right now you need to give her to me so that you can go after that boat."

Elizabeth stilled and moved just a little away from Everett, although her hand was still gripping his arm. "You'll find out who that is riding in my daddy's yacht?"

"I will, but not until I'm sure you're ready for me to let you go."

Elizabeth drew in a shuddering breath. "I'm ready."

Everett helped her to her feet, and then, reluctantly it seemed, he led her to Reverend Gilmore, who took Elizabeth's hand in his as he leaned down and wiped the tears from her face, smiling rather sadly at her.

"I think you and I should go for a stroll, my precious child."

"Are you going to tell me why God took my parents away and won't bring them back?"

Millie raised a hand to cover the sob she'd almost let escape.

Reverend Gilmore shook his head. "I don't have all the answers, Elizabeth, but I promise you this — I'll explain God and His loving ways, and where I believe your parents are, and maybe then you'll find some peace."

Elizabeth stared at him for a long moment, but then she nodded. Turning, Reverend Gilmore led her down the beach, his soothing voice trailing behind him.

Abigail turned and took Thaddeus out of Lucetta's arms. "I think you and I, Dorothy, should take Thaddeus and Rose up to the cottage," She nodded at Everett. "You did well, Everett, very well . . . and . . ." Abigail stopped speaking as her voice cracked, her eyes filled with tears, and with a nod to Dorothy, the two ladies turned and began walking away.

Millie moved closer to Everett and took his hand in hers. "Abigail was right. You did well with Elizabeth."

Everett locked anguish-filled eyes with hers. "I never realized until just now . . . how much those children have lost." He brushed tears that had fallen out of his eyes away with his free hand. "I never truly mourned my friend, never thought about how his death really affected his children. Why were they taken? Fred and Violet were good people, good parents, and . . . those children didn't deserve to lose them."

"They have you," Millie whispered.

"I'm not good enough to raise them."

"You will be," Lucetta said, stepping up to join them with eyes that were rimmed with red. "Don't sell yourself short, Everett. You're much more than you think you are, but right now . . . you have a yacht to find."

Everett squeezed Millie's hand. "I hate to ask this of you, but would you consider coming with me? I have no idea what I'm going to find, and you have an amazing ability of keeping your head under disastrous situations, even when mad peacocks are running amok, and . . ."

"You don't need an explanation for why you want me to come with you, Everett," Millie interrupted. "I would have insisted on doing just that if you hadn't invited me."

He smiled just a ghost of a smile and nodded to Lucetta. "You'll come as well?"

"This really isn't one of those moments where you have to be polite, Everett," Lucetta said. "I wouldn't have been offended if you hadn't invited me."

Everett's ghost of a smile turned into a genuine one. "I wasn't asking you to be polite, Lucetta. I don't know if Millie ever mentioned this to you, but she has suspicions about Fred's death — something I really should have taken more seriously — and . . . you've been known to addle gentlemen's minds when you simply step into a room. That might just come in handy today if the person riding on Fred's yacht turns out to be a little questionable and . . . a man."

"Be still my beating heart," Lucetta said, raising a hand to dash a stray tear off her cheek before she smiled. "I hope you won't take this the wrong way, Everett, but I actually like you — not that I'm exactly sure why."

"He doesn't get addled in your presence," Millie pointed out.

"Hmm . . . You're right, he doesn't," Lucetta said as her lips curled and she nodded to Everett. "That's exactly why I like you, and I do thank you for that. Although, let us hope, if we do run a scoundrel to ground today, he won't be immune to having his wits addled by me." She stepped closer and took Millie's other hand in hers. "Shall we get out of these wet clothes and then be on our way?"

Squaring her shoulders, Millie squeezed Lucetta's hand, and then, with Everett still keeping a firm grip of her other hand, they turned as one and headed for Abigail's cottage.

14

Less than thirty minutes later, Everett drove his buggy toward the harbor, still shaken by what had happened with Elizabeth.

Her despair had been soul deep, and he'd longed to stay with her to offer whatever comfort he could, but Reverend Gilmore had been right — he needed to track down the person sailing Fred's yacht.

He should not have disregarded Millie's suspicions so easily.

Something *was* definitely amiss, and it was past time he discovered what that something was.

"If you would stop wiggling, I'd be able to get you buttoned properly."

Glancing out of the corner of his eye, he found Lucetta struggling to get Millie buttoned into her gown. Both ladies had barely taken any time at all to throw off their bathing attire and don dresses before they'd jumped into his buggy. When he'd voiced his amazement about how quickly they'd been able to leave Abigail's cottage and get on their way, they'd proclaimed, somewhat indignantly, that it was not exactly the moment to primp.

Caroline and her friends wouldn't have stepped so much as a toe out of their homes unless they were coiffed to perfection. But there was something charming about barreling down the road with ladies missing stockings and shoes, although he was a little ashamed of himself for sneaking a bit of a peek when Millie had rolled stockings up her legs.

It wasn't well done of him, that peeking, but . . . he was only human after all, and . . . she had lovely legs. Although, it wasn't well done of him, either, to be looking at any legs other than Caroline's, not that he'd actually seen Caroline roll stockings up her legs. But since Caroline had disclosed such disturbing notions only hours before, he couldn't help wonder why he hadn't ended their alliance right then and there, which would have made his —

"Scoot closer to Everett. I don't have enough room to work," Lucetta said.

"I'm practically sitting on the poor man's lap as it is," Millie countered, although she did scoot another inch in his direction, that scooting leaving him with a strong desire to throw himself off the buggy seat because her knee was now firmly pressed against his leg.

Resignation settled in as he realized there was no longer any denying the fact, whether appropriate or not, he was attracted to Millie.

When he'd first touched her in the bathing machine, a shock of something sweet had coursed through him, that sweetness almost causing him to lose all good sense and . . . kiss her.

That he hadn't given in to that concerning urge was a miracle. But, instead of immediately diving back into the sea and putting as much distance between them as possible, he'd proceeded to torture himself further by teaching her to swim.

Every time he'd touched her after that had been somewhat agonizing, but he hadn't stopped, unwilling, or perhaps unable, to resist being in her company . . . to resist having an excuse to touch her.

His behavior was completely irrational, but he just couldn't seem to help himself. And it wasn't as if he was only physically attracted to her, now that he considered the matter. She made him laugh and want to strangle her at times, but she also had an incredibly kind heart, and —

"If all of my sensible clothes hadn't gone missing, or if Mrs. O'Connor hadn't conveniently shredded my last skirt and blouse in that wringer — something I'm still not convinced was an accident — it wouldn't be so difficult getting dressed," Millie grumbled as she suddenly stuck a hand on his leg when the buggy ran over a rut in the road. Immediately snatching her hand back, she blew out a breath. "I do beg your pardon, Everett."

"Think nothing of it," he managed to respond in a voice that sounded a little high-pitched.

"There," Lucetta proclaimed. "You're completely buttoned. Now all we have to do is fix your hair, and you'll be perfect."

"I don't know how you're intending to fix my hair, especially since it's still soaking wet, and . . . stiff with sea salt."

"I'm an actress. Fixing appearances is my specialty." Lucetta looked a little smug as she adjusted the large hat she'd plopped over her head. "My hair is salt-soaked as well, but no one will notice since I've arranged my hat just so, lending me a rather mysterious air."

"You could plop a bowl of fruit on your head and you'd still look mysterious," Millie said. "I wish I had one of my caps handy. That would solve my hair crisis nicely."

Everett caught Millie's eye. "I never liked your caps."

"They're practical."

"And ugly," Lucetta added, smiling over Millie's head at him. She pulled a hat from behind her on the seat that was a little squished, and stuck it on Millie's head, pulling a pin out of the bodice of her dress and sticking it through the hat. "There — you're adorable."

"I doubt that, but it's not as if I'm overly concerned about my looks at the moment." Millie turned front and center again, shifting just a bit in an obvious attempt to get comfortable. Her shifting had Everett fervently wishing he'd thought to ask Abigail for the use of her carriage. A carriage would have afforded the ladies an appropriate place to change while also —

"Is that the harbor up ahead?" Millie asked, drawing Everett from his thoughts.

Looking to where Millie was staring, Everett nodded. "It is . . . and . . ." He squinted against the glare of the sun. "There's the yacht with the pink flag."

Steering the buggy through the wagons and people milling around the harbor, Everett brought them to a stop in front of a hitching post. After securing the horse, he turned to help Millie and Lucetta down from the seat but found them already on the ground.

"I could have helped you," he said, moving up to them and extending Millie, then Lucetta, an arm.

"As Lucetta mentioned before, this isn't exactly the time to be worried about proper manners," Millie said, taking the offered arm. "Besides, since we are at the docks — even though we're in Newport — Lucetta and I need to look like we can take care of ourselves, which means we need to look intimidating."

"You couldn't look intimidating if you were sporting a rifle and held a knife between your teeth."

"I'm sure I would look intimidating under those circumstances."

Everett's lips twitched. "Well, since I don't *have* a rifle or a knife, we'll just have to hope that all these men milling about the docks find *me* intimidating."

"I can look intimidating," Lucetta said as she took his offered arm, right before she drew in a deep breath, closed her eyes, and when she opened her eyes again, she looked . . . different. Gone was the quirky woman with the ready grin and sharp wit, replaced with a lady who was aloof, mysterious, and . . . a little scary.

"How do you do that?" he asked.

"Don't ruin the mood" was all Lucetta said before she sent Millie the smallest of winks and started forward, leaving Everett no option but to keep pace with her, since both ladies were holding his arms.

An eerie silence settled around them as they walked, brought about no doubt by the presence of Millie and Lucetta at the docks. Men stopped moving and gawked their way, but Lucetta, Everett noticed, didn't appear to notice them. Millie, on the other hand, was swiveling her head from side to side, taking in everything as her moss-green eyes sparkled with curiosity.

"It's fascinating down here, all the different types of people, and . . . look, the yacht with the pink flag has a name." Millie stopped, which had Everett and Lucetta stopping as well. "*Adoring Violet* — what a charming name for a boat."

As Everett focused on the words *Adoring Violet* painted in black, he suddenly found it difficult to breathe. "Elizabeth was right," he finally said. "This is Fred's yacht, named after his wife."

Lucetta took a step forward. "He must have loved her very much. I know it's little consolation, but at least they're still together."

"Without their children," Everett added.

Millie squeezed his arm. "Their children have you."

"I'm rapidly coming to the conclusion I'm not worthy to have been given that honor."

Lucetta swatted him with her hand. "Don't be so melodramatic, Everett. Fred obviously chose you for a reason, which means you're worthy. The children adore you now, and maybe someday you'll figure out exactly why Fred and his Violet wanted you to have them."

"Now probably isn't that time though, since someone's getting off the yacht," Millie said with a jerk of her head back to the yacht.

"I need the two of you to wait here." Ignoring the mumbles of protest that statement caused, Everett strode forward without the ladies, making his way directly for the man who'd just gotten off the *Adoring Violet*. "I wonder if I might have a moment of your time, sir," he said as the man drew even with him. "Could you tell me who the owner of the *Adoring Violet* is, and if that owner happens to still be on board?"

"I'm afraid I'm not at liberty to disclose that information."

"Why not?"

"It's a matter of privacy, sir, now . . . if you'll excuse me." The man brushed past Everett, but before Everett could go after him, Lucetta stepped forward. She was no longer the aloof and somewhat mysterious Lucetta. Instead, she was smiling brightly at the man, obviously having decided that her skill at playing the coquette would serve her well at this particular moment.

"Forgive me, sir, but I wondered if you might be able to lend me just the smallest amount of assistance?" Lucetta actually fluttered her lashes at the man, which immediately had him stumbling before he headed straight for her.

"I would be happy to help you, Miss . . . ?"

"Plum. I'm Miss Lucetta Plum."

"Are you really? As in . . . the actress?"

Everett shot a glance to Millie and found her rolling her eyes right before she turned around and seemed to take a great interest in her surroundings.

"The last time I checked, I was, indeed, Lucetta Plum," Lucetta said with a hint of what sounded exactly like exasperation in her tone. "But tell me, what is your name, sir?"

"I'm Captain . . ." The man's voice cracked. He cleared his throat, then continued in a very deep, very masculine voice. "Captain Jonathon Jarvis, Miss Plum, at your service."

"Lovely to meet you, Captain Jarvis, but getting back to that assistance. My friends and I spotted the *Adoring Violet* as it sailed past the cottage I'm visiting. We, or rather Mr. Everett Mulberry, the man standing behind you, knew Fred Burkhart, you see, so . . . we're a little curious as to why his yacht is in Newport, given that Fred, well . . ."

Captain Jarvis spun around and set his sights on Everett. "You're Mr. Everett Mulberry?"

"I am."

Striding over to stand in front of Everett, Captain Jarvis inclined his head. "Begging your pardon, Mr. Mulberry, I had no idea who you were, and . . . may I just say that I'm very sorry about the loss of Fred and his wife."

"Thank you," Everett returned. "Because you're aware of Fred's passing, you must understand why I'm curious about the passengers aboard Fred's yacht."

"Since you're actually the reason we've come to Newport, Mr. Mulberry, I feel no hesitation whatsoever in telling you I've been sailing Mr. Duncan Victor and his

351

wife, Florence, around the world these past several months." Captain Jarvis shook his head. "We, myself and the Victors, were quite distressed to learn of Mr. and Mrs. Burkhart's untimely demise when we made port in Boston a few days ago."

Everett frowned. "May I inquire as to why Mr. Victor was sailing around the world on Fred's yacht?"

"There's no mystery to that, Mr. Mulberry. Mr. Burkhart sent Mr. Victor off to meet with a variety of inventors, all of whom were trying to solicit funds from Mr. Burkhart, and Mr. Victor as well, for their inventions."

The hair on the back of Everett's neck stood up. "And . . . was this a normal occurrence, Fred sending his attorney off to peruse new inventions?"

Captain Jarvis shook his head. "I'd never taken Mr. Victor before, sir, but it's my understanding that Mr. Burkhart had obligations at home which demanded his attention, thus the reasoning behind sending Mr. Victor in his stead."

"And . . . where would I find Mr. Victor at the moment?"

"He and Mrs. Victor were going to dine at a place called the Newport Casino, but then I do believe they're planning on seeking you out at Seaview Cottage." Captain Jarvis smiled. "We got the directions for your cottage when we stopped at your house on Fifth Avenue before learning you were in Newport. I have to imagine Mr. and Mrs. Victor will show up at Seaview in an hour or two."

Everett inclined his head. "Thank you, Captain Jarvis. You've been most helpful."

Captain Jarvis inclined his head in return. "If I may say so yet again, Mr. Mulberry, I truly was sorry to learn about Mr. Burkhart. He was a good man, and if you don't mind my asking, do you happen to know much about how he died?"

"He and Violet were in a buggy accident, but . . . didn't Mr. Victor tell you that?"

"I'm afraid Mr. Victor doesn't know many details surrounding Mr. Burkhart's death, which is one of the reasons he's here to speak with you."

"I wonder what the other reasons are," Millie said as she appeared by his side, obviously not content to stay put for long.

"I'll be certain to ask Mr. Victor just that question once we track him down." Taking her arm, he began walking back toward Lucetta.

"It was very nice meeting you, Miss Plum," Captain Jarvis called after them. "I'll be sure to look in on you the next time I'm at the theater."

Everett felt the tension in Lucetta's arm when he took hold of it, and didn't miss the temper that clouded her eyes for the briefest of seconds before it disappeared. "I know that took a lot on your part, flirting with him like that, and do know that I appreciate it, Lucetta. Would it make you feel better if I offered to buy you a new frock . . . or hat . . . or whatever else you may desire?"

"I'm really not keen about the whole paying me for favors given, Everett," Lucetta drawled. "But, if I ever truly need your help . . ."

"I'll be there, no questions asked."

Lucetta smiled, and this time it was a genuine one. "I'll keep that in mind. And thank you for realizing I don't like to flirt."

"Lucetta's a little sensitive about people drooling over her all the time because of her looks," Millie said. "But it was very well done of you to realize she doesn't care for flirting, Everett." She patted his arm. "Very well done indeed."

With his arm feeling rather warm where she'd patted him, and his heart feeling rather warm from her compliment, Everett reached the buggy and helped Millie into her seat before doing the same with Lucetta.

Untying the reins, he climbed up on the seat and urged the horse into motion, steering it back on the road and toward the Newport Casino.

Silence settled over the buggy, broken only by the clip-clop of the horse's hooves, and before he realized it, the Casino loomed into view.

Millie let out a sigh. "I'm really not looking forward to going back in there again."

"Why not?" Lucetta asked.

"Did I forget to mention to you that I played a little tennis here the first day we arrived in Newport, and . . . it didn't exactly go well?"

"You played tennis . . . at the Newport Casino?"

"I did."

"With Everett, I hope?"

"No, with Caroline and her friends, Gertrude and Nora. And I have to say, Nora Niesen is really rather lovely."

"You played with ladies?"

"I'm not saying it was the brightest thing I've ever done, but . . . Caroline annoyed me."

Lucetta caught Everett's eye. "If you haven't figured this out, Millie's really competitive, and you shouldn't — as in ever — encourage her to play anything against

355

ladies, unless it's . . . cards . . . or knitting."

"I don't think you can play at knitting," Millie said. "Besides, I don't know how to knit."

Grinning as he pulled the buggy to a stop, Everett handed the reins to the member of the Newport Casino staff who'd come running up to them. Climbing down, he turned and offered a hand to Millie, then to Lucetta, his grin widening when neither lady balked at having him assist them out of the buggy.

"We do know how to behave in public," Millie whispered before she squared her shoulders, took his arm again, waited for Lucetta to the take the other, and then began moving forward.

Unfortunately, the closer they got to the Casino, the more Lucetta seemed to be dragging her feet.

"Is something the matter?" he asked when they ended up barely moving because she'd almost come to a complete stop.

Lucetta looked at the Casino and shrugged. "You know, I don't think it's a good idea for me to stroll in there on your arm. Perhaps I'll just wander around to the back and take in the sights, or maybe I should just go back to the buggy."

Everett tilted his head. "You're not worried that I don't want to be seen with you here, are you?"

Lucetta let out a huff. "Really, Everett, I was trying to give you a discreet way *out* of being seen with me, one that would allow you to retain your gentlemanliness, and . . . here you went and ruined it."

"Am I really that shallow?"

When Lucetta and Millie exchanged a rather telling look, his mouth went slack. "You think I'm shallow?"

Millie patted his arm again. "You're a gentleman of society, Everett. You're bound to be a little . . . Well, I wouldn't say you're *shallow,* not exactly, but you are a bit of a snob, something I do think I've pointed out before. Having said that, Lucetta and I both know you're not used to being seen in public with ladies like . . . us."

Tightening his grip on their arms, Everett prodded them forward. "There's nothing wrong with either one of you, and just so you know . . . I've recently come to the conclusion that I might very well be a snob, but I'm trying to work on that."

Not giving the ladies an opportunity to balk, Everett increased his pace, practically dragging them beside him as he moved through the door and into the entranceway. Glancing around, his temper began to simmer when he realized that every guest was sending him covert glances, even as they pretended they hadn't noticed him.

His temper went from simmering to boiling in a split second.

Their behavior was completely unacceptable, but . . . how many times had he witnessed his friends giving people they considered undesirable the cut direct? How many times had he witnessed abuses directed at domestics working in different houses, yet never once objected to that abuse, at least not aloud?

"We really don't have time for you to make some sort of a stand, something the expression on your face seems to suggest you're contemplating," Lucetta said, amusement lacing her words. "But if you're determined to make some sort of spectacular stand at a later date, I could see if we can find you a small part in my play. That would show them."

"I'm not finding the attention, and all that goes with that, humorous at the moment."

"But if you can't find humor in this," Millie whispered, "it'll simply make you mad. You don't have the luxury to allow your temper to get away with you, so ignore the slights. I always do."

That Millie and Lucetta were so matter of

fact about the clear snubs they were receiving sent additional temper, mixed with shame, straight through him.

It truly was deplorable, the behavior of the people he'd always considered good company. Millie and Lucetta were both kind, intelligent, and remarkable ladies, but because they didn't possess the right social status, they were ostracized, and that —

"Mr. Mulberry, how delightful to see you again."

Shifting his attention from a circle of fashionably dressed young ladies who'd taken to tittering behind their hands, Everett settled it on an anxious-looking gentleman, a gentleman Everett thought might be one of the managers of the Casino.

"Ah, Mr . . ."

"Mr. Bancroft," Millie finished for him as he struggled for the manager's name. "It's me, Miss Longfellow. I don't know if you remember or not, but we met over a week ago, when I was here to play tennis. You found me a spare racquet." She beamed at the man.

"Ah, well, yes, of course I remember you, Miss Longfellow," Mr. Bancroft said, looking just a little pained. "How could I forget a lady who knocked another lady right off her feet?"

To Everett's surprise, Millie sent Mr. Bancroft a wink. "Bet that had everyone talking for a good long time."

"Oh, they haven't finished quite yet." Mr. Bancroft turned back to Everett. "What may I help you with this afternoon?"

"We'd like a table for three in the dining room," Everett heard come out of his mouth as Millie and Lucetta gaped at him.

Mr. Bancroft began to turn red as he lifted his hand and tugged on his tie. "I'm afraid the dining room is full at the moment, Mr. Mulberry, but I do have a nice, private room that might suit you better."

"We'll wait for a table to open up."

"Honestly, Everett, stop being difficult," Lucetta muttered before she breezed past him and smiled at Mr. Bancroft right before a throaty laugh escaped her lips. "Don't mind Mr. Mulberry, my dear Mr. Bancroft. We're not here to dine but to speak with a Mr. Victor. He's newly arrived in Newport, but we've been told he might be here at the moment." Her smile widened as she batted long lashes Mr. Bancroft's way.

"He's in a private room, dining with his wife," Mr. Bancroft said in a voice that was barely audible. "Would you like me to show you to him?"

"That would be kind of you."

Before Everett could badger the manager further — something he really wanted to do, just as he really wanted to sit down and order a five-course meal in the middle of the dining room with Millie and Lucetta — he found himself trailing after the ladies as every guest turned their way.

Knocking once on a closed door, Mr. Bancroft opened it and stuck his head in. "Begging your pardon, Mr. Victor, but Mr. Mulberry would like to speak with you. May I tell him you're available?"

Everett didn't hear the response, but since Mr. Bancroft opened the door fully and stepped aside, he assumed Mr. Victor had agreed to see him. Moving into the private dining room, he stopped and took a moment to consider the gentleman now rising from the table and staring back at him.

He was younger than Everett had expected, no older than midthirties, and he was polished and incredibly well dressed, with every dark hair on his head perfectly in place and his tie tied to perfection. Everett glanced to the left and found an elegant lady sitting at the table, her hair coiffed in an elaborate fashion, one that had certainly been coiffed by a servant, and wearing a stunning day dress cut in the latest style, designed by Worth, if he wasn't much mistaken.

A million questions crowded his brain, but he forced a smile and moved forward to shake the hand Mr. Victor was now extending him.

"Mr. Victor, I'm Mr. Everett Mulberry."

Mr. Victor squeezed Everett's hand a little harder than was strictly necessary, and then released it, nodding to the lady sitting at the table. "My wife, Mrs. Victor."

Everett walked over to Mrs. Victor and took her hand, kissing it properly before he nodded to Millie and Lucetta, who were standing right inside the doorway. "My friends, Miss Long-fellow and Miss Plum."

Not taking his attention away from Everett, Mr. Victor simply waved a hand in their direction, that action causing Everett's hands to clench.

"The captain of the *Adoring Violet* told us we could find you here," Everett finally said when Mr. Victor didn't bother to speak.

"He should have told you I was intending to come to your cottage after my wife and I dined."

"He did tell us that, but I found I didn't care to delay our meeting. I've been waiting a very long time to meet you, Mr. Victor, ever since Fred and his wife died, in fact."

Everett frowned. "Why is it that no one

could locate you?"

Mr. Victor shrugged. "Fred sent me to far-off places, with no set schedule. Believe me, if I'd gotten wind of Fred's accident, we'd have returned to the States posthaste." He narrowed his eyes on Everett. "However, I'm here now, so I suppose we might as well get on with things."

"We certainly do need to get on with *things* as you put it, especially matters concerning Fred's estate."

Taking a step toward Everett, Mr. Victor's eyes began to glitter. "Matters of Fred's estate don't concern you at all, Mr. Mulberry, and you should know that I'm here for one reason and one reason only."

"And that reason would be?" Everett asked slowly.

"To fetch the children home, of course."

For a second, Everett thought he'd misheard the man, but only for a second. Stepping closer to Mr. Victor, Everett forced a smile. "I'm afraid you're in for a bit of a disappointment, then, because the only way you're going to do any fetching of Fred's children is over my dead body."

15

"Strangely enough, when I imagined finally being given the opportunity to enjoy a lovely glass of lemonade at the Newport Casino, I never pictured myself enjoying that refreshment from the midst of a storage room," Millie said to no one in particular before she took a sip of tepid lemonade and glanced around.

Everett was sitting in a hardback chair, a wet rag covering his entire face, while Mr. Duncan Victor slouched down in a chair similar to the one Everett was sitting in, wiping his nose with another wet rag. Both gentlemen had one of their hands tied to those chairs, and both gentlemen had yet to speak a single word to each other, even though they'd been held in the storage room for a good ten minutes while management waited for the authorities to arrive.

"It's unfortunate Lucetta and Mrs. Victor aren't here to enjoy such delightful surroundings," Millie continued, her words drawing a grunt from Mr. Victor.

"My wife had the good sense to dive under the table when fists began flying," he said. "As for Miss Plum . . . Well, the only reason she's not here is because she batted those lovely eyes of hers at the staff, even though I told them that the plate she was holding in her hand was aimed directly at me." He lifted his head and sent a look filled with disgust at Everett, one Everett missed since his entire face was still covered. "I'm remarkably confused as to what an actress was doing accompanying you, Mr. Mulberry. Although given that I've come to the conclusion you're nothing more than a dirty scoundrel . . . I probably shouldn't be all that confused."

Setting the glass of lemonade aside, Millie rose to her feet, grateful she, at least, had not been tied to a chair. "If there's any scoundrel in this room, sir, it's obviously you. In fact, if you ask me, the only possible explanation behind you throwing the first punch at Everett was to divest guilt from yourself."

"Divert," Everett muttered through the cloth covering his face.

"Exactly right, *divert guilt* is what I meant to say." Millie took a step toward Mr. Victor, stopping immediately when a rather large member of the Newport Casino staff folded beefy arms over his chest and shook his head at her.

"I wasn't going to hurt him," she told the man, earning a huff of clear disbelief from Mr. Victor in the process.

"You broke my nose," Mr. Victor snapped. "Which really does beg the question of why you've been allowed in the same room with me." He narrowed an eye on her that was rapidly turning an interesting shade of black. "It is never permissible for a lady to punch a gentleman, not proper in the least. Although . . . given that you seem to be acquainted with Miss Plum as well, you're obviously not a proper sort of lady."

"I've never claimed to be a proper lady, Mr. Victor. In fact, I'm just the nanny."

"You *are* a proper lady," Everett said as he reached up and pulled the rag off his face, sporting not one but two black eyes. "And you're not *just* the nanny."

Warmth began traveling up Millie's neck to settle on her face, but before she could so much as get a word of appreciation out of her mouth, Mr. Victor let out another grunt.

"Do not tell me, Mr. Mulberry, that this woman, the one who recently broke my

366

nose, has been hired to watch Fred's children? Surely you must realize that putting those precious scamps in the direct vicinity of a woman prone to violence is hardly in their best interest." He mopped at his nose again. "She hit me in a manner that suggests she's spends quite a bit of time pummeling people. That clearly proves she's unstable — and proves you're not fit to see to the children's basic needs, since you hired her as a nanny in the first place."

"I've hardly spent my life pummeling people, sir," Millie said before Everett could reply. "Well, there was this one boy at the orphanage, Freddy Franklin, but . . . I digest from the topic at hand."

"Digress," Everett said right before he laughed. "I hate to point this out, Millie, but it might benefit you to go back through all the D words, since they seem to be giving you trouble today."

Millie's lips twitched. "And that explains why I was so dismayed — another D word that I know means *upset* — about not having my sensible clothing available. My aprons come in remarkably handy for holding my dictionaries." Additional warmth spread over her when Everett smiled.

Hoping that his swollen eyes made it difficult for him to see that she was blushing, she turned back to Mr. Victor, who was looking a little confused. "As I was saying, sir, I would not have felt the urge to enter the brawl if you would have stopped trying to do Everett in. If it escaped your notice, he's rather brawny and could have made mincemeat of you, but he was acting far too much the gentleman. That forced me to put an end to your nonsense before someone lost an eye or, heaven forbid, a brain, which is what I think you were intending when you lifted up that water pitcher. Quite frankly, if anyone possesses an unstable nature, it's clearly you. You attacked Everett with no provocation, which I know means *goading,* or something close to that."

Mr. Victor stopped mopping his nose. "He told me he'd only relinquish the children over his dead body. I thought it would expedite matters nicely if I took it upon myself to arrange that for him. If he's dead, it'll save me the trouble of seeing him arrested. He has, if you're not aware of this, stolen three children in what I've come to believe is a dastardly attempt at getting his hands on Fred's vast estate."

"What are you talking about?" Everett demanded as he squinted in Mr. Victor's direction. "I have no design on Fred's estate — don't even know the extent of it, by the way — and . . . even if it is as vast as you claim, all of it will be put into trust for the children."

"A likely story." Mr. Victor sat forward. "If you don't have an interest in Fred's estate, why, pray tell, did you abscond with his children? I have Fred's last will and testament in my jacket pocket — a will that clearly designates me as guardian of the children and executor of Fred's estate."

Everett ran a hand through hair that was standing on end. "And I, Mr. Victor, have a will back in New York that's dated a mere month and a half before Fred died, giving me custody of the children and naming *me* as executor."

Mr. Victor's face darkened. "You're lying. I was Fred's attorney, and he never had me draw up a second will."

"An attorney by the name of Mr. Samuel Colfax drew up Fred's last will," Everett said. "I assure you, it was all done very properly, and done, given what I've been able to piece together, after you left Boston on that mission you claim Fred gave you."

Mr. Victor's brows knit together. "Mr. Colfax made up a new will?"

"Are you familiar with the man?" Millie asked.

"We're casual associates, and he is a well-respected attorney in the Boston area, but . . . why would Fred have done that?" Mr. Victor asked. "Besides being his attorney, I was also Fred's business partner, and . . . I considered Fred to be one of my closest friends. That's why he wanted me to have guardianship of his children if anything ever happened to him and Violet."

Millie bit her lip. "Maybe he didn't trust you in the end, maybe he thought you were up to no good, and . . . maybe he knew you were considering . . . murder."

For a second, silence settled over the storage room, until Mr. Victor laughed.

"Murder is not amusing, Mr. Victor," she said with a sniff.

"But a nanny with an overactive imagination certainly is." He pressed the rag against his nose again. "I was not even in the country when Fred died, but on a yacht, halfway across the world."

"On Fred's yacht," Millie pointed out. "And forgive me, but it's somewhat suspicious that you were conveniently on Fred's yacht when the poor man died. And why are you only now coming to collect the children?"

"Fred made up a list that had no less than fifty names on it of inventors he thought worthy of further investigation. Those inventors were spread throughout the world, but Fred believed their inventions, at least on paper, warranted a second look. Since Fred was in the process of working with numerous inventors here in the States, he did not have the time to travel the world — thus he asked me to do it."

Everett leaned forward. "Weren't you concerned your law practice would suffer, being out of Boston so long?"

"Fred was my only client, and . . . as I said before, we were business partners as well. I invested my own money in the most promising inventions, and shared in the profits when those inventions became lucrative."

Speculation sparkled in Everett's blackened eyes. "And did many of those inventions turn lucrative?"

Mr. Victor shrugged. "Some did, most did not, but it was the allure of the next big invention that drew my interest, Mr. Mulberry."

"Allure doesn't cover the cost of gowns from Worth, Mr. Victor," Everett said softly.

"Are you insinuating that I'm only here to collect the children because I want to get my hands on Fred's estate?"

"I don't believe I'm *insinuating* anything."

Mr. Victor shot out of his chair and began

dragging it toward Everett, who jumped to his feet and clenched his free hand into a fist. Darting between the two gentlemen before the burly staff member of the Casino could move, even knowing it wasn't exactly a prudent move, Millie spread out her arms and stood her ground as Mr. Victor stumbled to a stop, glaring at her.

"Get . . . out . . . of . . . my . . . way."

"Not likely," Millie said. "Although I must say, you've now firmly convinced me you're unfit to raise Fred's children, given that temper of yours. That probably explains why Fred sought out another attorney and had that attorney draw up a new will."

Mr. Victor glared at Millie for a long second before his gaze darted around her and settled on Everett. "Tell me this, Mr. Mulberry — in addition to having Mr. Colfax draw up a new will, did Fred give him the ledgers pertaining to all of his investments?"

"Fred's ledgers have been nowhere to be found," Everett admitted.

Mr. Victor plopped right back down on the chair he'd been dragging behind him. "What do you mean? Fred had numerous ledgers, all organized by date in the office he kept at home, and . . . I had copies of those ledgers, which I found missing when I opened my office after arriving in Boston. Quite honestly, I thought you'd taken them."

Everett retook his seat. "Contrary to what you seem to believe about me, Mr. Victor, I'm not the type of gentleman to break into someone's office. That's why I mailed a letter to your law office, giving you my direction and telling you I'd taken the children."

"There was no letter from you when I returned," Mr. Victor shot back.

"I certainly don't know what to tell you about that, but . . . if you didn't receive my letter, how did you discover that I'd taken the children to New York, and then here to Newport?"

"It was not without difficulty," Mr. Victor admitted. "After stopping in at my office, where I immediately discovered all of Fred's ledgers missing, I hurried to Fred's home, stunned to find the house closed up and seemingly abandoned. I looked through a window that hadn't been fully obscured by the drape and was horrified to see all the furniture covered in linen." He blew out a breath. "One of Fred's neighbors, apparently the suspicious sort, confronted me, and it was through that man that I discovered Fred had died."

"That must have made for quite the

shock," Millie said.

"I was completely stunned, heartbroken over the loss of my good friend, and . . . confused beyond belief when the neighbor told me that you, Mr. Mulberry, instead of keeping the children in Boston, had taken them back to New York with you."

"I live in New York," Everett said. "Taking the children with me was my only option."

"You should have kept them in Boston."

"As a businessman, I'm sure you understand, given that most of my extensive real estate investments are in New York, why I moved the children there."

"And those extensive real estate investments are exactly why Everett doesn't need to get his hands on Fred's money," Millie added with a nod. "Which puts your interest in Fred's money in question again, Mr. Victor."

"I don't need Fred's money either, Miss Longfellow."

Before Millie could question Mr. Victor further, the door to the storage room burst open. Standing in the doorway was none other than Caroline, her expression livid as she set her sights on Everett and marched into the room.

"So the rumors swirling around Newport are true. You've been in a brawl, and done so right in front of our friends." Caroline stalked closer to Everett, coming to a stop directly in front of him. "Did you even consider the embarrassment you were going to cause me before you so foolishly engaged in a fight?"

Everett narrowed a black eye on Caroline. "I'm afraid those thoughts never entered my head, my dear, considering I didn't have much time to think about anything once Mr. Victor attacked me."

Letting out a sniff, Caroline looked to Mr. Victor before returning her attention to Everett. "You couldn't have been taken completely by surprise, given the condition of that gentleman's nose."

"I was responsible for the nose, Caroline," Millie said.

Caroline drew herself up. "Do not presume to address me so informally, Miss Longfellow, but . . . surely you're not suggesting you were brawling as well, are you?"

"I couldn't very well just stand by and watch Everett get smashed over the head with a pitcher of water now, could I?"

"Ladies should never . . . brawl. It's unseemly."

"Then it's a good thing you weren't here, Miss Dixon, or else Everett might no longer be in possession of his wits."

"My head appreciates your interference, Millie," Everett said, his words having Caroline immediately looking his way again.

"I simply don't understand what could have possessed you to engage in a rowdy round of fisticuffs while our friends were trying to enjoy a peaceful respite."

"I didn't intend on entering a brawl when I got up this morning, and the brawl happened in a private dining room, not the public one." Everett nodded to Mr. Victor. "He attacked first, and all because he believes it's his right to take the children away from me to live with him."

Caroline's eyes grew round before she actually smiled at Mr. Victor. "Those are marvelous words to hear, sir, but . . . why in the world would you want those children?"

"He's not taking the children," Everett said before Mr. Victor could answer her. "Fred clearly left the care of his children to me, which means Mr. Victor has no right to them."

"That still remains to be proven," Mr. Victor said.

"You wouldn't happen to be Mr. *Duncan* Victor, would you?" Caroline asked as she began walking closer to him.

"I am Mr. Duncan Victor."

For some reason, Caroline looked

absolutely delighted to hear that. "But Mr. Victor, our families have been introduced before, although it's been a few years. I'm Miss Caroline Dixon, of the New York Dixon family."

She sent Everett a frown. "Why would you punch — or allow Miss Longfellow, from the sound of it, to punch — a gentleman who comes from one of the oldest and most distinguished families in Boston?"

"You know Mr. Victor?" Millie asked slowly.

"I thought I made myself clear, Miss Longfellow. I don't want you to address me further, but yes, I know Mr. Victor, only as a slight acquaintance, of course, but . . ." Caroline smiled at the gentleman in question. "You actually *want* to take Fred's children?"

"Of course I want to take them, but . . . it remains to be seen whether or not I will be given that privilege. Mr. Mulberry told me Fred left a will that's dated after the one I have in my possession, so . . . I'll need to see that new will, and then . . . we'll go from there."

Caroline gave an airy wave of her hand. "Oh, I don't think that'll be necessary." She turned and arched a brow at Everett. "Will it, darling?"

Millie watched as Everett simply sat there for a long moment, looking at Caroline as if she'd suddenly sprouted horns on her head.

"You want me to just hand the children over to Mr. Victor?" he finally asked.

"That would solve all of our problems very nicely indeed."

"For some reason, I don't believe it will." Everett glanced to the door. "But since it does appear as if the authorities have arrived, why don't you meet me back at Seaview in an hour or two? We'll discuss everything then."

"If you'd have bothered to check your schedule, you'd know you're supposed to be dining with me this evening at Mr. and Mrs. Olmsted's cottage."

"Besides the fact that I'm not in any condition to dine out this evening, I was under the belief that our plans had been canceled since you're put out with me again."

"I don't need to be in accord with you in order to enjoy dinner with good friends, Everett," Caroline said. "But since you obviously don't want to escort me, I'll have Dudley step in, something he's been gracious enough to do numerous . . ." Caroline's words trailed off as a man in uniform stepped into the room.

After introducing himself as Officer Peterson, he walked over to Everett, pulled out a knife, and before Millie could so much as gasp, sliced it through Everett's bindings before he did the same to Mr. Victor.

"Begging your pardon, gentlemen, but the manager here has decided he does not want to press charges against the two of you, so you're both free to leave." He turned to Millie. "You, however, miss, are going to accompany me down to the station."

"You're . . . arresting me?" Millie breathed.

Officer Peterson nodded. "From what numerous members of the Casino have stated, *you're* responsible for the mayhem that recently occurred. You were also responsible, from what I've been able to gather, for another troubling incident that happened here just over a week ago." He shook his head. "We don't tolerate mayhem here in Newport, miss, so . . . I'm taking you in."

Everett rose to his feet and moved to Millie's side, taking her arm and giving it a reassuring squeeze. "Miss Longfellow was in no way responsible for what recently transpired here, which means you have absolutely no grounds for an arrest."

"Everett, don't be ridiculous," Caroline

snapped. "Of course Miss Longfellow should be arrested. She admitted to punching Mr. Victor in the nose, and I still bear the marks of her assault on me." She lifted up her hat and showed Officer Peterson her forehead where just the faintest trace of a bruise remained. "Shall I give you a statement now, or would it be possible for me to do that at a later date since I do need to get on my way to prepare for a dinner party I'm attending tonight."

"Being hit in the head with a tennis ball hardly constitutes assault, and it is certainly no reason to have someone arrested," Everett said between teeth that seemed to be clenched.

"I have no idea why you're constantly taking her side," Caroline said right before she threw herself into the nearest chair and began sobbing . . . enthusiastically.

"Since I see no valid reason to arrest anyone today, I'll just bid all of you farewell," Officer Peterson said right before he bolted from the room, followed by the burly man who'd been guarding everyone.

Sending Millie a look filled with clear exasperation, Everett moved closer to Caroline and knelt down beside her. "Caroline, there's no need for such dramatics."

Caroline raised her head, yet oddly

enough, there was not a single tear on her face. "No need for dramatics? You've caused us to become the source of rabid speculation by escorting Miss Longfellow and Miss Plum to this establishment, embarrassed me to no small end by getting into a fight, and . . . I have no idea how I'm going to be able to face all of our guests in just two days' time at the ball you and I, if you've forgotten, are hosting together."

"Perhaps we should consider canceling the ball," Everett said softly.

In the span of a split second, Caroline's eyes turned dangerous. "We will consider no such thing. I've worked for years to build up my position within society, and this ball . . . our ball . . . is what is going to cement that position for me. That you could even suggest such a thing is completely unacceptable, and . . . you've made me promises, promises I'm going to demand you honor."

She let out a laugh that sounded anything but amused. "I have been the most sought-after lady within society for years, yet I gave *you* the privilege of attaching your name to mine. You will not abandon me now, especially not for . . ." She turned her head and pinned Millie with a glare that was so hot Millie could almost feel the heat from it even though she was standing several feet away from Caroline.

Drawing in a deep breath, Caroline turned back to Everett. "You've made some grave errors in judgment these past few weeks, my *darling,* but now it's time for you to do what's right for both of us."

"It's only a ball, Caroline."

"It's not, and you know it."

Everett reached out and put a finger under Caroline's chin, raising it so that she was forced to meet his gaze. "Considering the strife between us at the moment, the ball is not going to be the crowning moment of the season, and I wouldn't count on any surprise announcement at the conclusion of it."

Prickles of something alarming shot down Millie's spine when Caroline's lips thinned as she stared at Everett for what seemed like forever.

Then, to Millie's surprise, Caroline smiled rather sweetly at Everett, pushed herself up and out of the chair, and headed for the door, turning when she reached it. "Of course there will be a surprise at the end of the ball, darling, and shame on you for saying differently." With that, she turned on her heel and headed through the door, the

distinct sound of her laughter trailing after
her.

16

"I had no idea, Everett, when your mother asked me, along with Reverend Gilmore, to track you down, that our tracking would culminate with finding you hiding in the dark depths of the Reading Room, buried behind a newspaper."

Folding the newspaper over the copy of *Pride and Prejudice* he'd been trying to discreetly read, Everett lifted his head and found his father staring back at him.

"Have you forgotten that you're hosting a ball in only a few hours' time?" Fletcher asked as he lowered himself into a chair right beside Everett.

"I'm hardly likely to forget that, since I was woken up this morning at a completely unacceptable hour by Miss Pickenpaugh and ordered to either stay out of her way, or roll up my sleeves and help with the preparations."

"And I take it you decided there was

something wrong with rolling up your sleeves?" Fletcher asked.

"Since I'm paying Miss Pickenpaugh a small fortune to organize what I'm firmly coming to believe is a disaster in the making . . . yes, I had a problem with the idea of being put to work. Did you mention something about Reverend Gilmore?"

"He'll be along directly. We ran into Millie, Lucetta, the children, and those adorable, yet incredibly misbehaving, puppies wandering down this very street. Reverend Gilmore is speaking with them now, but I'm sure he won't be long." Fletcher smiled. "Thaddeus still seems a little fascinated over some story you told him about this particular club. For some reason, he asked me if I thought Chip, his puppy, would be large enough to ride by next summer."

Everett settled back in the chair. "He's talking about the story I told him about how the Newport Casino came to be — the one that had Captain Candy riding his horse into this very establishment."

Everett smiled and shook his head. "It's probably a good thing that — what with the way this summer season is shaping up — I'm not all that keen about returning to Newport anytime soon. Although, considering the reputation I've been gaining of late, I don't think anyone would be too surprised if one of my wards tried to ride a dog into the Reading Room. I have to say, though, considering Thaddeus's fascination with this place, I'm surprised you didn't bring him in here with you."

"I extended the darling boy that very offer, but Thaddeus thinks it's not fair his sisters, or Millie and Lucetta, aren't allowed in here. That's why he's manfully trying to suppress his curiosity." Fletcher laughed. "I'm not certain about this, but I think Millie might have tried to sneak a peek in one of the downstairs windows, because she had telling flower petals on her clothing, petals that just happen to match the bushes surrounding this place."

"Her curiosity is going to get her into real trouble someday."

"I'm sure you're right, but it was a stroke of genius on her part to get the children and puppies out of the house, since Caroline seems to be in quite the state today."

"Why in the world would Caroline be in any type of state at all? She's getting exactly what she wanted — the ball of her dreams to impress her friends. And because Miss Pickenpaugh brought in an entire army of people to set up and staff the ball, Caroline really doesn't have to do much of anything."

"She decided at the last minute there needed to be more impressive gifts to give the guests."

"I thought the plan was to give the ladies fans and the gentlemen handkerchiefs."

"You still *will* be giving those out, but Caroline wanted something a little . . . grander, and something that would leave a lasting impression after the ball is over."

"Do I even want to know what that 'something grander' is?"

"Since you're footing the bill for this added touch, you should want to know."

Everett closed his eyes. "Go on then, tell me what I'm paying for."

"To give Caroline credit, it's a very clever idea, although costly, and the sheer stress of pulling this daunting feat off properly is sure to leave Miss Pickenpaugh with a nervous condition for the rest of her life." Fletcher cleared his throat. "You'll be pleased to learn that every guest will be given a children's pail, filled with sand."

Everett's eyes shot open. "That doesn't sound as if it will be too costly."

"In that sand is a miniature shovel," Fletcher continued. "That shovel has been placed at a precise angle, something Reverend Gilmore can attest to since he got coerced into placing those shovels just so before I dragged him after you."

"Why is there a miniature shovel in all the pails, and why was it so important that it has to be placed so precisely?"

"The placement is, of course, for effect, but the shovel will be used to help your guests dig up the trinkets Caroline had sent over from . . . Tiffany's."

Everett sat straight up in the chair. "She ordered trinkets for over two hundred guests from Tiffany's?"

"I'm afraid she did. Jeweled combs and bracelets for the ladies, and jeweled stick pins and small snuff boxes for the gentlemen."

"I have half a mind to refuse to pay the bill and make her pay it instead."

"You and I both know you can't do that, no matter how wrong Caroline is about the matter."

Everett raised a hand and began rubbing at an ache that was developing behind his temple. "She must still be very annoyed with me regarding the brawling incident."

"Of course she's annoyed with you, and not only about the brawling, if I were to hazard a guess."

"She has nothing else to be annoyed about."

"There is Millie," Fletcher said slowly.

"You mean the woman who has been deliberately avoiding me ever since the brawl?"

"Your mother *thought* something was amiss between the two of you."

"Well, she's right, but as for what that something is, I certainly don't know." He slouched down in the chair. "Millie's odd behavior began when we walked through the Casino after the unfortunate brawling incident to get to my buggy." A trace of temper shot through him. "All of the members of the Casino were gawking at us as we walked, sending Millie, Lucetta, and me looks of what can only be described as disdain. And . . . the society ladies were tittering behind their gloved hands, some of those titters rather loud, and none of them very kind in regard to Millie or Lucetta."

"Do you think Millie's upset because you did nothing to stop the tittering?"

"I told the crowd to mind their own business, which didn't go over very well, since they started tittering about me — and nothing pleasant, I must admit. But, instead of appeasing Millie, my attempt at protecting her and Lucetta from the harsh words seemed to aggravate her."

"Hmmm. . . . Well, good for you for making a stand, but as for why that would aggravate Millie, I must confess myself a bit perplexed."

"She's a complicated woman."

"All women are complicated, son. You should simply accept that for fact and be prepared to be confused for the rest of your life."

"I'm certainly confused at the moment."

"I don't blame you." Fletcher settled more comfortably in the chair. "You've never been one to seek my advice, and I blame myself for that since I was not available to you in your youth." Fletcher blew out a breath. "Your mother and I have recently come to the vastly uncomfortable conclusion that we've failed you as parents, but I hope you'll allow me to make amends for that, and give you some advice now."

"You and Mother did not *fail* me as parents. I was given everything a person could want."

"Except for our time, Everett. We never gave you enough of that."

"I was hardly at a disadvantage considering no parents in our social world spend much time with their children. You gave me the best education money could buy. And I was always surrounded by friends of the same social class, which meant I grew up with people holding the same values I do as well as sharing the same interests."

"Which only proves how much of a disservice I've done you," Fletcher countered. "As you said, you've been surrounded solely by like-minded individuals — and that has not given you a proper perspective of life. That right there is why you don't know how to proceed with that life in a way that's certain to make you happy."

"I'm happy."

"You're conflicted, not happy, and I take full responsibility for that confliction." Fletcher smiled. "I can only thank the good Lord above for finally allowing your mother and me insight into how wrong we've been."

"*God* showed you the errors of your ways?"

"In a very subtle, yet effective manner." Fletcher's smile widened. "Your mother and I were given the supreme pleasure of staying with this delightful family in France, and because of that stay, we were granted a new view of life." He crossed one ankle over the other. "We met Lord and Lady Davenport at a luncheon and quickly became friends with them. When they invited us to join them at their country home, we accepted, and that's what led to our decisive conclusion about our parenting abilities, or lack thereof."

"Lord and Lady Davenport told you that you and Mother were horrible parents?"

"Of course not, but you see, they were parents to five children, and . . . all of those children went to the local school and even ate dinner every night with their parents. They were included in all conversations, shown vast amounts of affection, whether it be a kiss from their parents on the forehead or skipping along on a walk as they held onto Lord or Lady Davenport's hand. But I think the greatest blessing these children were receiving was seeing how their mother and father held a strong belief in God. Lord Davenport was very comfortable talking about his faith, something that I readily admit made your mother and I very *uncomfortable* at first."

"We've always gone to church."

"Sitting in a pew, listening to words but not really listening to words, does not make one a person of faith. Your mother and I, even though we were raised in the church, always found talk of God to be rather . . . odd, as did most of our friends. What we discovered with Lord and Lady Davenport, though, was that we'd been wrong. Once we truly opened our hearts, things began to change for us. Our marriage grew stronger, which has been lovely since neither one of us married for love all those years ago, and then . . . Dorothy began having those dreams about you, dreams that finally sent us home."

Fletcher nodded. "I've come to believe that those dreams were God's way of showing us that you, even though you're grown, might still need us."

"I don't know how anyone can help me right now."

"I think what your father is trying to say, Everett, is that God can help you, but you're going to have to ask Him for assistance, and you're going to have to trust Him."

Looking around, Everett found Reverend Gilmore walking up behind him, holding Thaddeus's hand.

"I'm supposed to give the girls a detailed report about this place," Thaddeus said as he slipped out of Reverend Gilmore's hold and marched his way over to Everett's side. "But there's nothing really to report, and Miss Millie's going to be disappointed when I tell her I didn't find many books, even though you told her that from the very beginning."

Rising to his feet, Everett tucked the newspaper that was concealing *Pride and Prejudice* firmly under his arm before he took Thaddeus's hand in his own. "How about if I give you a quick tour and then we will rejoin *the girls* as you called them. But we need to do it quickly, before those girls get themselves into any mischief."

"They're across the street, sitting on a bench," Thaddeus said. "Miss Lucetta didn't like the way some of the gentlemen were looking at them from that second-floor balcony, so she said she was going to put some distance between them before she got an urge to hit someone."

"How about if I promise to bring you back here another day for a tour?" Without giving Thaddeus time to answer, Everett hustled the little boy out of the room, down the hallway, and out on the porch — a porch that just happened to be filled with gentlemen, all of whom were staring rather intently across the street.

"Oh . . . dear," Reverend Gilmore mumbled from behind Everett. "I should not have left the ladies alone."

"But Miss Millie insisted," Thaddeus said. "And we wouldn't want to disappoint Miss Millie, would we?"

Reverend Gilmore smiled. "She is difficult to resist."

"Everett, did you see?" a gentleman Everett was casually acquainted with by the name of Mr. Lewis asked as he nodded toward the street. "That's Miss Lucetta Plum over there."

Bending down to pick Thaddeus up, Everett gave him the newspaper and book to hold before shouldering his way through the crowd, anger beginning to stir when some of the comments the gentlemen were making caught his attention.

"She's a looker, she is."

"Haughty, though, especially for an actress."

"I heard she gets ten dozen roses on a slow night, more on a busy one."

"It's said she's particular about who she keeps company with, which is rich for a woman in her profession."

Stepping through the crowd, not caring about the gentlemen he pushed out of his way and the feet he trampled, Everett made it to the front of the porch, walked down the steps, and strode across the street. Handing Thaddeus to Millie, whose eyes were rather wide, no doubt that circumstance brought about because he was literally shaking with anger, he turned and stalked across the street again.

"Miss Lucetta Plum is a very good friend of mine, and I dare any of you to say one more disparaging thing about her in my presence," he said between gritted teeth.

"Looking for another brawl are you, Everett?" someone shouted.

"Oddly enough, I do believe I am." With that, Everett balled his hand into a fist and leapt up to the porch.

"You have got to stop doing this." Millie slapped a cold piece of meat over Everett's face, and slapped it none too gently, at that, as he sat in a chair in Abigail's kitchen.

"I was not going to stand by and let them say horrible things about Lucetta."

"Which was very noble of you," Lucetta said as she glided into Abigail's kitchen and moved to stand in front of him. "But really, Everett, the things those gentlemen were saying were things I've heard a million times before, and believe me, I've heard worse."

"It doesn't matter if you've heard them before, Lucetta." Everett readjusted the meat on his face. "Those gentlemen were being inappropriate, and don't even get me started on the fact they were practically shouting those insults your way as the children were within listening distance."

"The children didn't understand what they were saying," Lucetta argued. "You should have ignored the insults to me."

"You're a kind, compassionate, and far-too-sensible lady for your own good, Lucetta. I would have been no gentleman at all if I hadn't fought for your good name."

Everett watched out of the eye that wasn't covered in meat as Lucetta's eyes turned suspiciously bright before she blinked rapidly, sniffed just once, and patted his arm. "You're a good man, Everett. I don't care what anyone else says."

A laugh caught him by surprise even as his father let out what sounded remarkably like a snort from where he was sitting on the other side of the table, a piece of meat slapped over half his face as well.

"I must say I do agree with everything my son is saying, Lucetta," Fletcher began. "Those men were not behaving as gentlemen should behave. I, for one, will be discontinuing my membership at the Reading Room and plan to never step foot in it again."

"Has everyone lost their minds?" Millie asked as she looked up from blotting Reverend Gilmore's puffy lip with a wet towel. "The Mulberry family has worked hard over the years, building their real-estate empire and their position within society, but today's event has put that position in dire jeopardy."

"The Mulberry family, I'm sorry to say,

has not always behaved in an upstanding fashion, Millie," Everett said as he held her gaze. "We've made more money than we can ever spend, but ever since you questioned me a few weeks ago about some of our real-estate investments, I've been questioning the integrity we've used to amass our fortune."

"I'm not sure I understand what you're saying," Millie said slowly.

"We own land in Five Points, Millie," Everett bit out. "Land that tenement houses sit on, and even though we're not slumlords, well . . . we collect rent from those slumlords, which doesn't make us any better than them."

"Why are you telling me this?"

"Because I finally understand what *you* were trying to tell me a few weeks ago. That even though I've proclaimed the fact that the money I collect on rents is in no way comparable to what slumlords do, that's not true." He nodded to his father. "When you handed over the family investments to me, you gave me leave to manage them to the best of my abilities. I'm now hoping that you will be in full agreement with me when I tell you that I no longer find it acceptable to take money from the poor. That's why I'd like to buy up the tenement buildings that are built on land we own, and then go about the business of improving those buildings, hopefully improving the circumstances of the people who are unfortunate enough to live there."

"Good heavens, those men really did hit your head hard, didn't they?" Millie pressed the wet cloth into Reverend Gilmore's hand before heading Everett's way. Reaching out, she plucked the meat off his face and peered into his eyes. "Your pupils seem to be working all right, but . . . perhaps we should summon the physician to make certain you haven't been grievously injured."

"My wits aren't addled."

"I imagine that'll change once Caroline hears about your latest foray — which means *venture* — into brawling."

Everett simply stared at Millie for a long moment before he laughed.

"There's nothing funny about this, Everett. Caroline is determined to pull off the ball of the summer season tonight, and she'll be hard-pressed to do that if everyone at the ball spends their time discussing your recent activities."

"She probably won't even notice the new bruises I incurred today."

"Do you think she's not going to notice that your father is sporting bruises as well, and Reverend Gilmore's lip is twice its normal size?"

"I wasn't planning on attending the ball, dear," Reverend Gilmore said. "And I was only punched because one young gentleman got a little too enthusiastic when the mayhem began."

Fletcher smiled but then winced as if smiling caused him pain. "That certainly did put an end to everything rather quickly, once everyone realized an elderly gentleman — and a man of the cloth, at that — had been pulled into the fray."

Reverend Gilmore suddenly looked a little smug. "I'm sure the local churches will see an increase in their attendance, especially since I just couldn't seem to resist suggesting all those gentlemen repent and make reparations for speaking such vile things about my lovely Lucetta."

Everett grinned. "That was the best part of the whole brawl."

Reverend Gilmore returned the grin. "I do still have my uses, son, but . . ." He rose slowly to his feet and sighed. "I think I'll go have a nice lie down. As Fletcher so kindly pointed out, I am an elderly gentleman, and brawls can be rather taxing on us, even though, truth be told, I've never been in the midst of one before today."

Everyone watched as Reverend Gilmore left the room, and then Millie turned to him again. "Caroline's going to be livid with you — and with me, as well, since it's my fault in the first place. I shouldn't have let my curiosity get the better of me, but I just wanted to see what that Reading Room was all about."

"Don't be silly," Lucetta said. "Women of any station in life should not have to be concerned about walking past a gentlemen's club. The word *gentlemen* implies real gentlemen will be in attendance, but honestly, I do think the Reading Room really should look into making their qualifications for membership a little more difficult."

Abigail suddenly breezed into the room, looking a little harried but smiling at everyone once she plopped herself down into the nearest chair. "The children have been bathed and are resting in one of the guest rooms upstairs. The girls are waiting for you, Lucetta, to help them with their hair. I've had the dresses we fetched from Seaview laid out on their beds, and do make certain to use the right ribbon with the right dress. I want the girls to look perfect tonight."

"You still believe it's a good idea to take

401

the children to the ball?" Millie asked.

"But of course. We'll attend the ball as planned, a united front, if you will."

Millie's eyes widened in clear horror. "I'm not going to the ball."

"Of course you are," Everett argued before Abigail had the chance. "My mother is counting on you being there, and I'd look at it as a great privilege if you'd honor me with a dance."

"I don't know how to dance. And I never intended on *attending* the ball. I thought I was simply supposed to escort the children, and then stay with them as they peeked through a banister. Although . . . I do think that window off the side terrace might be a better choice, given that it's far away from where any guests will be."

Everett narrowed his eyes as much as he could, which wasn't much, since they'd taken to swelling. "I'm not comfortable with the idea of you hiding in the shadows, Millie. You've become an integral part of my family, and as such, I'd like you at the ball."

Millie drew herself up and suddenly looked rather fierce. "If you've forgotten, this is Caroline's ball. She's been looking forward to it for months, which means it would not be fair to her to have me anywhere near the ballroom. My presence would only ruin her evening, and I'm sorry, but I won't be responsible for that."

Everything and everyone except Millie faded to nothing as Everett simply stared back at her.

She'd been soundly abused by Caroline ever since she'd met the lady, and yet she didn't want to ruin Caroline's evening.

She'd been badgered into playing tennis and then shouted at when she'd had the audacity to win.

She'd also been responsible for changing the children into complete darlings, but on her own terms, and . . .

A finger snapping in front of his eyes had him leaning back.

"Where did you just go?" Millie demanded.

"Nowhere. I'm still sitting in the same spot, aren't I? But getting back to the subject of the ball. . . . You, as the children's nanny, will be expected to be there, at least while they join me in the receiving line."

"I am not going to be anywhere near the receiving line. You must know that Caroline would have my head if I even attempted such nonsense."

"She does make a most excellent point," Abigail said. "So in the interest of allowing

Millie to keep that lovely head of hers, I'll bring the children into Seaview, and I'll stand off to the side and keep an eye on them while the guests are being greeted."

"And while Abigail's doing that," Millie added. "Lucetta and I will retreat to the side terrace where the children can join us after they're done doing whatever you need them to do."

Abigail seemed ready to argue with that, but Millie held up her hand and smiled. "It's not up for debate, so don't even bother trying."

As Abigail immediately began looking a little grumpy, Lucetta headed for the door. "I'd better go see about getting the girls ready." She made it almost through the door before Abigail's next words stopped her in her tracks.

"I've left a nice little frock on your bed, Lucetta, and even though you won't be actually attending the ball, I'd still like you to wear it."

Lucetta arched a brow Abigail's way. "Did you leave a little frock out for Millie as well?"

"Of course, and both of you will wear what I've laid out, given that I am an elderly, dear, dotty thing, whom both of you would surely hate to disappoint this evening,

404

given the very great disappointment I've already suffered since you're going to be spending the night on the . . . terrace." Abigail's look suddenly changed from grumpy to . . . pathetic.

Shaking her head, Lucetta blew out a breath. "You're a bit elderly, Abigail, I'll give you that, but I don't think you've ever been dotty in your life, and I'm certainly not finding you dear at the moment — more like diabolical." Lucetta's lips curved ever so slightly. "I'll wear that frock just to appease you, but don't think I'm going to be happy about it." She turned and stomped out of the room.

"Don't forget the tiara I left beside the dress," Abigail called. "Or the sparkly shoes that are right on the floor, dear."

"I'm not wearing a tiara," Lucetta yelled back.

Abigail grinned. "She's such a dear, sweet girl. Possessed of such a quiet and delicate nature." She looked at Millie. "Well, aren't you going to go get ready as well?"

"It's still two hours before the ball."

"Hardly any time at all for you to primp."

"I never take time to primp."

"Yes, I know, it's one of your greatest faults — slightly endearing, mind you, but still . . ."

Leaning closer to Everett, Millie lowered her voice. "Just remember, this was your idea, and I'm telling you right now, it's not a very good one."

"It'll be fine."

"You say that now, when Caroline and all your friends aren't around, but tonight could very well put a nail in the coffin that was once your social position." Not bothering to wait to hear his reply, Millie marched from the room and disappeared, loud mutters about disasters trailing after her.

17

"Forgive me for complaining," Lucetta began as she limped across the side terrace of Seaview and plopped down on a stone bench before sending a glare Millie's way. "But why in the world did you insist on being let off clear at the end of the drive, instead of allowing Davis to drive us up to the front door?"

"Because all of Everett's friends were gathered in that long receiving line, and I thought it might be for the best if we avoided a scene before the ball even began." Millie glanced around the terrace. "I do think this will do very nicely this evening, especially since the weather seems to be holding."

Lucetta completely ignored the last part of Millie's statement. "You and I are wearing heels and Everett's drive is remarkably long. My feet are killing me, as I'm sure yours are as well."

"My shoes are in my reticule, along with my stockings, so my feet are feeling very well indeed."

"Good heavens, I didn't even realize you consider that bag you have slung over your neck a reticule. I thought you'd brought it along because it has things for the children stuffed inside it, but . . . it hardly compliments your outfit."

Millie patted the bag that was hanging low on her hip. "While it's quite clear you find my nonexistent sense of fashion appalling, I'm a nanny, which means ugly and large bags are something I cannot live without. Of course I have items for the children stuffed inside, such as a few changes of clothing, toy soldiers, a doll, paper and pencils to write with, and rags in case someone suffers an accident. Besides, Abigail didn't leave a fancy reticule out for me to use this evening, so I didn't think it was required."

"Pure negligence on her part, and do remind me to point out that negligence to her after I get the feeling back in my feet and am able to track her down."

Swallowing a laugh, Millie moved across the terrace and set her bag down on the stone bench Lucetta was sitting on, bending down to rustle around the contents until she located her shoes and stockings. Sitting beside her friend, she took a second to roll the stockings up her legs. Slipping into the sparkly shoes that she secretly found completely enchanting, she rose to her feet and shook out her skirts. "There, I'm put together once again."

Lucetta smiled. "You look lovely, even if you did forget the tiara Abigail left out for you to wear."

"I didn't forget."

Lucetta grinned. "I didn't really think so, and a tiara would have looked downright silly in your hair, darling, especially with those lovely sprigs of flowers we added. As it stands now, you look exactly like a fairy princess, but a princess of the woods, something that suits you to perfection."

Glancing to the house, Millie caught a glimpse of her reflection in one of the windows. Staring back at her was a slip of a lady, wearing a lovely gown of soft blue that reminded Millie of how the ocean looked around Newport when it was at its calmest. It was beautifully crafted, with lace framing the square neckline of the gown, a neckline that wasn't overly modest, yet modest enough to not draw attention to charms Millie didn't possess in any abundance.

Pulling her attention away from her reflection, she settled it on Lucetta, shaking her head as she looked her friend over. "It really is a shame you and I have decided to limit ourselves to the terrace this evening. We're looking remarkably well turned out, if I do say so myself. Poor Abigail's efforts to see us looking spit-spot are sadly wasted."

"I'd love to be able to claim I'm disappointed about that, but . . . hmm . . ." Lucetta said as three little bodies came flying around the corner of the house, bodies that belonged to Elizabeth, Thaddeus, and Rose.

"Where have you been?" Elizabeth demanded as she skidded to a stop right in front of Millie, looking completely adorable in a white dress of lace adorned with bows, the purple ribbon in her hair exactly matching those bows. "We've been searching every terrace for what seems like forever, and we were starting to get worried the two of you went back to Abigail's."

"Millie felt the need to stroll up the drive instead of being let off at the door," Lucetta said as she scooped little Rose up into her arms and gave her a loud kiss on the cheek. "We would never leave the three of you here alone to deal with all this madness."

Thaddeus nodded. "It is madness, Miss Lucetta, and it was strange, walking into Uncle Everett's house and . . . Miss Dixon acting like we were guests."

"Maybe it wasn't such a good idea to have you three get ready over at Abigail's," Millie said slowly.

"It *was* a good idea," Rose argued as Lucetta set her back on her feet. "I heard Grandmother Dorothy talking to Miss Abigail in the receiving line, and she said Miss Dixon and Uncle Everett got into a big fight when he got back to Seaview."

"Caroline must have gotten wind of what happened in the Reading Room," Lucetta mumbled.

"I knew word about that would travel fast," Millie said before she frowned at Elizabeth. "But speaking of the receiving line, why aren't the three of you still there? I thought that was the plan. Abigail was supposed to escort you into the house, and then the three of you were supposed to stand with Everett and greet the guests."

Elizabeth rolled her eyes. "Miss Dixon didn't want us to join them. She shooed us away after we said hello, but there's no need to look angry about that, Miss Millie. It's not fun to have to stand still for so long, and we really just wanted to come find you and Miss Lucetta."

Pushing aside the anger that had begun to bubble up inside her, Millie summoned up a smile. "And Lucetta and I are completely delighted about that, since I'm sure we would have begun getting rather lonely out here."

Elizabeth, for some reason, took to looking a little shifty. "Now that we've found the two of you, we need you to come with us into the cottage. We didn't get a chance to greet many people, and you've told us before that we shouldn't forget our manners."

"While it is true that manners are incredibly important, darling, I'm afraid I can't come with you into the cottage. This is Caroline's night, and it wouldn't be fair to her to do something that I know will annoy her."

"But . . . she's clinging to Uncle Everett's arm like he's the best gentleman in the whole world, and that means they've made up from their fight. And she's dripping in jewels, wearing a gown that's very lovely, and . . . what if Uncle Everett goes ahead and does something . . . awful?"

"Like ask Miss Dixon to marry him," Thaddeus whispered. "We don't want that to happen."

Millie's heart gave an uncomfortable lurch she tried her best to ignore. "Your uncle is a grown man, children. If he decides he wants to marry Miss Dixon, I'm certainly not the

412

lady who is going to be able to change his mind."

"If he sees you looking like that, you might be," Rose argued. "You look just like a fairy princess tonight, and Uncle Everett likes you, Miss Millie . . . likes you a lot . . . and we'd really rather have you as our aunt than Miss Dixon."

The sight of the three sets of eyes gazing at her so hopefully had Millie smiling even as she shook her head. "I'm just the nanny, children, and that means I'm the least-suitable woman on the planet for your uncle."

Elizabeth plunked her hands on her slim hips. "But . . . he likes you and . . . you like him."

"Your uncle and I have become friends of a sort, but . . ."

"She'll send us away to boarding school," Elizabeth whispered.

"Did someone mention something about boarding school?"

Spinning on her sparkly heel, Millie discovered Caroline standing on the edge of the terrace, and couldn't help but wonder how long she'd been standing there. "Miss Dixon, don't you look lovely tonight?" she forced out of her mouth.

Fluttering a jeweled fan in front of her

face, Caroline inclined her head, a head that had a huge tiara attached to it, one that seemed to match the diamond stomacher that was placed over her bosom, and matched the five strands of diamonds strung around her throat.

"Thank you, Miss Longfellow. I do believe I look rather nice indeed, as do you. Although I must admit I'm a little confused as to why you're wearing . . . a ball gown. Surely you weren't expecting me to invite you to *enjoy* the ball, were you?"

"I think we both know I would never expect that, Miss Dixon — which is why I'm spending my evening on the terrace. As for why I'm wearing this particular gown, well . . . Abigail purchased it for me, and the children thought it would be great fun if Lucetta and I dressed up, so . . ."

Caroline stiffened and swung her attention to Lucetta. "I wasn't aware you were coming tonight, Miss Plum."

"Believe me, I'd rather be anywhere else, but . . . Everett insisted I attend, and it would have been churlish to refuse his kind offer."

"My Everett certainly can be kind when he sets his mind to it. Misguided, but . . ." Caroline drew in a deep breath, slowly released it, and then smiled. "Well, no matter, the two of you *are* here, and it would be churlish of *me* to insist you leave. However, I've come to fetch the children, to introduce them around, so you, Miss Longfellow, will be expected to accompany us, walking the required three feet behind me, of course."

Millie frowned. "Why didn't you simply introduce the children in the receiving line, like everyone expected you to do?"

Caroline waved the question aside with a flick of her fan. "Surely you, Miss Longfellow, being such an esteemed member of your profession, know that children are highly unlikely to behave properly if they're made to stand still for too long. I, being a rather magnanimous sort, excused them from such a dreary obligation. But now it's time for them to put adorable smiles on those three little faces and allow me to show them off properly."

"We're not pets," Elizabeth muttered.

"That's debatable, but . . ." Caroline moved closer to the children and looked them up and down. "All of you, surprisingly enough, turned out very nicely this evening. Why, those dresses, with all their frills and lace, are too precious, and . . . look at you, darling Thaddeus, wearing pants, and well-tailored pants at that." She smiled again.

"You'll do me and your uncle proud this evening, and if you behave, I'll give you a wonderful surprise at the end of the ball."

"What kind of surprise?" Rose asked.

"It wouldn't be much of a surprise if I told you, Rosetta."

Rose immediately turned stubborn. "My name is Rose."

"It's not. Rose is a common, nasty name, so you'll go by Rosetta, thank you very much. Now, take my hand. You may take my other one, Elizabeth, and you, Thaddeus, may walk beside your twin."

"I want to hold Miss Millie's hand," Thaddeus argued.

"That would not be proper, dear. Miss *Longfellow,* not Miss *Millie,* is the nanny, so she does not get to have the honor of holding your hand, especially since I expect her to trail after us."

"I'll trail with her," Lucetta said, stepping up to Millie.

"I don't recall inviting you to join us, Miss Plum."

Lucetta drew herself up, and right there and then, in a blink of an eye, she turned . . . haughty. "Surely you must realize that I'm not the type of woman who waits to be invited for anything, Miss Dixon."

For a second, Millie thought Caroline was

going to argue, but she looked at Lucetta for a long moment, seemed to realize she'd met her match, and shrugged. "Fine, but make certain the two of you stay three feet behind me."

Lucetta dipped into a cheeky curtsy. "As you wish, Your Highness."

Not bothering to address the cheek, Caroline folded up her fan, grabbed hold of Elizabeth and Rose's hands, and without speaking another word, stalked for the house.

"Do you remember when Everett offered to purchase me something for my assistance and I refused his offer?" Lucetta asked, twining her arm with Millie's.

"Changed your mind about that, have you?"

Lucetta grinned. "I have indeed, and I think we might just have to ask him for an added bonus for you as well." Her grin widened. "That diamond collar Caroline's wearing is nice. Perhaps we'll insist Everett buy us two of those."

"I highly doubt I'll ever be invited to an event that requires something so fancy."

"Good point, but stop frowning, dear. People are beginning to take note of us."

Glancing to Lucetta out of the corner of her eye, Millie found her friend had changed from haughty to aloof, although her eyes were sparkling and her lips were curled rather intriguingly right at the corners, lending her a most mysterious air. "How do you do that?"

"Years and years of practice, but . . . smile."

Summoning up a smile, even though her lips had turned remarkably stiff, Millie held fast to Lucetta's arm as they traveled down a hallway — the requested three feet of space being carefully maintained — and into the ballroom. Pretending not to notice everyone staring her way, Millie kept her gaze on the children. Pride flowed through her when they used proper manners with everyone Caroline introduced them to, leaving quite a few guests smiling fondly after them when they moved on to meet other people.

"Everett's over by that wall," Lucetta whispered with a nod to the left.

Pulling her attention away from Thaddeus, who seemed to be telling a well-dressed lady all about his tin soldiers, Millie suddenly felt her stomach clench when her gaze settled on Everett.

He was looking . . . well, certainly not dashing considering the state of his bruised face, but he was laughing at something a young lady was saying to him and then nodding appreciatively at a gentleman who spoke to him next.

"He doesn't seem to be suffering any lasting effects from those brawls. In fact, he seems to be enjoying himself, and no one seems to be giving him the cut direct," she said.

Lucetta squeezed her arm. "I never imagined anyone would cut him, Millie." She waved a hand in the air. "Look around. We're right smack in the midst of proof of exactly how large the Mulberry fortune is, something no guest here, I assure you, has neglected to notice. The decorations alone had to have cost a sizeable fortune, and you can smell the tempting aroma of dishes that I'm going to assume will be extraordinary."

Taking a moment to look around her surroundings, Millie found that Lucetta was exactly right. Gold tulle was strung from the ceilings, sparkling with what she hoped weren't real diamonds, and exotic hothouse flowers were spread all over the room, their delicate scent mixing with that of the delicious food Lucetta had mentioned. Chandeliers sparkled, and crystal was everywhere, while members of the staff Miss Pickenpaugh had brought in served glasses of champagne off of silver trays. Fountains were tinkling from every corner of the room, and an entire orchestra was set up on the far side, the members of that orchestra formally dressed and even now beginning to tune up their instruments.

She'd never felt more out of place or more inconsequential.

This was Everett's true world, filled with sparkling people, sparkling surroundings, and sparkling conversation.

She was simply an orphan who came from poor parents and never had anything sparkling to say, unless it revolved around children.

"Millie, are you all right?"

"Of course I am," she finally managed to whisper.

Taking a very firm grip on her arm, Lucetta pulled Millie up to Caroline, who immediately bristled. "What happened to the three feet?" Caroline hissed under her breath.

"Millie isn't feeling well, so I'm taking her back to the terrace." Lucetta nodded to the children. "You may stay here, but when Miss Dixon is done with you, go to your Uncle Everett or come back to us. We'll be just outside."

"Millie, Lucetta, there you are."

Drawing in a steadying breath, Millie soon found herself being given an enthusiastic hug by Abigail, right before Dorothy replaced Abigail and gave her a good hard squeeze.

"You look absolutely breathtaking, my dear, as do you, Lucetta," Dorothy said with a smile.

"They neglected to wear their tiaras," Abigail grumbled.

"You expected them to wear tiaras?" Caroline's face began to darken. "That is . . ."

"I was just about to take Millie outside," Lucetta interrupted. "I think the closeness of this room has made her a little light-headed, so if you'll excuse us . . . ?"

Without bothering to wait for anyone to reply, Lucetta spun around with Millie still attached to her arm and began strolling ever so casually through the crowd, although she somehow managed the stroll at a rather rapid rate of speed. Pulling Millie through the door, she hustled her back to their obscure terrace and pushed her down on the stone bench. "What happened?"

Tears blinded Millie for a second before she dashed them away. "I've been so silly."

"I don't understand."

"I tried to pretend otherwise, but deep down I thought there was a chance . . ."

"For you and Everett?"

Millie waved a hand rather helplessly in

the air. "I told you — I've been silly. It's just that he's been so . . ."

"Interested in you?"

Millie blinked. "I don't know if I'd go that far, but he has been nice, but . . . I suppose that's just his nature."

"Everett is nice, but he's not *that* nice, and he *is* interested in you. He's just been fighting that interest."

"That makes me feel *so* much better."

Lucetta smiled down at Millie. "He's your Mr. Darcy."

"That's just a fairy tale, Lucetta. Real gentlemen don't put their social position in jeopardy because they've fallen for someone not of their station."

"Oliver fell for Harriet."

"Since she turned out to have a fairly illustrious ancestry, that's probably not the best example to use." Millie's shoulders sagged. "Did I ever tell you that I went back to the orphanage I was raised in a few years ago?"

"I don't recall you ever mentioning that to me."

"I was hoping, you see, to find out more about my parents, hoping to find out I had a few siblings here or there, but . . . no one could find any record of me having been raised there at all. Since I'm not even sure my surname really is Longfellow, I'll never find a real family like Harriet did."

"I'm your family, Millie. I've been your sister since the moment we met."

Tears blinded her once again, and she didn't bother to wipe them off her cheeks when they slipped out of her eyes. "That's lovely of you to say, Lucetta, but it doesn't change the fact that I'm missing the whole proper pedigree business that's essential in Everett's world."

Sitting beside her on the bench, Lucetta took her hand. Music from the orchestra began spilling out of the open windows moments later, and for a long while, they simply sat and listened to it.

Finally drawing in a shuddering breath, Millie patted Lucetta's hand and was about to go see where the children were when Davis, dressed in a smart set of formal livery, came out on the terrace, carrying one end of a table while Johnson, another footman, carried the other. Sending Millie a grin, Davis deposited the table off to the side, then nodded to some maids who'd followed him, maids who seemed to be holding table linens, cutlery, and dinnerware in their hands.

"Good heavens. What's all this?" Millie asked, rising to her feet as the maids went about the business of setting up the table.

"Mrs. Mulberry thought it might be pleasant for the two of you, and the children as well, to enjoy dinner out here on the terrace," Davis said. "Dinner won't be served for hours yet, but since all the guests are getting ready for the cotillion dances to begin, our services won't be missed right now."

"How kind of Mrs. Mulberry to realize the children would be more comfortable out here," Millie said softly.

"Indeed," Davis said right as Elizabeth, Rose, and Thaddeus ran out on the terrace again and sent Millie grins.

"Miss Dixon's done with us," Thaddeus proclaimed in clear delight. "We came back here to do some dancing even though Elizabeth might have wanted to watch that cotill . . . whatever it's called."

"Cotillion," Elizabeth supplied. "And I did want to watch it since I'm not really sure what it's all about."

Lucetta rose from the bench and walked over to Elizabeth's side. "A cotillion is a special dance, performed by a select group of young ladies and gentlemen, all of whom have spent hours learning the proper steps at a dance academy."

Elizabeth looked a little wistful. "I sure

hope I'll be able to learn a cotillion dance someday. The ladies all looked beautiful and their partners were very dashing."

Lucetta shook her head. "You say that now, darling, but once you've been forced to practice the same dance over and over and over again, well, it becomes somewhat tedious."

"You've practiced for a cotillion?" Elizabeth asked slowly.

For a second, Lucetta's eyes clouded, but then she laughed, took hold of Elizabeth's hand, and twirled her around. "How about if I show you a few simple steps?"

Watching Lucetta twirl Elizabeth around the terrace, Millie wondered once again about her friend's past, a past Lucetta avoided talking about, but a past Millie knew full well held secrets.

"Do you want to dance with me, Miss Millie?"

Shaking out of her thoughts, Millie grinned down at Thaddeus, who was holding his little arm out to her. Unable to resist his sweet offer, she bent down and took the arm, laughing in delight as they shuffled around the terrace, completely at odds with the beats of the music pouring out of the windows, but having a grand time nevertheless.

"Someone needs to dance with me," Rose complained from the sidelines.

Stepping immediately up to her, Davis presented Rose with a bow, and grinning from ear to ear, the little girl dipped into a remarkably fine curtsy, before she threw herself at the footman and he whirled her away.

Time slipped by as they danced to one tune after another, and during a pause in the music, feeling a little breathless, Millie shook her head at Davis, who'd just offered to show her how to waltz.

"I really don't dance, Davis, but thank you for the offer."

"I don't actually know the steps, Miss Millie, but it seems a shame that you and Miss Plum are looking so lovely tonight, but haven't been given the opportunity to waltz."

"It's a shame indeed."

Millie's breath left her in a split second as Everett strolled across the terrace, smiling her way and looking remarkably handsome, at least to her, even though his face was still a bit of a disaster. Coming to a stop right in front of her, he nodded to Davis.

"Perhaps you could offer Miss Plum a dance instead?"

Davis's eyes widened. He leaned closer to

Everett and lowered his voice. "Miss Plum scares me, Mr. Mulberry. That's why I asked Miss Millie. She's safer."

"I'm completely safe, Davis," Lucetta said with a huff before she took the poor man by the arm and grabbed hold of his other hand. "Allow me to teach you the basic steps of the waltz."

With Davis turning bright red, Lucetta sent Millie a wink and then spun Davis around, not giving the man an opportunity to refuse her demand of a waltz.

"That'll be something he'll be able to talk about for years," Millie said, catching Everett's eye, which immediately had all the breath leaving her again.

To her confusion, Everett frowned. "I must beg your pardon, Millie. I rather rudely stepped in between you and Davis. It has not escaped my notice that he seems a little . . . keen to be around you, and . . . if you're, ah, keen to be around him, I won't stand in your way."

Millie scrunched up her nose. "Davis has been secretly seeing one of the maids, Ann, for over a year now, so any keenness on his part has probably just been a ruse to hide that relationship. But don't go letting anyone know about that relationship, and don't even think about letting either Ann or

Davis go from their positions."

"Since you told me you're planning to tell Harriet about Davis and his tailoring skills, I have a feeling he won't be in my employ long, but of course I won't let him or Ann go."

"Wonderful, and . . . thank you for that."

"You're welcome, and since that's settled . . . shall we waltz?"

"I should warn you that what we're about to do will not remotely be considered a waltz, not given my two left feet."

"We'll see about that." Laughter rumbled in Everett's chest but the rumbling died a sudden death when he pulled her close, his breath fanning her face. "Did I tell you how lovely you look tonight?"

"I don't believe so," Millie managed to whisper.

"Well, now you know, and . . . we're waltzing."

Millie blinked and realized she was, indeed, gliding over the uneven stones of the terrace, Everett's strong arm pressing her a little too close for comfort as he steered her around, his steps perfectly timed with the music. A glance over his shoulder found the children clapping their hands, while Lucetta flashed her a grin as she pushed Davis through the steps of the dance.

"I, ah, couldn't help noticing that some of your guests seemed to be very friendly with you tonight," she said after Everett dipped her in his arms, the action sending butterflies fluttering about her stomach.

"Of course they're friendly, Millie. They've been invited to what will surely be deemed the ball of the summer season, and . . . I do hold a bit of power within society."

"You enjoy that power, don't you."

Everett slowed his steps and stared into her eyes. "I'm not that fussed about it anymore."

"But . . . you'd miss it, wouldn't you, if that power, or your position within society went away?"

"I think it would be next to impossible for that to happen. I'd have to do something really foolish for society to turn its collective back on me." Everett pulled her even closer and slowed their steps until they were barely moving. "This is nice."

Edging a little away from him, she lifted her head and found her breath catching in her throat when his gaze suddenly locked on her lips.

Tingles spread over her entire body even as her knees began to give out, and then . . .

"Everett, there you are. I've been searching all over for you."

Everett's arm dropped away from her, and
when Millie turned, she found Caroline,
strangely enough, smiling at them from the
edge of the terrace, although there was
something odd resting in the woman's eyes.

Before Millie could get so much as a
squeak out of her mouth, Caroline turned
and let out a laugh. "Doesn't this just prove
how devoted my darling Everett is to his
wards? Why, little Elizabeth wanted to see
how a proper dance was done, so what does
my Everett do? Shows her by teaching . . .
the nanny."

The last two words sounded somewhat
forced, but Millie didn't dwell on that, not
since she was being faced with what looked
to be all two hundred of Caroline's guests,
all of whom had assembled on the back
lawn, and all of whom were watching her
with rather daunting expressions on their
faces.

A gentleman Millie recognized as Mr.
Dudley Codman stepped out of the crowd,
and a mere moment later he was standing
right beside them, a smile on his face but
anger in his eyes. Taking hold of Everett's
arm, he let out a hearty laugh.

"Caroline has decided, since your guests

are so curious, to hand out the pails sooner than expected. Since this is *your* ball, and *you* provided your guests with the treasures inside those pails, well, you should be present when your guests are given their pails." Dudley lowered his voice. "Do not even think about declining, Everett. You're walking a fine line here, and embarrassing Caroline in the process. This is her night, remember that."

For a moment, Everett looked as if he wanted to argue that point, but then nodded to Caroline. "Shall we attend to our guests?"

Caroline smiled far too sweetly back at him. "I need to have a little word with the nanny first, but then I'll join you."

The hair on Millie's neck stood to attention.

Everett shook his head. "I don't believe that's necessary."

"I wasn't asking your permission, Everett."

Looking back to the crowd that seemed to be edging closer, Millie squared her shoulders. "I'll be fine. You should go see to your guests."

"I don't think I should leave you."

"Don't be ridiculous, Everett. I'm not going to do anything to her." Caroline smiled. "If you must know, I need the help of the children for an extra little surprise I've planned for later on this evening, and need to talk to their nanny about it. We'll only be a short time."

"We'll be fine," Millie told him again.

"I'll walk with you, shall I?" Dudley asked as he practically pushed Everett forward. Thankfully, once Everett began walking through the crowd, that crowd turned and followed him back into the house.

"It's amazing how cooperative people can be when there's the added lure of treasure," Caroline drawled before she set her sights on the children. "I need the three of you to go up to Elizabeth's room, and do not leave that room until I come to fetch you."

"I'm not comfortable having them out of my sight," Millie said slowly.

"They'll be less than comfortable if you keep them out here, especially since I have a few things to say to you that might not be appropriate for . . . tender ears."

Lucetta stepped forward. "Millie doesn't have to listen to anything you feel you need to say."

"Shut . . . up."

Millie caught Elizabeth's eye. "Darling, I need you to take your brother and sister to your room for just a little bit. I'll join you as soon as I'm able."

Looking close to tears, Elizabeth nodded, took hold of Rose and Thaddeus's hands, and hurried across the terrace and out of sight.

"Horrible creatures," Caroline muttered before she turned and set her sights on Millie again. "Now, you and I, my dear, need to come to an understanding."

"An understanding?"

"Exactly." Caroline lifted her chin. "You must find Everett's interest in you very romantic, but surely you must know that he'll end up with me in the end. He's a tried-and-true gentleman at heart, raised to adhere to the rules of society, no matter what those rules demand of him. Because of that, he certainly won't deny me, especially in front of the highest members of society, what he's been promising for years."

Millie drew in a breath. "You're going to go through with announcing your engagement tonight."

"Of course I am, in fact . . ." She lifted her hand, fumbled with the clasp of a small reticule that was looped around her wrist, then pulled out a box. "This is the ring I'll be wearing by the end of this night. It's an engagement ring I picked out, and an engagement ring that will soon be joined by a wedding band."

"Everett didn't mention anything about a ring he was going to give you tonight," Lucetta said. "And why would you be holding on to it?"

Caroline ignored Lucetta, keeping her attention squarely centered on Millie, who was beginning to feel a little queasy. "You didn't think he was going to throw everything away for you, did you?" She had the audacity to laugh. "He may be overly fond of you, my dear, but gentlemen like Everett don't marry the women they're fond of . . . they amuse themselves with them for a bit, then move on to the next amusement."

Lucetta's lips curled into a snarl. "Everett doesn't think of Millie as an amusement."

"Shut . . . up." Caroline turned her gaze back on Millie. "It pains me, it truly does, to see that hurt on your face, dear, but you're not good enough for Everett, and since you seem somewhat intelligent, you must realize that." She let out a sigh. "He was coming out here to tell you of our upcoming engagement, but . . . being a man, he apparently decided to cushion the blow by dancing with you first, something that was not well done on his part since it, I believe, allowed you false hope."

"You would have me believe that Everett came out here to tell me about his upcoming engagement, and then . . . decided to waltz with me to *cushion the blow*?"

"Society gentlemen do rather odd things at times, my dear, but . . . allow me to spare both of us any further drama. This is my ball, Everett has made promises to me that I expect him to honor, and it is past time you took your leave."

For a second, tears blinded her, but then Millie drew in a breath and squared her shoulders. "I can't leave the children."

"Do you honestly want to stay and watch Everett and me become engaged, because believe me, dear girl, given your obvious affection for the man, it won't be pleasant for you." She smiled. "As for the children, I really am intending to have them help me with a bit of an extra surprise I've arranged. I'll either have a maid see them settled tonight here at Seaview, or, if they turn difficult, I'll send them home with Abigail. But, they're not your responsibility, my dear, no matter how much you wish they were, and — just so we're clear — as of this moment, you may consider yourself dismissed from your position."

With that, Caroline reached up and patted Millie's cheek, before she headed for the cottage and vanished from sight.

Tears blinded Millie once again and she could barely see Lucetta's face when her friend came up beside her. "Are you all right?"

"Do you really think they're going to go through with their engagement tonight?"

Lucetta bit her lip. "I'd love to be able to say with certainty that she was lying, but . . . members of society are different from us. Because of that, I can't know for sure if Everett would be willing to risk his position in that society by not going through with the promises he apparently made Caroline."

Millie's shoulders drooped. "I thought . . . Well . . . it no longer matters what I thought, but . . . I need to get out of here."

"I'll bring the buggy around," Davis said, stepping out of the shadows and looking uncharacteristically solemn as he nodded to Millie and then walked away.

"I'm not at ease leaving the children, though," Millie whispered.

Lucetta rubbed a soothing hand down Millie's arm. "Don't worry about them. I'll find Abigail, tell her what happened, and then I'll stay with the children."

"That's a lot to ask of you."

"It's not." Taking Millie by the hand, Lucetta smiled a rather sad sort of smile. "I'm sorry, Millie. I was hoping things would turn out differently."

Millie straightened her spine. "As was I, if I'm being completely honest. But, if nothing else, I've finally seen exactly how ill-suited Everett and I are for each other. I may still find him incredibly appealing — especially since I've discovered he's not nearly as insufferable as I used to think — but I need to face reality. He's not my Mr. Darcy, no matter how much I might have tried to convince myself he was, and I need to accept that and move forward with my life — a life that does not include Mr. Everett Mulberry."

18

Anxiety settled in and refused to disperse the longer Caroline was absent from the ball. Nodding distractedly at a lady who was thanking him for the jeweled bracelet she'd found in her pail, Everett made his way across the crowded hallway, dodging numerous guests who'd brought their pails out there, probably in the hopes of finding a bit of room to enjoy their treasure hunting since the ballroom was a true crush. Spotting his mother beside an ornate fountain Miss Pickenpaugh had positioned right in front of a window, Everett headed her way.

"Did Caroline invite every person in Newport to this ball?" Dorothy asked as she fanned her face with one of the fans he'd thought were going to be the only favors given out to the ladies.

Everett smiled. "Mr. McAllister is responsible for the guest list. And I wouldn't be surprised to discover he's also the one responsible for giving Caroline the idea about the treasure pails."

"Which I'll be certain to speak with him about," Dorothy said as a lady pulled a sparkling bracelet from her pail and let out a squeal of pure delight. "But since I don't want to dwell on how much money Caroline's little treat to the guests is costing you, especially since I'm quickly coming to the conclusion she did it out of sheer spite, we should talk of something pleasant. Have you seen Millie lately?"

"I have, out on the terrace, but . . . I'm afraid I might have made a bit of a blunder, leaving her out there with Caroline and all, especially after Caroline, along with a lot of our guests, found me teaching Millie how to . . . waltz."

"Oh . . . my." Dorothy sent him a rather sad shake of her head. "That was a blunder, dear, and if I may give you some motherly advice, you need to go back to the terrace, immediately."

"I don't think Caroline would do anything to her," he said slowly.

"Which just goes to show how truly negligent I've been with teaching you the intricacies of a lady's mind, but . . . off you go now, and . . . good luck."

Taking a second to kiss his mother's

cheek, Everett headed back down the hallway, but before he had a chance to get to the terrace, the orchestra stopped playing and . . . Dudley's voice rang out.

"If I may have your attention . . . Miss Dixon is about to present her great surprise. We'll need everyone in the ballroom."

The next thing Everett knew, his arms had been taken by two giggling ladies, both of whom were sending him knowing looks as they steered him down the hallway and into the ballroom. Additional looks were immediately sent his way by all of the guests assembled around him — looks that had expectation written all over them.

As the two ladies released their hold on him and stepped back, he found himself standing there, in the midst of a very large crowd but not feeling like a part of that crowd. As if the sun had finally come out from beneath a very dark crowd, truth settled over him.

He could not, tonight or any night in the future, fulfill society's expectations for him and Caroline, because . . .

He didn't love Caroline.

She didn't love him.

And . . . he was fairly sure he was head over heels in love with Millie.

His lips began curving just as the idea

struck that this was probably not the best moment to have had such an epiphany, but . . . at least he'd had it before Caroline made her big announcement. That would have been horrible for both of them, and would have ended up embarrassing Caroline no small amount in front of people she only wanted to impress.

"There she is," someone called out, causing Everett to shake himself from his thoughts and direct his gaze to where everyone was now staring.

Caroline was framed in the entranceway of the ballroom, looking remarkably sparkly as the many diamonds she was wearing caught and held the light from the chandeliers. The crowd scooted backward, leaving her a clear path through the ballroom, and as she began walking, Everett started toward her, stopping in his tracks though when she lifted a hand and shook her head ever so slightly in his direction.

"Since everyone has been on pins and needles to learn about my little surprise, I thought I'd put all of you out of your misery and disclose my surprise sooner than planned," Caroline called as applause rang out through the room.

Caroline waited for it to end, and then she waved a hand and servers immediately appeared, bearing trays with fresh champagne. Smiling as the servers began to hand out the drinks, Caroline caught his eye and sent him a wink, but held up her hand again when he started moving her way.

"You're fine right where you are, dear," she called as laughter immediately spread throughout the room.

When everyone had a drink, Caroline held up her champagne flute. "Before we get to my little announcement, let us raise our glasses to Mr. Everett Mulberry, our host for the evening."

"Hear, hear," someone called, and then glasses were lifted to lips and champagne sipped.

Caroline sent another lovely smile his way, which he found less than reassuring, before she waved a hand to the crowd which had them falling silent again. "Now . . . on to the surprise. Darling, would you do the honors?"

Everett's feet remained rooted to the spot, but then, oddly enough, Dudley strode out of the crowd, across the ballroom floor, stopped by Caroline's side, turned, and smiled.

"Treasured friends, it is with great pleasure that I'm finally able to announce, here at Mr. Everett Mulberry's ball, that

Miss Caroline Dixon has agreed . . . to become *my* wife."

The silence was deafening as every single guest turned disbelieving eyes on Everett. For the span of a split second, he had no idea what to do, but then, he allowed himself the luxury of doing exactly what came naturally . . . he laughed.

His feet were suddenly able to move again, and he turned those feet in Caroline's direction. Reaching her side a moment later, he leaned forward, ignored the triumph lingering in her eyes, and kissed her soundly on the cheek, earning a hiss from her in response which he also ignored.

"Thank you, my dear, for giving me the greatest gift possible . . . my freedom."

When Caroline began sputtering, he looked to Dudley. "Well played, old friend, well played indeed. I wish you the very best of luck." Turning, Everett faced the crowd. "A toast — to Dudley and Caroline, soon to be Mr. and Mrs. Dudley Codman. May they enjoy a happy life together."

The guests slowly raised their glasses and then sipped their champagne, gazing back at him in obvious shock. Everett caught his mother's eye and found her beaming at him, while his father nodded in clear approval. Abigail was practically hopping up and down in delight, but before he could so much as send her a grin, Caroline was whispering furiously in his ear.

"You might think you've won this, Everett, but I assure you, you haven't."

Looking down at her, Everett kept a smile on his face even as his eyes narrowed. "What do you mean?"

"Did you truly believe I'd allow her to win? Allow a little nobody nanny to steal my gentleman away from me? I set her straight, I did, got her to see the truth about you, and . . . I might have mentioned that you and I were going forward with our engagement plans."

"You lied to Millie?"

"I did you a favor," Caroline corrected.

"Where is she?"

"She scurried off back to that dreadful Mrs. Hart's cottage. If you leave right now, you might be able to catch her. However . . . I don't think she'll listen to any sappy words you might want to tell her. I was very, very . . . convincing. Oh, and I dismissed her as the nanny, so, now that I think about it, she might already be heading out of Newport since there was no reason for her to take the children with her when she left Seaview."

"Where *are* the children?" he asked.

Caroline shrugged. "I told them to stay up in Elizabeth's room, but since those children don't exactly like to behave, they could be anywhere by now."

Swallowing the words he wanted to say, words that were not very gentlemanly at all, Everett brushed past Caroline and headed out of the ballroom, unmindful of the titters that followed him. Deciding his first order of business was collecting the children, he turned for the stairs and took them two at a time, the thought coming out of nowhere that Caroline had mentioned something about them being in on the surprise. Hoping she hadn't filled their little heads with her lies, he reached Elizabeth's room, but found it empty. Striding onward, he checked Thaddeus's room next, found it empty as well, and then moved on to Rose's room.

"If you're looking for the children, they're no longer here."

Spinning around, he found Miss Gertrude Rathbone standing in the doorway.

"What are you doing up here, Gertrude?"

"I saw you heading up the stairs, knew you'd be looking for the children, so thought I'd let you know they've left with Miss Plum." She began inspecting her nails. "I believe they were heading off to Mrs. Hart's cottage."

"Do you know if Caroline spoke with them?"

Gertrude raised her head. "Caroline loathes the little beasts. I doubt she would've had much to say to them, although I'm sure she's absolutely thrilled by the idea that she won't have a ready-made family waiting for her when she marries Dudley. Caroline does enjoy being the center of attention, don't you know, and with Dudley, well, he'll make certain she's always the center of his universe."

"I could almost feel sorry for him if he hadn't just broken every rule of friendship there is," Everett returned. "But how do you know for certain Lucetta was taking the children to Abigail's?"

Gertrude smiled. "Honestly, Everett, I would have thought by now that you'd know I'm very good at eavesdropping. How else would I always have such delicious gossip at my disposal?"

Realizing right there and then that Miss Gertrude Rathbone was not the good company he'd once thought her to be, Everett sent her a nod and headed out of Rose's room. He moved back down the stairs, meeting his mother when he reached the bottom.

"Goodness, but that was . . . interesting.

But . . . what were you doing upstairs?"
Dorothy asked.

"I was going to get the children, but Lucetta's apparently taken them over to Abigail's, so I'm off to fetch them now — along with Millie, of course."

Dorothy reached up and patted his cheek, causing him to wince since his face was still a little tender from all the brawls he'd been in of late. "There's hope for you yet, my darling."

Leaning closer to his mother, Everett kissed her cheek, stepping back to discover that Abigail had joined them.

"I must say that balls are certainly turning out to be far more interesting these days," Abigail said. "Why, I thought that what happened with Harriet at the ball I held just a short time ago would be enough to keep society all atwitter for ages, but . . . I think society will shove that incident aside and replace it with the drama that just unfolded here."

Everett leaned down and kissed Abigail on the cheek. "While I'm certain you're right, we'll have to discuss the pertinent details at a later date. I've been told Millie went back to your cottage. And since I've also been told that she's suffering under some false information, I need to get to her as quickly as I can."

"How wonderful, dear. Well, not the part about Millie suffering from false information. But when you see her, do make certain to tell her I'll be expecting an apology from both of you over your lack of confidence pertaining to my matchmaking abilities."

Sending Abigail a grin, he didn't bother to address that annoying bit of truth as he strode down the hallway. Not wanting to run into any of the curious guests he knew were probably lying in wait for him, he headed through the kitchen, out the back door, and turned toward the stables.

Reaching his destination in a relatively short period of time, Everett was forced to stop in his tracks when Davis suddenly stepped in front him. His footman was not looking his normal affable self but was glaring at Everett, and . . . the man's fists were clenched.

"Is something the matter?" he asked slowly.

"I would say so, sir, but since you are my employer, it wouldn't be proper of me to tell you what that something is, or tell you where I think you should go at the moment."

"I was intending to go to Mrs. Hart's house."

"You're not done misleading Miss Millie?"

Everett stepped closer to Davis, stopping when the man actually raised one of his clenched fists. "Were you, by chance, present when Miss Dixon spoke to Millie?"

"I was, and good thing too, sir, since I was able to fetch Miss Millie a buggy straightaway so she could get away from . . . you."

"Miss Dixon lied, Davis. She admitted to me she told Millie we were still going through with our engagement plans this evening, but I had no intention of asking Caroline to marry me tonight. And as odd as this may sound, Caroline is now happily engaged to Mr. Codman."

"I beg your pardon?"

"I wish I could explain more sufficiently, but now is not the time. I need to find Millie."

"Miss Dixon told Miss Millie you only see her as an amusement."

Temper began to boil directly underneath Everett's skin. "I swear to you, I've never looked at Millie as a source of amusement. Granted, I do find her amusing almost all the time, but that's completely different."

"What are your intentions toward her, sir, if I may be so bold to ask?"

"I think it would probably be better for

449

me to discuss those intentions with Millie first, although I can assure you, they are completely honorable."

Davis regarded him for a long moment before he nodded. "Well, that's all right, then, but I do think you need to find Miss Millie straightaway. She was close to tears when I summoned a buggy for her, and I don't believe Miss Millie is a lady who is normally prone to tears."

"You're certain she went back to Mrs. Hart's cottage?"

"I had Johnson drive her, sir, so yes, that is where he was told to take her."

"And may I hope Miss Plum and the children were in that buggy as well?"

"They were not. The last I saw of Miss Plum she was heading off to attend to the children, but I haven't seen her since."

"She never called for a carriage or buggy?"

"No, but she might have made use of one of the carriages parked out front. I did see a carriage traveling down the drive not too long ago, but I'm sorry to say I didn't take note of who was inside it."

"Well, I'm not doing any good standing here. I'm sure Lucetta's got the children well in hand, but if you see her, tell her to meet me at Abigail's."

"Very good, sir. I'll have a groom ready a

horse for you straightaway."

It was a mark of how competent his staff was that a horse was led out to him only a few minutes later. Thanking Davis again, Everett climbed into the saddle, urging the horse into an immediate trot. Turning toward Abigail's cottage, he tried to get his thoughts into some type of order.

The first thing to pop to mind was the realization that he'd narrowly escaped a nasty future. Caroline was not the woman he'd always hoped her to be, but was instead mean, vindictive, and quite honestly, a little disturbed. Being married to her would have turned into torture over the years, and as a great sense of relief settled over him, he lifted his head to the sky.

"You certainly do have an odd way of going about things, Lord, but thank you for helping me avoid a nasty future . . . without hurting Caroline in the process. And, if you could just watch over Millie for me until I find her, that would be greatly appreciated."

Urging the horse into a gallop, Everett soon found himself in front of Abigail's cottage. Easing out of the saddle, he looped the reins over the front porch railing and climbed the steps. He was raising his hand to knock when the door suddenly opened, revealing Mr. Kenton, Abigail's elderly butler.

Unfortunately, given that Mr. Kenton seemed to be holding some type of bat in his hands, a bat he was now raising at Everett rather threateningly, Everett got the immediate impression the man might not exactly be happy to see him.

"Good evening, Mr. Kenton," Everett finally said when the butler remained mute, something Everett was fairly sure went against every proper bone in the man's body. "I was, ah, well, I was wondering if I might speak with Miss Longfellow."

"She doesn't want to speak with you."

Before Everett could get another word past his lips, Mr. Kenton stepped back and shut the door in Everett's face.

Squaring his shoulders, Everett moved forward and knocked rather determinedly on that door.

The sound of the lock clicking into place was the only response.

He knocked again.

A minute passed, the door remained stubbornly shut against him, so . . . he knocked once more.

This, to his annoyance, became a trend. He'd knock, a minute would pass, and he'd knock again.

Finally, when his knuckles began burning, he turned and stalked down the steps. Just as Millie had done at the Reading Room, he began to peek in all the windows, hoping to find one that might be unlocked.

Unfortunately, Mr. Kenton had apparently already thought of the whole unlocked-window business, because Everett heard windows ahead of him being slammed shut.

Pushing through the shrubbery he'd been forced to climb behind, he jumped when a flock of peacocks suddenly flew out at him, screeching in a manner he was far too familiar with, right as the sound of barking puppies could be heard from inside the house. Knowing full well those puppies would be with Millie, who couldn't refuse cuteness if she tried, Everett followed the sound as the peacocks began trailing after him.

Stopping at the back of the house, he pushed his way through yet another shrub, peered through the window, and smiled.

Millie was standing by a roaring fire with a book in her hand, something he would never tire of seeing. His smile widened, until . . . she glared at the book right before she tossed it into the fire.

Unable to stop himself, he leaned forward

and rapped on the window.

Because she jumped a good foot into the air after the rap, he knew perfectly well she'd heard it, but Millie did not turn.

"Open the window."

Bending over, she straightened with another book in her hand, which she immediately tossed into the flames.

"What are you doing?" he yelled.

Turning, she narrowed her eyes, marched over to the window, unlocked it, and then pushed it up. "Go away."

"I need to talk to you."

"We have nothing left to say."

"We have plenty left to say. At least I do."

"You should be saying things to Caroline, not to me."

"Caroline and I have nothing else to say to each other."

"You're both from the same world. You should have plenty to say. Whereas you and I, well . . . we're just too different." Millie began pushing down the window.

"I didn't propose to Caroline, and from what I've been able to learn, she lied to you about everything."

Millie stopped pushing. "Why would she do that? I'm just the nanny."

"You were a threat, and one she wanted to get rid of, so she lied. Told you all sorts of horrible things."

"She also allowed me to see the truth. You'll be ostracized from all of your good friends if you continue associating with me."

"That doesn't bother me in the least."

Millie let out a snort. "It does, or at least it will when you're friendless."

"I'm not friendless. I have you, Lucetta, Oliver and Harriet when they get home, and I could go on and on."

"You've run out of names, haven't you?"

"May I come in?"

Frowning, Millie leaned closer to him. "Why didn't you just use the door in the first place?"

"Mr. Kenton slammed it in my face."

Millie grinned. "How delightful! But . . . oh, very well." She pushed the window open again.

"Couldn't you simply go and open the door for me?"

"And incur the wrath of Mr. Kenton? Not likely."

Grumbling a little under his breath, especially when the shrub seemed to take that moment to attack him, Everett hauled himself through the window and landed on the floor. Before he had a chance to shut the window though, a peacock hopped up on the sill and jumped into the room, followed by two of its friends.

Mayhem ensued when the puppies spotted the peacocks and apparently decided a nice game of chase was in order. By the time Everett had rounded the peacocks up and carried them one by one back to the window — where he had to very gently, per Millie's request, lower them to the ground instead of just tossing them out and hoping for the best — he was breathing somewhat heavily. He was also sporting a good deal of puppy slobber on his trousers, left there by Thaddeus's puppy, Chip, a far too enthusiastic scrap of motley adorableness that seemed to have a hankering for fabric.

Turning away from the window to what was now a peacock-free parlor, Everett found Millie standing in front of the fireplace again, holding another book in her hand and contemplating it rather intently.

"Surely you're not going to destroy another book, are you?"

"I've decided my obsession with reading has gotten me absolutely nowhere, so . . . I'm tossing all the nonsense out of my life and intend to travel forth with less baggage."

"You love to read."

"And I'll occasionally indulge that love, but enough is enough." She held up her copy of *Pride and Prejudice.* "This, for all intent and purposes, is a fairy tale. I'm done with fairy tales for good, as well as anything by Shakespeare. I loathe his stories, don't understand most of what he's written, and I was only reading them because of any future children I hoped to have. But since I'm destined to remain a spinster forever . . . I'm chucking them into the fire."

"What do Shakespeare and any children you might have in the future have in common?"

Millie sent him a look that clearly said she found him a little dense. "I wanted to be knowledgeable so that my children wouldn't suffer any embarrassment because of my ignorance and lack of education."

Everett's mouth dropped open before he had the presence of mind to snap it shut when she shot him a glare. Bracing himself in case she got it into her head to punch him as she'd done Mr. Victor, Everett stepped closer to her and pried the copy of *Pride and Prejudice* out of her hand.

"Any child would be lucky to call you mother, Millie. You're smart, well-read, curious about everything, and have a true love for children."

Staring at him for a long moment, Millie tilted her head. "I knew we should have summoned the physician to take a look at you after your last brawl."

"My wits are not addled, Millie. Quite honestly, my mind is clearer right now than it's been in years." He brought her hand up to his lips and kissed it, relieved when her eyes widened just a bit. "And I have to tell you something else."

"What?" she asked in a voice that sounded somewhat breathless.

"I can't allow you to burn any Jane Austen book — but especially not *Pride and Prejudice.*"

"That's what you have to say to me — that I can't burn a silly book?"

"I finished the story, Millie. I read *Pride and Prejudice* from cover to cover, and . . . I'm your Mr. Darcy and you're my Lizzy."

"You . . . finished . . . the story?"

"Indeed. And if you didn't hear me the first time, I'm Mr. Darcy."

"I'm fairly certain Mr. Darcy would have had an English accent, but since Lizzy did enjoy reading, I suppose it's not too much of a stretch to compare me with her, although. . . ."

As Millie continued talking, really rapidly at that, Everett simply watched her, taking in every detail of her face. Her green eyes were sparkling and her cheeks were flushed a delicate shade of pink. Brown curls had begun to escape the pins someone had put in her hair, and a spray of flowers that had been tucked into that hair was hanging somewhat forlornly over her ear. Her lips were still moving incredibly fast, but the second his gaze settled on them, he couldn't seem to look away. They were delightful lips, just the right shade of pink, and . . .

Everett leaned forward and claimed those rapidly moving lips with his own.

For the briefest of seconds, they continued moving, but then Millie stiffened, but before he could release her and beg her pardon, her lips softened under his, and she let out the smallest of sighs. Putting his arms around her, he drew her closer, loving the feel of her small form, loving the . . .

A loud clearing of a throat broke through the pure delight Everett was experiencing, and then he heard the distinct sound of someone slapping their hand against something wooden — something he was almost positive was going to turn out to be a bat.

Pulling his lips from Millie's, he grabbed hold of her hand as he stepped just a few inches away from her, pleased in spite of himself to see Millie was looking a little dazed when she finally opened her eyes.

His pleasure evaporated into thin air, though, when he lifted his head and locked eyes with Mr. Kenton, finding that man looking anything but pleased. In fact, the elderly man looked downright menacing as he continued to slap his hand against the bat.

"Explain yourself, Mr. Mulberry."

Suddenly feeling as if he were a mere boy instead of a full-grown man, Everett decided on the spot that charm might just be the way to handle this rather troubling situation.

"I was . . . well, you see, I know it was a little improper, kissing Millie and all . . . but she's completely irresistible to me, and . . . I'm rather afraid I lost my head for a moment."

"Try again."

"Ah . . . hmm . . ." was all he could come up with to say.

"I thought so." Mr. Kenton stopped slapping the bat against his hand and moved forward, a rather intimidating sight, even given that the man was positively ancient. Coming to a stop right in front of Everett, Mr. Kenton sent Millie, who was a lovely shade of pink, a fond look, before his eyes hardened as he directed his attention back to Everett.

"I'm going to be perfectly frank with you, Mr. Mulberry. Miss Millie is an orphan, and as such, she has no father to look after her interests. Having said that, I'm telling you right now that you will view me as her fatherly figure at this particular moment in time. You will also explain to me exactly what your intentions are for this fine, fine young lady who deserves better than to be hurt by a scoundrel like you."

Right there, as he was being threatened by an elderly gentleman, one who still retained possession of a rather sturdy-looking bat, Everett knew, without a glimmer of a doubt, that he was truly and irrevocably in love with Miss Millie Longfellow.

Whether it was her warmth or natural zest for life, she had a way about her that drew people in, and . . . he could no longer deny his feelings for the woman.

Unable to stop the grin that was spreading over his face, he nodded to Mr. Kenton, but when he opened his mouth, he was interrupted by the sight of another man walking across the parlor.

To his relief, he discovered that Reverend Gilmore wasn't clutching a bat.

"I didn't realize the ball had ended early," Reverend Gilmore said before he shook Everett's hand, kissed Millie's cheek, and then stared at Mr. Kenton, who'd taken to muttering under his breath. "Oh, dear, have I missed something yet again?"

Mr. Kenton let out a very uncharacteristic grunt. "I caught Mr. Mulberry kissing Miss Millie."

With barely a blink of an eye, Reverend Gilmore smiled. "How delightful."

"He has yet to declare his intentions."

"Only because I haven't been given the opportunity to do that yet," Everett said, taking a moment to send Millie a smile when he heard her suck in a deep breath.

Mr. Kenton slapped the bat again, just once. "Well, get on with it, then, Mr. Mulberry. Reverend Gilmore and I aren't getting any younger."

Bringing Millie's hand once again to his lips, Everett kissed it but then froze. Sending her a smile, he kept hold of her hand even as he released a bit of a sigh. "I need to speak with the children before I say another word."

Millie, to his very great surprise, beamed at him, lifted their clasped hands, and placed a very gentle kiss right on his bruised knuckle. "I think you're exactly right, and . . . you remembered that it's always about the children."

"I need to make certain they're in full

agreement with what I'm about to do."

"Of course you do."

Everett laughed and hugged Millie to him, releasing her quickly when Mr. Kenton began slapping the bat again. Squeezing her hand, he was just about to ask where the children were when Lucetta rushed into the room with Abigail at her heels.

Lucetta came to a stop as she rubbed her side and gasped for air. "Something dreadful has happened."

Millie dropped hold of his hand. "Where are the children?"

With eyes suddenly bright with tears, Lucetta lifted her chin. "Caroline gave them to Mr. Victor, but if we hurry, we might be able to catch them at the docks."

19

Millie's mind went curiously blank, and she simply stared at Lucetta for what felt like forever until a thousand questions replaced the blankness.

"Caroline . . . gave the children to Mr. Victor?"

Dashing away tears that had fallen on her beautiful face, Lucetta nodded. "She did, and . . . we have to hurry, before Mr. Victor takes them out of Newport."

"The carriage is right out front," Abigail said before she nodded to Everett. "I expect you to find those precious children, Everett, and" — she nodded to Lucetta — "I'm expecting you to take over my role as Millie's chaperone, since I'm old and will only slow everyone down."

"You're worried about Millie having a proper chaperone right now?" Lucetta asked, even as she bent over and pulled her shoes off her feet. "In case you've neglected to notice, we're in the midst of an emergency."

Abigail waved them to the door. "Emergencies are no excuse for abandoning proper protocol, dear. Now go."

With Everett's hand once again in hers, Millie ran beside him out of the parlor, Lucetta keeping pace by Millie's side. Hurrying down the front steps, they reached Abigail's carriage, and while Everett gave the driver directions, Millie and Lucetta climbed into the carriage, Millie scooting over on the seat when Everett joined them a moment later.

" 'Emergencies are no excuse for abandoning proper protocol'? Honestly, if we weren't facing such a dastardly situation, I'd find myself amused." Lucetta drew in a deep breath and slowly released it. "But enough about that. You probably want to know what happened."

Everett took hold of Millie's hand and leaned forward. "That might be helpful. How do you know Caroline gave the children to Mr. Victor?"

"After Millie left Seaview, I went in search of Abigail, intent on telling her about what had transpired between Millie and Caroline on the terrace. However, when I saw that Abigail was in the midst of a crowd of guests, I didn't want to draw undue curiosity by pulling her aside. Instead, I decided to go get the children. But when I reached the top of the stairs and started down the hallway, I ran into a little difficulty, that difficulty being two ladies — Miss Gertrude Rathbone and some woman named Bird something or other."

"Birdie?" Everett asked.

"Indeed." Lucetta's eyes narrowed. "They were standing in front of Elizabeth's door, looking almost as if they were guarding it, and when I tried to pass them, that Birdie lady stuck out a crutch and brought me to the ground. At first I thought it had to be an accident, but when she proceeded to hit me with that crutch and Gertrude stuffed a handkerchief in my mouth to muffle my yells, I realized something was horribly wrong."

"Birdie hit you with her crutches?" Everett asked in a deadly voice.

"Numerous times. I know this isn't exactly the moment to point this out, but . . . you have dreadful friends, Everett."

"They're not my friends."

"Wonderful, but to proceed with my story . . ." Lucetta absently tucked a stray strand of hair behind her ears. "Before I knew it, I'd been trussed up like a holiday turkey, with what I think were someone's stockings, and dragged into a closet, where I was stunned to find Miss Nora Niesen trussed up in exactly the same way."

She gave a sad shake of her head. "I've since learned that she tried to step in and stop Caroline, but that pesky business only resulted in her being accosted. Because our hands were tied, as well as our feet, we were in a rather precarious state. We tried to draw attention to our plight, hoping some passing servant would hear us as we mumbled through our handkerchiefs, but I think Caroline had made certain to let the staff know she was not to be disturbed as she spoke to the children."

"Do you know what she said to the children?" Millie asked.

Lucetta nodded. "I do, and you're not going to like it. The closet Miss Niesen and I had been thrown into abutted Elizabeth's room, and when I stopped mumbling, I heard Caroline speaking. She told the children that she and you, Everett, were announcing your plans to wed that very night, and then . . ." Lucetta blew out a breath. "She told them that you found the children to be a burden and did not want to take care of them anymore. Because of that, Caroline said that she'd arranged for them to go off with Mr. Victor, a man she claimed adored the children and would take them home to Boston."

Everett's hold on Millie's hand tightened. "And the children believed her?"

Biting her lip, Lucetta frowned. "I don't think they did. Elizabeth started arguing, but Caroline cut off the arguments — slapping her, I think — and then . . . Rose started crying. And that's when Caroline really turned nasty."

Millie leaned forward. "What did she do?"

"It was dreadful. After Rose started crying, there was the sound of another slap before Caroline told the children that if they didn't cooperate, she would not give them to Mr. Victor, a kind and loving man, but would see them sent off on the first orphan train she could find."

Temper bubbled up and out of Millie. "She's a monster, and I swear to you, when I get my hands on her . . . Well, what I did to Mr. Victor's nose will look like child's play."

"And I'll be there with you, darling," Lucetta said. "But first we have to find the children. I'm afraid they might have left the harbor, given that it was quite some time after I heard Caroline leading the children away that I managed to get free. That Birdie lady came back into the closet not long after Caroline left and stood over us, brandishing her crutch in a very threatening way, that brandishing making it unwise for me or Miss Niesen to make so much as a squeak when we heard you, Everett, come up to look for the children.

"After you left, Birdie left, and that's when Miss Niesen and I finally took to banging our tied legs against the door, but it was quite some time before Mr. Macon found us." A ghost of a smile flitted over Lucetta's face. "The poor man was completely appalled to find us in such a state, but he rose to the situation magnificently, fetched Abigail straightaway, then her carriage, and . . . if I'm not much mistaken, he was going after Caroline once we got on our way."

Leaning back against the seat, Everett sighed. "I just cannot believe Caroline would go to these lengths to hurt me. I thought I knew her well, but it seems as if I didn't know her at all."

Millie caught his eye. "She's a spoiled woman, Everett, used to getting her way, and she must have been simply beside herself when you weren't cooperating."

"And when you were forming a very charming attachment to our dear Millie," Lucetta added. "We mustn't forget about that." She sent a pointed look to Millie and Everett's clasped hands. "I have not heard the full story yet, but I'm assuming the two of you have straightened matters out?"

Millie felt her face heat, but before she could respond, Everett responded for her.

"After I left the ball, I found Millie in the process of burning her beloved books, so I did the only thing I could think of . . . I kissed her. Mr. Kenton then threatened me with a bat, but we can't discuss anything further with you until after we find the children." He smiled. "We want them to be included in any and all of our future decisions."

As Lucetta stared back at them in clear delight, the carriage turned off the main road and began jostling over ruts, coming to a stop a few moments later. Everett was out the door in a split second, helping Millie and then Lucetta to the ground before he took them by the hand and headed for the docks.

They checked every boat in the harbor, but the *Adoring Violet* was nowhere to be found.

Pulling her and Lucetta beside him, Everett headed for his own yacht, bellowing loudly that he needed to board. A plank was lowered almost immediately, and as Everett talked to the captain, a man who looked as if he'd just been woken from a sound sleep, preparations to pull anchor began immediately.

Sinking into a chair on the deck, Millie waited until Everett and Lucetta joined her and then lifted her chin. "What are we going to do if we don't find Mr. Victor in Boston?"

"Where else would he go?" Lucetta asked slowly.

"Well, I'm not sure, but considering he is an attorney and must know that kidnapping is a grave offense, don't you think he might expect us to follow him to Boston and decide to head somewhere else?"

Everett rubbed a hand over his face. "You're exactly right, Millie, but since we don't know where else to begin looking for the children, we'll start in Boston. I had the captain send a boy off with a message for Abigail, telling her we didn't find the children at the docks. I'm sure that won't relieve any of the anxiety she's feeling, but at least she'll know what city we're heading for." He blew out a breath. "If we don't find them in Boston . . . Well, we'll worry about that when the time comes."

Settling back in the chair, Millie shivered as the sea breeze picked up, but before she could even comment on the chilly wind, Mr. Andrews, the steward she'd met when she'd first traveled to Newport, was suddenly standing in front of her, handing her a blanket. Before she could do more than smile her thanks at the man, Everett was pulling his chair closer to her, even as he sent Mr. Andrews a rather knowing smile.

With a shake of his head, Mr. Andrews actually returned Everett's smile, released a sigh of obvious disappointment, and looked to where Lucetta was sitting right as his mouth dropped open. Instead of handing Lucetta the blanket he was still holding in his hand, he thrust it Millie's way and made a hasty retreat.

"I would love to say that doesn't happen often, but . . ." Lucetta smiled a small smile, took the blanket Millie held out to her, and settled into her chair.

Silence descended over the deck as everyone seemed to get lost in their own thoughts. Leaning her head back, Millie gazed at a sky filled with stars, and reached out to God. He would guide them . . . and hopefully keep those precious children safe.

Closing her eyes, she lifted her heart in prayer.

By the time they reached Boston, docked

Everett's yacht, found a carriage to hire, and inquired at the Victors' home, the morning was completely gone.

Millie had not been able to catch much sleep, and given the weariness on Everett's face, as well as Lucetta's, she assumed they hadn't slept much either.

"At least we know that Mr. Victor came back to Boston," Lucetta said as the rented carriage trundled down another Boston street. "I don't think I've ever been so excited to see a boat before. The sight of the *Adoring Violet* anchored in the Boston harbor had goose bumps traveling down my arms."

"But unless his entire household staff is lying, neither he nor Mrs. Victor have been home for almost a week," Everett added, raking a hand through hair that was now completely standing on end.

"They've taken the children to their old home," Millie said again. "I know they have."

Everett lifted her hand to his lips and pressed a quick kiss on it. "I hope you're right, but I have to admit, I have doubts about that. It's too obvious. And as you said, Mr. Victor has to know he's broken the law by stealing away the children."

"It might be too obvious, but . . . I just

have a feeling that's where we'll find them."

Looking out the carriage window, Millie took in the tree-lined street and the dignified houses spread out along that street, each house with a large lawn, while a dense forest ran the length of the neighborhood. When the carriage began to slow, she turned back to Everett. "You told the driver to let us off a few houses away from Fred's house?"

"I did."

"Good. We don't want to allow Mr. Victor an opportunity to flee if he does turn out to be here."

When the carriage pulled to a stop a few moments later, everyone climbed out. Millie waited as Everett gave the driver further instructions, and then they began walking down the street — Millie hobbling just a bit because her sparkly shoes had begun pinching her toes.

"Don't you think the neighbors are going to find three people strolling down the street in formal attire a little odd?" Lucetta asked.

Millie's lips curved. "Probably, but it wasn't as if we had time to change."

Falling silent when Everett slowed his pace, Millie glanced to the handsome house sitting back from the street. It was three stories high and made of red brick, and even though the drapes were firmly drawn and the house had a slightly abandoned air to it, she could tell it was a home that had known much love. There were flower boxes attached to every window, and the porch held inviting chairs with cushions that were worn yet comfy looking.

"I hope the spare key is where I left it," Everett whispered. He strode over to the side of the house, ducked around the corner, and reappeared a moment later holding up a key. As they stood by the front door, he blew out a breath and suddenly looked a little . . . determined.

"I want you and Lucetta to wait out here for me. I'll come get you after I make sure it's safe."

Lucetta let out a snort. "Not likely. If you haven't figured this out yet, Everett, Millie and I are not fainting flowers, willing to stay back while the brave, brawny hero scouts out the dangerous situations. Besides, you might need us — especially since it seems someone really is here." She nodded to the door. "The door's cracked open, which makes that key in your hand unnecessary now."

Millie's nerves immediately began to jangle as Everett slowly pushed open the door and stepped into the house. Following him a second later, they moved down the hallway, splitting up to check different rooms. Feeling more and more unsettled with each empty, linen-draped room she looked into, Millie reached the end of the hall and stepped through another door, completely taken aback by the sight that met her eyes.

Whatever she'd been expecting to see, it had not been finding the children tied to straight-backed chairs, with . . . Mr. Victor and his wife tied right beside them.

"Good heavens, what is going on?" she asked, abandoning any attempt at caution when she noticed the tears streaming down Rose's face.

"Run, Miss Millie, run," Elizabeth yelled. "He'll be back any minute, and you have to get . . ."

Millie felt Everett come right up behind her, but as she glanced over her shoulder, she found him looking furious, and then Lucetta was suddenly thrust forward. Looking past them, she saw a thin man wearing gold-rimmed spectacles right behind Lucetta, carrying not one, but two pistols in his hands and smiling back at her.

"How delightful, more guests. I must say I wasn't expecting additional company, but . . . into the parlor with you, if you please, and do hurry. I have a vast amount of things on my schedule today, although I think that schedule is going to get completed faster than I thought, now that I have people I can ask questions of instead of searching this house and the barn on my own."

The man craned his neck and nodded at Mr. Victor. "Imagine my delight when Mr. Victor just happened to bring the children back to their old home just as I was becoming incredibly frustrated that my search has not been going very well at all. Why, if you ask me, it's one of those delicious coincidences we're only fortunate to see once or twice in a lifetime." The man released a laugh that held a note of clear insanity in it.

Millie soon found herself tied to a chair, Lucetta tied to the chair right next to her, and Everett secured to the leg of a table.

"There, all safe and snug." The man picked up his pistols and moved away from Everett. He smiled around the room, his gaze lingering on Lucetta.

Lucetta held the man's gaze for a long moment, before her eyes widened, then closed, then snapped back open. "You're Mr. Franklin Robinson, aren't you? The mad inventor who sold my theater faulty electric lights."

The man presented Lucetta with a bow. "I've heard rumors about that ironclad memory of yours, Miss Plum, and do allow me to say I simply adore watching you take the stage." His smile dimmed. "Unfortunately, I'm afraid you won't be taking the stage ever again. It's a shame you recognized me, but don't fret over that. I wouldn't have left any of you breathing, even if you hadn't just told everyone my name."

He used one of the pistols to scratch his nose. "I'm much too savvy to leave loose ends lying about, which is why I'm back in Boston — to clear up the last of the loose ends."

"You're going to . . ." Millie shot a look to the children before she returned her attention Mr. Robinson. "Do away with us?"

"I wish that wasn't the case, but I have no intention of going to jail, or of being hunted for the rest of my life, so . . . sorry."

"But . . . why?"

Mr. Robinson shrugged. "Fred Burkhart was supposed to endorse my electric lights. However, the man turned out to be far too curious for his own good and ran numerous experiments on them. When he discovered the lights weren't perfect quite yet, given that some of them would burst unexpectedly into flames, he refused to give me additional funds — and was going to go public with his findings. I couldn't very well allow him to do that, not considering how much money people were throwing my way as they purchased box after box of my lights. So . . . I had to put a stop to him once and for all."

"I thought he died while testing a new buggy," Everett said.

"There was nothing wrong with that buggy, although I do feel slightly bad for the inventor of that creation. . . . He's been under quite a bit of scrutiny since Fred and Violet were found dead in his invention."

Elizabeth's face turned completely white. "You killed Daddy and Mommy," she whispered. "You're a. . . . monster, a. . . ."

Mr. Robinson sauntered across the room and slapped Elizabeth squarely across the face. "Shut up."

Millie shot a glance to Everett and found him struggling against the ties that bound him. His eyes were filled with rage, but before she could warn him not to make a scene, especially since Mr. Robinson still had possession of the guns, Mr. Robinson let out a laugh that had the hair standing straight up on the back of Millie's neck.

"I didn't *relish* the nasty business I was

forced to enact. Although . . . once a person has taken one life — or two, as the case may be — it's much easier to contemplate further deaths, but back to business." He strode to the middle of the room and studied the children for a long moment before he swiveled around and arched a brow at Mr. Victor.

"I've been here for days, going through all of the ledgers Fred left here, as well as the ones I took from your office, Mr. Victor. I also helped myself to a bit of your mail as well — although that really had nothing to do with me. I was just curious to see who'd been writing you. However, I have not found the documents I know Fred made up, itemizing the problems with my electric lights. Those documents, I'm sure, are . . . dated. If word gets out I knew there were problems with the lights before that theater Miss Plum works in caught fire, or the other fires that have been caused by my lights, well . . . it won't be pretty for me. That's why I've returned to Boston and the scene of the crime, so to speak. I need those documents now, before people at Miss Plum's theater start turning nasty."

"I never saw a document regarding faulty electric lights," Mr. Victor said slowly.

Mr. Robinson tapped one of the pistols

against his leg. "Hmm . . . I thought Fred was becoming suspicious of you — that suspicion completely my fault since I led him to believe you were fully behind my invention. Perhaps, when Fred started getting the idea someone was out to harm him — those carriages trying to run a person down in the streets more than once can bring those suspicions to mind — he began wondering if you and I just might be . . . in cahoots."

"That explains why Fred made up a new will," Everett said.

"I was never in a partnership with this man," Mr. Victor said, catching Everett's eye. "If Fred would have only told me of his concerns, I —"

"You would already be dead," Mr. Robinson interrupted. "I expect his suspicions are what sent you off on that worldwide trip. But . . . the day is growing short, and I'm on a tight schedule. I need to know where that document is."

Mr. Victor shook his head. "I told you — I never saw a document regarding your lights."

Mr. Robinson raised a gun, and for a second, Millie thought he was going to shoot Mr. Victor. Instead, to her horror, he turned and leveled the gun on Rose.

"Children, from what I saw, all of you were very close to your father. Which means, he probably told you everything."

"They're just children," Everett said, his voice decidedly lethal. "Leave them alone."

"Oh, I won't shoot them — at least not yet — but I have the strangest feeling they, or at least one of them, knows where that document I'm looking for is." Mr. Robinson nodded to Elizabeth. "Well?"

Shaking her head, Elizabeth blinked back tears, her face bearing a distinct handprint where Mr. Robinson had slapped her. "I don't know. I never saw Daddy put a document anywhere except in his safe. Did you check there?"

"Of course." Mr. Robinson turned to Rose, who simply shook her head, apparently too frightened to even speak. Nodding politely to the little girl, he directed his attention to Thaddeus, who was glaring back at him and looking stubborn.

"That leaves you, dear boy. Do you know where your Daddy stashed that pesky document?"

Thaddeus little lips quivered, he opened his mouth, but then he snapped it shut.

"Ah, you do know, don't you?" Mr. Robinson smiled, moved in front of Thaddeus, ruffled Thaddeus's hair, then, calm as you please, turned the gun on Rose again and began pulling back the trigger.

"Don't shoot her!" Thaddeus yelled.

Lowering the gun, Mr. Robinson quirked a brow. "I won't if you tell me what I want to know. Did you see your daddy hide what I'm looking for in the barn?"

With his face wet with tears, Thaddeus shook his head. "I didn't see him hide anything in the barn, but he buried a box out in the forest. He told me not to tell anyone unless it was . . . necessary he said, but I didn't know what that meant." Thaddeus rubbed his nose. "Daddy wanted to mail it, but . . . he said something about running out of time. The box is under a big tree that Daddy carved a cross into, clear past my treehouse and straight back into the forest."

"Wonderful." Mr. Robinson ruffled Thaddeus's hair again before he made for the door. "If all of you will excuse me for just a moment, I need to see if young Thaddeus is right and if what I seek is buried out past his treehouse." With that, Mr. Robinson disappeared from sight.

"I hope Daddy — if he's watching us right now — isn't mad at me for telling," Thaddeus whispered.

"Of course he wouldn't be mad at you,

darling," Millie said softly. "You've been very brave, and now I understand why you buried your pants."

"Daddy told me it's what you do when you don't want anyone to find your things, or when you don't have time to mail them to someone else."

"Which is all very enlightening, but we need to figure out how to get out of here," Mr. Victor said. "He'll be back, and I think all of us know exactly what he has planned."

"Which is why it's a good thing I am proficient at getting untied — as are the children." Millie exchanged a look with Elizabeth, who was smiling just a bit. As Millie began twisting her hands, Elizabeth began rocking her chair back and forth, using her toes to help her hop her chair right up next to Rose.

"So that's how you did it," Millie said, slipping her hands free a second later, as Rose's binding fell free as well, and Elizabeth grinned. "Ingenuous, you're simply ingenuous, darling."

Hurrying across the room, Millie soon had Everett untied, and before many minutes had passed, everyone was free and standing on their feet.

"You and Lucetta get the children to safety, Millie," Everett said. "I'll go deal with Mr. Robinson, although it would be nice if I had a weapon."

Elizabeth scampered over to him and tugged on his sleeve. "Daddy kept guns in a concealed safe behind a bookshelf in the library." She smiled. "I know the combination."

"Of course you do," Everett said, taking her hand as they rushed out of the room.

"You go with Miss Longfellow and Miss Plum," Mr. Victor said to his wife, a woman who was looking terrified and had yet to speak a single word. "I'm going with Everett."

Millie narrowed her eyes on the man. "I hardly trust you to have Everett's back, given that you stole the children away from him and are responsible for landing those children in this troubling circumstance."

Mr. Victor exchanged a look with his wife before he shook his head at Millie. "We didn't steal the children from anyone, Miss Longfellow. Miss Dixon sought me out as I was preparing to leave Newport and told me Everett had had a change of heart. She said, since they were soon to be married, Everett didn't want the burden of raising three children, so bade me come and fetch them."

Lucetta let out a snort. "You didn't think

fetching them in the middle of the night from a ball was a little suspicious?"

"Miss Dixon said Everett wanted an opportunity to say a proper good-bye to the children, and wanted to allow them the treat of watching him propose to her during the ball."

Millie picked up Rose, who was looking close to tears again, and snuggled her close. "Do you honestly believe that Fred would have left these little angels to a man who would carelessly toss them aside?"

Mr. Victor stared at her for a moment. "No, he wouldn't, and I now believe that Fred left the children to Everett because he knew his friend would guard them carefully."

"I've done a poor job of that."

Millie looked up as Everett and Elizabeth reentered the room, Everett carrying a pistol in one hand and a rifle in the other.

"There was no possible way you could have known the danger the children were in," she said softly.

"I know it now." He moved up to her, and even though she was still holding Rose, bent close and pressed his lips briefly against hers. "You'll see them safe?"

"Of course."

Nodding to her before he kissed Rose's

forehead, Everett turned. "I'll need someone to summon the authorities." .

Mrs. Victor surprised everyone by saying, "I'll do it — even if I have to knock on every door to find a neighbor who'll assist me." She placed her fists on her hips and nodded at Everett. "Duncan's going with you, and before you argue with me, he can be trusted."

With her heart in her throat, Millie watched as Everett, followed by Mr. Victor left the room. She headed for the door, motioning Elizabeth and Thaddeus to join her. Lucetta scooped Thaddeus up in her arms, Mrs. Victor took hold of Elizabeth's hand, and they hurried toward the front of the house, even as Millie prayed Everett would be safe.

"I don't know if all of you saw this or not," Elizabeth said. "But Uncle Everett just kissed Miss Millie right on the lips."

"It was disgusting," Thaddeus proclaimed.

"Disgusting or not," Elizabeth continued, "if we get out of this alive, I think Miss Millie might just become our new aunt."

20

Rage such as he'd never felt before traveled through his veins, clearing Everett's head and leaving him with a clear purpose.

Franklin Robinson had murdered two innocent people, taking Fred and Violet from their three precious children, and for that . . . he would pay.

Spotting an abandoned pail lying on its side right next to what had surely been a sandbox at one time, although now it seemed to be filled with dead leaves, Everett's sense of rage increased. That Fred had provided that sandbox for his children, there was no doubt, but he'd never again be able to enjoy watching his children play in it.

With every step he took, Everett saw additional signs of how much Fred had invested in his children's lives, from the swing hanging forlornly from a tree, to the miniature house patterned after Fred's real house sitting right before the beginning of the forest. White curtains hung in the playhouse windows, and miniature chairs rested on the small covered porch, seemingly waiting for the children to once again return to sit in them.

"Do we have a plan?"

Glancing to his right, Everett found Mr. Victor looking incredibly somber, yet fierce at the same time. "We can try to capture him, but if he balks, I'm shooting him."

"Don't shoot to kill though, Everett. Mr. Robinson needs to be held accountable for his crimes, of which I'm sure there are many."

"I wasn't planning on killing him, even though he seems to have no remorse for murdering Fred and Violet."

"A nice leg wound might do the trick. I've heard those are incredibly painful. But he will pay for their deaths, Everett. I am an attorney, after all, and I promise you, that man will never again see the light of day, except through a very small window from a very small cell."

Nodding, Everett led the way through the trees, using the sound of a shovel plying industriously at the ground as a guide. Slipping up behind a large tree, he waited as Mr. Victor joined him. He then drew in a breath, sent up a quick prayer, something he was beginning to find very reassuring, and stepped from behind the tree, the pistol he'd taken from Fred's safe held in front of him.

"Find what you're looking for?"

Mr. Robinson froze in the act of shoveling, but only for a second. Throwing the shovel directly at Everett, Mr. Robinson dove for his gun right as Everett fired.

Dirt and leaves scattered about as the gun Mr. Robinson had been diving for skittered across the ground, stopping out of the man's reach. A blur that turned out to be Mr. Victor rushed past Everett, and satisfaction flowed freely when the attorney reached the gun before Mr. Robinson did. Mr. Victor snatched it off the ground and calmly aimed it in Mr. Robinson's direction.

"That was a great shot," Mr. Victor said, with just the barest trace of a grin on his face.

"Not really. I was aiming for his leg."

Mr. Victor laughed. "Might want to spend some time practicing, because —"

"Everyone drop your weapons, get down on the ground, and keep your hands where we can see them. We were contacted by the neighbors that something suspicious was going on, and clearly, they were right, but we . . . Mr. Victor, what you doing here, sir?"

Before Everett could blink, let alone comply with even one of the demands the police officer had yelled his way, he found himself surrounded by additional policemen.

Raising one hand into the air, he was about to drop his gun, when all of a sudden, Mr. Robinson rushed at one of the policemen, trying to wrest the man's gun away from him. As they began to struggle, there was a deafening bang, and then . . . Mr. Robinson crumpled to the ground.

"Everett!"

Turning, he found Millie racing toward him, screaming at the policemen not to shoot, and before he could reassure her that he was unharmed, she jumped into his arms, her entire body shaking as she held him tightly.

"Thank God, thank God," she kept saying over and over again. "We heard the shots as we were leaving in the carriage, and . . ."

"It's all right, Millie," he said, soothing her with a hand to her back.

"I thought I was going to find you dead," she whispered in his ear.

"I'd hardly be much of a guardian to the children if I stopped breathing."

"Would someone please explain what's going on?"

Pulling Millie to his side, Everett looked at a policeman who was rising to his feet, the same policeman who'd been struggling with Mr. Robinson. "Is he dead?" he asked with a nod in Mr. Robinson's direction.

"No. Just fainted, I think," the policeman said. "An unfortunate condition brought about due to the fact the fool shot himself in the leg." The policeman dusted off his hands. "However, we need a detailed explanation as to what transpired here."

Everett nodded. "I don't have time for many details just now, but the long and short of it is this — that man, Mr. Franklin Robinson, crazed inventor it seems, murdered Fred and Violet Burkhart, and was intending to murder . . . well, quite a few more people." He caught Mr. Victor's eye. "Would it be possible for you to take over explaining the rest of what we know?"

Mr. Victor tilted his head. "You're anxious to get to the children."

"They've been through quite a bit in the last day."

Taking a step closer, Mr. Victor paused. "You'll be taking them back to New York?"

"Most likely."

Moving closer, Mr. Victor held out his

hand. "They belong with you. I see that now, and I cannot apologize enough for not speaking with you before I brought the children here. Miss Dixon was just very convincing, but . . . that's no excuse for me not gathering all the facts."

"Since you helped bring down Fred's killer, I think we'll just forget that nasty business of the children disappearing, me losing years off my life, and —"

"I like you too," Mr. Victor said before he shook Everett's hand, nodded to Millie, and then turned and went to speak with the police.

Taking Millie's hand in his, they walked back through the forest. When they reached the edge of Fred's lawn, the swing captured his attention, and he stopped and stared at it before blowing out a breath.

"We have much to discuss, Millie, you and I."

Millie squeezed his hand. "We do, but not just yet."

Looking down at her, he smiled, but his smile faded when she reached up and pulled his head toward hers. The second their lips touched, the horror of the day faded away, and as he pulled her closer to him, he knew without a doubt that he was in the very best of company, the company of the lady he loved.

"The children are playing with their toys in the nursery," Millie said thirty minutes later, as she rejoined everyone in the drawing room, a room Lucetta had already stripped of the dustcovers. Moving over to a settee done up in yellow, Millie took a seat. "Since they haven't seen those toys in quite some months, I think we'll have plenty of time to speak of matters they really don't need to hear."

"Did you tell them about Mr. Robinson?" Lucetta asked as she walked across the room to join Millie on the settee.

"I told them he's going away forever, but I left it at that. They don't need to know more about that depraved gentleman, at least not until they're older." She pushed some bothersome curls out of her eyes. "It's been quite the day."

"It's been quite the summer," Lucetta corrected. "And here I thought I'd be getting a lovely rest away from the theater, but I'm not exactly feeling rested."

Footsteps coming down the hallway had Millie turning in that direction. She smiled when Everett came into the room, her smile dimming when she noticed the expression on his face. "What is it?"

"We finally found what Fred buried."

"And?"

"Everett hasn't opened it yet, because the box is locked," Mr. Victor said, sending Millie a small smile before he joined his wife on a chaise placed at an angle in front of the fireplace. "We're hoping Fred left a key for it in his desk, unless you, Miss Longfellow, know how to pick locks as well as get untied from bindings in dastardly situations."

Pulling one of the few remaining pins from her hair, Millie grinned. "Please, call me Millie, and of course I know how to pick locks."

Handing Everett the small box a moment later, a box that had probably been used at one time to store letters, Millie sat beside him as he opened it and began pulling out papers.

"These look like the documents Mr. Robinson was looking for." Everett handed the papers to Mr. Victor before returning his attention to the box. He reached back into it, pulled out a letter, and then stilled. "It's addressed to me."

Placing the letter on his leg, Millie watched as Everett took a finger and slowly traced it over the name Fred had written across the envelope. "He always did have horrible penmanship." Sliding a finger under the flap, Everett pulled the letter out of the envelope and cleared his throat before he began reading.

"I hope this letter has found you, Everett, although if it has, I'm probably dead, as is Violet. I've been hoping whoever is out to do me in spares her, but . . . time will tell.

I should have contacted you when I first began having suspicions someone was out to harm me, but . . . you must remember I'm a stubborn sort and thought I could handle this on my own, especially when I contacted the authorities and, since I didn't have any substantial proof, they acted as if I'd lost my mind.

I've sent Mr. Duncan Victor and his wife away. Their safety is probably in jeopardy as well, but I will be honest and admit I don't entirely trust Duncan. My suspicion might turn out to be unfounded, and if it does, and if you happen across him someday, tell him I'm sorry for doubting him."

Everett looked up from the letter and smiled sadly at Mr. Victor, who was blinking through tears that had filled his eyes. "Fred's sorry about not trusting you."

"So I gather," Mr. Victor said in a rather raspy voice.

Bending his head again, Everett continued.

"I'm sure you were surprised that Violet and I left you the children. I know you'll be confused by that, and perhaps even angry, but I know your heart, Everett. You'll protect my children from the evils of this world. I just wish I hadn't had to ask you to do me such a favor. I wasn't intending to give you such a responsibility, but I had this dream as I felt danger closing in around me. You were in that dream, Everett. You were holding Thaddeus in your arms, and smiling at my girls, and when I woke up, I knew what I had to do.

Love them well for me, my dear friend. Tell them how much Violet and I loved them, and help them live happy lives. They're the greatest treasures of my life, and I wouldn't trust them with anyone but you.

May peace be with you, Everett, and know that Violet and I, if we are, indeed, gone from this earth, will be watching you from above.

With my sincerest love and gratitude.

Your friend,
Fred

And . . . if it is not Everett reading this, but Franklin Robinson . . . you'll have to meet our Maker in the end, something I don't believe you're going to enjoy."

Millie watched as Everett stopped reading yet didn't take his eyes off the single page Fred had left him. Two tears trailed down Everett's face, but he didn't brush them away. He simply sat there, rereading Fred's letter.

"He must have thought very highly of you, Everett," Lucetta said softly, "to have given you the care of those precocious scamps."

Everett drew in a shuddering breath. "I'm humbled and honored beyond belief."

Millie rubbed his arm, and leaned closer to him, but before she could speak any words of comfort, someone was pounding on the front door, the sound causing everyone to jump.

"Who could that be?" she asked, heading for the hallway. "Do you think the authorities have more questions for us?"

"It's Grandmother Dorothy," Elizabeth shrieked as she raced down the stairs, slid on the wooden floor, regained her balance and headed for the front door. "We saw from the window, and she's brought. . . . everybody."

"She even brought the puppies!" Thaddeus yelled as he rushed past Millie.

"I didn't see my peacocks." Rose charged after her siblings. "They're going to be mad at being left behind."

Breaking into a run, Millie soon found herself on the front porch, blinking in surprise at the vast number of people grinning back at her.

Dorothy and Fletcher were standing on the porch, Dorothy already holding Rose, while Fletcher hugged Elizabeth tightly. Thaddeus was on the lawn, being licked enthusiastically by Chip, while the other two puppies yelped mournfully by his side, until Elizabeth and Rose ran down to greet them.

Abigail was standing with Mr. Kenton on one side of her and Mr. Macon on the other, and Davis, Ann, Mrs. O'Connor, and what seemed to be the entire staff from Seaview and Abigail's cottage filled up the front lawn, all of them smiling back at Millie.

"We got Everett's note, the one telling us you were heading for Boston," Reverend Gilmore said, stepping out of the crowd.

"Since we needed to make certain you were safe and had found the children, here we are."

"But . . . why didn't you just wait for us to return to Newport, or wait for us to send a telegram?" Millie asked slowly.

"Because we're your family, Millie, and families don't wait."

With tears blinding her, Millie was soon enveloped in one lovely hug after another. Her heart was filled to bursting, and she realized for the very first time in her life that she wasn't truly an orphan. She might have a family made up of the oddest assortment of people — from society matrons, to footmen, to dear, precious children, and Lucetta and Everett, of course — but they were her family, and she loved them dearly.

"Mr. Victor!" Abigail barked. "Rose just told me who you are, sir, but why aren't you in jail?"

"He wasn't the villain we assumed him to be," Everett said, hefting Thaddeus up in his arms. "However, even though we have much to tell everyone, there is a matter of great importance that must be addressed immediately, and in order for me to be able to do that, I need to speak with the children. If all of you would gather out in the backyard, I'll be with you directly."

Lucetta grabbed hold of one of Millie's hands while Abigail took hold of the other, and with anticipation beginning to swirl through her, Millie led the way across the lawn with the puppies now scampering at her feet.

"I must say the two of you are looking rather bedraggled," Abigail said with a nod to Lucetta and then to Millie. "Dorothy and I packed bags for both of you, so you'll be able to change soon."

"Should I ask what you packed for us?" Lucetta asked with an arch of a brow.

"Lovely gowns of course, with a few pairs of pants tailored by our very own Davis for you, Lucetta, since I do know how you like to be comfortable, if not always fashionably acceptable."

Lucetta grinned. "You really are a dear, sweet woman, aren't you."

"Of course I am," Abigail returned as they rounded the house and moved across the backyard. "And I'll be sure to remind you that you made that claim after we get back to the city and . . . Well . . . no need to delve into that."

She turned away from a now-sputtering Lucetta to settle her attention on Millie. "Mr. Kenton told me about the kiss you shared with Everett. The poor man was completely baffled about how to handle the situation, although he did mention something about a bat being involved, and not the type of bat that flies through the air at night."

Millie's lips curved into a grin as she looked to Mr. Kenton, who smiled back and sent her a wink. Looking around the backyard, she was about to thank everyone for coming such a long way when Everett and the children reappeared, the children grinning from ear to ear and Everett looking rather . . . determined.

He strode across the lawn and came to stop directly in front of her, silence descending as he took hold of her hand. Giving that hand a little squeeze, he smiled.

"I was not comfortable saying anything until getting the approval of the children, but now that that has been fulfilled . . ." He dropped to his knees, but then, surprisingly enough, frowned. "Good heavens. This isn't right. I don't have a —"

"I have one right here, darling." Dorothy hurried up, pressed a small box into Everett's hand, muttered something about it being a family heirloom, and then sent Millie a rather misty smile before she hurried back to Fletcher's side. "You may continue."

"Thank you, Mother." Everett looked up and smiled at Millie. "Where was I?"

"You were getting ready to ask Miss Millie to marry you," Thaddeus called.

"Yes, quite right, thank you, Thaddeus."

Swallowing a laugh, Millie bit her lip as Everett grinned, but then he sobered a second later. "Miss Millie Longfellow, I know we've had our differences, and I know I've been a complete idiot with you, but as the esteemed Mr. Darcy said, or said something like this — through the pen of Jane Austen, of course — you are my reason for living, and I'd be beyond honored if you'd agree to become my wife."

"That's not what Jane Austen wrote in her book," Lucetta called. "Not even close."

"And you forgot to tell her you love her," Elizabeth added.

Everett turned and arched a brow at Lucetta. "I understand you have this gift for memorization, but honestly . . ." He directed his attention to Elizabeth next. "And as for your comment, I thought the whole 'you are my reason for living' covered that."

Elizabeth crossed her arms over her chest. "It's not the same."

Sending Elizabeth a wink, Everett looked back up at Millie and smiled. "Well, there you have it. So I suppose all that's left for me to say is . . . I love you."

With knees that were distinctly wobbly and a heart that felt ready to burst, Millie smiled back at him. "I love you too."

"And you'll marry me?"

"Of course."

Slipping the ring Dorothy had provided over Millie's finger, Everett rose to his feet. Pulling Millie close to him, he smiled at the crowd watching them so intently, and then . . . he kissed her.

As applause and cheers filled the air, Millie knew beyond a shadow of a doubt that God had blessed her greatly. Not only had He given her a gentleman to love, and one who loved her back, but He'd given her an entire family to call her own.

When Everett pulled slowly away and smiled his oh-so-charming smile back at her, she realized that she, Miss Millie Long-fellow, had somehow ended up with her very own Mr. Darcy, and knew they were going to be granted their very own happily ever after.

Epilogue

October 1882

Standing in the very back of the theater, Reverend Gilmore looked around, having chosen this particular spot because it afforded him the best view of what was truly important.

Sitting in a private box above him sat Everett and Millie, their heads bent together as they chatted before the show. They were in New York for this specific performance, Lucetta having arranged for the children to make a special appearance in her latest play — something the children had been talking about for weeks.

Everett and Millie had moved the children back to Boston, after they'd had him marry them, of course. It had been a simple ceremony on Abigail's private beach in Newport, with only the people Everett and Millie considered to be good company in attendance. Every member of Abigail's and

Everett's staff had been there, along with Miss Nora Niesen, Everett's parents, three puppies, and an entire flock of peacocks.

Millie had been concerned that Harriet would be disappointed missing the wedding, but he'd reminded her that Harriet wanted to hold her own second wedding ceremony when she arrived back in the States, which had Millie deciding she'd do the same.

Ushers suddenly appeared in the theater, and Reverend Gilmore smiled as they hurried around, snuffing out the candles management had decided were safer than electric lights. The crowd quieted immediately, and then a cheerful tune began to play, right as three little fairies on wires swung out over the stage.

"Uncle Everett, Aunt Millie, look at us," Thaddeus yelled as he waved his hands around before he let out a yelp when the wire pulled him back.

Glancing back to Millie and Everett, Reverend Gilmore found them on their feet, clapping wildly and completely ignoring the disdainful stares of the people who'd once called Everett friend.

When the children got reeled in, the silence turned deafening, and then Lucetta was gliding out onto the stage. She was beautiful in a lovely gown of gold, her gown accented by the diamond collar she was wearing, the style of the necklace matching the tiara in her hair and the diamond stomacher attached to the front of her gown. The diamonds had been a gift, or so it was said, from Caroline, who had obviously been feeling remorseful — or scared to death — after Abigail had had a little chat with her.

As Lucetta began pacing around the stage, Reverend Gilmore leaned back against the wall and lifted his gaze to the ceiling.

Once again you've surpassed my greatest hopes for my precious Millie, Lord. You've provided her with a vast and loving family, and provided the children with a woman who'll love and cherish them forever. You've given Everett a second chance at becoming the gentleman he was always meant to be. I do believe we'll see great things from him in the future, especially since he's going to become involved with improving the state of the tenement slums.

Reverend Gilmore pulled out the cross he always kept near and closed his hand around it.

I know I must sound a little greedy, asking for more when you've given me so much, but . . . if you have a few minutes, I'd love to discuss . . . Lucetta.

ABOUT THE AUTHOR

Jen Turano, the author of six novels, is a graduate of the University of Akron with a degree in clothing and textiles. She is a member of ACFW and lives in a suburb of Denver, Colorado. Visit her website at www .jenturano.com.